THE REBEL

KELSEY CLAYTON

Cover Image by Michelle Lancaster
Editing by Librum Artis

To Melissa
My favorite little eggplant.
Thank you for being such an amazing friend.
I love you.

CONTENT WARNING

This book deals with sensitive topics that may not be suitable for all readers. As some readers have said they find descriptive trigger warnings to be spoilers, I have provided a link to where you can find all of the trigger warnings for each of my books. Please read safely.

For trigger warnings: Please go to www.kelseyclayton.com/triggerwarnings

Tessa

The pain that pierces through my head is the equivalent of being hit with a truck—not that I know what that feels like, but it sounds comparable. You'd think I would learn by now about drinking to the point where I don't remember my own damn name. However, that's clearly not the case. My agonizing hangover is proof of that.

I pull a sweatshirt over my head, hoping it'll help shield me from the light peeking through the blinds. No luck. The only thing I can think of that might save me from this misery is a steaming hot cup of coffee. Taking a couple of Tylenol from my en suite bathroom, I swallow them down and head for the kitchen.

"I don't know where she is, to be honest." My father's voice echoes out into the hall. Ugh. I was really hoping I wouldn't have to see him today, or at least not until I got some caffeine in me. "One thing I can tell you, though, is she's going to have to answer to me as soon as she gets home."

As I turn the corner, the sight of my dad sitting at the island with my Uncle Dominic catches me off guard. He rarely comes over, let alone at ass o'clock on a Sunday morning. Still, I smile politely and try to hide how gross I feel.

"Good morning," I tell them.

Both their heads turn to me, and my father seems genuinely surprised.

"I'll be damned." He focuses back on my uncle. "Hell must have frozen over if we've reached a day where Tessa came home and Delaney is the one who stayed out all night."

"Delaney didn't come home?"

Shaking his head, they both stare me down. "You don't happen to know where she is, do you?"

"No." Not that I would tell you if I did. "She probably slept over Savannah's or something."

Thankfully, my dad lives under a rock. Being too stuck up on his high horse, he has refused to have any kind of conversation with Mrs. Hayworth. If he had, he would know that Sav—Delaney's best friend —has been living right across the street with Mrs. Hayworth and her son, Savannah's boyfriend, Grayson. Instead, he's too absorbed in his own little world to acknowledge anyone else.

"Perhaps. If you talk to her, tell her to get her ass home." His tone is light but I can sense the threat lingering in his words. "And I better not find out she's hanging around that scumbag again."

I roll my eyes, knowing that nothing I say about Knox Vaughn, or anyone from that side of town, will get through to him. Even my own boyfriend isn't allowed at our house because he doesn't drive a Porsche and his name doesn't hold a social standing fit for a king. Although, that doesn't stop Easton from sneaking in my window late at night. What daddy dearest doesn't know won't hurt him.

Uncle Dom clears his throat and stands up. "Well, I came here hoping to take my two favorite nieces out to breakfast, but I can't exactly do that when one of them is missing."

"I'm telling Ainsley," I singsong.

He chuckles. "I bet you will, you little shit."

My uncle and I have always had a good relationship. He's the only relative I have that doesn't treat me like I'm still seven years old and still playing with dolls. It's something I respect about him. He treats me like the grown-up I'm in the process of becoming.

"Oh well. More food for me." Plastering a playful smile on my face, I turn to leave the room. "Let me just get dressed and then we can go."

It only takes a few minutes for me to change my clothes and throw my hair up into a messy bun. Some girls might cringe at the thought of leaving the house without looking like they just left a photo shoot, but

I've never been like that. Sure, I like to get dolled up occasionally. Who doesn't? I just don't feel like I need to put on makeup in order to be seen in public.

By the time I get back downstairs, Uncle Dom is waiting by the front door, exchanging hushed words with my dad. As soon as they see me, the conversation dies immediately, and they brush it off like they aren't hiding anything. Typical.

"Ready to go?" my uncle asks, and I nod.

Just as I'm about to walk out the door, my father calls my name. "If you hear from your sister, tell her I want her home, pronto. I mean it, Tess."

I don't justify that with an answer. Delaney, my twin sister and literal other half, has been my best friend since birth. Meanwhile, my father has basically made it his mission to ruin my life. There isn't any possible situation where I would take his side over hers. If I manage to get in touch with her, the only thing I'll be doing is giving her the heads-up to stay away until he doesn't have a stick up his ass.

"So, where are we going?"

Uncle Dom buckles his seatbelt and pulls out onto the road. "To a place called The Underground."

My brows furrow. "The Underground? That doesn't sound like a restaurant."

"Nothing gets by you, does it?"

A heavy feeling settles in the pit of my stomach. Something isn't right. I don't know what kind of Dr. Jekyll and Mr. Hyde shit he's pulling, but my uncle went from the loving man I've known all my life to someone completely different in a matter of seconds.

"You know, I'm actually not feeling so hot. Maybe we can do breakfast some other time."

He laughs, with the look on his face displaying how sinister he really is. "Silly girl. We're not going to breakfast. Your sister and her boyfriend are hiding from me, and I bet you're just the thing I need to lure them out."

Panic sets in and I go to open the door, but it's safety locked. "Let me out of the car."

"Not going to happen, darling."

I turn, kicking at the window to try and break it. Yet still, it doesn't budge. It was like this car was made to withstand some sort of onslaught.

"I wouldn't do that if I were you."

My head whips around to face him, and I narrow my eyes to slits. "Fuck you."

Again, he lets out a humored laugh. "Suit yourself."

He turns his focus to the rearview mirror and nods subtly. I don't get a chance to see what he's looking at, however, before two arms come from behind and firmly hold a cloth over my mouth. It only takes a few seconds until everything goes black.

I gasp for air as I wake from my terrifying dream. The familiarity of my room does very little to calm me down. All the events replay in my head like a horror movie I can't seem to escape from. None of it may be happening right now, but the scars are very real.

Knowing the last thing I want to do is be alone right now, I get up and head across the hall, quietly slipping into my sister's room. As soon as I'm next to the bed, Delaney scoots over and pulls back the covers for me.

"Another nightmare?" she questions tiredly.

I sigh and cuddle up next to her. "Yeah."

The best part about having a twin sister is how connected we are. She doesn't say anything else, simply because she understands I don't want to talk about it. That day is something she and I have both tried to leave as far in the past as possible, but as the age old saying goes: some things are easier said than done.

I WAKE IN THE morning to the sound of my sister quietly moving around her room. She takes stacks of clothes from her drawers and places them into her suitcase, reminding me she's leaving tomorrow. The irony that I should be doing the same isn't lost on me. Unfortunately, I made some idiotic choices last year and now I'm required to repeat half of my senior year. I guess that's karma's doing, and man is she a bitch.

"Can't you take me with you? Hide me in your suitcase or some shit?"

She chuckles, walking to the side of the bed to sit beside me. "You know I would if I could."

The two of us learned early in life to rely on each other. When our parents would argue. When our sister tried bossing us around and then lied to get us in trouble when we didn't let her. When our best friend showed up at school after vanishing for years, only to act like she had no idea who we were. It's always been her and me—the one constant thing I knew I could count on.

"What am I going to do without you?" I murmur sadly.

"The same thing you always do—make dad want to rip his hair out and laugh as you do it."

I laugh, partly because it makes me sound like a maniac and partly because it's true. It's no secret that I'm the menace of the family. Delaney and our older sister Ainsley have always been the ones destined for greatness, but me? I've made it a game to see how many times I can get on my father's shit list. I know they say to love your family and all that nonsense, but whoever said that never had a dad like mine.

My phone vibrates on the nightstand, and my heart sinks when I see the name. *Easton*—my boyfriend, at least for now, anyway. In a few days, he'll be leaving for college like everyone else, and I'll be stuck here. We've both been avoiding the inevitable conversation, but it looks like time has run out. I take the device into my hand and swipe it open, seeing exactly what I thought I would.

> We need to talk.

We need to talk. Four words every girl loves to hear. Lucky for me, I've always looked at this relationship exactly for what it is—something to pass the time. Don't get me wrong, Easton has helped me through a lot, but it would be naive of me to think we have any chance of making long distance work. I'm better than letting some high school fling turn into me being cheated on for months.

> The lake. One hour.

Delaney watches as I drop my phone into my lap and run my hands over my face. The comforting touch she places on my back tells me she's here if I need her, but this is something I have to do on my own. Besides, as of tomorrow, I won't have my sister to lean on for emotional support anymore. *Sink or swim, bitch.*

"Are we still on for the club tonight?" I ask, getting up from the bed.

"Yeah. I think Sav said she wants to leave around nine."

I nod and head toward the door, only to be stopped.

"Tess?" Laney calls, causing me to glance back at her. "I love you."

A small grin spreads across my face. "I love you, too."

With that, I go to get ready for my unavoidable breakup.

AS SOON AS I pull into the parking lot, Easton can hear me coming. That's the thing about having a jet-black Lamborghini Aventador—it's a bit noticeable. As much as I love this car, it was a birthday present from my parents. Sometimes, that makes it feel more like a ball and chain than a luxury.

"You look good," he tells me as soon as I climb out of the car.

I smirk. "Don't I always?"

The tension between us is so thick I could choke on it. It's like we both know exactly where this is heading but neither of us want to be the one to say it. I run my fingers through my long brown hair and look him up and down. There are a lot of things that attracted me to Easton in the first place, the main being his tendency to not give a single fuck about authority. His brunette locks are brushed away from his face, and his matching brown eyes are an aching reminder of all the time I spent staring into them. I walk around to the front and sit on the hood of my car.

"So, when do you leave?"

He looks down at the ground and lightly kicks a rock. "The day after tomorrow."

I press my lips into a thin line, nodding. "That's cool."

The two of us don't say a word as we look out at the water and hope for something to offset the awkwardness. If I'm being honest, the silence is excruciating. I take a deep breath. Since he clearly doesn't have the balls to do it, I'm going to have to.

"So, it was fun, right?"

His brows furrow. "What?"

"This." I gesture between the two of us. "We had a good time while it lasted."

As soon as he realizes what I'm saying, he exhales. "We're breaking up."

"Easton, don't act like you didn't see it coming. You and I both knew what this was." I hop off the car and wrap my arms around him. "No hard feelings."

He kisses the top of my head, releasing me as soon as I move to back away and walk to the driver's side.

"Are you ever going to settle down?" he calls out. "Let someone make an honest woman out of you?"

The question almost catches me by surprise. *Almost*. I bite my lip to suppress my grin. "What's the fun in that?"

I can hear him chuckle as I get in and shut the door. The engine roars to life before I back out of the space. With one last soft smile at Easton, I drive out of there, never looking back. It isn't that I don't care about him. He helped me get through some pretty rough times. But I've made it a rule not to let anyone get close enough to hurt me. It's the best way I know to stay unbroken. The single tear that slides down my cheek is the only one I'll allow myself to shed.

THE CLUB IS PULSING with energy as the music vibrates through the walls and the floor. I slide my fake ID back into my wallet and wait for my sister and friends to do the same. Knox, Delaney's troublemaker boyfriend, wraps his arms around her from behind, making her smile. The two of them were the most unexpected couple, being as my sister was practically a nun before she met him, but they work in the best possible way.

"All right, bitches," Grayson says in his best valley-girl voice. "Someone come with me to get a beer. I'm ready to get shwastey."

We all laugh as Knox smacks him in the stomach. "Remind me again why I'm friends with you?"

Gray falls into Knox's arms. "Because I'm your soulmate and you love me."

"Aye, watch it." Delaney levels him with a single look.

He stands up and raises his hands in surrender. "Uh-oh. Looks like I made your little Bambi mad."

Savannah rolls her eyes. "You're not even drunk yet, and I'm already wanting to take your ass home."

"Ooh," he coos, bouncing his eyebrows. "For some hanky panky?"

As Grayson goes in to kiss Sav, she stops him with her hand on his forehead. "Call it hanky panky *one more time*."

Knox chuckles and grabs Gray by the arm. "All right, let's get you that drink before you make Savannah realize how much better she is than you."

As they walk away, Delaney and Savannah watch them, looking so loved up it almost makes me sick. I'm happy for them, of course, but I just don't understand how you could feel *that* much for someone. To let them in like that—giving them the ability to destroy you at the snap of their fingers—it just doesn't seem worth it to me.

"Is he drunk already?" Lennon questions.

Sav shakes her head. "Nope, high. Knox thought it would be *hilarious* to convince Gray to smoke a blunt with him before we left."

"I mean," Delaney tilts her head side to side, "it is pretty entertaining."

"No," I interject. "Entertaining is the fact that you got *Knox* to agree to follow you across the country."

Her eyes widen and she looks around quickly. "Shh, not so loud! He's like a scared animal. One wrong move and he'll run for the hills."

I don't know what's more amusing—the fact that she referred to the guy who literally took a bullet for her as a *scared animal* or that she honestly believes he would allow her to move thousands of miles away without him by her side. I personally witnessed the change in Knox as he fell in love with my sister, and there isn't a damn thing in this world that could keep him from her.

I SIT AT THE bar with Delaney, Lennon, and Savannah, while Knox and Grayson are off somewhere being a bunch of idiots. It was cute at first, watching both their stoned asses make fools of themselves, but it quickly got old.

As I take a sip of my drink, I catch sight of someone over my glass. He's sitting across the bar, looking every bit like a fantasy of mine—older, muscular, fucking gorgeous. He looks at me with a darkness in his eyes that is exactly my type. Just the expression alone is enough to put every one of my senses on high alert. Unfortunately, another girl steps up next to him and his attention is pulled off me and onto her. *Ugh*.

"I don't want you to leave tomorrow." I lay my head on Delaney's shoulder, letting my buzz control my level of honesty.

"I know, but you'll be okay. Besides, you can come visit any time you want."

I huff. "You better be available whenever I want. You're supposed to be my ride or die and you're leaving me."

Savannah, being the brat she is, looks over Laney and at me with a smirk on her face. "Are you actually sad because Delaney is leaving, or because you broke up with Easton?"

Fuck. Of course Laney told her about that. Meanwhile, I hadn't gotten around to telling Lennon, so I cringe as she gasps and her head whips toward me.

"You broke up with Easton?"

If I didn't want to smack Savannah a couple hundred times before, I definitely do now. "He's going away to college, and I'm not stupid or naive enough to think we can make the whole long-distance thing work. It's not fair to him or me."

If there's one thing that I love about Lennon, it's that she's like Laney in the sense that she can tell when I really don't want to talk about something. Even in the short time I've known her, she's figured out how to read me and uses that to her advantage. She smiles and nudges me with her elbow.

"Well, good. You can be single with me this year."

Savannah and Lennon banter back and forth, but I can't be bothered to listen. Instead, all my focus is back on the mystery man who, despite having some supermodel level bimbo trying to hang all over him, can't keep his gaze off me. I only catch the end of the conversation.

"Weeds out all the pussies."

"Speaking of pussies..." I bite my lip, causing him to lick his own, and that's the only sign I need. "Mine needs a change of pace. Excuse me."

I ignore the shocked and confused looks on their faces as I get up. It only takes a few seconds to get to where he is, and as soon as I do, I rudely slot myself between him and the girl trying desperately to seduce him.

"Uh, excuse me," she whines, but I can't be bothered.

Two perfect emerald eyes are locked with my own. His dirty blond hair looks like he just ran his fingers through it to push it from his eyes. The black T-shirt he's wearing is tight, and his muscles bulge through it. He looks like he could toss me around just for the fun of it, and I'm totally on board.

I take what's left of his whiskey and throw it back like a shot while he watches me, completely enamored.

"Tessa Davenport," I lie, handing him the empty glass.

He smiles as he takes it back and places it on the bar, his sights still on me. "Asher Hawthorne."

Asher

Two Weeks Earlier

THERE WERE ALWAYS TWO THINGS I WAS SURE about in life. One was that I was going to marry my high school sweetheart, and the other was that I would have a long career playing in the NFL. When I found out my fiancée was cheating on me every time I left for an away game, it hurt, but I knew I'd survive. The end of my career, however, is another story.

When I was younger, my father was my coach—which meant if I wasn't the best damn player on the field, I didn't belong on it at all. He was tough on me, but that only made me better. Weekends were spent at practice and evenings consisted of running solo drills in the yard. Some of my friends thought it was crazy. No one could play football *that* much without getting sick of it, but I loved it.

I'll never forget the look on my dad's face the moment I got the call. I was a first-round draft pick for the San Francisco 49ers. It was the best day of both our lives—all our hard work, physical exhaustion, and sacrifice crystallized into a single moment of triumph. It wasn't just me who accomplished my dream, it was *us*.

"Hey." One of my teammates, Anthony, pats me on the back. "Sorry to hear, man. We're really going to miss you around here."

I nod a silent thank you, not able to say anything with the

disappointment still pulsing through me. The wound is too fresh after finding out that everything I worked toward for as long as I can remember is over after only six short years.

As I pack up my locker, people come in and out—getting ready for practice and heading out to the field. Each of them stop by to share their condolences, but it's obvious none of them really know what to say. After all, it's not them. They're still in perfectly good health and their careers are firmly intact. Mine, however, is in shambles.

"All right, enough of the pity party," Colby jokes as he comes into the room. "You're clearing out your stuff, not going to a funeral. Cheer the fuck up."

Somehow, he manages to pull a laugh out of me, but it dies quickly as I glance up at the TV screen in the corner and notice the headline.

Asher Hawthorne's Career Ending Injury.

It's right there, on replay, the moments in which I threw the ball down the field at the last second, only to get sacked from two directions at once. You can see my shoulder slam against the ground, my arm contorted beneath my body. Even through my helmet, you can see the agony on my face. Just watching it now makes me cringe as I remember the pain.

My shoulder was dislocated and my rotator cuff was fully torn. As I sat in the hospital bed, listening to the doctor explain to me that I was going to need surgery and weeks of intense rehab, all I could think about was getting back on the field.

I did everything I was told. Took all my medication as directed. Faithfully followed the excruciating exercise routine my physical therapist prescribed. I even wore that obnoxiously uncomfortable brace, despite everything in me wanting to take it off. But it wasn't enough.

They tell you all about the rare complications that could happen going into surgery. There's always a chance of something going wrong—a bad reaction, stroke, or even death. No matter how much they warn you, though, you never think it's going to happen to you. Unfortunately, I was one of the unlikely cases that ended up with nerve damage caused by the surgery, and until they figure out how to fix it, I'm not fit to play.

It could be months; it could be years. Hell, it could be until I'm too old and have lost my ability to perform to the standard they require. All I know is that even while being in the best shape of my life, my body failed me.

"Don't pay attention to that," Colby pulls my attention away from watching the last moments of my career on a loop. "You'll end up back out there. I know it."

I snort and shake my head. "You a doctor now, Hendrix?"

"Damn right, I am. Certified and all by WebMD."

As I finish putting the last of my stuff into the bag, I turn around to face my best friend. It only takes a second before I notice the dark purple hickey placed in the dead center of his neck.

I flick it with my finger, making him wince. "You better cover that shit up. You know how Coach feels about you partying on nights before practice."

He rolls his eyes but does exactly what I said, knowing that if he doesn't, he'll be running until he vomits all the alcohol he consumed last night.

It doesn't surprise me, honestly. Colby Hendrix has always been a ladies' man. His brown hair and baby face make him look innocent enough to be trusted and the digits in his bank account drive it home. He's one of the best wide receivers in the league, and he's not beneath bragging about it. Especially if it helps get the girl of his choosing into bed with him. I've never cared to ask, but I'm sure if I did, he'd tell me that his motto in life is "less stress, more sex."

I watch as he dabs on more of the tattoo grade cover-up,

making me laugh. "Who the fuck did you sleep with, a goddamn vampire?"

His eyes meet mine through the reflection of the mirror and he simply winks. If I didn't know him any better, I'd think it was the typical I-don't-kiss-and-tell answer that respectful guys throw around. However, I *do* know him, and that wink was his way of getting out of answering questions he doesn't know the answer to. Having to guess, I'd say he either kicked her out last night or woke up with her this morning and ditched before she had a chance to ask him to stick around. That's usually his M.O. as the reigning king of one-night stands.

"All right, well you have fun with that. I'm going to head out."

His brows furrow. "You're not sticking around to watch practice?"

Slight laughter bubbles out of me. "Do I look like the type for self-inflicted torture?"

Colby smiles, displaying the dimples that match my own —our secret weapon, as we like to call them.

"Okay, touché. I'll catch you later."

I grab my bag and go to leave, when he opens his mouth once more.

"Oh, by the way, there's a swarm of media outside. Just a heads-up."

Groaning, I pull my sunglasses over my face. The last thing I need right now is to get berated with questions by people who don't deserve the answer. It's like rubbing salt in my wound. Sure enough, as I turn the corner, there they are—standing around like vultures waiting for their next kill.

My phone vibrates in my pocket. *Trent Englewood*. I swipe it open and bring it to my ear.

"Hello?"

"Hey," he greets me, sounding relieved that I answered. "I saw the news. I'm so sorry man. I had no idea."

I shrug, even though he can't see me. "It wasn't really something I wanted to talk about. I think I was in denial about it for a while."

"I get it, man. That's really rough."

Trent is an old friend, someone who has been in my life since we were kids. I wouldn't call him my *best* friend, since Colby would slaughter me if anyone else held that title, but he's definitely my *longest* friend. He's the kind of guy I can go months without talking to, and nothing changes. We pick right back up where we left off and it's like no time has passed. He's probably one of few people I'll answer the phone for right now.

"Give me a second. I have to walk through a wall of money-hungry assholes trying to get the inside scoop."

He chuckles. "Don't get skinned alive."

I pull the phone away from my ear and use my arm to shield my face as cameras flash and questions are all but screamed in my face.

Asher, is that all your stuff?

How do you feel about not playing football anymore?

Do you think you'll ever recover?

If it wouldn't get me thrown me in jail, I'd probably run them over with my car for sport. The whole group of them follow me all the way from the doors to my black Range Rover and the questions don't even stop when I'm safely inside. As I start the car, my phone connects to the speaker.

"You still there?"

"Yeah," Trent responds. "That sounded brutal. How many of them were there?"

I look in my mirrors, just to make sure there's no one in my way, then pull out of the parking spot. "Not sure, and I'm not sticking around to count."

He sighs. "Anything I can do to help?"

"You can talk about something else. What's new with you?"

"Ash, you know there's never anything to talk about on my side. I'm still teaching a bunch of kids who think their parents' money is the key to success, and in the summer, I hang out by the pool."

I can't help but laugh. "You make that last part sound like a bad thing."

"It could be more eventful, that's for sure."

"I don't know. I could use a little R&R by the pool."

To be honest, I can't remember the last time I let myself just breathe. It was probably back in high school when my family and I took a trip to the Bahamas. Wait, nope. Even then, my dad had me running drills on the beach. I take that back.

"Well, you're always welcome to come chill by mine," Trent offers, then pauses for a second. "You know, that might be a good idea."

"What? Sulk at your place and force you to listen to me bitch and moan?"

He snickers. "No, asshole. Come stay with me for a bit. You know they're going to be camped out at your place for the next couple weeks, just waiting for a chance to get the inside scoop. At least they won't know to look for you here."

It's not a bad plan, but a part of me is hesitant. "I'm not sure I'd be the best company right now."

"Do you think I give a shit?" he quips. "Layla is out of the country for the summer and I've got the place to myself. We can be bad company together."

As I turn the corner toward my building, I realize just how right he is. I can already see all the news vans and photographers gathered around outside. While I usually enter through the elevator in the parking garage, I'm sure it's only a matter of time before they infiltrate that as well.

"Alright," I cave. "Just until all this dies down and they focus on the next poor soul."

BY THE TIME I grab a few of my things and get to Trent's, I'm exhausted. It's only two in the afternoon, but all I want to do is collapse onto a bed and sleep for the next week. However, in honor of being a decent house guest, I force myself to stay awake as Trent and I sit in the living room and drink a beer.

He tells me more about the school he teaches at, Haven Grace Prep. To be honest, it sounds like my own personal hell: a place filled with spoiled brats who think that because their parents are rich, it means they have some kind of upper hand. I've met a few trust-fund kids in my time, and the worst thing about them is that there is nothing you can say to pop their false security bubble. Not a single one of them is prepared for the real world, and it's bound to eat them alive.

"I don't know how you do it," I tell him. "You couldn't pay me enough to deal with all that nonsense."

He chuckles and takes a swig of his beer. "They're not all bad. At least the son of the district attorney graduated this past June. *He* was a handful."

"God, I can only imagine. Rich *and* powerful. A lethal mix in someone who, for all intents and purposes, is a child."

"Hey, I seem to remember a certain someone going through a power trip at the age of twenty-two."

I throw my head back laughing. "Could you blame me? I became a starting quarterback in the NFL. Shit, I was on top of the fucking world. It felt like nothing could bring me down."

Those were the good times, before two players with a vendetta knocked me on my ass and ruined my life in the process. I swear, if I ever get a minute alone with one of them, there's no telling what I'll do, but I know it won't be pretty.

Trent and I use the rest of the day to catch up and watch recordings of our high school football games. It's bittersweet, but doesn't sting nearly as much as I thought it would. I might even consider it fun, taking that trip down memory lane. One thing's for sure, this is definitely where I need to be right now.

THE NEXT COUPLE WEEKS are spent doing everything and nothing all at the same time, and I've never felt more relaxed. Between lounging around the pool and eating all the things I was never allowed before without consequences, it's the closest I'm getting to happiness. Unfortunately, all good things must come to an end.

An incessant knocking on the door forces me to open it, being as Trent's in the shower. However, the second I do, I wish I hadn't. Standing on the other side is Blaire—my publicist—and if looks could kill, I'd be dead on the floor.

"Asher," she says with a glare.

I roll my eyes and open the door further to let her inside. "Blaire. Aren't you a sight for sore eyes."

"Cut the shit, Hawthorne. Flattery will get you nowhere."

Rubbing the back of my neck, I smirk. "A lot of women would beg to differ."

Her expression suggests she's anything but amused by my antics. "You're a difficult man to find these days."

"Uh, yeah. Sorry." I quickly come up with a lie. "I turned

my phone off when I got here. I just needed some time away."

"Oh, really?" She raises one brow, taking out her phone and pressing a button before putting it to her ear.

I drop my head and let out a breathy laugh as mine starts to ring in my pocket. "All right, you caught me. Why don't we cut the shit and you just tell me what you're doing here so you can fuck back off to whatever hell you came from?"

It may be rude but Blaire is nothing but a thorn in my side. She was hired by my ex while we were still together, and I was too busy to have any say in the matter. Everything was happening so fast, and all we knew was that I needed one. The only reason I haven't fired her ass is because she's damn good at her job.

"Your disappearance has caused an uproar," she snaps. "What did you think, that you can just vanish at a monumental point in your life and no one will care? Your fans need to hear from you. They need to know you're okay."

I cross my arms over my chest. "Why? They're just going to move on to the next guy with a good arm and even better aim."

She rolls her eyes. "Wow, Colby wasn't kidding. You really are throwing the world's biggest pity party."

"Screw you."

The corner of her lip raises in a scowl. "No thanks. I don't get in bed with guys who have slept with more women than their IQ."

She thinks she's hit me where it hurts, but I only smile. "Now who's lying? You think Colby didn't tell me about the two of you at that party a few months back?"

Her cheeks pink, and she instantly becomes flustered. "Can we get back to the point, please?"

"By all means."

"You need to be doing something that your fans can

admire. Something that gives them the opportunity to see what you're up to and that you're giving back. Otherwise, if you ever get the chance to go back to playing professional football, they really *will* be too focused on the next guy with a good arm and better aim. They won't even give you a second look."

I groan, sitting on the arm of the couch. "And what is it you suppose I do?"

The smug look on her face makes me fear the next words to come out of her mouth. "You're going to coach the team at your friend's little school, Haven Grace Prep."

Asher

I GLARE AT THE BRICK BUILDING IN FRONT OF ME like it's personally played a major part in ruining my life. If it weren't for Blaire on one side and Trent on the other, I'd run so fast in the opposite direction. I don't like kids, let alone want to teach a bunch of we-know-it-all brats the right way to play football. All the money in their parents' bank accounts can't buy them the skills they need. It takes practice, dedication, and effort—and something tells me these kids have never worked for anything in their spoiled little lives.

"I can't believe I'm doing this," I grumble.

Trent sighs and puts his hand on my shoulder. "It won't be that bad."

I shake him off me. "Don't talk to me, traitor."

"Me?" he asks in disbelief. "What about her?"

Blaire stands there with an arrogant look on her face, which only pisses me off more, but I can't be bothered with her right now. Instead, I narrow my eyes on Trent.

"I pay her to be all involved in my business and make me do things I don't necessarily want to do. *You* involved yourself, and did it behind my back."

"Oh, come on!" He throws his hands up. "I told you. *She* called *me*."

I shake my head and turn to Blaire. "How did you get his number, anyway?"

"Phone records, Babycakes. Apparently, you never changed the password after you and Nicole split."

My stomach drops at the mention of my ex's name. "You went to Nikki?"

She doesn't look up from her phone as she shrugs like it's no big deal. "You disappeared without saying a word. It left me with no other choice."

Even the concept of her knowing any of my business is enough to make me see red. It was two years ago when we split, and it wasn't exactly on the best of terms. How could it be after I walked into the house I bought for us, only to find her fucking some other guy in our bed? She screamed, he tried to jump out the window, and I put my fist through the wall. Eight years and two hundred grand on a spring wedding down the drain, but at least I found out when I did. It saved me from a pricey divorce, I'm sure.

"All right, we need to get in there," Blaire says. "Mr. Hyland is expecting you."

I murmur a few obscenities under my breath but shove my hands in my pockets and follow dutifully into the school. It's prestigious, that's for sure, with a giant crest on the floor of the main foyer. The lockers are gold and the walls a deep burgundy. It's all flawless, making me wonder how much time they spend making sure everything looks top of the line.

Trent leads us through the lobby and into the main office, where an older man stands waiting. His gray hair contrasts with his black suit, giving away the fact that he's closer to retirement than not. As he lifts his head and spots me, a grin spreads that's too big for his face. *Great, a grown fan-boy.*

"Mr. Hawthorne. It's so nice to meet you," he greets me, extending his hand. "I'm Jon Hyland, but you can just call me Jon."

"Thanks for having me," I lie.

26

If he can tell that I'd rather be literally anywhere else, he doesn't say anything about it. "The pleasure is all mine."

I lean against one of the desks and wait for Trent to finish introducing Blaire to Jon. When they're finally finished, I get straight to the point. It's not like I'm trying to be disrespectful, but the last thing I want to do is sit around this place all day and exchange fake pleasantries. I can only force a smile on my face for so long.

"So, what exactly does this coaching gig entail? I show up a couple times after school and to the games on Friday night?" *Please tell me that's all it is.*

The wary glance he shares with Trent tells me that couldn't be further from the truth. "Not exactly. While we're thrilled that you're willing to coach our team and surely lead them to a long-awaited championship, the policy states that all coaches must be members of the faculty."

"Aw, damn." I feign disappointment. "I guess that rules me out then."

"Well, let's not jump the gun. We do have an opening for an English teacher that I'm prepared to offer you, which would make it so you meet all the necessary coaching requirements."

My brows raise, and I instantly shake my head to try to wake myself from this real-life nightmare. "No offense, Jon, but I don't know fuck-all about being a teacher."

He crosses his arms over his chest. "Maybe not, but from what I gather, you and Trent are quite close, and he's one of the best teachers we have. I'm sure he could show you the ropes."

"I'm not qualified," I begin, but of course, he has an answer to everything.

"You have a degree from when you attended Notre Dame, correct?"

"Yes, but—"

"Then you're qualified."

My jaw locks and my teeth grind together harshly. It's all I can do to keep from shouting out what I really think about this whole ordeal. Judging by the way both Trent and Blaire refuse to look at me, it's obvious I'm the only one who wasn't previously informed of this minor detail. Just knowing they ambushed me into this makes me want to tell both of them to fuck themselves.

As if Blaire can read my mind, she finally speaks up. "Asher, you need this."

"I don't *need* anything."

"You do if you want a chance in hell of getting back onto the field when you're well. You know teams aren't just looking for talent when they pick a quarterback."

Groaning, I lace my fingers into my hair and tug, hard. I'm sure Colby is going to get a kick out of this—his best friend going from one of the league's best quarterbacks to a fucking English teacher and coaching high school football. I can only imagine the jokes he'll make at my expense.

"Well, I guess I don't have a fucking choice, now do I?"

Blaire smiles like the cat that caught the damn canary, while Trent and Jon both sigh in relief. *Douchebags, all of them.*

I grudgingly sign the paperwork Jon needs to officially hire me, and *ironically*, Blaire comes prepared with all the required documents. If she wasn't a woman, I'd probably lay her out just for the fun of it. When we're finally done, I can't seem to leave the school fast enough—ignoring Jon as he calls out about what an honor it is to have met me. As far as I'm concerned, he's just had me sign my goddamn death certificate.

Here lies Asher Hawthorne's dignity.

"Am I free to leave?" I ask Blaire.

It's obvious she's trying to hide her amusement by the way she swallows down a laugh. "For now. I'm going to be setting up an interview—over the phone, so no one can see your lack of enthusiasm for your new profession. I'll have all the questions and your responses faxed over to your penthouse later this week."

"Fan-fucking-tastic."

I don't wait for her to say anything else as I get in my car and slam the door. Trent jumps in just before I pull away, which is good for him, because I was about to leave his ass here. Today went from bad to worse. One wrong word out of his mouth and I just might snap. Luckily for him, he stays quiet as I drive back to his place.

"I'm going to get my things and stay at a hotel for the night," I tell him as I pull into the driveway. "I'm still not ready to go back to my penthouse just yet, but I sure as hell can't be here."

He frowns. "Come on, man. You don't need to do that."

I shake my head adamantly. "I do. I'm not in the mood to hang out, and if I stay here, I'll end up saying shit I don't mean. Trust me when I say, it's best if I go."

It looks like he wants to argue it, but he knows better than to push me right now. So instead, he nods and gets out of the car. *Thank fuck.* At least *something* went the way I wanted in the last twenty-four hours.

OKAY, SO MAYBE BEING alone wasn't the smartest choice. The suite I got is massive, and all I've done since I got here is pace. The rug will probably have track marks in it by the time I leave.

How the fuck did this happen? How did I go from having the world by the balls—both literally and figuratively—to this? Some washed-up quarterback making less money in a year than I used to make in an hour. It's almost laughable.

My phone rings on the table, and Colby's name flashes across the screen. I'm not stupid enough to ignore him. If I do, he'll only make it worse for me.

"What?" I answer, not even bothering to hide my sour mood.

The chuckle he lets out makes me imagine punching him in his stupid, little, baby face. "Well, I was going to tell you about this crazy rumor that started circulating today, but judging by *that* greeting, I'm going to go out on a limb and say it's not crazy at all."

"Fuck off, asshat."

Laughter booms over the line. "Aw, come on. Is that any way to talk to your best friend?"

I roll my eyes. "I don't have a best friend. Only people I hate less than others. Right now, you're not on that list."

"Sure, I'm not. Okay, but in all seriousness, what the fuck?"

Throwing myself onto the bed, I groan. "Honestly, I've been asking myself that for the last two hours. This was all fucking Blaire's doing."

He exhales loudly. "Why don't you just fire her ass?"

"Because that would be publicity suicide right now and you know it. She's good at her job, I just don't like her tactics."

"Well, if you ever need someone to show her the door, I'm your man."

"You mean like you showed her to yours? Oh wait, that's right—you didn't. You fucked her, then patted her cheek a couple times and *pointed* to the door."

I can practically hear the amused grin spread across his face. "I was tired, but I sure as hell didn't want her thinking she could stay. She wasn't good enough in the sack to deserve that luxury."

Now *that* manages to pull a laugh out of me. "Whatever

you say, Playboy."

"Maybe that's what you need," he suggests, like he's just solved world hunger. "When's the last time you got laid?"

"I'm *really* not in the mood for company."

Colby grumbles in frustration. "I'm not asking you to go speed-dating, fuckface. I'm saying just go to the nearest club, find a chick, and screw her until you're a little less wound up."

It's not the worst idea, and he may have a point. It's been at least a few weeks since I brought someone to bed, the last being some girl at a party Colby threw. The way she acted when we woke up, however, put me off the idea for a little while. It's as if sleeping with her meant we were secretly married or some shit. I literally had to change my phone number to get her to stop calling.

Tonight could be different, though. I'm not drunk, nor desperate, and can take my time picking. Really make sure she isn't completely certifiable before I bring her back to my hotel room.

I ponder it for another few seconds before finally caving. "Yeah, all right."

"Yes!" my idiotic best friend cheers. "That's my man!"

"Okay, I'm going to pretend you didn't just celebrate me agreeing to get laid more than you did winning the last game."

He snickers. "I appreciate it."

The two of us get off the phone and I grab a towel before heading for the shower. I guess my plans for tonight have changed.

THE CLUB IS FILLED with a ton of women who make no effort to hide the way they eye-fuck me—at least not until I spot one from across the bar. She's sitting with a few of her friends, or is that one her sister? They look alike enough to be twins, but still different. Her brown hair flows down over her chest, bringing my direction straight to her cleavage. Her red dress is low cut enough to entice but still leave enough to the imagination.

I take a sip of my whiskey as I watch the way she laughs at something. *God, she's gorgeous.* Like she can feel my gaze on her, she looks up and her eyes meet mine. I can see the moment her breath hitches, and she glances down before focusing back on me. She pulls the straw of her drink into her mouth and her cheeks hollow as she sucks in, making my dick twitch inside my pants.

"Hey." A woman greets me, placing herself unnecessarily close and ripping my attention from the bombshell I was just silently flirting with. "You're Asher Hawthorne, right?"

Fuck. "No, sorry, I just look like him."

"Really? I could have sworn you were him." Her shoulders deflate just slightly.

"Nope. Besides, I hear he's a major dick."

She gasps as if I just kicked her damn puppy. "Don't talk about him like that! I heard he's a total sweetheart."

Is that what people are saying about me? Shit. I should really fix that.

"If you say so." I brush it off, taking another swig of my drink.

I was hoping for this girl to get the hint that I'm not interested, but unfortunately, she's a bit dense. She comes even closer and places a hand on my arm while bending forward enough to practically shove her tits in my face.

"So, if you're *not* Asher Hawthorne, who are you?"

I shrug. "Just a guy having a drink."

"Oh, mysterious," she coos. "I like that in a man."

I'm sure you do, Barbie. I'm sure you do.

The thorn in my side starts blabbering about something I can't bother to listen to when I find myself once again in a staring contest with the only one in this place to grab my attention. She says something to her friends before biting her lip in a way that makes my cock harden in a matter of seconds. My tongue juts out slightly to moisten my own lips, and she instantly catches the underlying message.

All the girls she was with look confused as she gets up and walks around to me, inserting herself in between me and the blonde who doesn't know how to shut her mouth. It's a ballsy move, but doesn't compare to her next one. She grabs my glass off the bar and downs the rest of it in one fluid motion.

"Tessa Davenport," she says, returning the now-empty tumbler.

I can't help but smile. "Asher Hawthorne."

It's probably stupid, telling her my real name after I just lied to the chick standing right behind her, but it slipped. In a matter of seconds, this girl has me totally off my game. Confidence radiates from her in waves as she stands tall and lets her eyes rake over me with zero shame.

"I thought you said you *weren't* Asher!" whines the pest that doesn't know how to take a hint.

Tessa rolls her eyes hard before turning around. "He's a little busy, okay? So, run along and find some other poor soul to torture."

As if no one has ever called her out before, she recoils like she was just punched in the face then turns to me. "Whatever. You were right, you *are* a dick."

With that, she storms away and leaves Tessa and me exactly how I wanted to be in the first place—alone. She chuckles at the dramatics, and the sound is one I wouldn't mind playing on a constant loop for hours on end. Is there anything about this girl that *isn't* perfect?

"How did she know who you are?" she questions, completely surprising me.

"You don't?"

She raises one brow. "Should I?"

And okay, that's hot as fuck. It's not often I come across a woman who doesn't already know me. Whether it's because their ex or even current boyfriend watches football or because they're a straight-up gold digger, they usually all at least recognize me. This one, however, seems to be shocking me at every turn.

"Well, if you don't know, I'm sure as hell not going to tell you."

Pulling her lip between her teeth again, she doesn't seem to mind the fact that I don't plan on clueing her in. "Okay."

"Okay?"

"Yeah." She shrugs. "I'm not going to hassle you out of information you don't seem to want to share."

Wow, all right. So, not only is this chick the most breathtaking woman I've seen in a while, but she's probably also the most down to earth. Maybe Colby was right. This was a fucking brilliant idea.

"Okay, then. Do you want to dance?"

Her gaze meets mine, and I can already see something sinful brewing behind those brown eyes of hers.

"No, because I don't believe for a second that *dancing* is what you came here for."

Now, I'm intrigued. "Oh? And what did I come here for?"

She moves in closer until her lips are at my ear and her breath teases my skin. "To find someone who makes you want to strip their clothes off, then take them back to your place and do exactly that." Pulling away, she levels me with a look that threatens to flip my whole damn world upside down. "So, are we leaving or not?"

Tessa

WE BURST THROUGH THE DOOR IN A TANGLED MESS of body parts. Asher pushes me against the wall, breathing me in as his lips connect with mine once again. It's sexy, the way he takes complete control and doesn't offer up a single ounce of it. His hands skim down my sides, leaving a lingering burn in his wake and making me feel alive.

"You are so goddamn sexy," he murmurs as he moves to my neck.

My head lolls to the side to give him more room as he kisses, licks, and nips at the sensitive skin. A breathy moan emits my mouth at how he ignites every single one of my nerve endings.

"How attached are you to this dress?"

I look down at the red fabric that clings to my body then back up to meet his jaded eyes. "Not enough to care what you do to it."

He smirks. "Good."

In one fluid motion, he grips the top of my dress and tears the fabric in half, literally ripping it off me. His muscles flex with the movement, and his gaze rakes over my newly exposed body. He licks his lips as he pulls the remaining scraps down my arms until it pools on the floor.

"Fucking perfect," he whispers.

Our mouths meet again in a feverish kiss, with our tongues tangling and him grinding against me. He lifts me with ease and pulls me from the wall. As he carries me through the suite and into the bedroom, my already intense arousal grows.

He puts me down, and I pull the shirt from his body while my eyes take in the sight of his abs. Every single one is perfectly toned, making him look like he was carved out of stone. I bite my lip. There is nothing sexier than a guy who works hard for himself, and there's no way this body came naturally.

"Like what you see?" he asks, cockily.

I look up at him and smirk. "I'll like it a lot more when I see what it can do."

He chuckles. "You're not going to try to get to know me first? Ask me where I grew up or what I do for a living?"

"No." I shake my head. "Because I honestly don't give a fuck. Why don't you use that tongue of yours for something a little more useful?"

A dimpled grin appears on his face, rendering me completely defenseless. "Gladly."

Before I have a second to brace myself, he picks me back up and tosses me onto the bed. Then, he stalks toward me like a lion to its prey. He grabs the small fabric of my thong and slowly pulls it down my legs. *Well, at least he didn't destroy that, too.*

Climbing onto the bed, he kisses his way up the inside of my thigh slowly—teasing and torturing me with the anticipation of what's to come. Then, once he reaches his destination, he glances at me for a second before diving in.

The second his mouth meets my sex, my head is thrown back in ecstasy. He licks and sucks on my clit with a practiced skill, knowing all the ways to make me scream. I bring my hand down and lace my fingers into his hair to grip onto something. He moans at the tension, which only pushes me further.

"Your pussy tastes so fucking good."

Groaning at the momentary loss of contact, I arch my hips and pull his head back down. He chuckles against me.

"That's it, baby. Grind against my face. I want you to come on my tongue."

He slips two fingers inside me and I'm a fucking goner. Pleasure explodes throughout my body, and I scream out as he works me through it, not relenting for a single second. It has to be the fastest orgasm I've ever had, and I'm already sure it won't be the only one tonight.

Asher backs away and licks his lips as he savors the taste of me for a little bit longer. He unbuckles his belt and pulls the rest of his clothes off in one move, leaving me to gawk at the size of him. He's huge—at least nine inches and the biggest I've ever seen, let alone done anything with. The chances of him ripping me in half are high, but I welcome the challenge.

He hovers over me and reaches into the nightstand to grab a condom. *Of fucking course, it's a magnum.* Ripping it open with his teeth, I watch as he slides it over his thick cock. Once he's done, he lines up at my entrance and sinks inside me in a single thrust.

"Fucking fuck," he growls as he bottoms out.

The pain of being stretched open stings, but it's the most pleasurable pain I've ever felt in my life. I dig my nails into his lower back, mentally begging him to do something, and he smiles as he gets the message.

Thrusting into me relentlessly, the moans coming out of both our mouths are animalistic. He fucks me like he isn't afraid to break me—like I'm anything but fragile—and I'm living for it. We both may be in pieces by the time this is over, covered in bruises and scratch marks, but neither us seem to care. We'll ride this out to sunrise.

I WAKE IN THE morning feeling sore in all the best places. The heavy arm draped across my stomach reminds me that Asher is sound asleep beside me. Allowing myself a moment, I run my eyes over his face and take in each one of his features. He's flawlessly gorgeous, and if I didn't know exactly what last night was, I may even consider sticking around.

Carefully, I slip out from under his hold and tip-toe to the bathroom. My reflection stares back at me from the mirror, in nothing but underwear, completely unashamed of what took place a few hours ago. I run my fingers through my hair to remove any knots and use a tissue to fix my face. When I'm done, I creep back into the room. The last thing I want is for him to wake up and think he needs to let me down easy. I'm not some fragile little thing, and I don't need to be treated as such.

I manage to find my dress on the floor. As I pick it up, however, I remember how he literally tore it off me. Sexy as fuck, yes, but it doesn't make for a very easy getaway. I spot his black T-shirt draped across the back of the chair and nearly cheer in victory. Pulling it on, the shirt hangs so low on me, it could be considered a dress. *Perfect.* I grab my heels and go to leave the room when I hear Asher from behind me.

"Leaving already?" he asks, voice laced with sleep in a way that makes me want to relive last night all over again.

"Yeah. I have a thing I need to get to this morning."

Nodding, he looks me over once and his brows furrow. "Is that my shirt?"

"Yeah," I tell him, doing a twirl to show how much better it looks on me than him. "I'd wear my dress, but you kinda ruined it."

"Shit." The smirk drops right off his face. "I forgot about that. Let me pay for a new one."

As he reaches for his wallet, the sheet covering him falls

to his waist, and the sight of his abs is enough to keep me locked in here for the rest of the day, learning more of the sinful things he can do with that tongue. But I can't. Delaney is waiting for me, and I can't let her down. It's not an option.

"That's *really* not necessary."

He looks up after pulling a massive wad of hundred-dollar bills, and okay, what the fuck? "Are you sure?"

With my luck, he's probably some kind of mafia boss or something. No one *that* hot comes without trouble. It's practically a proven fact. And as tempting as it is to stay and figure him out, I have to go.

"Positive. I was only going to wear it once anyway."

He seems confused for a second, and then tosses the cash onto the bed. "Well, at least let me walk you to the door."

Apparently, having to see his abs again wasn't enough. The universe has to torture me with seeing him in his boxers, walking toward me with fuck-me-eyes and a smirk that could melt the clothing right off my body. I swallow hard and try to focus on literally anything else as he places his hand on the small of my back and leads me to the door of the suite.

He steps in front of me, blocking my exit. His knuckle goes under my chin, and he lifts my head up to face him. I stand completely still as he bends down and kisses me once more. It's slow and calculated, but there's an underlying want in the way he moves his lips against mine. There isn't a doubt in my mind that if I could stay, the two of us would spend hours exploring each other's bodies and bouncing between reality and sexual sub-space.

"It was nice meeting you, Tessa Davenport," he says seductively.

"You too, Asher Hawthorne."

With that, he opens the door and I walk out—knowing I'll never see him again.

AS I STAND IN in my driveway, I don't think I've ever dreaded something so much in my life. Delaney and Knox are putting their suitcases into the trunk of Laney's car. Once they're done, my sister turns to me and my heart drops. I can already see the waterworks building in her eyes.

"Don't," I plead. "If you cry, I'm going to cry."

She chuckles, but it doesn't stop the tear from escaping and sliding down her face. "I am going to miss you *so* much, Tess."

"You're not going to have a chance to miss me, because I'm going to come see you every fucking chance I get."

Wiping her cheek with the back of her hand, she pulls me into a tight hug. "I'm holding you to that."

We stand there and hold each other for a while, neither one of us wanting to let go, until our parents come out to say our goodbyes and we're forced to part. While she focuses on them, I turn my attention to Knox. He's standing by the car with his hands in his pockets, patiently waiting for Laney to get done. I walk toward him until we're no more than a foot apart.

"Tessa." He says my name like he's completely unaffected, but I can hear the sadness in his voice.

I stand tall in a way that says I mean business. "Do you remember when Ainsley threatened to kill you if you ever hurt Delaney?"

He raises a single brow. "Yes?"

Smirking, I take one step closer. "Let me find out you ever do anything that makes her the slightest bit upset, and I'll do things to you that will make the shit we went through this past year seem like a dream world."

A wide grin spreads across his face, and he wraps his arms around me. "CBP, I'm going to miss your crazy ass."

I can't help but laugh, despite the fact that he's using the nickname he refuses to tell me the meaning of. "Even after I almost burned your house down?"

"Even after that," he promises.

As I take a step back, Delaney and our parents come up behind us. I hug my sister one last time and watch as our dad, who used to despise Knox with a passion, shakes his hand. I guess your opinion of someone changes when they literally take a bullet to save your daughter's life.

"I swear to God, Delaney, you better text me every single day," I tell her, my head resting on her shoulder.

"And I swear to God, you better answer every single day," she retorts.

Knox's focus moves from my dad to my sister, and you can see the love and admiration in his eyes. I can't decide if it's adorable or vomit-worthy. The one thing I can appreciate, however, is the fact that I know he will always do whatever it takes to protect her. He's more than proven as much.

Delaney steps toward him with the biggest smile on her face. I'm happy for her, I am. But I'd be lying if I said my heart doesn't crack a little with every bit of distance that spreads between us. They both wave goodbye and climb into the car, and I do my best to hold it all together as I watch them drive away. Once they're gone, however, all bets are off.

"Tessa?" my mom asks as I turn around and race inside the house.

"Just give me some time," I beg. "Please."

Thankfully, neither of my parents make another attempt to stop me as I run up the stairs and into my bedroom. The second the door shuts behind me, I lean my back against it and slide down until I'm sitting on the floor. Sobs rip through me, the pain practically unbearable.

I've never had to know what life is like without my other half—never had to know how much it sucks to not have her

43

close by all the time. And now, she's moving to the other side of the country. A place where there is a three-hour time difference and thousands of miles between us.

I get up and crawl into my bed, letting the tears soak my pillow. It's weak, and pathetic, and everything I never wanted to feel like, but I can't help it. Everything is different now.

"How am I supposed to get through this without her?" I cry to no one but myself.

"By being the badass you know you are."

Lennon's voice catches me off guard, and I turn around to find her standing by my door. Her blonde hair is tied up in a bun, and the sweats she's wearing show she plans on staying with me through every second of this massive pity party.

"What are you doing here?"

She shrugs, dropping her purse and coming to lay beside me. "Your sister may have told me you'd need someone today."

I groan. "Fucking Delaney."

Lennon and I stay in my bed for what feels like hours, with neither one of us saying anything. I'm too lost in my thoughts, and she's smart enough to know that nothing she says right now can make me feel any better. But that's the thing about her—she stays anyway and doesn't complain once.

THE TASTE OF MINT chocolate chip ice cream coats my tongue as I laugh at Lennon's impression of Principal Hyland. Okay, so we may be a little drunk, which is probably the reason she stumbles and falls to the ground. She lays on the floor, giggling, while staring up at the ceiling.

"This rug is like heaven," she slurs.

"If that rug is heaven, you've never had good sex."

I can practically hear her eyes roll. "Accurate, because I've never had sex at all. Oh, but how was last night? You disappeared pretty quickly."

Thoughts of Asher fill my mind, and I find comfort in the distraction. The way he ran his hands over my skin, as if he was worshiping my body...even remembering it sends chills down my spine. It was hands down the most mind-blowing sex of my life.

"Do you know what the best part about being with an older guy is?" I question dreamily.

"No, but I'm sure you're about to tell me."

"They're experienced. They know exactly what to do and how to do it in a way that makes you scream."

A small laugh bubbles out of her. "So, I'm guessing it went well then."

"*Extremely* well, but the one thing I can't seem to get out of my head is his face when he found out I don't know who he is. It was like I should have, and the fact that I didn't was a total shock to him."

Getting to know Asher wasn't on my agenda for last night. It was purely sexual—a release for both of us and nothing more. But today, I'm curious.

"You don't think he's famous, do you?"

I shake my head. "Why would a famous person who looks like *that* be in a club without a bodyguard? That's just idiotic."

Lennon gets up and sits on my bed next to me. "You know how people get, though. There are like a million books and movies about them ditching their security to have a little unmonitored fun."

"Len, this is real life, not a movie."

She shrugs. "Well, the idea had to come from somewhere." Reaching over to my nightstand, she grabs my laptop and places it in front of me. "You remember his name, don't you?"

I nod, almost laughing at the question but stopping myself. "It's literally burned into my brain."

"Then it's time to meet Google."

It takes a minute of me thinking it over, not sure if I want to know the truth behind the guy who rocked my entire world last night. Yet, if I don't find out now, I know it's going to eat me alive, and eventually I'll do it anyway. It's better to skip the hard part and give in now.

I open my computer and put in the password. Once it's powered to life, I pull up the search engine.

"Asher Hawthorne," I whisper to myself as I type in his name.

The second I hit enter, thousands of results load—most of them being recent articles. His picture sits on the right side of the screen, those same green eyes making me question why I let myself walk out that door without at least getting his phone number. Maybe we could have made a thing of it. Nothing serious, of course, just a little fun. Oh well, too late now.

Scrolling down, I read over the headline of the first article.

Asher Hawthorne's Career is Over Due to Injury

"Holy shit," Lennon breathes. "You went and fucked an NFL player."

I continue to scroll through the mounds of information. "I guess I did."

She sighs, throwing herself backward and lying down. "Only you would score some sexy ass famous quarterback and be totally nonchalant about it."

The urge to see him again squeezes my chest, but I know it's not possible. What am I supposed to do, march back up to his hotel room like a total stage-five clinger? No, thank you. I have a bit more dignity than that. Well, at least I'll have plenty of pictures I can use to relive last night in my mind.

THE REST OF THE summer passes in the blink of an eye. The next thing I know, I've gone three weeks without waking up to Delaney right across the hall. It's difficult, of course, but it's getting easier. Especially because we still talk almost constantly. She's enjoying college and living with her boyfriend, while I'm stuck here—repeating my senior year of high school. *Lucky me.*

I walk down the hall toward my locker with Lennon by my side. This girl has very quickly become one of my best friends, and I love her for that. After Savannah introduced us a few months ago, we've been practically inseparable.

"Well, if it isn't my two favorite firecrackers," Kellan greets, stepping in between us and draping an arm over our shoulders.

Kellan Spencer is basically the spitting image of his cousin, Carter Trayland—Haven Grace Prep's favorite golden boy, who graduated last year. He ruled the school easily, with girls basically fainting just from him winking at them, and Kellan isn't much different. His blond hair and aquamarine eyes only accentuate the jawline that looks like it could be used to cut glass. He's hot, and he knows it.

"Hey Kellan," I respond, snickering at the way Lennon blushes.

She can pretend all she wants that she doesn't have a major crush on him, but it doesn't take a dating expert to see it. Any time he's around, she goes quiet—and that girl is nothing if not outspoken.

As we approach our lockers, I can't help but notice Charleigh, Skye, and Adrianna all huddled around, excitedly gossiping. Lennon and I share a confused look before intruding in their conversation.

"What are you guys up to?" Len questions.

Charleigh is the first one to speak. "Rumor has it, we have a hot new English teacher."

"It's *not* a rumor," Skye remarks. "I saw him myself. He's fucking gorgeous."

My eyes roll. While these girls aren't the worst, if they think that they have a chance in hell with our new teacher, they're delusional. He's a teacher, which means he's at least four years older and probably has morals that would keep him from messing around with a student. It's like the typical fantasy pipe-dream. However, at least I'll have something pretty to look at it in the mornings, because English is our first class.

"Eh, I learned this summer that gorgeous to *me* and gorgeous to *Skye* are two completely different things," I turn to smile at her. "No offense."

After she hooked up with one of the nerds at a party, during what she calls a momentary lapse in judgment, I've learned not to take her advice. Granted, he was probably one of those guys who looks better if you take off his glasses and remove the gel from his hair, but knowing that's how he *chooses* to look makes me question his sanity.

The bell rings, making Charleigh smile. "Well, looks like it's time to find out once and for all."

Lennon and I walk down the hall with the rest of them, ignoring the guys talking about football this year. The last time I tried to insert my opinion, they told me the most I should know about their team is whatever I learn from the sidelines, slinging pom-poms. Needless to say, I punched Tanner in the arm so hard it left a bruise. Cheerleading is *not* my thing.

Just as I'm about to walk into the classroom, Kellan grabs my wrist to stop me.

"What are you doing?"

He places one arm next to my head, leaning off the wall in a way that's supposed to be sexy and seductive, but I just don't see him that way. One, because I'm pretty sure my best friend has a thing for him, and two, because I don't mess around with younger guys.

"You and I should hang out later," he tells me.

I shake my head. "Sorry, Kellan. I'm not interested."

Slipping out from under him, I turn and enter the room. However, as soon as I do, I stop short. Kellan crashes into my back, but I barely even feel it. I'm frozen completely in place, staring straight into the green eyes I've pictured more times than I'd like to admit since the night we spent together. My jaw drops as everything sinks in.

Holy shit. Asher Hawthorne, the one-night-stand that will go down in history as the best sex of my life, is my new English teacher.

Tessa

I SIT AT MY DESK, UNABLE TO FOCUS ON ANYTHING but Asher. The look on his face when I walked in the room was unlike anything I've ever seen—furious, frustrated, and somehow hotter than fucking ever. It took a minute before I snapped out of it and went to sit next to Lennon. Still, he's yet to look at me since.

"All right," he grumbles, standing up and walking over toward the chalkboard. "My name is Mr. Hawthorne, and trust me when I say, I want to be here even less than you do."

A round of chuckles fill the air as they think he's cracking a joke, but judging by the way he rolls his eyes, he isn't. Skye raises her hand with a cocky grin on her face. He raises a brow at her, giving her permission to speak.

"What's your first name, Mr. Hawthorne?"

A bunch of girls fail at masking their giggles while Asher looks entirely fed up. "*That* is not information you need to know. You are a high school student, and I am your teacher. It'll do you good to remember that."

Skye pouts but my focus stays on the way Asher glances over at me and then down at the ground. Something tells me that little speech wasn't meant for her, but for me. I can't help the dull feeling of disappointment at his words, because seeing him again…I fucking want him, bad.

"Let's get back to business, shall we?" He walks back over to his desk and sits down. "I'm going to take attendance.

You're all seniors in high school, so I don't think I need to explain how this works." Looking at his computer, he starts to call out names. "Tanner Ackerman."

"Here," Tanner calls back.

"Lennon Bradwell."

"Here."

"Tessa Da—" As he stops short, I realize he almost called out the fake name I gave him that night. He swallows, hard. "Sorry. Tessa *Callahan*."

I drop my head down, feeling uncomfortable for the first time in a while. "Here."

He continues as if nothing happened, but the way my heart is racing proves otherwise. If this is how the next few months are going to go, Jesus take the wheel.

THE WHOLE CLASS IS spent with Asher avoiding looking at me at all costs, yet I'm still afraid that when the bell rings, he's going to ask to speak to me—which is something I can't handle. When I woke up this morning, the absolute *last* person I expected to see today was him, and I just need a minute to get my head on straight. So, the second the bell rings, I grab my things and blend in with the crowd, careful not to make eye contact with him as I leave.

"Ugh, the rumors were true," Skye sighs as she grips her book. "He *is* gorgeous."

Charleigh laughs. "Didn't you hear him? Messing around with one of his students doesn't seem to be on his bucket list."

"A girl can dream, okay?"

I look over at Lennon and can practically see the gears turning in her head. It's obvious she hasn't caught on yet, but it's only a matter of time until she puts the pieces together.

"Honestly, he seemed like a major hard-ass," Adrianna offers.

Kellan snorts and shakes his head. "You think *that* was him being a hard-ass? You should see him at practice. He almost made Tanner vomit."

"He did not!" Tanner whines. "I told you. I was already feeling sick before I got there."

"Sure you were, buddy." Kellan pats him on the back twice before jumping away as Tanner goes to smack him in the stomach. He focuses on Lennon. "What's up with you? You're quieter than usual."

Turning the corner, Lennon sighs. "He looked so damn familiar, but I just can't put my finger on it."

"You've probably seen him on TV or in a magazine." Tanner shrugs. "He's a former record-breaking quarterback for the 49ers."

And there it is. Lennon's eyes double in size as she stops and turns to me. I push her up against the wall and cover her mouth with my hand to keep in whatever she might blurt out. The girls keep walking, but Kellan and Tanner stop. Their brows furrow, but I smile sweetly.

"You go ahead. We'll catch up," I tell them.

Thankfully, they don't ask any questions as they continue their trek to our next class. Once they're out of earshot, I remove my hand.

"Tessa!" Lennon whisper-shouts. "What the fuck?"

"I know."

"He's the guy from the club!"

"I know."

"You've had sex with our English teacher!"

I roll my eyes, but I can't hide my amused grin. "I know. I realized who he was as soon as I walked in."

She runs her fingers through her hair as she lets it all sink in. "Do you think he remembered you?"

"Trust me, there's no way he didn't."

I lean against the wall next to her and let my head tip back. *What am I going to do?* I can't just continue to go to class every day, pretending I don't know how good his hands feel against my skin and the magical things he can do with his tongue. Just today alone I spaced out three different times as I replayed that night inside my head. But the look he had when he realized I'm a high school student wasn't only surprise—it was pure, unadulterated anger.

"So, are you going to try talking to him?" Lennon questions.

I exhale heavily and then shake my head. "I don't know. If I do, it certainly won't be right now. I obviously need to say something; I'm just not sure what."

WE'RE HALFWAY THROUGH LUNCH when Oakley and Micah finally decide to make their appearance. Them showing up late is completely unsurprising, especially on the first day of school. However, when they learn that their new football coach is their first period teacher, both their cocky smiles drop off their faces.

Oakley is a lot like Kellan, but with morals. He's your typical jock who only has love for football. Sure, he's hooked up with his fair share of girls. They practically flock to him, with his hazel eyes and toned body. Plus, he plays on the fact that his eyes change color in the light. However, he's always been very clear about the fact that his future in sports is his sole focus right now, and that there's no room for anything, or anyone, else.

Micah is more of the shy, quiet type. He's been Oakley's

best friend since they were in first grade, which is why he's just as into the dream of playing in the NFL, but he's nothing like him personality wise. For example, when I met them both over the summer, it was at a party. Oakley was doing body shots off some girl he didn't remember the next morning, while Micah was reading a book in the middle of a crowd of people.

"Shit, and we have practice today, too," Oakley whines. "All right, we say we had a doctor's appointment."

"Both of you?" Kellan raises a brow.

Oakley looks over at Micah and grins. "Quick, pretend you're pregnant."

The whole table laughs, since it's such an Oakley thing to say. He's always been the one to make a joke of things. It's nearly impossible for anyone to be in a bad mood around him, including myself.

As I'm talking to Tanner, Lennon subtly elbows me to get my attention, nodding her head toward the door. I can feel his eyes on me before I even see him. When I glance over at him, my chest tightens. He's standing near the entrance and talking to another teacher, but his eyes move to mine every few moments, glaring hard.

A part of me considers marching up to him, demanding to know what his problem is. However, I don't think the middle of a crowded cafeteria is the place for that kind of conversation. Instead, I just sit here, unable to look away.

"What are you looking at?" Kellan asks, starting to turn around.

Thankfully, the bell rings at the perfect time and breaks both mine and Asher's concentration. Lennon chuckles and shakes her head as I take a deep breath. It's only been a few hours, and there's already been a close call. I'm sure that means I'm fucking doomed.

We all get up and filter out of the cafeteria. I try looking around to see where Asher went, but he's nowhere to be found. Honestly, it's probably for the best.

"Who wants to skip third and fourth?" Oakley asks, and each one of us looks at him like he's lost his mind.

"Oak, you just got here," Tanner replies, snickering as he shakes his head.

Oakley just shrugs. "The first day is useless anyway."

I walk over to my locker to get my things, but as soon as I open it, a folded piece of paper falls out. My brows furrow as I bend down to pick it up. After a quick glance to make sure no one is looking over my shoulder, I open it.

Meet me after school.
- A. H.

My heart instantly starts to pound inside my chest, to the point where I wonder if anyone else can hear it. There's no question as to who it's from, and the small hope I had that he doesn't remember me is long gone.

Re-folding the note, I shove it into my bag and grab the stuff for my next class.

———

THROUGHOUT THIRD AND FOURTH periods, I can't seem to focus on anything but the piece of paper practically burning a hole through my bag. Even the way he wrote it, all scrappy and hard, shows his frustration. The only thing I know right now is that I'm running out of time to figure out what to say.

I take my time at my locker and wave goodbye to my friends as they leave. Lennon gives me a hug and makes me promise that I'll call her as soon as I get home. Then, once the hallways clear out, I swallow the lump in my throat and head to Asher's classroom.

It's now or never.

Asher

I PACE BACK AND FORTH IN FRONT OF THE chalkboard, running my fingers through my hair and pulling in frustration. How the fuck did I end up in this mess? It was one thing having to come and teach these brats, but to find out that one of them is the girl who gave me a night I can't seem to fucking forget? This all feels like a bad joke, like I did something to royally piss off the universe.

After Tessa left that morning, I couldn't get her out of my head. I thought maybe it was the environment. Every inch of the hotel room reminded me of her: the way we crashed through the door and practically fucked against the wall; the sounds she made that filled the air. It was like I was drowning in the urge to have her again.

So, I went back to my penthouse—and the thoughts came with me. I started picturing all the places I would fuck her in there. The way she would look if she were naked in front of my fireplace, wrapped in a thin, white sheet. No matter what I did, she was there, in the center of my mind, with no intentions of going anywhere.

Hell, I even went back to the club hoping to see her again. That happened more times than I'd like to admit, and Colby eventually told me I need to get over myself. That if I did find her, there's no guarantee she would still be interested. What we had was clearly a one-night stand. She knew it as well as I did.

When I got to work this morning, I was already in a bad

mood. I spilled coffee on myself right before I left the house. Colby decided it would be fucking hilarious to replace my sugar with salt, so when I took a sip of my morning liquid gold, needless to say, it tasted like shit. I spit it out and in the process, poured it down the front of me. *Douchebag.*

It's like he gets some kind of kick out of messing with me. He's been up my ass lately about cheering the fuck up and not walking around like my entire life got screwed in a matter of a couple months—but it did. He still has his dream. He has no idea what it's like to have everything you've ever wanted in the palm of your hand, and watch it get ripped away.

A quiet knock sounds against the door, bringing my attention to it before Tessa steps inside. Even just seeing her again has my blood boiling. She closes the door behind her, straightens her shoulders, and turns around.

"Hey."

My eyes widen. "Hey? That's all you have to say to me right now?"

She crosses her arms over her chest. "What else should I say? You called this little meeting."

"Oh, I don't know. Maybe *Hi, Asher. I'm so sorry I lied about my age and didn't tell you I was a student in high school before we fucked.*"

"Shh! Someone might hear you, dumbass." Stopping for a second, she lowers her own tone as well. "And I didn't technically lie. You never asked me how old I am."

My jaw locks. "I didn't think I had to! You were in a club, drinking alcohol. That normally means you're at least twenty-one."

The way she scoffs shows me she's not taking this as seriously as she should. Then again, why would she? It's not her freedom hanging in the damn balance.

"Like you've never used a fake ID."

Truthfully, I haven't. Sure, I drank underage—almost everyone has—but it was at house parties or in college. There was never a need for me to get a fake ID, let alone time to use one. I take a deep breath, trying to rein in my anger before asking the question I'm afraid to know the answer to.

"Are you even legal?"

She smirks for a moment, and then drops the façade. "Yes. I turned eighteen in January."

Eighteen. She's fucking eighteen. At least I didn't break any laws, but Jesus fucking Christ, she's so young. Instead of dwelling on that, I give myself a minute to breathe. I'm *not* going to jail for statutory rape.

Leaning against my desk, I shake my head. "I'm practically old enough to be your father."

"Okay, first of all, ew," she chuckles. "And second, unless you were having kids at age ten, that's a lie."

I cock a brow, turning to look at her—which is a big fucking mistake because she still looks just as gorgeous as I remember, and the prep school uniform is not helping one bit. "How do you know how old I am?"

She rolls her eyes. "Because *Grandpa*, there's a thing called Google. Maybe you've heard of it? Or are you too old for that kind of technology? The internet can be tricky for the elderly."

Leave it to Tessa to make me laugh. She's just as sassy as I remember, which is exactly why I need to keep my distance. Tell her to leave, transfer her out of my class, and avoid her at all costs.

"You Googled me?" *Okay, so my brain didn't get the fucking memo.*

Pushing the hair from her face, I partly expect for her to shy away, but she once again surprises me by standing taller.

"Don't flatter yourself," she says with a snort. "Some girl

at the bar knew who you were, and you were so surprised that I didn't. Of course, I Googled you."

"And what did you manage to find?"

"You're twenty-eight, single, and an insanely talented quarterback."

A tightness forms in my chest as I stare at the ground. "I *was* a talented quarterback."

"Asher," Tessa breathes, putting her hand on my shoulder. "Just because an injury screwed your career doesn't mean who you are changes. You're still a gifted football player. You just have something holding you back a bit."

My gaze meets hers, and I'm instantly drawn to her. I glance down at her lips, and her tongue juts out to moisten them, only making me crave her more. *No.* Bad *fucking* idea. I force myself to look away.

"You should go, before someone sees you in here."

Her breath hitches, as if that wasn't what she expected, and she takes a step away. Just when I hear the door open, however, I call out.

"And Tess?" She turns back to look at me. "Make sure no one finds out about this."

"Whatever you say, *Mr. Hawthorne.*"

I can't help but watch as she walks away, wondering what the fuck I've gotten myself into.

COLBY'S LAUGHTER ECHOES THROUGHOUT the room. He throws his head back and grips his stomach as he cracks up at my misfortune. I take the stress ball in my hand, throwing it directly at his balls. A smile grows on my face as I hit my target dead on and watch him hunch over in pain. Serves him right. *Bastard.*

"The fuck, man!"

"Oops?"

His eyes narrow to slits. "Asshole."

The second I left the school, I called Colby and told him to meet me at my place ASAP. I needed someone to talk to about my perpetually bad luck, and being as he's the only one who knows about the girl from the bar, he was the one I called. Thankfully, he answered and told me he'd be right over. Then again, he's not exactly helpful right now.

"I'm so glad you find this amusing."

He continues to chuckle as he wipes the tears from his eyes. "I'm sorry. It's just, this shit would only happen to you."

Getting up, I go over to the wet bar in my living room and grab another glass of whiskey. It's well needed, and well deserved, after the day I've had. Before this morning, a part of me still hoped I'd run into her again at some point. I didn't plan on starting anything serious, mainly because she doesn't seem like the type to want monogamy but also because I've tried giving my heart away once, and it didn't end well for me. To put myself through that kind of shit again, I'd have to be a goddamn idiot.

"So, how did you find out?" he questions. "You looked over your class lists the other night. You didn't recognize her name?"

I shake my head. "The first name, yeah, but the last name was different. I know she's not the only Tessa in the world, so I thought it was just a coincidence. Turns out, she lied."

"Damn." He takes a sip of his beer. "What are you going to do?"

It's a question that has been running through my mind all day. I know what I *should* do. I should go to Jon Hyland and tell him I need Tessa transferred out of my class. However, he's going to ask why, and being as it's only the first day of school, I can't exactly use the excuse that she's disruptive in

CHAPTER 6

class or anything. There's also the insanely fucked-up part of me that *wants* to see her every morning. To be able to sneak glances at her when no one is paying attention. To analyze her handwriting like some sort of fucking creep.

I know it's a recipe for disaster, and bound to bite me in the ass, but maybe if I can manage to keep enough distance, it won't be so bad.

***

THAT NIGHT, DESPITE HOW intoxicated I got while Colby was here, I lay in bed wide awake and unable to get comfortable. No matter what I do, nothing can shake the thoughts of Tessa from my mind. Even after finding out she's a student, she remains that breathtaking, confident bombshell I spent a crazy, sex-filled night with. The way she stood there today, completely sure of herself and every one of her actions, fuck! It was hot.

As I get in the shower and turn the temperature to ice cold. All I can think about is how many ways this can go wrong. The only thing I can do is hope it doesn't blow up in my face.

Like I said, *recipe for disaster*.

***

THE NEXT MORNING, I get to school and head into the teacher's lounge. Trent is already there, going over lesson plans while he drinks his coffee. I pour my own cup before going over to join him.

"Hey, Asher," he greets me. "How'd your first day go yesterday?"

I shrug. "It wasn't the worst thing in the world."

"No one gave you a hard time? Sometimes these kids try

to see how far they can push the newbies, learn what they can and can't get away with."

"Eh, nothing too bad. I think it helps that I coach the football team, so all the players know not to mess around."

He nods. "That's a good advantage to have. You should've seen the seniors from last year."

"That bad?" I ask, taking a sip of the brightest part of my morning.

"One of them, the captain, was the one I told you about. He was the son of the district attorney. Therefore, he thought he was invincible. He and his friends always came to class late and didn't even care that they were being disruptive."

Sounds like how I was in high school. "You didn't discipline them?"

"I couldn't," he sighs. "Carter's dad had Hyland in his back pocket. It was stupid to even attempt to stand against those kids. They even managed to corrupt my favorite student, Delaney Callahan. Though, she still managed to graduate valedictorian, so maybe there's hope for her after all."

The name catches my attention. "Callahan? As in *Tessa* Callahan?"

Trent looks up and cringes. "Ah, so you're the sad soul that ended up with Tessa in your class."

"She's in my first period."

He nods. "Well, yeah. Tessa is Delaney's twin sister. She should have graduated last year as well, but she skipped too many days and ended up needing to repeat part of her senior year."

Twins. So, that would explain the girl she was at the club with—the one who looked just like her, only not as confident and daring. It also explains why she's turning nineteen in a few months and still in high school. Okay, at least I know she wasn't lying about her age, *again*.

"What's her deal?" I inquire, trying to get some more information on her, even though I know I shouldn't. "What makes her so bad?"

Tapping his pen against the table, he leans back in his chair and locks his gaze with mine. "Tessa Callahan is like a forest fire—reckless, unpredictable, and nearly impossible to manage."

Tessa

"Oh, come on. You have to come. It's like a senior's rite of passage. We get the best seats this year," Lennon argues.

I shut my locker and roll my eyes. "You're forgetting, I've already done the whole *senior year* thing."

"No, you *skipped* the whole senior year thing, hence being here again and not at college."

My brows furrow. "Remind me again why I'm friends with you."

She grins sweetly. "Because I'm amazing and you love me."

I snort and go to walk away, but she moves with me.

"Please? I really want you to come with me."

"I don't know, Len."

As we stop outside our first period classroom, I can see the moment it clicks for Lennon. She peeks in and spots Asher sitting at his desk, then turns back to me.

"You know, Mr. Hawthorne is the football coach this year."

Groaning, my head thumps back against the wall. "And, your point?"

"Meaning, he'll be at the game."

She bounces her eyebrows seductively, knowing all about my lady boner for our English teacher. In my defense, he was my one night stand *weeks* before he became my teacher. However, I'd be lying if I said the whole person-of-authority thing isn't a turn-on. Between the way he took control the night we spent together, and the way he looks in that suit— it's a lethal fucking mix.

"Fine," I cave. "But we're taking my car."

Lennon chuckles. "Yes, because I'm going to complain about riding in your expensive-ass Lamborghini. That thing is better than sex."

"You've never had sex."

"Ugh," she groans as we turn into the classroom. "Just rub it in, why don't you?"

I'M ONLY HALFWAY THROUGH class and ready to rip Skye's eyes out of her head. I swear to God, the way she gawks at Asher, unashamed and like she's mentally undressing him in her mind— it's fucking infuriating. Doesn't she know to be discreet?

It's been five full days of having to sit in here with him for an hour and a half every day, and each time it gets harder. He's the most laid-back teacher I have, probably due to the fact that he doesn't want to be here in the first place, and if the sight of him didn't make me want to jump his bones, he would probably be my favorite. However, how can a teacher be your favorite when they absolutely refuse to even look at you?

Sometimes, when I'm trying to focus on the assignment he gave us, because redoing my senior year for a *third* time isn't something I'm up for, I can feel someone's gaze burning into me. It's intense, with a tension there that's completely unmatched, but whenever I look up, it goes away, and I don't find anyone staring back at me.

Does he really have to look *that* good all the time? I'm honestly not sure what's worse—having to look at him in a suit every day, or knowing exactly what he looks like underneath it.

"Okay, who can tell me the main plot of the book so far?" he asks, walking around to lean against the front of his desk.

As he crosses his arms in front of his chest, the fabric of his shirt stretches across his bulging muscles. I bite my lip to suppress the moan that wants to leave as I remember what those babies can do. The way he held me up against the wall, and then carried me across the hotel room. *Fuck.*

I'm so lost in my pornographic daydream that I don't even notice I was called on until Lennon nudges me with her elbow. I look around and realize that all eyes are on me, including Asher's for the first time since our little spat in this very room.

"I'm sorry, what?"

He clears his throat. "The plot of the book. What is it?"

The answer is there, right at the tip of my tongue, in the front of my mind, but it's blocked by images of him doing magical things to me with his mouth and the way his muscles flex when he cums.

I shrug. "I have no idea."

"See me after class, Miss Callahan." He shakes his head and moves onto someone else.

Oakley leans toward me with his fist covering his mouth. "Way to go, firecracker. First week of school and you're already in trouble."

"Says the guy who has already skipped four classes. Who are you trying to be, me?"

"That depends," he smirks. "Are guys like you your type?"

"Mr. Beckett, something you'd like to share with the class?"

The grin drops right off Oakley's face, as if he actually finds Asher to be intimidating. Then again, I'm yet to see what he's like during football practice. If it's anything like the way he is in bed, all bossy and demanding, they're screwed. *Shit,* there I go again, thinking about what he's like in bed. Ugh.

Oakley shakes his head and centers himself in his seat. "No, sir."

Asher nods slowly. "Keep your attention on me and off her, or you won't be starting in tonight's game. Got it?"

"Yes, sir."

The bell rings and everyone gets up. I take my time, knowing I won't be leaving just yet. Lennon gives me a look that silently wishes me luck as she walks out the door with the rest of the class. Once they're gone and we're left alone, Asher turns to face me. I grab my things and make my way toward him.

"You wanted to see me?"

He hums then looks out the door to make sure no one is around. "You need to pay more attention in class."

I snort. "Is that all?"

"No. You also need to refrain from biting your lip—at least while you're in here."

At the sound of his words, a whole new dose of confidence flows throughout my body. I take a step closer and let my eyes take over his body. *I bet that suit would look a whole lot better on the classroom floor.*

"And why's that?" I ask, biting my lip teasingly. "Can't handle it?"

His Adam's apple bobs as he swallows hard. "Tessa."

It's difficult to contain my amusement, but I manage to do it as I run my hand down his arm. "What's wrong, *Asher*?"

In a swift move, he grabs my wrist and holds it firmly away from his body. "Stop. This isn't the time or the place to play your little games."

"And when *is* the time? While we're making flirty eyes across a bar, or when you get me alone in a hotel suite?" I stick my tongue out seductively while he watches, not saying anything. "You remember that night, don't you? The way you made me scream for hours?"

Just when I think I'm starting to get somewhere, he releases me and steps away. "Not going to happen, Callahan. Now go, you have a class to get to—part of being a student."

Rolling my eyes, I turn on my heels and walk out of the room. Asher may think he's the one in control, but he just slipped up. Now I know one of his weaknesses, and I'm going to use it to play him like a violin.

I PULL UP TO the dance studio, ignoring all the people who gawk at my car as I get out. The music from inside can be heard from the sidewalk, and I can see Lennon dancing through the window. She's so talented, with the things she can do with her body. It's incredible.

And then there's Brady. Twenty-three years old and looking like a fucking God, Brady Laurence is everything sexual fantasies are made of—and as straight as a circle. Maybe if he was flamboyant and had rainbows and glitter coming out of his ass, it would be easier to not be attracted to him. Unfortunately for girls everywhere, that's not the case. He's 180 pounds of muscle and pure manly man, except for maybe the fact that he's a better dancer than most. Although, in his defense, that's what happens when you grow up with your mom owning the studio.

"Oh, hey," Lennon greets me as soon as she sees me standing in the doorway. "Is it five already?"

"Five-thirty."

Her eyes widen. "Shit. Okay, let me change, and we'll go."

She disappears into another room, leaving Brady and I alone together. He walks over to the side and picks a water bottle up off the floor. The way he wipes the sweat off his forehead shouldn't be nearly as sexy as it is.

"Hey, Tess."

I shake the thoughts from my head. "What's up, Brady?"

"Oh, you know. The usual." He walks over and pulls his iPhone off the base. "Have you heard from Savannah lately?"

Ah, Savannah. She used to dance at this studio, too—until she graduated with a full ride to Juilliard. She and Brady have been best friends for years, ever since Sav's father went all dead-beat-dad and Mrs. Laurence was the one to give her something to strive for. Hell, the two of them even fake dated for four years. The dedication to masking their truths was a little excessive, if you ask me, but their loyalty to each other is something I can appreciate.

I shake my head. "She's more Delaney's friend than she is mine."

He chuckles. "That's not true. I remember the three of you being the best of friends when you were kids."

"Yeah, well, that was before she vanished for years and then came back with a *new year, new me* attitude."

"You're still holding that against her?"

I shrug, breaking our eye contact to look at the ground. "You didn't see what that did to Delaney."

The topic is one of few that I shy away from. My sister is the most important person in my life, and seeing the way she was destroyed by Savannah's refusal to acknowledge her after being gone for three years—let's just say Delaney may forgive her, but it's going to take a lot more than an apology and some groveling before I do.

"Touché." Brady smiles and drops the subject.

A few minutes later, Lennon emerges again, dressed in jeans and a HGP hoodie. She gives Brady a quick hug goodbye and then links her arm in mine and heads for the door. I pull the keys from my pocket, unlocking the door. The second we get in, Lennon sighs.

"God, I've missed you."

My brows furrow. "You saw me a few hours ago."

She turns to look at me and smirks. "I was talking to the car."

"You're a bitch," I snicker.

"I know," she says with pride. "It's the main reason you love me."

THE BLEACHERS ARE FILLED with students excited to attend the first football game of the year. Most of them are dressed in the school's colors. Even Lennon has eye black on her face, though of course she pulls it off better than anyone else here. It's the blonde, curly hair and petite figure that makes her gorgeous, but it's her personality that makes people actually fear her. She's a total spitfire, which is why we get along so well.

I watch Kellan and Oakley run across the field like they own it while Tanner throws the ball in a perfect spiral. Kellan catches it and takes off, dodging every player trying to take him down. He stops short, and the guy charging toward him misses and falls to the ground, only for Kellan to jump over him. Oakley's shoulders bounce as he laughs and the touchdown is scored.

Glancing over at Asher, he seems pleased, but still has that stone-cold look plastered across his face. It's like he has no feelings. No pride. No joy. He just stays completely stoic, even as the buzzer sounds and Haven Grace is announced the winner.

"At least blink while you stare. Jeez, Tess."

I roll my eyes and turn my attention to Lennon. "I can't seem to figure him out."

She smiles sadly. "I don't think you're meant to. He's not just the guy from the bar anymore. He's our teacher. It changes the dynamic between you two."

A part of me knows she's right. I should stay away. Involving myself with him would lead to trouble. It's completely against the rules, and yet, I've always been the rebel. The more forbidden he is, the more I crave him. I'm sure there will be consequences, but I can't seem to care. I'm not going to stop until I get what I want.

ALCOHOL IS FLOWING THROUGHOUT the house as everyone celebrates the football team's win. Kellan's place is big enough to fit the entire school, but thankfully, not everyone was invited. At least that boy has sense enough not to allow the freshmen in. For one, they're fourteen and have no business being at parties like this, and second, they're always so overbearing and desperate.

"Tess, come take a shot with me," Charleigh calls, but my attention is currently being pulled elsewhere.

Scrolling through the Asher Hawthorne hashtag, I happened to come across a video of some girl talking about the party currently going on at Asher's penthouse. A brilliant idea comes to mind and I stand up, pocketing my phone before going to find Kellan. As expected, he's surrounded by girls, with one on each arm. They all have to be juniors. Lord knows he's already worked his way through the whole senior class over the last couple years.

"Hey, where's your football roster?"

His brows furrow. "In my room. Why?"

I shoot him a sweet, innocent smile. "No reason. Thank you!"

As soon as I get into Kellan's bedroom, I thank my lucky stars he's not as messy as Easton. That boy's room always looked like a bomb went off in it. While I doubt Kellan cleans, the neatness of it makes it easy for me to spot what I need sitting right on the desk. I grin triumphantly when I open it up and spot Asher's address right at the top. *Bingo.*

I take a picture of it with my phone and then put it back in its place before heading downstairs to find Lennon. She's laughing at something Oakley said when I come over and whisper in her ear.

"Come on. We're leaving."

"What?" she asks, confused. "Where are we going?"

I bite my lip as I think of how tonight could go. "Stopping at my place to change, then downtown. Let's just say I'm on a mission, and I'm not willing to lose."

Asher

I DRIVE ACROSS TOWN, WANTING NOTHING MORE than to get home and crawl into bed. Between dealing with bratty teenagers the whole week and the pressure of making sure we won tonight, I'm exhausted. I never thought I would be so anxious over a fucking high school football game. If they lost, people would have started to question my abilities. This win wasn't just preferred—it was *necessary*.

Parking my car, I get out and walk over to the elevator. After I put in the code for the penthouse, it starts to bring me to the top. However, the higher up I get, the louder the music becomes. *What the fuck?*

The doors open, and I'm instantly faced with nearly fifty people in my living room. They're all drinking out of fancy glasses, while the music sounds like we're in a club. There's only one person who could be responsible for this, and I'm going to kill him.

I push through the crowd of people, ignoring those who try to get my attention until I find Colby leaning against the kitchen island. As if he can feel me glaring at him, his eyes meet mine and he grins.

"It's about damn time you got here!" he shouts happily.

"Dude, what the fuck?"

Looking around as if he's oblivious to the problem, he turns back to me. "What?"

I wave around, gesturing toward all the people. "Uh, the party?"

"Oh," he chuckles. "I figured you need a night to let loose, and since I can't seem to drag you out of this place lately, I decided to bring the fun to you."

"Yeah, no." I shake my head. "Get them out of here."

Colby throws his head back and whines. "Aw, come on! Don't be like that."

"I'm not being like anything, Hendrix. I'm just not in the mood to entertain a shit-ton of people tonight."

"You're never in the mood," he argues. "You've been walking around the past few months with a stick shoved up your ass. At first, I dealt with it. You had shit you needed to work out on your own and I respected that, but fuck, Asher. You can't throw the rest of your life away because things didn't go the way you hoped." He reaches behind the bar and grabs a beer from the ice-filled sink. "Drink this and chill the hell out."

Okay, so maybe he has a point. Before my injury, I craved nights like this, where I could just let loose and hang out— embracing the feeling of living on top of the world. Once I got hurt, however, everything changed. My main priority became getting back on the field. Nothing and no one else mattered. I guess I just never left that mindset. And well, since the party is already here…

I'M STANDING WITH A few of my former teammates, laughing while Griffin tells me about how Colby got chewed out after Coach found him passed out in bed with two women. Apparently his alarm didn't go off and he missed practice. Instead of calling him, Coach decided to wrangle up the whole team and show up at his house.

"I tried telling you that your sex life is going to get your ass in trouble."

Griffin chuckles and shakes his head. "Wait. It gets better."

I groan. "Oh no."

"So, the girls both wake up and the one *screams*. I'm talking ear-piercing, blood-curdling scream."

"Why, because the whole 49ers football team was seeing her practically naked?"

"Nope," he grins at Colby. "Tell him who she is, Colb."

Colby's head drops as he refuses to look at me. "Coach's niece."

I hunch over, laughing hysterically. Not only did he catch him in bed with his niece, but he caught them in what was obviously a threesome. I couldn't dream of anything more embarrassing than that.

"What did you say?"

Griffin snorts and gives me the answer Colby is too afraid to say. "He asked Coach to get him a beer because he was too hungover to get it himself."

Jesus Christ. If anyone could take an already horrible situation and make it impossibly worse, it's my idiotic best friend. I look over at him with tears in my eyes from laughing so hard and shake my head.

"You're a special kind of dude, you know that?"

The corners of his mouth raise. "Yeah, it's part of my charm."

A few minutes later, we're all talking about the kids I'm currently coaching and if I see any NFL potential in any of them. Honestly, I could see Oakley making it. He has the mindset and determination to get him there, *and* he doesn't let anything get in his way. I heard him talking to Kellan in the locker room tonight. He was telling him the best way to stay focused is to not give yourself anything else to focus on. It's actually pretty smart, when you think about it.

"Goddamn!" Colby practically chokes on his drink. "Who is *that?*"

As my previous thoughts disappear, I follow his gaze and when I find what he's looking at, my chest tightens. Stepping through the elevator is none other than Tessa Callahan, and *fuck* she looks good. The black dress she's wearing clings to her perfectly shaped body. Her brown hair is messy, like she just ran her fingers through it, and it reminds me of how she looked all sexed out and sprawled across my bed. *What the hell is she doing here?*

I slam my beer down onto the counter and quickly march my way over to her. The second she sees me, the amazed look she had as she glanced around the room vanishes, and all that's left is the confidence that seems to drive me crazy.

"What the fuck do you think you're doing?"

She shrugs. "Coming to a party, what does it look like?"

"You just *happened* to show up at a party at *my* house?" I deadpan.

"Oh, this is *your* place? I had no idea."

I cross my arms over my chest. "Cut the shit, Tessa. You need to leave." Looking to her side for the first time, I recognize the blonde standing with her as another one of my students. "And you brought Lennon with you? Have you lost your mind?"

"Easy, Cujo." She holds up a hand. "Lennon already knew about us. She was with me the night we met."

Just when I was starting to feel like maybe tonight was a good idea after all, the one thing that tortures me on a daily basis has to show up and take my frustration level from a steady four to a rapidly increasing twelve.

I try to take a breath to calm myself. "Who even invited you?"

"Yes, please tell me so I can thank them," Colby says as he steps up next to me.

Tessa's jaw drops as she stares at him in shock. "You're Colby Hendrix." She looks to me and points at Colby. "He's Colby Hendrix."

I arch a single brow. "Oh, so you don't know who *I* am but you know who *he* is?"

"You weren't voted Sexiest Man Alive two years in a row, Asher." She smiles and blatantly checks him out with not even a single ounce of shame.

"Tessa," I growl, not liking the jealousy that courses through my body. "Don't."

A bark of laughter leaves Colby's mouth. "So, *you're* the infamous Tessa. I've heard a lot about you."

"Have you now?" She shoots me a look of delight. "And what exactly have you heard?"

"Enough to know you're trouble, and I happen to like trouble."

It's obvious Colby is only doing this to get a rise out of me. He can be a douchebag, but one thing he's always been adamant about is not sharing chicks. Still, that doesn't stop me wanting to rip his head off when he places his arm around her.

"Let's get you a drink."

I put my hand out to stop them, and she rolls her eyes. "If you don't want to see me having a good time, fine. Just don't look."

With one last smirk at me, Tessa lets Colby lead her through the party and over to the kitchen. Lennon stays put, not nearly as ballsy as her friend. Unfortunately for me, I seem to lack the ability to be a total dick.

Sighing, I glance at her. "You're not going to take pictures and brag on Monday about how you spent the weekend partying with your English teacher, are you?"

She shakes her head rapidly. "No way—and not just

because I don't want to get you fired, but because my dad would kill me."

Good enough. "All right, go make sure Tessa doesn't jump in bed with dumbass over there."

As she goes to join them, I take a deep breath and try counting to ten like my therapist told me to. I only get to six before I say fuck it. Where the hell is my whiskey? I'm going to need a glass or four.

WATCHING OAKLEY HIT ON Tessa in class earlier today was hard. I wanted to do everything in my power to keep him as far away from her as I possibly could. However, all of that pales in comparison to the things going through my head as I watch her with Colby. He may be doing it to mess with me, but fuck, it's working. He's my best friend, and yet every time he makes her laugh or smile, I want to grab him by the throat and watch as he struggles to breathe. If he doesn't cut the shit, I just might do it.

It's obvious Tessa is drinking a little too much wine by the way she starts swaying. I keep an eye on her from across the room, careful not to get too close. It's not like I haven't noticed all the not-so-subtle glances she's been throwing at me. If I go anywhere near her, especially while she's intoxicated, it won't lead to anything good. At least not good for me.

Colby leaves her side for the first time all night and comes to get her a bottle of water. It's disgusting how much just the sight of her getting dizzy starts to worry me. The party is starting to die down by now, being as it's two in the morning, which means that Tessa has been drinking for at least the past three hours.

"Is she okay?" I question, unable to hold back.

He chuckles quietly. "Yeah, she just had a little too much champagne."

As he takes the cold bottle into his hand, he goes to walk away but I stop him. "What do you think you're doing?"

"What do you mean? I'm just being a gentleman."

"You don't have a gentle bone in your body," I counter. "Cut it the fuck out. I'm not kidding."

Shrugging, he gives me his best boyish, yet devious, grin. "What's wrong, Ash? Feeling a bit jealous?" He takes a step closer. "If you want her, go get her. She's right there."

"I can't," I bite out through gritted teeth.

"Why not? She's legal. She's hot as hell. And, she wants you." He backs away and holds up his drink-filled hands. "But hey, your loss. Just don't blame me for not making the same mistake."

"Colby—" The tone of my voice is a warning, but it only causes his smile to grow.

"What? She's not *my* student."

The second he turns away, I snap. My hand flies out to grab him by his shirt, and I yank him backward until he slams into the bar. I maneuver my body in front of him so he's trapped and put a hand on his chest to hold him in place.

"You so much as *think* about taking advantage of that girl, and I swear to God I won't be the only player taken out of the NFL by an injury this year."

Despite the fact that I'm close to snapping his neck, Colby starts to laugh. It's then that I realize I just played directly into his game. He wanted to see just how much this girl gets to me, and he got exactly what he was looking for. I let him go and run my fingers through my hair.

"Fuck you, Hendrix."

That only makes him even more smug. "Hey, don't hate

me because you're so hung up on her that you're ready to hurt anyone who threatens to take her from you."

I shake my head. "She's not mine to be taken from."

"And who's fault is that?"

Someone clears their throat, breaking the intense conversation Colby and I were just having. I turn my head to see Lennon standing there with a sheepish look on her face.

"Uh, I don't mean to interrupt, but we have a bit of a problem." She nods her head toward the living room, where Tessa is curled up on the couch and fast asleep. "She mumbled something about the room spinning and being sleepy, then laid down and passed out."

Fuck, okay. I rub my hands over my face as I try to think of what to do. I could have Colby take her home, and I would if he didn't spend the last few hours flirting with her just to screw with me. I could get her home myself, but judging by the amount of alcohol she's had, it would probably require carrying her inside. I can only imagine what her parents would do if they saw me bringing their wasted daughter home from *my* party. Nope. Next option.

I run through all the possible solutions in my head, but one by one they each get ruled out for one reason or another. Finally, I'm only left with one, and fuck if Colby isn't going to be a cocky little prick about it.

"Clear everyone out of here," I tell him, then turn to Lennon. "You, come with me."

We go over to the couch where Tessa is curled into a ball. I bend down and carefully scoop her up before carrying her into my room and placing her on my bed. It takes a second for me to find the smallest pair of sweatpants I own and a T-shirt, but once I do, I hand them to Lennon.

"I'm going to help Colby. Help her change and come get me when you're done."

She nods and I leave the room so they have some privacy.

Thankfully, by the time I get back in the living room, most of the stragglers are gone, and the rest are grabbing their things and heading toward the exit. I take a garbage bag from under the sink and start cleaning up. Sure, I could wait until my housekeeper comes in the morning and leave it for her to do, but to be honest, I need something else to focus on. Otherwise, I'll think about the fact that Tessa is currently being undressed right now in my bed—and neither my brain, nor my cock, can handle that right now.

"So, what's the plan?" Colby asks as Lennon comes out.

I take a pillow and blanket from the linen closet and toss it onto the couch. I could sleep in the guest room, but it's too far away to hear if Tess gets sick in the middle of the night.

"You're going to take Lennon home."

"And Tessa?"

"She's staying right where she is."

It requires every ounce of strength I have not to react to the teasing look on Colby's face, but I manage to pull it off. I walk them both to the elevator and promise Lennon I'll have Tessa call her in the morning while Colby calls his driver to tell him they're on their way down. Then, when they're finally gone, I quietly make my way into my bedroom.

Tessa is dressed in my clothes, making her look even smaller than she normally does. Her hair is covering her face as she snuggles into the pillow. I gently brush it out of the way and cover her with a blanket. Once I've convinced myself she's comfortable, I glance at her one last time and turn off the light.

"Goodnight, beautiful."

Tessa

Lifting me, Asher places my ass on top of his desk and spreads my legs open to stand between them. His hand slides up the inside of my thigh slowly, teasing me with every inch. Each touch is like fire, and the wait for him to reach where I want is fucking excruciating. I throw my head back and moan.

"Tessa," he whispers with the softest pressure against my clit.

"Fuck, Asher," I breathe.

He clears his throat and says my name again. "Tess."

My eyes fly open, and I instantly wish the whole damn world could just swallow me whole. Standing in front of me is no other than Asher himself, and judging by the look on his face, he knows exactly what I was just dreaming about.

"I, uh, made breakfast," he tells me, then turns around and walks out—leaving me to deal with the embarrassment.

As I sit up, I realize that I'm dressed in Asher's clothes, the dress I wore last night is folded neatly on the chair, along with my shoes and my purse. *What the hell happened?* I go over and dig a hair tie out of my bag. Then, once I tie my hair back and fix my makeup, I venture out of the bedroom.

The second I open the door, the smell of breakfast wafts throughout the penthouse and infiltrates my senses. My stomach growls at the thought of eating something that will absorb the alcohol and ease the pounding in my head. Hangovers always have been a bitch.

Approaching the kitchen, I'm graced with the vision of Asher cooking a full damn buffet. He's got scrambled eggs and bacon on the stove, pancakes on a skillet, and he's chopping some fresh fruit on the counter. My brows furrow as I wonder who the hell he's feeding.

"Please tell me your parents aren't coming over or something. What's with the feast?"

He looks up, and I can tell he's trying not to smile. "No, I was just hungry, and I figured you could use something to eat."

I nod, sitting on the bar stool directly across from him. Looking around, however, something occurs to me.

"Where's Lennon?"

"I had Colby take her home last night," he grumbles.

The fact that he won't even look my direction isn't lost on me. I start to wonder if something may have happened last night—something he regrets. For the first time in what feels like forever, an uncomfortable heaviness consumes me.

"We didn't do anything, did we? You and I?"

Okay, so maybe I should have waited to ask that until he wasn't tasting the eggs. At the sound of my words, he practically chokes, coughing violently and pounding his fist against his chest. When he's done and can breathe easily again, he shakes his head.

"No, Tessa. Drunk and unconscious isn't exactly my type."

Relief washes over me. It's not that I don't want to do anything with him, because Lord knows I do. It's just that I'd hate for it to happen and me not remember it. I'm a greedy bitch, especially when it comes to him.

I smirk and lean forward with my elbows on the counter. "Oh yeah? And what *is* your type?"

His gaze locks with mine, and he slowly walks around until there's nothing but air in between us. "Gorgeous, smart, confident..."

He pauses just inches away from me and glances down at

my lips. I'm frozen in place, wondering if he's actually going to give me what I want, until he slips a piece of strawberry into my mouth.

"...and out of high school."

My shocked look turns to a glare as he shoots me a wink and steps back. "You're an asshole."

Chuckling, he grabs the remote and cuts the music off. "You're just figuring that out?"

He plates the food and puts one in front of me before sitting down, with a full empty seat in between us. I roll my eyes as I take a bite. Could he be any more childish? Not even able to sit next to me. It's like we're in preschool and he thinks I have cooties. Meanwhile, I'm nearly having an orgasm over the fact that this guy can cook.

The two of us eat in awkward silence and when I'm done, he grabs my plate for me and puts it in the sink.

"Here," he says, handing me two Advil. "Take them."

"Yes, sir."

It's meant to be murmured under my breath, but judging by the way his hand tightens on the counter, he heard me loud and clear. More importantly, he's affected by it. I file that little fact away and swallow the pills down with my glass of orange juice, then lick my lips deliberately as I watch him.

"You okay?" I tease. "You seem a little...flustered."

He narrows his eyes to slits and shakes whatever thoughts he was just having from his head. "Do you need a ride home?"

"No, I drove here, but that reminds me." I hop off the stool and stand in front of him. "Why did you let me sleep in your bed? Why not have Colby take me home with Lennon?"

His jaw ticks and I can see the subject of his best friend makes him angry. "Because I don't want you anywhere fucking near him."

"What? Why not?"

He goes to walk away. "Nothing. Don't worry about it."

"Why, Asher?" I press, following closely behind. "Is it because of last night? Because I knew who he was and not you?"

"Don't." His tone is a mix between a demand and a plea. "Don't push me on this."

Yeah, no. Not good enough for me. "Do you think I want him for something? Is that it?"

"You just don't know when to stop, do you?" he snaps, whipping around to glare at me. "Drop. It."

"No. Not until you tell me why." When he doesn't respond, an idea comes to mind that's either brilliant or reckless. Either way, I'm going for it. "Fine, then I'll just ask him. Lennon had him put his number in her phone last night. Something about getting an autograph for her dad."

It's a total bluff, but I keep my poker face in position and pull my cellphone from my pocket, scrolling to Lennon's contact.

"Tessa—" He says my name like a warning, and I look up at him and smirk.

"Last chance, Hawthorne."

Turning away for a second, he grips at his hair and groans. "Because the thought of anyone within five feet of you makes me feel like my blood is on fucking fire." He spins back around and his eyes meet mine. "Is that what you wanted to hear? That it's not all in your head? That you drive me absolutely insane with how bad I want you sometimes?"

His admission surprises me, but I do my best to mask it. "Then what's stopping you? I'm right here."

A dry laugh emits from the back of his throat. "That's part of the problem! You're always *right there*. Always looking the way you do and tempting the shit out of me, but I can't give in, Tess. You're my student. There are rules."

"Fuck the rules."

For the first time since the morning I left the hotel, he smiles brightly at me—with his dimples rendering me speechless. He runs his knuckle gently down the side of my face.

"I wish I could have that mentality, I really do, but I can't. There's too much at stake." Coming closer, he presses a kiss to my forehead. "I'm going to get in the shower, and when I get out, you need to be gone."

With that, he spares me one last look, then walks away and disappears into his bedroom. And me? I'm left standing here, wondering what the fuck just happened.

———

THE STREETS ARE CROWDED as I hold the phone to my ear and navigate through the mess of people. Delaney is rambling about how much she's loving school and how well Knox is doing with his apprenticeship. It's nice to hear her this happy, Lord knows she deserves it, but I miss her. The selfish part of me wishes I could just fly to Rhode Island and kidnap her—force her to come back and never leave without me again.

"You have to come visit soon, Tess," she tells me. "You'll love it here."

"Yeah, definitely. I just have to figure out when."

I can hear her sigh, even with all the noise around me. "Are you okay? You sound a little off."

And there she goes, being able to read me just by the sound of my voice. To say what happened with Asher this morning was confusing would be the understatement of the century, but what made it worse was the thought that he's never going to throw caution to the wind. At least not for me anyway.

I reach the building and duck inside. "Yeah, I'm all right, but I just got to my class. Can I call you later?"

"You better," she threatens. "I mean it, Tessa. Don't make me come back there."

"Oh, is that an option?"

"Ha-ha. Very funny."

Chuckling, my eyes meet Jackson's, and he nods a silent hello. "I promise I'll call you after. Twin's honor. Love you."

"Love you, too."

We hang up, and I place my bag and my phone on the bench. Once I take a sip of my water, I toss it down and go over to Jackson, holding out my hands for him to tape them up.

"All right. Let's do this."

He gives me a friendly smile. "Was that Delaney?" I nod. "How's she doing?"

"She's good," I tell him. "Her and Knox seem really happy out there."

"That's great. They deserve it. They've been through a lot, and so have you."

I hum, but it's clear I don't really want to talk about it, so he drops the subject.

Jackson earned my trust this past spring, when he saved not only my life, but Knox and Delaney's, too. My uncle, who at one point in time was my favorite, had a secret side to him that Knox ended up involved with. When push came to shove, Delaney and I got caught in the crossfire. Thankfully, Jackson was there. Every part of me thanks Knox for saving Delaney's life, after he literally took a bullet for her, but Jackson was the one who saved us all.

"How's that feel?" he questions as he gets done taping me up.

I ball my hands into fists. "Perfect."

"Great. Go hit the bag for ten minutes to warm up."

As I follow his orders, I think about how lucky I am to have something like this as an outlet for my frustrations. Getting to hit something as much as I need without anyone actually getting hurt—it's perfect. And besides, learning self-defense is how I make sure I'll never end up in the same situation again.

Delaney worries about me, but I've got this under control.

———

BY THE TIME I get home, I'm utterly exhausted. It's one thing to work out while feeling good. It's a whole different game when you do it with a massive hangover. The Advil that Asher gave me wore off shortly after Jackson and I started, and everything only went downhill from there. When I vomited into the garbage can, he called it a day and told me we'll pick up where we left off on Wednesday.

I manage to stay upright long enough to shower, but as soon as I'm finished, I crawl into my bed with no plans to get out of it for at least the next eighteen hours. Quietly, I mumble the words that come with every hangover ever.

I'm never drinking again.

———

"WAIT, SO HE COOKED you breakfast, confessed to being crazy about you, and then all but kicked you out?" Lennon repeats, trying to understand the situation better.

I shush her and look around the crowded diner to make sure no one was listening. "Just tell the whole damn world, why don't you?"

She rolls her eyes and takes a bite of her toast. "It's not like anyone is paying attention. Take that guy for example."

95

She points to an old man sitting a few tables away. "I could flash him and he wouldn't even notice."

No part of me stands a chance in holding back my laughter at that idea. "Please do. I'd *love* to see how that goes for you."

Her head tilts to the side, as if she's actually considering it, before she shrugs. "Eh, not worth it. And besides, we're not talking about me. This is about you and Mr. Off-Limits. What are you going to do?"

Shrugging, I don't verbally answer. It's clear he feels something for me, even if it's just a physical attraction—he admitted that himself. The only thing standing in the way of me getting what I want is some stupid rule saying that this is wrong. Well, I don't buy it. I'm going to make him see that whatever this is between us, it's worth risking it all.

Asher

THE ONLY THING WORSE THAN A USUAL MONDAY, is a Monday where you have to teach a room full of arrogant teenagers at eight o'clock in the morning. It's like the universe imagined the most torturous life for me and came up with this—being an English teacher for a bunch of entitled pricks while having a stupidly strong attraction to a girl who may as well be a minor. I don't know who the hell pissed off, but damn do they hold a grudge.

I'm in the middle of discussing the events of chapter fifteen when a familiar laugh echoes through the room. I look toward the back of the class to see Tessa smiling brightly and chuckling at something Oakley said. He reaches over and brushes her hair out of her face. She lightly smacks his hand away, but it's obvious he's not giving up. I do my best to ignore it—until he picks up his desk and moves it so he's flush up against hers.

"Beckett," I growl, getting both their attention. "Since you're just so talkative today, why don't you come sit up here with me."

As I gesture to the desk at the front of the room, Oakley sighs and gets up. Tessa smirks in a way that says she knows exactly what she was doing. She wanted to make me jealous and she succeeded.

There are two things I learned the night I let her sleep in my bed. One is that my couch has the ability to cause the world's worst back pain, and the other is that Tessa Callahan may very well be my Achilles' heel. The way her voice sounded as she moaned my name in her sleep is burned into my memory and plays on a fucking loop. When I walked away from her in my living room, after admitting the one thing that should have never left my mouth, I knew I had screwed up. Letting her know she gets under my skin only fed her fire, and that can't be good for me.

When Oakley is securely in his new seat, as far as possible away from Tess, I continue on with the lesson—until they're once again interrupting the class with her giggling. My brows furrow as I wonder what the fuck is so funny now. It all becomes clear when I notice the two of them on their phones. *You've got to be kidding me.*

I walk over and snatch Oakley's straight out of his grasp before going to the back of the class. Putting my hand out, I give Tessa an expectant look and just wait. Her eyes meet mine, all confident and challenging. She's got that same fire she had the night we met, when we both waited for the other to make a move. I won then, and I'm sure as hell going to win now.

"Callahan," I say, voice firm with authority.

She rolls her eyes and slaps her phone into my hand before crossing her arms over her chest. I grin smugly then go to put both devices in the top drawer of my desk.

"If I start seeing notes being passed, you'll be sitting out the next three games," I tell Oakley, just so he knows I mean business.

"Yes, sir."

His words, while they don't have any effect on me, they *do* remind me of when Tessa said them two days ago. They were full of sarcasm and clearly not meant for me to hear, but fuck did they go straight to my cock. Control has never been one of my kinks, and yet, the thought of having her in the palm of my hand is enough to make me come undone. She's wild, uncontrollable, careless—and all I want is to make her beg for me while she's on her knees.

I shake the thoughts from my head as I realize this is not the time, nor the place, to be imagining things that will give me away. Instead, I plaster the same hard-as-stone look on my face that I've mastered over the years and sit behind my desk to hide my obvious hard-on. *Fuck, what this girl does to me.*

"All right. Take the rest of the class to read chapter sixteen and write down at least one theory you have about the book."

AT THE SOUND OF the bell ringing, everyone gets up, stopping at my desk to drop off their assignment before leaving the room. I hand Oakley his phone back as he passes, with a lowly spoken threat that if he doesn't knock it off, he'll risk losing his place on the team. His fear is evident as he swallows and nods. Something tells me he won't be a problem anymore.

Once everyone is gone, only Tessa and I remain. She walks up to my desk and all but slams the paper down on it, then turns to me with her head held high.

"Are you going to give me my phone back?"

I smirk. "Now, now. Is that any way to ask for something?"

She mumbles something under her breath before plastering the fakest smile onto her face. "May I have my phone back, *please?*"

Stroking the bottom of my chin, I make it look like I'm actually considering it. Then, I drop my hand and shake my head. "Yeah, no."

"What? Why not?"

"You know why," I say, leveling her with a look.

Her mouth opens to argue it but then Trent comes into

the room and she clamps her lips shut. She huffs, storming out and leaving me to snicker. Trent looks between me and the door she just disappeared through with an amused grin.

"What's got her all pissed off?"

I shrug. "She was disrupting my class, so I took her phone."

His eyes widen. "And she let you?"

"Yes. Why wouldn't she? I'm her teacher."

He shakes off the shock and chuckles. "She doesn't listen to anyone. I'm surprised she didn't tell you to fuck yourself."

Oh, she probably would have had you not come in here. I go sit down at my desk and rest my feet on top of it as I wait for my next round of trust-fund brats.

"So, did you need something, or are you just stopping by to see if I still want to punch you in the face for tricking me into this gig?"

"I didn't *trick you*," he argues. "I thought Hyland would make an exception. The fact that he wasn't going to is something only him and Blaire knew."

Fucking Blaire. That reminds me of the voicemail she left on my phone this morning. Apparently, I have an interview this week where I have to go and gush about how much I *love* my new job, and how coaching high school football is a calling I didn't know I had. It's all a crock of PR bullshit, but I understand the necessity of it. At least the one thing I have to look forward to is going to the game in a month.

As students start to filter in, Trent gives me an apologetic smile and leaves the room. It's not that I'm still pissed at him. Okay, maybe I am, but it'll fade in time. It's just a little difficult not to want to punch him when I'm standing in the middle of my own personal hell.

HALFWAY THROUGH THE DAY, Tessa's phone still sits in my drawer, tempting and taunting me. It's practically begging me to look at it. Invading someone's privacy is wrong, and something I used to *hate* when my ex did it to me. But the chance of knowing a little more about the girl who has managed to get the most response out of me in years is too difficult to pass up.

I pull the phone from my drawer and swipe to open it, only to feel disappointed when it immediately asks for a password. I rack my brain to try to think of what it could be.

123456. *No.*

543210. *Nope.*

With the obvious ones out of the way, I wonder if maybe it could be numbers that spell out a word. Lennon seems to be her closest friend.

536666 for L-E-N-N-O-N. *Access Denied.*

Fuck. What the hell could it be? I swallow down the lump in my throat as I try the next one and hope it hell it's not correct.

O-A-K-L-E-Y. 625539. *One more attempt before the phone locks.*

Sighing in relief, I never thought I'd be so glad to get it wrong. Okay, I've only got one more chance before it locks for the next five minutes—long enough for me to talk myself out of this moronic idea. Then, an idea comes to mind.

674276.

The phone opens instantly, and I can't help but laugh. The girl actually made *orgasm* her password. Why does that not surprise me? After checking to make sure no one is around, the first thing I do is go to her text messages with Oakley. It's pathetic how badly I need to know what they were talking about.

I'm serious, Tess. Come out with me on Saturday.

And why would I do that?

Because I'm the best. Duh.

Yeah, I've heard. The best at making a girl regret the night before.

Ouch. You wound me.

It ends there, making me glad I took their phones when they did. Then again, it looks like she had the situation completely handled. Oakley may want her, but she's not an option he has. Especially not if I have any say in the matter.

I know I should stop. I found what I was looking for and now I should put the phone back in my drawer where it belongs. My fingers, however, don't get the memo, as they go back and open up her text with Lennon. The thread seems never-ending, so I stop the first time I see my name.

Are you okay? I'm sorry I left you there, but my dad would have killed me if I wasn't back by the time he woke up.

It's fine, honest. Not a single part of me minded waking up in Asher's bed.

How'd that go?

The exact way I'd expect it to. His mouth says we can't but his eyes say something else.

Think you'll wear him down?

Have you met me?

A student clears their throat, and I instantly click off the screen and put it on my desk. Toby stands in front of me, looking confused.

"Can I help you?"

His brows stay furrowed. "Why do you have a rose gold phone?"

I grab the device and toss it into the drawer. "Why are you so goddamn nosy? Now, what do you need?"

Thankfully, he sighs and changes the subject, bringing it to something safer and more controlled—the assignment. I need to be more careful, but there's something about her that makes me forget who I am and what I want. And judging by those texts, she has no intention of stopping this little game she's playing.

THE PLAYERS BREAK INTO two teams, shirts and skins. Kellan is the captain of one, while Tanner is the captain of the other. It's always a good idea to take two of the best players and put them against each other. That way, no one team is necessarily better than the other. It'll push them to work harder and strive to win.

"Can I stop yet?" Oakley pants.

I shake my head. "No. You interrupted my class not once but twice. Another five laps and then ask me again."

He looks like he's ready to pass out, but I know he can handle a little more. He's only been running for forty-five minutes. Another fifteen won't kill him.

"You know," a voice sounds from behind me, "you can't just make everyone who hits on me run laps until they puke."

I hum as Tessa takes a seat on the bench. "Who said that's why I'm doing this? Maybe I just don't care for the blatant disrespect."

"So, if I told you that I'm going on a date with Kellan this Friday night…"

"I'd tell you you're lying. There's a game Friday night."

She smirks and looks down for a second then back up. "Then why are you gripping that clipboard so hard it might snap?"

My hand releases and I curse under my breath for once again letting her see how she affects me. Fuck. What is this girl doing to me? Am I losing the one ounce of self-control I have left? I take a deep breath but don't dare to look at her.

"Is it not enough that you know how completely crazy you make me, you have to use it against me, too?"

"What if I'm just trying to get your attention? What if that's how crazy *you* make *me*?"

I sigh. "You have it, Tessa, but that doesn't mean anything. You're my student, first and foremost. If we let something happen between us and people found out, you'd be that girl who had an affair with a teacher. Do you really want that?"

"It'd hardly be the worst thing I've been called," she mutters.

"What's that supposed to mean?"

Her hand waves off the topic. "Nothing. I just don't care what people think about me. And you shouldn't either. We're both legal adults."

"You're still a student. *My* student."

"Okay, then tell me this," she runs her fingers through her hair, "what if I met you as a freshman in college? If I wasn't *your* student. If I wasn't anything to you but a girl you met in a bar."

I turn my attention from my players and put it all on her. "I'd do things to you that would make whatever happened in that dream of yours look like a G rated movie."

With wide eyes, she swallows harshly. "Yeah, that. Do that."

Chuckling, I pull my focus back to its rightful place—not on her. "You said if you weren't my student, and you are."

"Fucking minor details," she groans. "Fine. Can I just have my phone so I can leave?"

"Giving up that easy?"

I can see the sexy smirk on her face out of the corner of my eye, and I know not to turn my head. If I do, I risk giving in, and I don't think the way to be discreet about this is letting the whole football team see the things I want to do to her. It's bad enough that she's here right now.

"No, Asher, but there isn't much I can do about it here. Now, phone." She puts out her hand and waits.

I pull the device from my pocket and hand it over. "Next time don't use it in my class."

"You're sexy when you're all authoritative."

"Tessa…"

The laughter that bellows out of her does something to me as she gets up. "I'm not someone who doesn't get what she wants. Mark my words, Hawthorne—I want you."

With that, she walks away, leaving me to process her words. And honestly, there's nothing surprising about them. That girl is a force to be reckoned with, and if I'm not careful, she just might get me to risk it all.

Tessa

I come to on the floor of some nasty-looking room. There's no windows, no furniture—just the hard, cold cement. My head is killing me as I sit up and try to remember how the hell I got here. Then, it all rushes back to me. My uncle. He was looking for Knox and Delaney. I have to get to my sister.

Struggling to find my footing, my eyes search for the door before they land on one in the corner of the room. I rush over to it, only to turn the knob and find it locked. What the fuck? I try again. No luck.

"Are you fucking kidding me?" I shout, hoping he can hear me. "You seriously locked me in here?"

My fist pounds on the door until I hear the click of the lock. The door flies open, and I jump back just in time to not be hit with it. Uncle Dom stands there, looking every bit like a villain. There is no trace of the man who helped teach me how to ride a bike or the one who sneaks me alcohol at family dinners. No, that man is gone, and this dark version is all that's left.

In a quick attempt, I go to rush past him but he steps in my way and pushes me back, laughing when I fall to the ground. My elbow stings with a fresh scrape, but I'm not about to let that stop me from getting out of here. I get up and try to force my way through, but he's like a fucking wall, firm and unwavering.

"What is wrong with you? Just let me go!"

He shakes his head slowly. "I can't do that. You're an essential part of my plan."

"What plan?"

Looking to whoever is in the hallway, he smirks, and the next thing I know, four guys are coming into the room. Each one of them have biceps the size of my head, and if this weren't such a terrifying situation, I'd probably hit on at least two of them. However, they all look like they could snap me in half with ease. I back away until I hit the wall and they corner me in.

"Tie her up," my uncle orders. "I don't need her trying to escape every five minutes."

One goes to grab me, but I'm faster than he is. I lean against the hard cinderblock and use all the force I have to kick him in the balls. He crumbles to the ground, groaning and clutching his damaged goods. Another one pulls me into his hold, but I manage to get one hard elbow into his ribcage.

Turning to get away from them, I quickly jab my two fingers into another one's eyes.

"Christ, you're feisty," the last one tells me.

My uncle chuckles. "That's why she's always been my favorite. She's a little fighter, this one."

"Fuck you," I spit.

He grins deviously. "I'm not keen on incest, sweetheart, but I'm sure Javi here would love to get a little piece of you."

Javi looks me up and down, licking his lips and making me feel like I'm going to vomit. The thought of him coming anywhere near me is repulsing. He takes a step toward me and I take one back, noticing the rest of the assholes are starting to recover. I may be tough, but there's no way I can fight off all these guys plus my uncle. Plus, I don't know who else is out there.

For the first time since I woke up, fear settles in my stomach, and I start to wonder if I'm going to make it out of here alive. The only thing I know is that in order to stand a chance, I need to cooperate as much as possible.

"Don't come any closer, or I swear to God, I'll rip your dick off and feed it to you," I threaten Javi and then turn to Uncle Dom. "What do you need me to do?"

"It's simple. Help me get your sister and her little shithead of a boyfriend here," he sneers.

My breath hitches, and I instantly shake my head. "No. I'll do anything you want. I'll lure Knox. I'll entertain your little brigade of goons. I'll even let you use me as your pawn. But you have to leave Delaney out of this."

He narrows his eyes on me but the corners of his lips raise. "I thought you'd say that, but you don't call the shots here."

In one quick move, he tosses what looks like a crowbar to one of his jacked-up idiots, and I don't even have time to duck as he swings it at my head and everything goes black once again.

I jolt awake, sitting up and clutching my head. The memories are vivid and play havoc on my nerves. I try to calm my breathing, but it only gets harder as everything tightens.

Short, rigid breaths are all I can seem to take, and each one hurts more than the last. I press my fist against my chest to put pressure on the pain but nothing seems to be helping. This panic attack is going to rip through me, and all I can do is let it happen.

THE NEXT MORNING, I wake up and realize I slept through my alarm. I'm not surprised, being as I was awake for hours after that nightmare. Usually, I would go into Delaney's room and be able to fall back asleep without too much issue. Unfortunately for me, she's about three thousand miles away and therefore not able to calm me during my 2:00 a.m. freakouts.

I head down into the kitchen to get something to drink, only to find my dad sitting at the island with an angry look on his face.

"What are you doing home?" he questions.

I shrug as I walk around him and head for the fridge. "I slept like shit last night. I had another nightmare and a panic attack."

"And that makes you think you can just skip school? Didn't you learn anything from having to watch your sister graduate and go off to college while your ass is stuck here?"

"No, but it just got to me. You have no idea what I went through that day."

He scoffs and rolls his eyes. "It was six months ago, Tessa. Suck it up and move on." Walking out of the room, he stops and turns back to look at me. "And get your ass to school, *now*."

I will the tears to stay back. When everything went down, my dad was actually supportive for the first time in my life. He put his opinions of Knox and Easton aside because he knew we needed them. He checked on me every night for three weeks. He was caring, loving, and sweet. But, as I predicted, he eventually fell back into his normal, cold-hearted self.

Ugh. I glance at the clock and notice class has only just started. If I hurry, I'll probably make it there with still half of first period left. Since not going apparently isn't an option, I may as well get to see Asher. Otherwise, it's just another boring day in Haven Grace hell.

TO SAY I LOOK like shit is putting it nicely, but after the night I had, I really don't care. The only thing I want right now is a tub of ice cream and a six-hour nap. Instead, I have to spend the next six hours at school, listening to lectures I couldn't care less about.

I take the late slip from the secretary and head to first period. As soon as I open the door, the whole class goes quiet. Handing the slip to Asher, he eyes me curiously but doesn't say anything. Then, I go take my seat between Lennon and Oakley.

"Well, well, well," Kellan teases. "Look who's falling into old habits already, and only a few weeks into the school year."

"Fuck off."

He smirks. "Mr. H! Did you hear what she just said to me?"

Asher rolls his eyes and crosses his arms over his chest. "Yeah, she told you to fuck off, and judging by the mood she seems to be in, I'd do as she says."

Everyone chuckles as I give Kellan my sweetest *I win* smile. Once the commotion dies down, we're all told to start doing the worksheet for chapter sixteen. However, being as I haven't read a single word of this stupid book, I take out my phone and start texting Delaney instead.

> Had a nightmare last night. I miss you.

Lennon, being the godsend she is, fills out the worksheet in a matter of minutes and hands it to me. I copy the answers down onto my own and hand it back just as a response from my sister comes through.

> Ugh. I'm sorry I'm not there. Next time, FaceTime me. Maybe it will help.

> Oh yeah. I'm sure Knox would just love that.

> He'll deal. You're my sister. You come first, always.

I can't help but smile, feeling slightly better just by talking to her, until I get another text that has me confused for a second.

Asher: Get off your phone, Tessa.

What the fuck? Since when does he have my phone number? Since when do *I* have *his*? I don't know whether to be excited or freaked out. Then, it clicks.

Okay first, Pot meet Kettle. Second, you put your number in my phone? Isn't that a little stalkerish?

I look up to see him smirking down at his phone. A little thrill runs through me that I was able to put that look on his face.

Coming from the girl who showed up at my house for a party she wasn't invited to. How'd you even get past security?

It's all in the attitude, babe. Act like you're meant to be there and people will believe you. And speaking of getting past things, how'd you figure out my password?

674276. Orgasm? Really?

A bark of laugher leaves my mouth, and I quickly move to cover it. Still, everyone side-eyes me for interrupting the silence.

Smooth.

Shut up. Don't you have a class to teach?

Don't you have a worksheet to do? Oh, no wait. That's right. You copied off Lennon.

I roll my eyes and glance up at him just long enough to see him wink.

> Your stalker tendencies are getting a little extreme. You should see about getting some help for that.

> Ha. Ha. You're just such a comedian.

> I know. I'm hilarious.

> So, with the risk of sounding concerned, is everything okay? Why were you late?

The thought of him caring enough to ask is heartwarming. I wonder if he realized I wasn't here before I came in late. Instead of being vulnerable, however, I keep that side of me hidden away.

> Aw, look at you caring about my wellbeing.

> Tessa.

> I'm fine, worry wart. I overslept. That's all.

As I press send, the bell rings and we all gather our things. I purposely take my time so that I'm the last student to leave the room. Asher is standing by the board and stops me just before I step out. He lightly wraps his fingers around my wrist. Just the touch is enough to ease some of the pain.

"You sure you're all right?"

I nod, hoping that my face doesn't give me away. "I had trouble sleeping last night. I'll be fine, really."

He looks like he doesn't believe a word I'm saying, but he's not sure he wants to push it. So, he doesn't. "Okay. Just checking."

THE CAFETERIA IS FILLED with chatter like usual, only this time, it's actually bothering me. I'm so tired, and all I want to do is sleep. If I wasn't afraid of my dad finding out, I'd sign myself out for the day and go home.

Tanner and Kellan are talking about the game this Friday when Charleigh shrieks. I cringe at the sound and turn my head toward her.

"Uh, Char, do you mind?"

She smiles sheepishly. "I'm sorry, but I think you'll be excited about this, too. My cousin is going to a frat party this weekend at NHU, and she said I can come."

I look at her like she's lost her mind. "And that would excite me, why?"

"Because you're coming with me, duh."

Okay, so maybe she's right. That *does* spark my interest. Things have been getting a little tense lately, and a college party at North Haven University may be just the thing I need.

Asher

FOR MOST OF THE WEEK, SOMETHING HAS BEEN OFF with Tessa. Something I can't exactly put my finger on. On Monday, she was her usual self, pushing limits at every turn and making me question my sanity for resisting her in the first place. Then on Tuesday, she came in late, and a totally different person. I could see it in her eyes; she's struggling with something. But it's clear she doesn't trust me enough to talk to me about it. Whatever it is, I hope she's all right.

Thursday afternoon, I walk out onto the field where all the players are waiting for me. They're stretching and warming up, which is exactly what I want them doing. Once they see me, they all line up and wait for my instruction.

"All right," I begin. "I know you're all nervous about tomorrow's game. It doesn't take being here a while to know how strong the rivalry is between us and North Haven High. It's been years since this team defeated theirs, but tomorrow night, all that's going to change."

A few of them look unsure, and Kellan even rolls his eyes.

"Something to say, Spencer?"

He sighs, tugging on the collar of his shirt. "No offense, Coach, but they beat us even with Grayson Hayworth as our quarterback. Tanner is good, but he's no Grayson."

"Fuck you too, ass," Tanner snaps back, but Kellan shrugs unapologetically.

"Okay, okay. Relax." I bring all their attention back to me.

"I don't know who this old quarterback is, but I do know we have one thing NHH doesn't."

"Yeah? What's that?" Oakley asks.

The corner of my mouth raises in a smirk before I bring my fingers to my lips and whistle loudly. All their eyes widen as Colby, Griffin, Anthony, and Leighton come around the corner, looking like a dream team. I exchange a handshake with each one of them, then turn back to my players and cross my arms over my chest.

"A bunch of pros to practice with."

I DON'T THINK I'VE ever seen these guys play as hard as they do with my former teammates. And the best part is that they all look happy doing it. The broad smiles never leave their faces even while sweat is pouring off them and they're panting heavily, trying to catch their breath.

I let Colby take over and go over to sit on the bench for a minute. There's something I've wanted to find out all damn day, but I didn't want to ask while school was still in session. I heard Skye talking about some frat party they're going to this Saturday at the local college, and while I shouldn't care, I want to make sure Tessa isn't going to be there.

> A little birdy told me there's a party this weekend.

Being as this girl's phone is practically glued to her hand, it doesn't surprise me when she starts to type back right away.

> Birds can't talk, Asher. And I'm sure there are plenty of parties this weekend. That's what kids do. They party.

I shake my head at her constant snappy comebacks, but can't help the smile that comes.

> Okay, smartass. I'm referring to the frat party at NHU. Tell me you're not going.

New fone, who dis?

> Tessa.

If I tell you I am, are you going to try talking me out of it?

> You're damn right I am.

Then no. I'm going to sit at home with my rosary beads and pray.

Chuckling, I try to imagine that, but there's no way in hell to even picture it.

> I mean it, Tess. Those parties are bad fucking news. You don't belong there.

😒 You do realize that had I not skipped more school than I attended last year, I would be going to those parties on the regular, right?

> Irrelevant. You DID skip all that school, and you're NOT a student there.

When she doesn't respond, I know I need to give her an excuse not to go. It may be a horrible idea, but it's all I've got, and I'll do anything to keep her away from that party. Places like that, they prey on the freshman—a high school senior would be like spilling blood in a pool of sharks.

> Come hang out at my place instead. I'll even let you drink.

> It's tempting, but I'm going to pass. I haven't gotten laid in weeks, and there's about a 110% chance that won't happen if I choose you. Sorry, babe.

The air is sucked straight from my lungs at the thought of her going there with the intention of letting one of those idiots take advantage of her. A little voice in my head argues that it would probably be Tessa taking advantage of someone else, but still. It burns all the same. Well, if I can't convince her out of going, I'll have to execute Plan B.

Colby comes over in perfect timing and takes a seat next to me.

"They're a bunch of great kids, and you're right. Oakley Beckett really has potential to go pro. Kellan Spencer, too."

I shake my head. "Kellan needs an attitude adjustment. Otherwise, the pressure will eat him alive."

He grins. "Isn't that what he has *you* for?"

"Don't remind me. I'm just not sure how to get through to him."

"You could always do what your dad did with you. Tough love and brutal honesty can go a long way."

I nod, knowing he has a point. "Thanks for coming out here. They really needed this pick-me-up."

"Of course, man." He pats me on the back. "I think I'll crash at your place for the night. I kind of want to see how they play tomorrow."

"Sounds good. You know the guest room practically has your name on it. You don't even have to ask."

He chuckles. "Oh, I wasn't asking."

A brilliant idea comes to mind, and I turn to my best

friend. "You know, now that I think about it, I may need one more favor."

"You're cashing them all in, aren't you?"

"Just about."

I WATCH THE TIMER count down, waiting for the buzzer to sound. Even Colby is screaming so loud that you can hear the roughness in his voice.

Five, four, three, two, one.

"And that's it!" the announcer shouts. "Haven Grace wins the game!"

The crowd behind me goes wild as all the guys on the field celebrate their monumental win against North Haven High. Not only did they win, they absolutely *demolished* them. The score of 41 to 7 stares me back at me from the scoreboard, reminding me of why I fell in love with football in the first place.

As the guys go in to change, I stay on the field. For the first time in almost a year, I feel connected to the game again, and I'm not exactly ready to give that up just yet.

"Well, look at you, pulling off the impossible."

I turn my head to see Tessa walking toward me. She's dressed in jeans and a black sweatshirt I'm almost positive isn't hers but don't have the balls to ask about.

"It wasn't impossible," I argue. "And I didn't do anything. It was all them."

Her grin widens. "Please. Those guys could barely run a play before you."

I laugh because she has a point. "Yeah, well. They worked hard."

"Aw, so the tin man *does* have a heart. Good to know." She

tilts her head to the side to look behind me. "Hey, Colby." Her syrupy tone gets my hackles up instantly.

"What's up, Tess? You're still driving this one insane, I see."

"Duh. It's like my favorite sport. You two have football. I have messing with Asher."

"Hey!" Lennon calls from the other side of the fence with Kellan and Tanner. "We're heading out. You coming?"

She nods and turns back to me. "I'll see you on Monday, *Mr. Hawthorne*."

Despite how much I know I should look away, my attention stays solely focused on her as she goes over to her friends and hops the fence. Tanner places an arm around her, and while I know it's just a friendly move, my nose scrunches at the sight.

Colby chuckles and places his hand firmly on my shoulder. "You, my friend, are so totally fucked."

"I don't know what you're talking about."

That's a lie. I do, and he's probably right, but I'm sure as hell not going to admit it. The second I breathe those words into existence, it all becomes way too real. Nope. They'll stay right where they belong—the vault inside my mind.

THE FRAT HOUSE IS big enough to get lost in. The music is so loud you can hear it down the street, and people are even drinking on the front lawn. There has to be at least 300 people here, Tessa being one of them. I already peeked at her social media and saw she posted a selfie with Lennon— drinks in both their hands.

"I cannot believe you dragged my ass here."

I roll my eyes. "Look, I don't want to be here either, but I had no choice. You know what goes down at these parties."

He shoves his hands into his pockets and snickers. "Yeah, I do, and you just had to be a knight in creepy armor. What the hell are we even going to do, stand there watching her like a bunch of strange bodyguards?"

"If that's what it takes to keep her safe."

The two of us walk up the steps and into the house. People are everywhere. Some are taking shots, while others are doing keg-stands. It's all part of the college experience everyone looks forward to. Even I had my fair share of it, before my coach and my dad laid into me about how I was throwing it all away for a few drunken nights I'd never remember.

"You know," Colby says teasingly, "for someone who has no interest in her, you sure are invested in her safety."

"My God, you gossip more than half my students."

He raises his hands in surrender. "I'm just speaking the truth, my dude."

We go over to grab a beer and then casually make our way throughout the party. The goal is to stay out of sight—to find somewhere I can keep an eye on her, without her ever knowing I was here. At least that way I'm keeping her safe while still keeping a safe distance. Unfortunately, that backfires when she sees me before I see her.

"Uh-oh. Hurricane Callahan headed this way."

My brows furrow as I follow his line of sight, and that's when my eyes meet hers. She looks like a mix between pissed off and intrigued. The shirt she's wearing stops about midway, showing off the belly ring dangling against her stomach. Further down, her jeans hug her hips perfectly. *Fuck me.* Half my mind wants to cover her up, while the other half wants to peel every inch of clothing off her until she's nothing but a quivering mess underneath me.

"I may have been kidding the other day, but I'm starting to think you really do have stalker tendencies."

Taking a sip of my beer, I shrug. "You turned down my invitation. I had nothing better to do, and a party sounded like a good idea."

She places a hand on her hip. "A party you told me I shouldn't go to? Really?"

"Wait, wait," Colby interrupts. "What invitation?"

Shit, I forgot he was there. Tessa smirks before completely blowing up my spot.

"*Mr. H* over here invited me to come hang out at his place if I agreed to not come here."

"Okay, when you say it like that, it sounds worse than it is."

My best friend starts to laugh at my expense. "Okay, I'm going to need a girl on my arm if I'm going to deal with this shit all night." It's then that he notices Lennon standing beside Tessa. He drapes his arm across her shoulders. "Hey, Lennon. You look good."

"I'm seventeen."

Jumping away as if she burned him, he fixes her shirt and hair so it looks like he never touched her. "The fuck. Shouldn't you be at home coloring or some shit? Where are your parents?"

Tessa and I chuckle while Lennon smiles sweetly. Colby mumbles something about needing another beer and walks away. Meanwhile, Tess gives me a look that makes me wonder if it was a mistake coming here at all.

"So, are we going to talk about why you're *really* here?"

I play it off as well as I can manage. "I already told you. I had nothing better to do."

She steps closer and runs a finger down the front of my shirt. "Are you sure? There wasn't some other reason?" I swallow hard. "Tell me, Ash, what would have happened if I chose you instead of here?"

"The offer still stands. Why don't we go back to my place and you can find out?"

Her tongue slips out to moisten her lips, and it's embarrassing how fucking drawn to it I am. I almost think she's going to take me up on it, until she steps away and shakes her head.

"Nice try," she tells me. "I came here for a reason, and it wasn't so I could leave and go play Scrabble with you and Colby."

"I was thinking more along the lines of Monopoly or Xbox."

"Yeah, not a chance." She loops her arm with Lennon's and looks me up and down once more. "Have fun stalking."

As soon as they leave, Colby steps up beside me. "Did you know Lennon was only seventeen?"

I can't hide the amused smile that spreads across my face, but my eyes stay on Tessa. "She's my student. What do you think?"

"And you just let me hit on her like that?"

"Oh, relax. I wasn't going to let it go anywhere." I turn to face him and lightly smack his cheek. "And besides, a little humility could do you some good."

EVERYTHING SEEMS TO BE going smoothly. I even start to enjoy myself and let my gaze leave Tessa for a bit. The only thing she's been doing is hanging out with her friends and eye-fucking me from across the room. Meanwhile, I make sure to stay sober to avoid falling into her spell. Having my guard up around this girl isn't just recommended—it's a goddamn necessity.

"I'm just saying, letting off a bit of steam could be good for you," Colby continues on his drunken tangent. "There are over a hundred girls at this party who would jump at the chance to sleep with Asher Hawthorne."

I snort and shake my head. "Thanks, but I'm good."

"No, seriously. I'm telling you. Watch!"

Before I can stop him, he grabs the first girl he can get a hand on and pulls her close. It's some blonde, obviously a college student, and probably in a sorority, but definitely not my type.

"Hey, babe. I'm taking a poll. Would you sleep with my friend here?"

She lets her gaze rake over me then purses her lips. "Yeah, why?"

He pushes her away like that's all he needed and now he's dismissing her. "See? If you weren't so wrapped up with resisting your not-so-unattainable girlfriend, you could be enjoying all the beautiful women here."

Lennon approaches with an unsure look on her face, but of course, Colby doesn't notice that. He points to her and narrows his eyes on me.

"But stay away from girls like her. They'll send you to prison, and trust me, you'll become someone's bitch in prison."

A part of me wants to comment on that last part, but the fact that Lennon is standing in front of me alone gives me reason to ignore it.

"You okay? What's wrong?"

She runs her fingers through her hair and glances around, then sighs and looks directly at me. "I can't find Tessa."

My body goes cold as exactly what I was afraid of becomes an alarming reality. "What do you mean you can't find her?"

"She started to feel really dizzy so she sat down. I went to get her some water, and when I came back, she was gone." Her bottom lip starts to quiver. "I'm really worried."

Asher

I PUSH THROUGH THE CROWD OF PEOPLE, LOOKING for any sign of the brown-haired pain in my ass. I fucking warned her not to come here, and now look what happened. She's God knows where, getting God knows what done to her, because she just didn't want to listen.

"She was sitting right here," Lennon points to the bottom of the stairs.

Glancing around, I don't see any sign of her. Colby leans against the railing and rolls his eyes. "She's drunk. She probably just wandered off somewhere."

"I really don't think she did," Lennon argues. "Tessa's my best friend. She wouldn't have gone somewhere else without telling me."

"Unless she did."

"Colby," I snap. "If there's ever a time in your life where you decide to shut the fuck up, let it be now."

He makes a face and takes a sip of his beer. "Someone's feisty."

I can't listen to this right now. I shake my head and continue the search for Tess. The line of people outside the bathroom tells me she can't possibly be in there. The kitchen has plenty of people in it, but she's not one of them. Finally, I spot Charleigh in the living room and march over to her.

As soon as she sees me, she looks like a deer caught in the headlights and quickly moves to hide her drink. "Mr.

Hawthorne. I didn't expect you to be here. I was...uh... holding this for a friend."

"I don't care that you drink, Charleigh." I resist the urge to roll my eyes. "I just need to know where Tessa went."

She glances over at Lennon and her brows furrow. "I saw her go upstairs with some guy like ten minutes ago. So, I'd assume she's still up there."

Fuck. I mumble a quiet thanks and rush over to the stairs. Just as I'm about to go up, Colby grabs my arm.

"Dude, think about this for a second," he pleads. "If she went up there willingly, you risk making yourself look like a crazy person who's just jealous and possessive over the girl you won't allow yourself to have."

I take a deep breath and turn my attention to Lennon. "You're sure?"

She nods immediately. "She would've at least texted me."

"That's all I need to know."

Ignoring the advice of my friend, I book it up the steps, taking them two at a time. As soon as I'm at the top, I start checking bedrooms. If I've learned anything from coming to parties like this, is that the ones doing something wrong are always the ones to lock the door. After catching way too many people in the throes of it, I finally find that one at the end of the hall.

"Shh! Quiet," someone whisper-shouts as soon as I try turning the knob.

I look behind me to see both Colby and Lennon standing there. Colby gives me a nod, silently telling he's on my side, no matter what. I back up just enough and then slam my foot full force into the door. It cracks in half and swings open, hanging only by one hinge.

"What the fuck?" a guy asks angrily as I push myself into the room.

As soon as I get inside, my stomach tightens and my rage

builds to unimaginable levels. Tessa lies on the bed, barely conscious, with her clothes in disarray. Two pricks I don't recognize stand there looking at me and Colby with pure fear in their eyes.

"Yo, this isn't what it looks like. She asked us to bring her up here."

"Yeah?" I grab the closest guy by his collar. "Was that before or after her clothes started falling off?"

He gulps and shakes his head rapidly. "I-I didn't know she was taken, man."

That only pisses me off more. Like the fact that she's single would make it okay for him to do whatever he damn well pleases.

"Colby, get Tessa and Lennon out of here."

He does what I say without question, picking up Tess and leaving me alone with these two pieces of shit. I ball up my fist and swing it directly into the closest one's stomach. He cries out as he hunches over, but I'm instantly pulling him back up.

"What the fuck did you give her?"

"I didn't give her anything!"

Throwing him to the floor, I turn my attention to the other shithead. "You, then. What was it?"

He steps backward and right into the corner. "Rohypnol. I slipped it in her drink. I'm sorry!"

A part of me knows I should walk away. I've got a girl that needs my attention waiting for me outside. However, as I go to leave, I realize I can't just let this little shit get away unscathed. I turn back around to find him trying to check on his friend. When he looks up at me, his eyes widen. In one swift move, I punch him directly in the face—finding comfort in the way his bone cracks beneath my knuckle. *Serves him right.*

"Let me find out you do this shit again, and I'll personally make sure both of your dicks no longer work."

I push through the crowd of people, not giving a damn when I make some guy spill a drink on himself. The second I get out the front door, I spot Colby and Lennon down the street, leaning against my car. Jogging over to them, I see Tessa lying across my back seat.

"Is she okay?"

Colby shrugs. "As okay as she can be. She's pretty fucked up."

I sigh and stretch out my now aching hand. "They roofied her."

"They what?" Lennon shrieks. "Like, the date rape drug?"

Nodding, I check her over. "One of them must have slipped it in her drink when she wasn't looking. How are you feeling? You okay?"

She wraps her arms around herself. "A bit freaked out, but I definitely don't feel like she does."

Thankfully, Colby seems to be sobering up a bit. The severity of the situation must have killed his buzz. Tessa groans in the backseat, and I know I need to get her out of here before she vomits in my car.

"How'd you two get here?" I ask Lennon.

She glances back at the house. "Charleigh drove."

"All right, well, you're definitely not going back in there, and I doubt Charleigh wants to leave yet. I'll give you a ride home if you want."

Seeming unsure, she looks upset as she watches her best friend. "Where are you bringing her?"

"Back to my place," I tell her. "I want to keep an eye on her. Make sure she's okay."

"Would it be okay if I come with her? It's not that I don't trust you to take care of her. I just don't want to leave her right now, and my dad already thinks I'm spending the night at Charleigh's."

It's risky, but I can appreciate her worry. "You're not going to tell anyone?"

"No. Of course not."

"Okay," I agree. "Text Charleigh and tell her you're leaving, and that she needs to be careful about her drinks. Hop in the back with Tessa. I want to get the hell out of here."

I PULL INTO THE parking space and get out of the car. Colby makes a move to grab Tessa, only for me to stop him. If anyone is holding this girl, it's going to be me. The only reason I didn't carry her out of that party is because I had two sad excuses for men that needed to be dealt with.

Opening the back door, I reach in and lift Tessa into my arms. Her head lolls against my chest. The only thing I find comfort in right now is the sound of her steady breathing.

Colby holds the elevator open for me and I step inside. Lennon watches me carefully, but I would too if this shit happened to my best friend. Tess may make some bad choices sometimes, but no one deserves this. I can only imagine what she's going to do when she wakes up tomorrow and realizes what happened.

The second we reach the top and the doors open, I carry Tessa straight into my bedroom and place her on my bed.

"Asher?" she murmurs as I go to grab her some more comfortable clothes.

"Shh. It's okay," I tell her softly, brushing her hair out of her face. "You're going to be okay."

She falls back asleep, and Lennon sits on the edge of the bed. "Will she really? Like, we shouldn't be bringing her to the hospital?"

"It's not the drug that's dangerous. It's the people who

135

slip you the drug that you need to be afraid of," I explain. "We got her out of there in time, luckily. Now it's just a matter of letting her sleep it off."

Pulling clothes from my drawer, I hand them to Lennon with a quiet chuckle of her knowing what to do. This seems to be a repetitive thing. She gets drunk, or in this case drugged, then Lennon changes her clothes, and I make her breakfast in the morning.

I leave the room to give Tessa some privacy. Lord knows she needs it after practically being defiled without her consent.

As I head straight for my wet bar, I pull out a bottle of whiskey and pour myself a glass. The liquid goes down like molten lava, and I relish in the pain of it.

"Stop doing that." Colby appears out of nowhere.

"Doing what?"

He grabs the bottle and pours some for himself. "Punishing yourself. This wasn't your fault."

My gaze locks onto the counter. "I shouldn't have taken my eyes off her."

"You didn't know this shit was going to happen!"

"Didn't I though?" I roar. "Isn't that the reason I didn't want her going in the first place? I went there to protect her from shit like this!"

"And you did!" he counters. "You found her, and you got her the fuck out of there. Don't beat yourself up over it. Whatever those assholes had planned for her didn't happen because *you* saved her from it."

His words make sense, but they're just not registering. I honestly don't think there is a thing he can say that will calm me down right now. I will spend all night worrying about her and hoping she's still the same Tessa when she wakes.

I'M SITTING ON THE edge of my bed, just watching Tessa sleep. Lennon is beside her, with her hand clutching Tess's. It's heartwarming to see someone care so much about her wellbeing. Whatever has been going on with her, I'm glad she has Lennon to lean on.

"Mmm," Tess groans, turning her head to the side and cracking her eyes open just slightly. "What time is it?"

"Almost four-thirty."

A low whine emits from the back of her throat. "What happened? My head is killing me."

"Someone slipped you something at the party, but don't worry. I got you out of there before anything could happen."

Her brows furrow in concern, but then lets her eyes drooped closed again. "My hero."

I play with her hair, careful not to keep her awake but needing to feel some kind of connection with her. Just when I think she's fallen back asleep, however, she sighs.

"Where were you the day he took me? Why didn't you save me then?"

My attention zeros in on her words. I know for damn sure she didn't mean to say them. She's still in a drunken and drugged haze, but I don't doubt for a second that there's truth to her statement.

What the hell happened to this girl?

Tessa

I WAKE IN THE MORNING, FEELING WORSE THAN I ever have in my life. The comfortable bed beneath me is familiar, but not mine. *Asher.* I faintly remember him sitting beside me in the middle of the night. At the time, I thought it was a dream. He was playing with my hair and being so sweet. The real Asher would never allow himself to get that close to me—not while I'm still his student, anyway.

As I peel my eyes open, the room instantly starts to spin. It only takes seconds before I'm jumping up and sprinting to the bathroom. I make it to the toilet just in time to empty the contents of my stomach into it. The heaving is so intense I don't even hear the door open behind me.

Two hands move to pull my hair out of the way. I glance back to see Asher standing there.

"No, go away," I whine. "I don't want you seeing me like this. It's *so* not sexy."

"Shush."

He drops down to his knees anyway, holding my hair back as I continue vomiting repulsively. His free hand strokes my back, and when I'm done, he rubs a wet washcloth over my face.

"How did I end up here?" I ask, still confused.

His brows furrow. "You don't remember?"

I shake my head slowly. "The last thing I remember is being at the party, and something about you running your fingers through my hair, but I think that was just a dream."

"It wasn't a dream, Tess."

"It wasn't?"

"No," he confirms and raises to his feet. "There's an extra toothbrush in the drawer. Get cleaned up and I'll meet you in the living room."

Left alone, I try to rack my brain for any indication of what the hell happened last night, but even the slightest thinking causes my head to hurt more. Instead of putting myself through more pain, I brush my teeth and tie my hair up.

Stepping out into the living room, I become even more confused when I spot Lennon and Colby sitting on the couch. They're both drinking coffee while Asher fucks around with something in the kitchen. Did Colby end up winning her over last night? No, he wouldn't even try. Not after learning she's still a minor.

"Lennon?"

She turns to me with the most relieved look on her face. "Oh, thank God."

Jumping up, she runs over and wraps me in a tight hug. The action just worries me more. *What the hell happened last night?*

"What's going on?" I question lightly.

Lennon looks confused and glances over at Colby. Meanwhile, Asher comes into the room holding a bottle of water and some painkillers.

"She doesn't remember anything," Asher explains to Lennon, then turns his attention to me. "Here. It's higher grade Tylenol. It'll help with the headache."

I thank him quietly and take the pills. I'm ready for anything to get rid of the throbbing.

Lennon and I sit down on the couch. She cuddles into me, and I welcome the gesture. There's something in my gut telling me that whatever they're about to tell me, I'm not going to like. Between the look Colby and Asher are giving each other, and the fact that Lennon spent the night at Asher's with me, it's got to be bad.

"Okay, someone spill, because nothing is worse than not knowing."

Both Lennon and Colby look at Asher, who sighs and comes to sit on the coffee table in front of me. He places a hand on my knee, which in any other circumstance would be exhilarating, but not today. Not now.

"Last night," he pauses to swallow, "you were drugged. Two guys slipped something into your drink and then led you upstairs."

My stomach drops, and the need to throw up surfaces again. "Did they..."

"No," all three of them answer my unspoken question.

Asher gives me a sad smile. "Lennon came to me and Colby, and we managed to find you before they could do anything. I don't know exactly what they did, but when I got to you, you were still fully clothed."

This is the second time I've been taken advantage of, and this one I don't even remember. For all I know, I could run into the guys again, and I wouldn't know not to trust them. My chest tightens the same way it has many times before, and I know I need to get out of here. I gently move Lennon and jump up off the couch.

"Excuse me," I murmur as I run out of the room.

The second I get into the bathroom, I shut and lock the door behind me—leaning against it and trying to catch my breath. My heart pounds like it wants to break out. My hands are clammy, my eyes wet with tears.

Why me? Why can't I just live a normal, traumatic-event-free life? Did I do something so horrible to deserve this?

This isn't the time or the place for this. Keep it in, swallow it down.

A light knock on the door grabs my attention, and for a second I panic.

"Tess?" Lennon asks softly.

I relax at the sound of her voice. "One sec."

Splashing some water on my face, I do the best I can to level my breathing. Then, I open the door and step out. My best friend stands there, watching me carefully. I can see the silent question in her eyes.

"I'm all right. I just thought I might throw up again, but I didn't."

She sighs and pulls me in for a hug. "Are you sure? You went through a lot."

"Please. You know me. It's going to take more than a couple assholes with shitty morals to bring me down." I put on my best fake smile and hope to hell she buys it. "Come on, let's get back out there before Asher sends the national guard to make sure I'm okay."

That makes her chuckle. "He really does get crazy protective over you."

We go back out to find Asher and Colby standing by the kitchen, speaking in hushed tones. As soon as his eyes land on me, Asher's attention to whatever Colby is saying vanishes. I give him a sad smile and nod once to let him know I'm fine. Well, as fine as I can be right now, anyway— but I won't admit that until I'm alone in my room.

THE FOUR OF US spend the morning, or at least what's left of it, goofing around and watching videos of Asher and Colby at some party a couple years ago. Apparently, Griffin thought it would be hilarious to get them both piss drunk and record everything they do, and well, he was right. It's the best thing I've ever seen.

Asher hangs off the balcony overlooking the living room, as Colby stands beneath him with his arms spread wide open, screaming "Let It Go" from Frozen. The whole party watches them like they're fucking insane, and you can tell Griffin is laughing hysterically by the way he can't keep the camera still.

"Promise you'll catch me?" Asher begs, looking down at Colby.

"I promise!" he calls back.

Finally, Asher lets go of the banister and falls straight through Colby's arms. He lands in a heap of limbs on the floor, groaning in pain as Colby stares at his empty arms in disbelief. When he realizes what happened, he falls over and clutches his stomach while laughing. Asher kicks him in the ass and calls him a douchebag before crawling to the kitchen to get another beer.

"I can't believe you let go!" I tell him in disbelief.

"Me? I can't believe he didn't catch me!"

Colby chuckles. "I thought I was going to, like in the movies, but then you hit the floor. Oops?"

Asher glares at him playfully. "Yeah, oops my ass."

It's nice, being here with him and seeing him this carefree. He's always walking around with a scowl on his face and keeping me at arm's length. But now? Now, he's sitting directly next to me, with his leg pressed against mine. It's probably because of what happened last night. The fear of something happening to me got to him in a way I didn't think it would. Still, I'm not about to complain.

"All right," Colby announces, standing up. "I've got to get going. Lennon, you said you need a ride home, right?" She nods, and then Colby turns to me. "Tess? You want a ride?"

My eyes meet Asher's, and his brows raise in question. The fact that he's not jumping at the chance to get me out of here is something to take note of. Whether it's because he doesn't want me to go with his friend or because he genuinely wants me to be here, I'm not sure. I can't help but smile as I look down at my lap and Asher answers the question for me.

"Nah, I want to keep an eye on her for a bit," he tells him. "Make sure she's okay and all that."

Colby snorts. "Yeah, we'll pretend that's why."

Asher flips Colby the bird, and Lennon gives me a hug before they both head out the door.

"So, now that they're gone..." He gives me a look. "Are you okay?"

No, but there's no way in hell I'm telling you that. "Yes. I mean, I want to find out who they are and rip their dicks off with my bare hands, but yeah. I'm okay."

He smiles brightly, and it's fucking infectious.

"What?" I question.

"You're like a cherry bomb—cute and little but fucking explosive."

I ponder it for a second before biting my lip. "Dangerous. I like it."

His eyes stay locked on my mouth a long time, and I consider doing it again, but decide against it. My stomach is still queasy, and the last thing I need is to finally get what I want, and throw up on him during it.

A bit of silence fills the room, but it's not nearly as awkward as it could be. Finally, I break it by laughing.

"I still can't believe you let go."

He throws his hands up in exasperation. "He said he would catch me!"

I shake my head. "If he had, you both probably would have gone to the ground."

"Yes, but I would have had him to break the fall."

"Using your best friend as a human cushion," I joke. "How nice of you."

Looking at me, he smirks. "You're feisty when you haven't had something to eat."

I roll my eyes. "No, I'm feisty in general. Don't act like this is a surprise to you."

"Touché," he says, and stands up. "But I'm making you something to eat anyway. It's noon, and the last thing you put in your stomach came back up this morning."

Grimacing, I sink down into the couch. "Don't remind me."

Asher snickers as he walks into the kitchen, and I pull out my phone to text Delaney. I know she's going to flip when I tell her what happened, but it's better she hears it from me than someone else. At least then she'll know I'm okay while she has a conniption.

AN HOUR LATER, ASHER and I are sitting in the kitchen, eating grilled chicken wraps. I would have been fine with a simple peanut butter and jelly, but he claimed I needed more protein than that after last night. I'm glad I didn't argue, because this is delicious.

"Where did you learn to cook?" I inquire.

As opposed to last time, he's sitting right next to me instead of keeping a whole bar stool between us. He finishes chewing, swallows, and wipes his mouth with a napkin.

"My mom taught me," he explains. "My dad and I had football in common, and I guess she got jealous. So, one day she woke me up in the middle of the night, and we started cooking. After that it became our thing. Every Saturday night, my dad would find us in the kitchen at two in the morning—cooking whatever we had the ingredients for."

Hearing him talk about his childhood is adorable, and I couldn't keep the smile from my face if I tried.

"She sounds like a great mom."

He nods. "She is. I got really lucky in the parental department. What about your parents?"

I shrug. "My mom is all right. Doesn't have much of a backbone though."

"And your dad?"

"He's a straight-up dick."

Nearly choking on his water, he laughs. "Well, damn, Tess. Don't hold back."

I give him a sweet smile that makes me look so much more innocent than we both know I am. "I never do."

"Is he really that bad though, or is it just that you're a teenage girl in her *you can't control me* phase?"

My thoughts instantly flash through all the times I've wished he would disappear and never be seen again. When he told me I'm a failure and that I'll never amount to half of what my sisters are. The morning he pulled me out of bed by my hair because I left the window unlocked when I snuck back in. The night he slapped me across the face when I told him I wouldn't stop seeing Easton.

"Hey." Asher brings my attention back to him with a soft hand on my face. "I was just making conversation. Don't get lost in that pretty little head of yours."

As if he didn't realize he was doing it, he quickly pulls his hand back and focuses back on his food. I grin lightheartedly in an attempt to defuse the situation. Things go quiet again while the two of us finish our lunch, but his words play in my mind repeatedly. For a second, I didn't think about our age difference or the fact that he's my teacher. I don't think he did either. It was just him and I, sharing a moment.

I'm putting my plate in the sink after finishing when he leans against the counter and sighs.

"Can I ask you something?"

It doesn't seem good, but I nod anyway.

"Last night, when I came in to check on you, you

whispered something about the day he took you. Who took you? What happened?"

My heart drops inside my chest, and I can instantly feel myself starting to shut down. "I was delirious and on drugs. Who knows what I was rambling on about."

He frowns. "See, I might have believed that, if it wasn't for the look on your face when I asked you about it."

"Drop it, Asher."

I go to walk away, but he grabs my wrist. "Come on, talk to me."

"There's nothing to talk about!"

"That's bullshit and you know it!"

A dry laugh leaves my mouth, and I roll my eyes. "What the fuck does it matter? Why do you even care?"

He narrows his gaze on me. "I'm just trying to figure out if saving you is going to become a regular task for me."

"Oh, I'm sorry," I coo, acid leaching from my words. "I didn't realize me being drugged was such an inconvenience for you."

"Don't be like that. You know that's not what I meant."

"Isn't it, though? How long have you been dying to say *I told you so*? Go ahead. Get it out of your system."

Running his fingers through his hair, he grunts. "You want me to tell you I was right? *Fine*. I was! I told you to stay away from that goddamn party, but no. You just *had* to go, and look where that got you!"

I scoff and cross my arms over my chest. "It was *one party*, Asher. I had too much to drink and got too comfortable. But that's not going to stop me from going to more."

"Of course it's not, because apparently, you have a tendency to run toward danger with open arms!"

I've heard enough. I'm not going to sit here and let him yell at me like this. I take a step back and shake my head.

"I already have one asshole dad. I don't need another."

147

Turning on my heels, I head for the door, but Asher is following closely behind.

"Tessa—" he tries, but I ignore him. "Don't leave."

As I approach, the elevator opens, and some woman in a business suit steps out. I look her over from head to toe. Her pin-straight blonde hair and Barbie doll figure catch my attention, and I start to wonder if maybe he has a girlfriend he failed to mention. However, she only glances at me for a second before narrowing her eyes on him.

"Blaire? What are you doing here?"

She holds up her phone and shoves it in his face. "A frat party, Asher? Are you out of your damn mind? You attacked two college kids at fucking frat party?"

He sounds pained as he groans. "Okay, they were hardly innocent. I was protecting my friend! Those shitheads drugged her!"

I step into the elevator and wave with a sickeningly sweet grin. "You enjoy that."

The look on his face as the doors shut is a mix between wanting to strangle me with his bare hands and wanting to fuck me senseless. I'd probably be okay with the latter if he hadn't just managed to piss me off. Then again, hate sex always is the best kind.

I get to the bottom and pull out my phone, grateful that an Uber is right around the corner. The sooner I get away from here, the better.

I WALK INTO MY bedroom after having yet another argument with my dad. Today is obviously not my fucking day. I lock the door and fall to the ground, finally allowing myself to process the events of the last twenty-four hours.

Sobs wrack through me so harshly that I don't even notice Lennon until she sits beside me on the floor.

"What are you doing here?" I ask, wiping the tears from my cheeks, only for them to be replaced by more.

"You may have said you're fine, but you're forgetting that I'm your best friend. I know you better than that."

I lay my head on her shoulder and let her hold me as I cry. She rubs my back and plays with my hair, whispering comforting words I'm not sure either one of us believes.

"You're going to be okay, Tess. We'll get you through this."

But I'm not sure I will be.

THE NEXT DAY, TENSIONS are still high. The whole time spent in Asher's class, the two of us refuse to look at each other. His *my life sucks* scowl is back in its rightful place, only with an extra hint of misery. A part of me wonders if it's because of that girl from yesterday, Blaire. I don't know who the hell she is, but I'm determined to find out. I may be a lot of things, but a home wrecker isn't one of them. If he has a girlfriend, I'm out—no matter how much I may want him.

I'm sitting in lunch when my phone vibrates in my pocket.

Are you okay?

I'm conflicted. On one hand, the fact that he thought to check on me and was the one to cave first makes me wonder if maybe he's a little more invested in whatever the hell is going on between us than I originally thought. The other, however, is incredibly pissed at him. Still, I can't let this go on.

I get up from the table and head out of the cafeteria. The walk to Asher's classroom feels like an eternity, and he might not even be there, but I'm not having this conversation via text. I open the door and find him sitting at his desk. His eyes meet mine, and I step inside, closing the door behind me.

"Hey," he says with a sigh.

"Hi."

"I take it you got my text."

I nod. "What makes you think I wouldn't be okay?"

He shrugs. "I was just checking on you. I didn't know that would be a problem."

"It's not."

The silence takes over. This time, however, it's awkward, and I fucking hate it. Finally, the question on my mind all morning comes out of my mouth before I have a chance to stop it.

"Is she your girlfriend? That woman from yesterday?"

He grimaces and shakes his head. "No. God, no. Blaire is just my publicist."

I'd be lying if I said I'm not the slightest bit relieved. "Oh. She's pretty."

"Pretty psychotic," he quips. "Colby hooked up with her once, and she was talking wedding dresses by the next day."

"Yikes. Poor Colby."

His snort alleviates some of the disgustingly thick tension. "Not poor Colby. He knew the shit he was walking into when he decided to sleep with her. He's heard the rumors."

I tilt my head from side to side. "Okay, then he asked for it. But she works for *you*. You've never considered it?"

He shakes his head with utmost certainty. "She's great at her job, but I wouldn't touch her with a laser pointer, let alone my dick."

An involuntary laugh bubbles out of my mouth, and somehow, it makes me feel better. I watch as Asher's shoulders relax at the sound.

"Listen," he starts. "I'm sorry about yesterday. I didn't mean to make you feel like what happened Saturday night was your fault."

"It's fine." I wave him off, but he's not having it.

"It's not. You did *nothing* to deserve any of it, and I shouldn't have thrown it in your face like that." He sighs and leans back in his chair. "The sight of you half conscious and completely defenseless in that bed is burned into my brain. I can't imagine how I'd feel if something had happened to you."

Walking over to him, I lace my fingers into his hair. "But it didn't. You made sure of that."

His gaze locks with mine, as if he's trying to get some kind of read on me. "What happened, Tessa?"

It doesn't take an explanation for me to know what he's talking about, and just like that, I'm retreating into the safe space inside my head.

"Nothing. I told you. I wasn't in my right mind."

He rolls his eyes with an attitude. "Oh, come on. You can't actually expect me to believe that, can you? Hearing the way you said what you did that night, you had the most honesty I've ever heard in your voice. It wasn't nonsense."

I back away and shake my head. "Why can't you just leave it alone? It happened! It's over now!"

"*What* happened?"

"Nothing!" I shout, not caring that we're at school where people can hear us. "Fucking Christ, Asher. Let it go!"

He stands up and starts pacing the room, then turns to look at me again. "How do you always stay so damn guarded all the time?"

I mask my vulnerability the best way I know how—with sass and sarcasm. "It's a practiced skill."

"Clearly."

Everything in me is telling me to leave, but for some reason, I stay in place. It's like I want to fight with him. I want him to press me for information I'm not willing to give. I want to see the look on his face as he tries to figure me out. The only thing I'm not willing to do is tell him what happened. If I do, he'll be just another person who sees me as broken. Fragile. Weak. And I'm anything but porcelain. I have to stay strong.

"So, that's just it? You're not going to tell me?" he tries again. "You'll just keep your secrets locked away for good?"

I shrug. "It's worked well so far."

His hand is clenched in a tight fist, like he's ready to punch the closest wall. Though, I don't recommend it. All the walls in this place are rock solid. Trust me, I'd know.

"You're fucking infuriating, you know that?"

Yes. "Me? You're the one obsessing over something that doesn't concern you!"

Laughing humorlessly, he puts his fists on the desk and leans over it, keeping his head down. "Oh, right. Fuck me for giving a shit."

This conversation is going nowhere. It's only going to escalate until one of two things happen—either he drops it, or I tell him what happened. I don't see him doing the former, and I'm not willing to do the latter, so we're at a stalemate.

I storm over to the door, wanting nothing more than to leave, but the second my hand reaches the knob, I stop. My body turns around and my back rests against the wood. I don't know whether I want to scream or cry. Asher glances at me for a second. He straightens his back and walks toward me, his arms caging me in, his eyes refusing to meet mine.

The only sound in the room is our heavy breathing. He's so close I can taste him, feel the intensity of whatever internal battle he's experiencing. Finally, his hand drops down and I hear the click of the lock. His sights finally lock on mine, with pupils blown from pure lust, and the two of us move at once.

Asher

OUR LIPS MEET IN A BRUISING, HEATED KISS, ONE that makes the night we spent together pale in comparison. All the pent-up aggression we're both holding is shown in the way her mouth moves against my own. It's messy, and angry, and fucking incredible.

Reaching down, I grab her ass and lift until her legs wrap around my waist. My tongue tangles with hers as I pull her away from the door and press her up against the chalkboard. The way she grips at my back and tugs at my hair tells me everything I need to know. She wants me just as bad as I want her.

The temptation to fuck her right here is so strong I could choke on it. All it would take is lifting her skirt, moving her panties aside, and slipping inside of her. God, it would be so easy, but I can't.

Reluctantly, I break the kiss and rest my forehead against hers—panting heavily as I focus on what little restraint I have left.

"I can't lose control," I whisper. "Not with you."

She whimpers slightly and I'm almost a goner when my eyes meet her pleading ones. But this is Tessa. She's no longer some girl I met in the middle of a night club. She's not just the girl I had a wild night with. She's my student. She's my friend. She's my Cherry Bomb.

The bell rings and I lower her to the ground, still coming to grips with what just happened. She seems just as confused as I am while she fixes her skirt and messes with her hair. I walk toward the door, but just before I unlock it, I bend down and kiss her once more—because apparently, my mind and my body are not on the same page.

"I'm sorry," I tell her. "I'll drop it, but I hope one day you'll tell me because you want to. Because you trust me enough to let me in."

She walks out of the room without saying a word, and I realize after she's gone that for once, Tessa Callahan is speechless.

———

THE REST OF THE day and all throughout practice, I can't get that fucking kiss out of my mind. And trust me, sporting a hard-on is insanely difficult to conceal in dress pants. My concentration is shot. The only things that run through my mind are the sounds she made and the way she tasted—like strawberries and sin.

I get out of my car and walk up to the door, not even bothering to knock even though this isn't my house. However, the minute I see a girl on her knees with her head bobbing up and down, I realize I probably should have at least warned him.

Colby is in his personal heaven, with his head thrown back on the couch and his hand in this chick's hair. The beer in his other hand is still cold, meaning he probably has no intention of finishing any time soon.

Dropping my keys onto the counter, they clatter loudly like I intended, and the two of them startle. Colby's eyes double in size as he grips and harshly rips her off him. He curls into a ball, clutching himself and mumbling nonsense as he rocks back and forth. My brows furrow as I glance at the girl and then back to him.

"The hell is wrong with you?"

He looks at me with tears in his eyes. "She fucking bit me."

There isn't a damn thing in the world that could keep the laughter from barreling out of me. I press my hand against my chest in an attempt to gain a little bit of composure, but the second I see the girl still sitting there with a sheepish look on her face, I lose it all over again.

"Sweetheart, you should probably go."

She nods at me and stands up. "Call me."

"He won't," I answer for Colby, since he's still muttering a bunch of nonsense and worrying about his favorite body part.

Once she's gone, I pull the blanket from the back of the chair and throw it to him so he can cover up. The last thing I need is to see more of Colby's dick. We've been best friends for years now. Trust me when I say that I've seen it enough.

As he calms down, he narrows his gaze on me. "You're an asshole."

I chuckle in response and raise my hands. "Hey, it's not my fault you got a blowjob from a piranha."

"Ugh, why am I friends with you?"

"I keep your life interesting."

He groans and stands up, giving me another show I never wanted as he pulls up his pants. "Is there a reason you're here, or was your intention just to get me damn near castrated with a side order of blue balls?"

I shrug. "Well, there was a reason, but that was a huge bonus."

"Prick."

He goes to the fridge and grabs two beers, being as the one he was drinking got thrown across the room the second teeth sunk into his manhood. I pop it open and take a sip, surprised he didn't shake it up first. The cold liquid flows down my throat and manages to slightly calm the need to bury my face between Tessa's legs.

"I kissed her," I blurt out.

Colby looks over at me and smirks. "Well, it's about damn time."

I shake my head. "Of course, you would think that way."

"Why wouldn't I?" he counters. "You're acting like you did something wrong. Tessa's eighteen, and unless something drastically changed in the last thirty-six hours, I'm sure she was a more than willing participant in your little game of tonsil hockey."

Thinking back, I know she wanted it just as much as I did. Hell, she would have gone further if I had let it happen. But nothing about that kiss changes the fact it's wrong, no matter how good it was. No matter how bad I want it to happen again.

"I can't," I tell him. "She may be legal, but she's still a student. There are probably at least fifteen rules against that kind of thing. Maybe laws, too."

"Ugh." He throws his head back and rolls his eyes. "You're like a walking, talking poster child for how to live the world's most boring life."

"Well, excuse me for having a moral compass."

"Yeah? And where has that gotten you? You wasted eight years on a chick you should have thrown to the curb the day you graduated high school."

Colby doesn't hold back when talking about Nikki, though I don't expect him to. Those two never got along, even when her and I were still together. He thought she was an uptight bitch and told me to fuck her in the ass to relieve some pressure, and she thought he was a pig who was going to corrupt me and make me like him. It's hilarious to think of how she's actually worse. At least Colby doesn't give anyone false expectations. He doesn't go agreeing to marry someone, only to cheat on them as soon as he gets the chance.

"Look, all I'm saying is that Tessa isn't some random high school student," he continues. "She's different. More mature. If you're worried about her going and blabbing to her friends about it, you don't know her as well as you should by now."

I sigh, leaning back in the chair. "If she were going to tell people, she would have already told them about the night we met. It's not that."

"Then what is it?"

"She's eighteen. She's just setting out on her life, and I've already lost a career," I explain. "Soon, she'll want a serious relationship. To settle down with someone and start a family. You and I both know I can't give her that. Not after the shit Nikki put me through."

While that breakup didn't destroy me anywhere near the way my injury did, it still hurt. I promised I'd never put myself in that position again, and it's one I've kept. I didn't become anything close to Colby. I swear, he'll fuck anything with a pulse. However, I did shut down the idea of spending my life with someone.

He tilts his head to the side. "I'm not entirely sure Tessa is the commitment type though."

"Maybe not yet, but she will be."

"And what exactly are you afraid of?" He leans forward and rests his arms on his knees, giving me a look that says he sees right through my bullshit. "That she'll become too attached, or that you will?"

"Colby," I warn, but he doesn't back down.

"What? Don't sit here and act like you're afraid she's going to want a future with someone. You're afraid she's going to want a future with someone *who isn't you*."

"Fuck you."

Laughing, he raises his beer at me and takes a sip. "Stop

torturing yourself. She wants you, you want her. Just make sure she doesn't bite your dick. That shit hurts."

I GET TO WORK in the morning, feeling just as conflicted as I did when I left here yesterday. Going to Colby's did jack shit. It just added to my inner turmoil. The only good thing to come out of that was the memory of the look on his face when she bit down. That's one I'll remember for the rest of my damn life.

After getting my coffee, I head for my classroom and start getting ready for the day. Don't get me wrong, this job still sucks, but it's becoming a little easier now that I've got the hang of it.

As students begin to fill the room, I feel her presence before I see her. Sure enough, I glance up from my computer to find Tessa walking in. She's talking to Kellan about something with Lennon at her side. However, whatever attention she had on him is gone the second her eyes meet mine. It's like the first day of school all over again, only so much more intense.

Lennon whispers something into her ear with a tug on her arm, and Tess snaps out of the trance she was in. The two of them walk to their desks, and I do my best to pull my attention away to avoid suspicion.

"Who here knows the story of Romeo and Juliet?" I question, and most of the kids raise their hands. "Jacki, what's the main dynamic of the relationship between the hero and the heroine?"

"That they're forbidden to be together," she answers.

"Good." I look around the room. "And Skye, why are they forbidden to be together?"

"Because their families are enemies and their parents won't allow it."

"Does that stop them?"

"No."

"Hell, yeah!" one of the stoners shouts. "Stick it to the man! Who needs parents? At least they get their happy ending."

Snickers echo throughout the room as I roll my eyes in amusement. "Sure, Matt, if you call a double suicide a happy ending."

His face drops for a second before he laughs, no doubt high off his ass.

I do my best to keep my attention off Tessa, but it's easier said than done when I can feel her eyes on me. I give in and look over for a second. She smiles, and I'm completely fucked because I instinctively smile back. It must last for longer than I intended, because Lennon purposely drops her book on the floor, pulling my focus back to where it belongs.

Away from Tessa.

OKAY, SO IF I thought it was hard to resist her before, it's drastically more difficult after I've broken that seal. Sleeping with her before I knew she was going to be my student was one thing. I could separate the two, almost like it wasn't actually her. There was the Tessa I met at the club, and the Tessa who sits in my classroom every morning for an hour and a half. But kissing her yesterday made it so the two molded together. The kiss, the way she tasted, the want and need behind it all... It was exactly the same as the first time, but more.

The final bell rings and the students from my last class gather their things and start to leave. Unfortunately for me, the juniors are even worse than the seniors with the way they shamelessly attempt to flirt with me. Just as a few of them bat their eyelashes at me on their way out, Tessa steps in. She shoots them a dirty look that has them scurrying away, and the sight alone makes me laugh.

"Do you enjoy having girls fawn over you all day?" she asks when we're finally alone and the door is shut.

"No," I tell her. "They're practically children."

Her brows raise, and I immediately know exactly what she's thinking.

"Okay, that's not what I meant."

She bites her lip to hide the smile. "Careful babe, your old is showing."

I can't help but laugh. "You're a little shit."

"I know," she tells me, popping a piece of chocolate from my desk into her mouth.

As I work on packing up my stuff, Tessa makes it more difficult by sitting on top of one of the student desks, scrolling through her phone.

"Okay, what is #PoorColby and why is it trending?"

I snort and shake my head. "You don't want to know."

Her legs dangle off the edge, and I'm almost positive her skirt is at least three inches shorter than it was this morning. Finally, when she can't wait any longer, she hops down and walks toward me.

I grab her hands from where they rest on my shirt. "Tess, we should talk."

She sighs, as if she saw this coming. "Why? So you can tell me for the millionth time how wrong this is? That it's against the rules and we shouldn't do it? Save it, Asher. You've said it enough. No need to waste your breath."

Turning, she goes to walk away and it triggers something inside me. I reach out and grip the back of her neck, spinning her around and instantly pressing my lips to hers. It's not anywhere near as feverish as yesterday's, but it curbs the craving just enough to focus.

"What was that for?" she breathes as we pull away.

I brush a strand of hair out of her face. "It managed to render you speechless yesterday. I was hoping it would work again so I could get a word in."

"So, you're not going to tell me why this can't happen?"

I smile. "Well, I was—that was the plan, anyway. Fuck, Tessa. We're playing with fire."

She steps even closer, and I have a clear view down the front of her shirt. "Isn't that the point? The part that makes it so tempting? The danger of it all is so fucking alluring."

"If we get caught..."

"We won't."

And just like that, my resistance snaps, and our mouths collide once more. Her arms go around my neck, and she presses herself against me. I explore her with my tongue as my hands slide up and under her skirt, gripping her ass. The breathy moan she lets out is enough to send me off the edge, but I hang on by a thread—a very irritating, moral integrity thread that the rest of me would really like to take a pair of sharp scissors to right now.

I move my hands to her hips and break the kiss, keeping her away as she tries to come back for more.

"Tessa. Tess!" I grit my teeth. "We can't."

"Why, because we're in the school?" She rolls her eyes. "Let's go back to your place then."

"No, that's not why."

Her face drops. "But you just..."

I sigh. *I'm going to fucking hate myself for this.* "I know, and we can kiss, maybe even fool around a little, but we can't have sex. We're already too attracted to each other to be discreet. Sex would only make it more difficult to keep it hidden."

163

She raises one eyebrow, like I just told her the most ridiculous thing she's ever heard. "What the hell kind of shit is that?"

"Some people would call this a compromise."

"Sounds more like a fucking tease."

I chuckle, bending down and kissing her softly. "Yeah, but you'll deal with it."

Tessa

All I can feel is Asher as we sit on his couch, in the middle of a heated a make-out session. His hands on my waist. His mouth moving against my own. His hair beneath my fingertips. Our tongues tangle together, and I can taste him. The smell of his cologne infiltrates my senses. I swear I could get high on him and him alone.

"Are you sure this is all we can do?" I murmur against him, sliding my hand over his crotch.

He shudders and grabs my wrist. "Don't. I'm so far past the point in my life where cumming in my pants is remotely acceptable."

I pull my bottom lip between my teeth. "Is someone having trouble sticking to his own rules?"

Growling, he pulls back only to kiss his way down to the left side of my neck. I tilt my head to the side to give him better access, but the instant his lips graze the skin, I'm blasted back to Saturday night.

"Look at you. It's like you were begging for our attention, weren't you baby?"

His hand runs up my side. I try to push him off me, try to get away, but I can't move. It's like my body is paralyzed. Why can't I fucking move? My mouth opens to scream for help but nothing comes out.

"We're going to have so much fun with you," the other one tells me and comes down to lick a stripe up the side of my neck.

I freeze at the memory, and Asher instantly stops. He looks at me with nothing but concern in his eyes.

"What? What's wrong?"

The small part inside me that's pleading for help tells me to be honest. To tell him to stop and take the time to figure out what's going on with me. But I can't. Talking about what happened and admitting that I'm affected by it gives them power. It makes them win. I won't allow that.

"N-nothing, I'm just ticklish on that side," I lie. "Try the other."

He gently kisses the right side of my neck and I moan in relief when it doesn't cause the same reaction. I drag my nails down the back of his shirt, wishing it would just disappear. His mouth sucks at the sensitive skin in a way I know is going to leave a mark, but I can't be bothered to care. It feels too good.

Now, if only I could get my mind under control.

WALKING INTO THE DANCE studio, I watch Lennon dance in the mesmerizing way she does. The things she can do with her body are out of this world. I've only ever seen two people dance the way she can—her and Savannah. Sav had talents that were so unmatched she was offered a full scholarship to Juilliard Academy of Dance. If Lennon wasn't totally loaded, she'd probably be offered one as well. She's already hopeful to join Savannah there next year.

Brady sits on the floor with his back against the wall, watching her closely for any mistakes or places for improvement. He might not be the owner of this place, but you can tell he loves being here just as much as his mom does. He's spent his life at this studio, and may be even more skilled than his mother. Mrs. Laurence focuses more on the younger students while Brady takes the older, more experienced dancers. At this point, he's more their friend than he is their teacher.

"Raise that leg higher, Lennon," he commands.

"If I raise it any higher, I'll dislocate it."

He gets up and walks over to her, placing one hand on her hip and the other under her leg. I've never been so jealous of my best friend in my life. It doesn't matter that he's gay. Brady Laurence is fucking hot, though he doesn't compare to Asher, so I really can't complain.

I watch as he moves her positioning just slightly, and Lennon's leg is able to be lifted a few more inches without causing her any pain at all. She rolls her eyes playfully and smacks his hand to release his hold on her. Then, she goes right back into the routine like she didn't miss a single beat. Brady chuckles and comes over to me.

"Hey, Tess. Here to pick up sassy pants?"

Keeping my eyes on my best friend, I nod. "Yeah, but I'll wait. We're having a girls' night."

He instantly pouts. "Why am I never invited to girls' night?"

My brows furrow. "Uh, because you're not a girl?"

Lennon is in the middle of an intense spin but laughs anyway. "Oh, please. He's more of a girl than I am."

"Hey!" Brady chucks his empty water bottle at her. "I'll have you know that Jake is the girl in our relationship, thank you very much."

Images that I'm mentally torn on play in my mind. "Wow. In just five minutes I've learned more about you than I ever wanted to know."

He throws his head back, laughing. "Right. Like every girl in this town hasn't wondered what he and I are like in bed."

Well, he's not wrong. When it first came out last year that he's been dating a guy for the past four years rather than

Savannah Montgomery, like everyone thought, we had a bet going on who bottoms. A part of me considers tracking down Carter and Jace to collect what I'm owed. As repulsed by the idea as they were, Carter said there was no way in hell a dancer was the manly one out of the two. I, however, knew Brady is nothing if not masculine.

Lennon finishes up a few minutes later. Brady and I clap as she finishes, simply because she deserves it. If I could do half the things she can, maybe getting Asher into bed with me wouldn't be so difficult.

"All right, jerk," she says to Brady. "I'll see you tomorrow."

"You better. Later, Tess."

"Bye, Brady."

We walk out of the studio and over to my car. As soon as we get in, she tosses her phone into the cup holder and turns to me.

"Okay, so tell me. Did you two talk about yesterday?"

I say nothing as I slide my sweatshirt down my neck. Her eyes widen the second she sees it.

"Holy shit! Is that a hickey?"

She pokes it and I flinch while knocking her hand away. "No, I put makeup on my neck to make me look like a ho. *Yes*, it's a hickey."

"Damn," she says, impressed. "I didn't take Asher for the leaving marks type."

"I'm not sure if he is. We went back to his place for a bit and I think he may have just gotten caught up in the moment."

"So, I take it you slept together?"

I put the car in drive and pull out onto the road. "Unfortunately, no, and it's not for a lack of trying."

She looks just as confused as I feel. "Then what happened?"

"Asher happened," I groan. "He basically declared us celibate. He said we can kiss, but that's it. Apparently, even though we've made out, he still thinks it's wrong for us to sleep together."

"He said that?" The amusement is clear in her tone.

"Don't laugh at me. A girl has needs, Len, and this *compromise* as he likes to call it, is getting in the way of having those met!"

Her hands raise in surrender and she chuckles. "I'm sorry. It's just funny. Most guys would kill to have a girl who wants sex as bad as you do."

I slam my head back against the headrest in frustration. "I know! Ugh. What is wrong with him?"

"Are you sure you're ready for this though? Even just doing *something* with him?"

My one brow raises. "Why wouldn't I be?"

She shrugs. "Well, you told me after everything with your uncle, it took you weeks before you could stand doing anything sexual with Easton. With what happened last weekend, I'm worried that maybe it's bad timing."

I get her point. I do. And I know she's only saying it because she cares, but no part of me is willing to let two douchebags' actions get in the way of this.

"I'm okay, really. It sucked, and it was hard to deal with, but I'm not going to let it get to me the way I did six months ago. I won't let someone else's choices have that power over me again. I refuse."

I don't tell her about the flashbacks, or how the nightmares have become so frequent that I'm barely sleeping. It's classic mind over matter. If I convince myself I'm okay, I will be. Plain and simple.

I'M SITTING AT MY desk, admiring the way Asher looks in that suit. Judging by the way he's struggling to stay focused, he's having just as much trouble as I am with pretending we don't want to jump each other's bones right now. Every few minutes, he glances in my direction, and I have to look away to keep from smiling. As a distraction, I fiddle with the scarf that hangs around my neck—a necessary accessory for today.

The bell rings and everyone stands up, collecting their things.

"Miss Callahan, can I see you for a second?"

He sounds all professional when he says it, but I know I've done nothing to attract the attention of Mr. Hawthorne, meaning instead I've attracted the attention of Asher. Kellan gives me an odd look, but Lennon, being the goddess she is, grabs his attention when she brings up the party he's throwing this Saturday. As soon as they're gone, Asher appears behind me.

His hand brushes against my side, and I instinctively lean into his touch.

"What do you think you're doing?"

My breath hitches. "What?"

"Take off the scarf, Tessa." The authority in his tone threatens to make me obey him without question, but there's still that little bit of resistance I hold onto.

"See, I would, but then everyone would see the hickey on my neck that makes it look like I had a make-out sesh with a vampire."

He reaches in front of me and removes the fabric himself, then moves his mouth next to my ear. "The fuck do you think I put it there for?"

I turn around, finding him standing so close I have to bend my neck to look at him. Despite how much I want to cave under his intense stare, I smirk.

"You're awfully possessive for someone who won't sleep with me."

He lets out a breathy laugh, licking his lips and checking me out for a second. "Just because I won't fuck you doesn't mean I can't get you to scream."

I bite my lip in the way I know he loves-slash-hates. "Oh yeah? Prove it."

The next bell rings, and he grins as he steps back. "Go to class, Callahan."

I do my best to cover the mark on my neck with my hair, just to irritate him. Then, I grab my books and walk out of the room, swaying my hips as I go. I don't need to look back to know he's got his eyes on my ass.

AS I COME TO, the thick smell of cigarette smoke fills the air. It only takes a second before I realize I'm draped across someone's lap as he rubs up and down my inner thigh. My head is pounding from the impact that knocked me out in the first place. I groan in pain and can hear everyone go quiet.

"So, the princess is awake," one of the assholes says. "Not such a badass now, are you?"

"Fuck off."

They all snicker, and the closest to me grips my leg tightly. "Now is that any way for a lady to talk?"

I shove his hand off me and go to move, only to be shoved to the ground. Before I can try to get up, I'm grabbed by someone else, who roughly fondles my breasts. The one I kicked in the balls positions himself in front of me.

"Unfortunately for you, Boss said we can do whatever we want, as long as we keep you alive." He grabs my jeans and yanks them down my legs, then rubs his hand over the outside of my panties. "This is going to be the best day of work yet."

A scream leaves my mouth as I'm blasted awake. I sink deeper into my bed as I repeat the usual mantra to myself in a whisper.

"It's not real. It's just a dream. You're okay."

But I don't know if that's the truth, because it *was* real. It *wasn't* just a dream, it was a memory. So, what makes me think that I'm actually okay?

———

LENNON AND I SIT on my bed, eating ice cream and scrolling through our favorite models on social media like we do at least once a week. Only difference is, the more I look, the more I want Asher.

It's been three weeks now of this PG-rated arrangement we've got going on, and every day that passes I get more and more sexually frustrated. How he's not damn near crippled from intense blue balls is a mystery to me, because I'm ready to explode.

"Ugh. I need sex," I whine.

She looks over at me and giggles. "I can't believe he's held out this long. I thought he'd break by the end of week one."

"You and me both!" I shout. "The only reason I agreed to this stupid compromise was because I figured it's better than nothing. Now, I'm not so sure that's the case."

"So, make him break." She shrugs, as if that's the easiest thing to do.

"You think I haven't tried? The furthest I've gotten is lightly grazing his dick, and that's only because I played it off like my leg was falling asleep."

Lennon sits up and looks down at me. "Oh, come on. You're Tessa fucking Callahan—the girl who went over to Knox Vaughn's house with a Molotov cocktail because you thought he betrayed your sister."

I chuckle at the memory.

"You're telling me you can't get a guy to sleep with you no matter how hard you try?" She turns her attention back to her phone. "Damn girl, you're losing your touch."

I WALK INTO ASHER'S with a newfound determination. His brows raise in surprise the second he sees me, and it's exactly the reaction I was looking for. I smirk, walking directly over to him and straddling his lap.

"Kiss me."

He smiles. "Gladly."

The second his mouth starts to move against mine, I grind down on him. His cock hardens beneath me in record speed, and he grunts before pulling away.

"Tessa."

I give him an innocent grin. "What?"

"What are you doing? We agreed."

"I said okay. I never said I was going to make it easy for you." I bend down and tease his earlobe with my teeth, making goosebumps raise across his skin and his dick twitch against my center. "Trust me, Asher. I won't just get my way. I'll make you beg for it."

Asher

I should've known I could only get away with this compromise for so long before Tessa started to push back. But my God, I never thought she would go this hard. It's my fault, really. The girl is a fucking knockout, with the kind of body every guy dreams about, and she *knows* it. It was only a matter of time before she came up with the idea to use it against me. Literally.

From the second she came over, threw herself in my lap, and practically declared war, my dick has been begging for me to bury myself inside of her. I walk around almost all the time with a perpetual hard-on. No amount of cold showers and jerk-off sessions are enough to compete against what Tessa Callahan does to me.

It started that night, when she kissed my neck, moaned in my ear, and rubbed her clothed pussy against me until I was damn near ready to burst. Then, right before I found relief, she got up, winked, and walked out—leaving me in a confused haze of blissful torture.

Over the next few days, she began doing little things. Stepping in front of me, intentionally making it so her ass rubs against my crotch. Sucking on a lollipop during class in a way that could put porn to shame. Sitting on my kitchen counter and asking if I think it's a good height for her to straddle me. *The answer was yes.*

In short, the girl knows what she wants, and she's not backing down. Take right now for example: I'm sitting on my couch while she proceeds to model her new lingerie to "get my opinion." As she steps out in a black lace bra and a matching pair of panties, I groan and adjust myself for the umpteenth time since this torture session started.

"Do you think this is cute?" she asks, like it's a legitimate question. "Too revealing?"

I stare blankly at her, doing everything in my power to mask how much effort it's taking to stay in this goddamn seat.

She tilts her head to the side. "What? If you're uncomfortable, I could just go find Oakley. I'm sure he'll let me model this stuff for him."

"If you think I'd let you get one foot out that door, you're out of your fucking mind."

Her gasp shows how caught off guard she is, and I use it to my advantage. Getting up, I stalk toward her until she's pressed up against the wall. My body hovers over hers as her breathing starts to quicken. I slide my hand gently down the front of her, stopping when I'm right where she wants me.

Putting the slightest pressure on her clit, she releases a moan that goes straight to my cock. I move my fingers in a circular motion while her eyes close in ecstasy. However, I only let it last a couple seconds before I pull away and leave her silently begging for more.

"Remember, babe," I wink as I take a step back. "You're not the only one who knows how to tease."

I'M IN THE MIDDLE of teaching a class, when I look over and notice Tessa's head is down on her desk. If my attention wasn't so constantly drawn to her, the increasingly tired look on her face might go unnoticed—but that's not the case. It seems like the more time that passes, the more exhausted she looks. Still gorgeous, but exhausted none the less.

Even last weekend, when she spent the night at my house after having one too many glasses of wine, I found her awake at three in the morning. She was scrolling through social media on her phone and gave me some half-assed excuse of not being able to sleep, but wouldn't tell me why. I've learned the hard way what happens when I press her for information, so I decided not to push the subject. Now I'm starting to wonder if I should have.

"Lennon, can I see you for a second?" I ask, holding a random piece of paper in my hand as a front.

She gets up from her desk and walks to the front of the room. As soon as she's standing in front of me, I glance over at a sleeping Tessa and back at her.

"Is she okay?" I whisper.

The look on her face tells me she's not. "I don't know. She's more irritable lately, but whenever I ask her about it, she says she's fine."

Just then, Tessa wakes up with a loud gasp and a terrified look on her face. It draws everyone's attention to her, including mine. As she gazes around the room, her shoulders relax and her expression gets wiped clean. She shoots me a shy smile before looking away. I look up at Lennon who sighs.

"I'll see what I can get out of her."

I WALK INTO MY penthouse with the phone held firmly against my ear. The whole drive home, I've been trying to get Colby to give me Lennon's phone number. After what happened in class, I'm worried about Tessa. And being as I can't exactly ask her for her best friend's phone number without looking super fucking suspicious...

"Colby, just give me the damn phone number."

He chuckles. "I don't know, Mr. Moral High Ground. I don't think it would be good for your *I'm the good guy* image to have a seventeen-year old's phone number in your phone."

"Cut the shit. I told you. I just want to check on Tessa. Something's wrong with her."

"Of course something is wrong with her," he says as if he's obvious. "She's sexually fucking frustrated, caused by a douchebag who wants her but won't let himself actually have her."

I roll my eyes. "Fuck you."

"No, Asher. Fuck *her*."

Dropping the subject, I listen as Colby goes into an overly long rant about how Coach needs to lay off his dick, and that as long as he's showing up for games and practices, his personal life should be his own choice. Clearly, he's still pissed off about the fact that Colby fucked his niece without a care in the world and refused to see her again after.

A half hour later, he's still going. I'm sitting on my couch when the elevator doors open and Tessa comes through them. She's wearing a black skirt that's short enough to leave nothing to the imagination, and a low-cut shirt. She looks like a fucking goddess, but that's not what gets my attention. It's the look on her face that tells me I'm in for it.

Instead of saying anything at all, she sits down on the chair across from me and spreads her legs. Her hand skates down her body slowly until she gets to the bottom of her skirt. She pulls it back and I watch as she slips her hand inside her panties. Her head leans back against the chair, but her eyes don't leave mine as she starts pleasuring herself, breathy moans punctuating her movements.

Colby's voice is still coming through, but I can't hear a

damn word he's saying. Every ounce of my focus is on Tessa and what she's doing right now. Before I have a second to question it, I unzip my pants and take my hard cock into my hand. She stares at me as I stroke it, and the way she licks her lips tells me exactly what she's thinking.

Without saying a word, I end the phone call and toss the device, not caring where it lands. Tessa smirks as I stand up and walk toward her. She glances between my face and where I'm still jerking myself off.

"Is this what you want?"

She nods.

"How bad?"

Her throat bobs with a harsh swallow. "So fucking bad. It's all I've wanted for weeks. My fingers aren't enough. I need something more to fill me."

By the time she finishes talking, I'm hovering over her. "Yeah? You want something thick inside of you? Something to clench around?"

"Yes. Fuck, yes."

She reaches for my dick but just before she gets there, I grab her wrist to stop her. Looking deep in her eyes, I smirk and plant a quick kiss on her lips.

"Then buy a dildo."

Her jaw drops and all her movements stop as she watches me walk away. I turn the lock as soon as I close my bedroom door. Suddenly, I'm in need of an ice-cold shower.

FRIDAY COMES QUICKER THAN I expected, and the plan is for Tessa, Colby, and I to all go to some new nightclub downtown. I'm not exactly a fan of Tess using her fake ID again, but when she argued that she was going with or without me, I didn't have much choice but to agree. After that last frat party, the idea of her going anywhere without me there to protect her puts an uneasy feeling in my stomach.

Colby shows up at my place a little after eight. He's dressed in jeans and a button down, looking like he's ready to score. Knowing Colby as well as I do, I know that outfit and the cologne he's wearing means he's looking to go home with not just one girl on his arm, but two. It's obnoxious how easily he manages to get what he wants.

"Let me just shower and get ready, and then we'll go," Tessa says, kissing me once before retreating to my room.

Colby whistles as he sits on the couch perpendicular to mine. "Look at you two, being all non-platonic. How's that going for you? Did you fuck her, yet?"

"No, douchebag," I take a swig of my beer, knowing I'm going to need it to deal with his ass. "And it's not like she hasn't been trying. I deserve a fucking medal for the shit I've resisted."

"I'm not sure I'd go with a medal," he says with a snort. "Certificate of Stupidity, maybe, but not a medal."

"Screw you. At least I'm not getting my dick nearly bit off."

He rolls his eyes. "First of all, that was *your* fault, and second—"

His jaw drops and his pupils dilate as he stares behind me. I turn my head to find Tessa walking out of my bedroom *stark fucking naked*. Every inch of her flawless body is on full display for both me *and* Colby to gawk at. Her brown hair flows down her bare back, and her ass jiggles deliciously as she walks.

She goes across the living room, through the kitchen, and into the laundry room. When she comes back holding a towel in her hand, she simply smirks.

"Forgot a towel," she says, without a hint of shame.

Colby is still sitting in shocked silence as she disappears back into my room. But me? I've never felt more fucking possessive.

"Colby," I growl, and he doesn't need any more than that.

"Yeah, nope. I got it." He stands up and immediately heads for the elevator. "I'll catch you later."

The second he's gone, I march through my room and into the bathroom, not even bothering to knock. Tessa's gaze meets mine through the reflection in the mirror, a wicked glint sparkling in her eyes. I press myself against the back of her naked body and wrap my hand around the front of her throat.

"Look at you, practically begging for trouble."

Her pupils are blown, telling me she likes it—my grasp on her neck, the deep tone of my voice. She's so turned on, and fuck it, so am I. I've never met someone who drives me as crazy as she does. From the way she looks at me to her utterly fearless demeanor. It's intoxicating, and I want nothing more than to get drunk on her.

"Who said there's anything wrong with a little bit of trouble?" she counters.

I kick off my shoes and, with my free hand, I undo my belt. "No one, but you've said it yourself. I'm a possessive fuck when it comes to you, and you just gave Colby the show of his lifetime."

"Did I?" The question comes out with a syrupy sweet tone, and she smiles. "Oops."

"Yeah, oops," I grumble.

Pulling myself from the tight confines of my pants, I use my grip on her throat to spin Tessa around and push her back against the counter. She whimpers, biting her lip to keep quiet, but fuck, I want to hear it.

"Don't be shy now, baby. Go ahead. Let it out." I press

myself up against her and rub my hand over her bare pussy. "No one can hear you but me."

As I push a finger inside of her, she clenches around the digit and releases the sexiest moan I've ever heard. I press my lips against hers and pull her closer, forcing her mouth open so I can taste her. She kisses me back with the same enthusiasm as always, except this time, it's mixed with the beautiful sounds of her pleasure.

Just as she starts to relax a bit, I slip another finger inside. The slight resistance is enough for me to know she hasn't had sex since the night we spent together a few months ago, and it's frightening how much I love that. I press my thumb against her bundle of nerves as my fingers pump in and out of her. Judging by the way her pitch changes, I know she's close.

"That's it. Cum all over my fingers. Let me feel you."

My grip on her neck tightens just enough, and that's all she needs. She screams with her release, and I nearly explode myself as I feel her clench around my fingers and her warm juices drip down my hand. I help her through it, practically holding her up as her knees quiver.

When she's done, I pull my fingers out and suck them into my mouth. The taste of her is everything I remember, and achingly addictive. She watches me through hooded eyes.

"You taste so fucking good," I tell her, moving my hand from her neck to her hair. "Now, be a good girl and get on your knees. It's time for you to learn what I taste like."

Tessa

I WAKE UP IN A GOOD MOOD FOR A CHANGE, DESPITE the fact that after Friday night, Asher went right back to his *only kissing allowed* shenanigans. We spent the whole weekend together, and somehow, I managed to sleep a little better. Don't get me wrong, the nightmares still come—they're just a little weaker than usual. It's like Asher was able to replace their touch with his own, and fuck do I want more of that. I *need* more of that.

Pulling into a parking spot, I'm more than ready to go inside and spend the next hour and a half staring at my man. Well, okay. So, he's not exactly *my* man, but we make out and spend more of our time with each other than anyone else. Honestly, I think that's the most either one of us can handle right now. It doesn't take a rocket scientist to see the way his ex fucked him up, and Lord knows I have enough of my own issues.

I'm walking around to the front of the school when I see two people I never expected to be here. I'm shocked, but I can't help the smile that comes to my face. The second they see me, they smirk. Both of them are looking like straight sex on legs. Let's just say there was a reason I skipped so much school last year.

"What are you guys doing here?"

Zayn is the first to open his arms and I go willingly, laughing as he spins me around.

"Well, *he* wanted to see you." Z nods his head toward

Easton. "And how was I supposed to turn down a chance to see my favorite girl?"

I look over at my ex, who drops his head and smiles at the ground. There is a faint tension in the air, being as we haven't seen each other since we broke up in August, but he's still Easton. Maybe not *my* Easton, but he's still the guy who helped me through a terrible time in my life.

"So, are you going to just stand there or hug me?"

He rolls his eyes playfully. "Get over here."

As he embraces me the same way he always has, I rest my head against his chest and breathe in his cologne. I wouldn't say I've missed him, but seeing him again also isn't the worst thing in the world. Pulling away, I run my fingers through my hair and he does the same—a nervous habit we both possess.

"What are you doing back in North Haven? Shouldn't you be at UCLA?"

Zayn snorts and Easton nudges him. "It's a lot to explain. Do you think maybe we can go somewhere and talk?"

I don't even have to consider the question to know the answer. Spending first period with Asher is the best part of my day, and I'm not about to pass that up. Instead, I give Easton a sad smile.

"Sorry, I can't," I tell him as I walk backward toward the school.

He arches one eyebrow. "Since when does Tessa Callahan refuse to skip class?"

I shrug with a smirk. "Since I don't want to be stuck here, again."

With that, I blow them both a kiss and walk into the school, no part of me wondering what my ex has to say. The only thing on my mind is getting to first period.

FOR SOME REASON, ASHER looks hotter than usual in the light gray suit he chose to wear today. The tie hanging from his neck looks like it would be perfect to tie me up with. He's clearly the type to do something like that, especially after Friday night. Feeling his hand wrapped around my throat—threatening the ability to cut off my air supply with the slightest squeeze—it was so goddamn hot.

My phone buzzes in my pocket, and I pull it out to see a text from Asher.

> Stop eye-fucking me and do your work. And for the love of God, take the pen out of your mouth. This isn't exactly a great place to have a boner.

I chuckle quietly as I type my response.

> Maybe I would if you'd actually fuck me.

He reads my reply but doesn't answer, and I keep chewing and sucking on the end of my pen just to mess with him. I may have gotten *something* out of him, but it still isn't what I want. And hey, at least it's not a lollipop. That one was cruel.

AS SOON AS THE bell rings, everyone jumps up. It's like they think the classroom is diseased and they need to get out as soon as possible. In actuality, the only place they're going is their next class, so what's the rush?

"Tessa, a word?" Asher asks.

I smile at Lennon as she leaves with the rest of our friends, and head over to his desk. The time between when his first class leaves and the next one comes in is short.

"Who were those two guys you were with this morning?"

My eyes instinctively peer out the window and I realize he probably could have seen us from his desk.

"Zayn and Easton," I answer. "Zayn is a friend, and Easton...well, Easton is my ex."

His jaw ticks and he gets that possessively jealous look on his face. Instead of waiting for him to answer, I step a little bit closer until I'm directly in front of him.

"Hey, no. It's not even like that. I don't want him. This"—I gesture between us—"is exactly what I need right now."

He shoots me a disbelieving look. "Even though I won't sleep with you?"

I bite my lip and let my eyes rake over him. "Having to work a little for it never killed anybody. Besides, keeps it interesting."

That manages to get a laugh out of him, and his demeanor relaxes. "There's no practice today. Are you coming over?"

"Is that even a question? An extra three hours of being teased and tortured? Why would I subject myself to that?"

He smiles. "So, you'll meet me at my place?"

"Of course." I wink, turning on my heels and leaving just in time for his next students to filter in.

AS I WALK OUT of the school, after what ended up being a rather irritating day, the only thing I can think of is getting to Asher's and throwing all my pent-up frustration into a steamy make-out session. Unfortunately, as I push through the doors, I realize life has other plans for me. Standing at the bottom of the steps is none other than Easton, and this time, he's alone.

"You know, most people graduate and make it their mission to stay as far away from high school as possible."

He snickers and shakes his head. "Most people don't have a reason to come back."

"And you do?"

"I'm looking at it."

Oh boy. I glance back at Asher's window for a second but they're one-way glass, meaning I wouldn't know if he's watching or not.

Pushing my hair out of my face, I focus on my ex. "What do you want, Easton?"

He raises his hands. "I just want to talk. Can we go somewhere?"

I don't want to. There are actually a million things I would rather do, but I know Easton. He won't stop trying until I hear him out, so I may as well get it over with.

"All right," I say with a sigh. "Let me get my car and I'll meet you at the lake."

Smiling, he walks around to the driver's side and climbs in, pulling away before I can change my mind. I let out a deep sigh as I turn around and head toward my car. Well, this isn't how I saw my afternoon going. I take out my phone and send a quick text to Asher.

> Easton wants to talk. I'm going to hear what he has to say and then I'll be over. Half hour, tops. 😬

I don't wait for his response before I shove the device back into my pocket. It's not like he's going to be happy about it. And honestly, I'm not either.

I TURN INTO THE parking lot and pull up next to Easton. Ironically, we're in the exact same spaces we were in when we broke up. If I didn't know any better, I'd think he's trying to rewrite the past or some shit.

"Okay, you have ten minutes."

His brows raise in curiosity. "Somewhere you need to be?"

I cross my arms over my chest as I lean against my car. "Something like that."

There aren't many times I've seen Easton nervous. Being best friends with Knox Vaughn and the rest of the guys, they ruled the school. Between the parties that Zayn threw and Knox screwing almost everything with a pulse, before he met my sister anyway, he's always been a cocky little shit—until now. He suddenly finds his shoes really interesting.

"Are you going to tell me, or…"

He groans and looks up at the sky. "I saw this going differently. I thought you would be excited to see me again."

Okay, now I feel bad. "I am, but you clearly have something you want to say to me. I'm just trying to find out what it is."

"I don't know where to start."

Ugh. "Well, you could start with why you're here and not at school."

Looking down at the ground, he lightly scratches over his arm. "I transferred to NHU."

"I'm sorry, you did what now?" I ask, unsure if I heard him right. "Why would you do that?"

He shrugs. "Because I missed my friends. Missed you."

And there it is. The underlying point of all this that I saw coming from a mile away. Hell, even Asher must have noticed it when he saw us this morning. Easton is anything but subtle with the way he looks at me, and I'm sure he picked up on it.

"Eas," I breathe, hating how vulnerable he looks right now.

"I know. You don't have to say it. I just thought that you missed me, too. I realize now I was wrong."

"It's not that," I backpedal, trying to save him some heartache. "I'm seeing someone."

His eyes widen. "Wow. That took you no time at all, huh? Did you even think of me the last couple months?"

Not really, but I'm not about to tell him that. "Easton, you knew what we were. It was only ever meant to be a good time."

"Bullshit!" he snaps. "It wasn't like that at all. At least not for me. I wanted to make it work! That morning we broke up, I was going to tell you that I wanted to try. I figured you'd give it a shot after all the shit I helped you through, but instead, you tossed me away like it was the easiest fucking thing in the world."

"Because it was!" The words come out of my mouth before I can stop them. "Don't you get it? I wanted to get rid of everything from that day, you included."

Laughing darkly, he rolls his eyes. "And what? Someone who played a part in it gets to stay simply because he's family?"

"Knox took a fucking bullet for Delaney. That's hardly the same thing, and I wasn't about to tell her she couldn't be with him. Besides, they moved across the damn country."

He shakes his head in frustration. "I'm not talking about Knox."

My stomach flips at his words, and not in a good way. "Who *are* you talking about then?"

"Nothing," he retorts, trying to take it all back. "Forget I said anything."

"No, Easton. What the fuck are you talking about?"

His hand moves to rub the back of his neck while he looks anywhere but at me. "Let's just say your dad wasn't the innocent victim he portrayed himself as."

I **STORM THROUGH THE** front door of my house, heading straight into my father's office. The only thing Easton would tell me is that my dad knew more than what he let on. He wouldn't budge on anything else, so, I'm taking matters into my own hands.

Sitting down at his computer, it immediately asks me for a password. *Fuck.* I type in a couple different things, like his mother's maiden name and the place he met my mom, but no luck. Finally, it comes to me.

Ainsley's birthday.

The computer opens in a second and I roll my eyes. Of course, it would be that. His stupid little pride and joy. Fuck the fact that he has two *other* daughters. Seriously, sometimes I wonder why my parents even had more kids. He was obviously happiest with the one.

I pull up the surveillance camera footage from that day, hoping it managed to pick up the conversations my dad had with my uncle before I came into the room. It took a long time before I learned how to maneuver around this place without being picked up by the cameras. Why this man feels the need to record the *inside* of his house is something I've never understood.

The second my uncle comes on the screen, I immediately want to vomit. It's been six months since I've had to see him, and I've liked it that way. Jackson putting that man in the ground was the best thing for everyone.

Watching through the footage, I don't hear anything suspicious—then I remember the hushed conversation they cut short the second I came back down the stairs. I switch the video over to the one from the foyer, and press play.

"My men looked for him all night but came up empty," Dominic says to my dad.

He leans against the wall. "Yeah, well, if he's with Delaney, then Tessa is the best way to lure them out. The girl may be smart, but when it comes to her sister, she'll do anything."

"It may get ugly. If Delaney doesn't think Tessa is in trouble, Knox may convince her to stay hidden."

"That's all right. Maybe you'll even get Tessa to start behaving. Scare her straight."

Dom scoffs. "Wishful thinking. She's a lost cause, that one. But I'll do my best."

My father nods. "Just promise me one thing—Knox Vaughn doesn't make it out of there alive."

I come into view with a smile on my face, having no idea what was about to happen and how it would ruin me.

I stop the video and my chest tightens like a vice grip, threatening to drag me down to the depths of despair. The urge to vomit surfaces as my stomach churns. The one person on this planet who is meant to protect me against the evils of the world led me straight to the slaughter without a second thought.

"What do you think you're doing?" My dad stands in the doorway, looking every bit like the man who raised me, but I'm seeing him in a whole different light.

I wipe the stray tears with the back of my hand as I stand up. "You knew."

"I beg your pardon?"

"Don't play fucking stupid. You knew!" I shout. "You knew what his plans were when he picked me up that morning and you let him take me anyway!"

He takes a hesitant step forward. "Tessa."

Picking up the closest thing to me—which happens to be a framed photo of our oh-so-happy family, *how fitting*—I throw it directly at him and he jumps back.

"Do you have any idea what they did to me that day? What *you* allowed to happen?" I throw something else—this

195

time, a paperweight. "I was locked in a room with four guys while Dominic let them have their fucking way with me! I spent hours being molested by men who were just as sick and twisted as he was!"

Raising his hands in defense, he stays in place. "I didn't know he was going to let it get that out of control."

"Oh, please! You practically fucking asked for it!"

I hit a button on the computer and it replays the part where he talks about scaring me into behaving. Listening to it once was hard, but hearing it a second time is absolute hell. The tone of his voice as jokes with the devil himself about what a lost cause I am, it feels like a knife straight to the heart. Every hope I ever had for a relationship with my dad dies in an instant.

He sighs. "All he told me was that he was going to use you to scare Delaney and Knox out of hiding. That's all I knew."

Everything coming out of his mouth is nothing but a goddamn lie. This house. This life. It's all a façade. He doesn't care about anyone other than himself. He proved as much when he threw his own daughters into the lion's den. I scan the office for an outlet for my fury. Rage builds up inside of me, and all I want is to make him feel even an ounce of the pain I've suffered.

I pull out the nine iron and inspect it carefully. *That'll do.* "No, see, I'm having a lot of trouble believing that. Especially because I listened to you order him to not let Knox out of there alive."

"Tessa," he tries again, but it's no use.

"He tried to kill Delaney!"

I grip the handle of the club, and his eyes widen as I swing it full force at his computer.

"He almost killed Knox!"

This time I swing at everything else on the desk, sending it all flying.

"His fucking intention was to kill us all!"

Bookshelf.

I take my dad's most prized possession—an autographed, gold-plated football that Ainsley bought him for Christmas one year—and hold it up in my hand.

"And then you had the audacity to play the part of a victim."

A humorless laugh echoes out of me as I toss the stupid thing into the air and whack it across the room, loving the sound it makes and the look on his face.

"Tessa, stop!" he yells, as if he has any say at this point.

The light coming in through the window glints off a piece of metal on the ground and catches my attention. *A key.* After picking it up and reading the label on it, I clutch it tightly in my palm and level my father with a look.

"Fuck you," I spit. "You don't get to tell me what to do. Not now. Not ever." I take a couple more steps until I'm right in his face. "You're a piece of shit, and I hope you rot in hell, right alongside your brother."

As I hand him the golf club, he watches in silence as I leave the freshly destroyed space and the house entirely.

I PULL DOWN THE long driveway to the secluded property. The familiar, oversized house sits at the end, taunting me. I grab the gas can from the passenger seat and climb out of the car. As I get closer, there's nothing flowing through my veins but the hatred I have for the man who lived here.

Slipping the key into the lock, the door swings open and I step inside. Everything looks exactly how I remember it: the furniture, the décor, the colors. Memories of Delaney and I running around this place as kids threaten to surface, but they're not memories I welcome anymore.

I walk around the downstairs, pouring gasoline throughout each room. Then, when everything is doused, I pull the matches from my pocket.

"No one gets to have something to remember you by," I say out loud. "You don't deserve it. Your memory gets to fucking die like you did."

Sparking a match against the pack, I let it fall to the ground and back away as the flames shoot across the trail of gasoline, imagining my memories burning along with this house.

Asher

I PACE ACROSS MY LIVING ROOM, NOT EVEN
finding solace in the glass of whiskey gripped in my hand. My
eyes glance at the clock for the hundredth time since I got
home. *An hour late.*

Seeing Tessa this morning with two guys I didn't
recognize spurred an uncomfortable feeling in the pit of my
stomach. It was clear by the way the one looked at her and
touched her that they share a history that she and I don't.
Colby would tell me I'm jealous—that I'm afraid to lose her
to someone her own age or some shit—but personally, I'm
enjoying what we have going on. Sue me for not wanting it to
come to an end.

I was just finishing up a short conversation with Trent
when I got her text telling me that Easton wanted to talk and
she'd be a half-hour late. I didn't necessarily like it, but I'm
not her keeper. If she wants to hear him out, that's her
choice. However, it's an hour after the time she said she'd be
here, and Tessa is nothing if not straightforward. If she
decided not to come, she would have told me.

The glass slams down onto the counter with a force I
didn't intend. Something isn't right. I take out my phone and
pull up her location. Okay, so maybe I turned that on without
her knowing, but it was after the party debacle and I was
worried she'd end up in another potentially dangerous
situation—like right now.

Her blue dot sits at a house that isn't her own, and my

paranoia grows tenfold. It doesn't take more than a couple seconds before I'm grabbing my keys and heading for the elevator.

THE SMOKE FILLING THE sky becomes thicker the closer that I get to her location. Dread flows through me the second I turn down a long driveway and see her Lamborghini parked at an odd angle in the drive. It's empty, but her phone isn't pinging from the car.

As the house comes into view, my whole body goes cold and my every fear magnifies. Not only is Tessa's phone signaling inside the place, but the whole thing is up in flames.

No.

No, no, no.

I jump out of my car and look around, hoping to see her anywhere except for in there.

"Tessa!" I scream in pure terror, but there's no response. "Tess!"

In a split-second decision, I run up to the door and kick it in. Smoke billows out just enough for me to see my girl sitting on the floor, watching everything burn around her. Relief floods through me as I use my shirt to cover my mouth and rush over to her.

"Tessa, baby, we have to get you out of here."

She blinks up at me, completely void of emotion. She seems like an empty vessel, but even through the soot and ash covering her face, I can see it. The red-rimmed eyes. The runny nose. She's been crying.

"Let me take care of you," I beg. "Please."

Holding my hand out, I look at her pleadingly. We need to get out of here before the whole damn thing comes down on top of us. A board falls behind me, and I flinch. Thankfully, Tessa takes ahold of me and I pull her to her feet. The two of us run outside and don't stop until we're standing by my car.

I check her over, making sure there are no injuries that require medical attention. She coughs a couple times but her eyes stay glued to the house, still barren of the life I've always found in them.

"What the hell happened in there?" I question, but there's no point. It's like I'm not even here.

Pulling out my phone, I dial the number of the one person who will do what I ask without any hesitation.

"Hey, man," he answers.

"Colby," I say, relieved that he picked up on the second ring. "Where are you?"

"Just leaving practice. Why? What's up?"

Thank fuck. "Good. I need you and Griffin to get in your car and come get Tessa's Lamborghini from the address I'm sending you. Once you have it, call 911 about the fire if no one is here yet."

"Wait, what fire?" He sounds alarmed but I don't blame him.

"I'll explain later. I don't even have all the answers right now."

Tessa's laughter meets my ears, and it's the first hint of anything since I found her. She's staring at the way the house is burning to the ground, a maniacal grin on her face. She laughs again and alarm trills up my spine.

"Is she laughing?" Colby asks.

I swallow hard, wondering what the hell happened today. "Just bring her car to my place when you're done."

No part of me waits for his answer as I hang up the phone and shove it back in my pocket. I lead Tessa around and put her in the passenger seat of my SUV.

"Stay here. I'll be right back."

Getting into Tessa's car, I peel out of the driveway and drive it a little down the road, into the woods and hidden from view. I send Colby the location and a picture of where it is, then sprint full speed back to my Range Rover. As I get in, Tessa is staring out the window, her eyes not leaving the house that will soon become a pile of ash.

I CARRY HER THROUGH the penthouse and into my bathroom. The whole drive home she didn't murmur a single word. She just sat completely still, eyes focused on my dashboard. No matter what I said to her, what part of her I touched, it was like I didn't exist.

Turning on the shower, I set it to a warm stream and step back. I approach Tessa with caution as I gently run a hand over her shoulder.

"You need to get cleaned up, babe."

I'm not sure if she even hears me, and I'm worried something's wrong that needs medical attention, but I'm scared of doing the wrong thing and making this worse for her. I drop my head when she doesn't answer and turn to leave.

"Don't leave me."

The words are so quiet, I almost wonder if I imagined them, but the pain in her voice is what stops me dead in my tracks. I pull my shirt over my head and toss it to the floor.

"I'm here," I tell her. "Okay? I'm right here."

With a delicate touch, I carefully remove her school uniform. She listens to everything I say, helping me get her undressed, but her eyes still won't meet mine. When she's finally naked, I quickly dispose of the rest of my attire and lead her into the shower.

The water flows over the two of us, rinsing the ash from her skin. I gently tilt her head back to wash her hair and let my hand run across her. She leans into my touch just enough for me to notice, and I realize she's still in there. Somewhere, in spite of whatever happened, she's fighting the terror she's dealing with.

"Tessa, talk to me."

Finally, her gaze meets mine, and my breath hitches at the torment you can see in those honey eyes. A sob rips through her, tears quickly flowing down her face. Her hand moves to grasp her chest, and I instantly fear the worst.

"What's wrong? Can you breathe? Should I bring you to the hospital?"

She shakes her head as she cries. "It just hurts."

"What? What hurts?"

Leaning back against the tile, she's visibly breaking right in front of me. This girl has always been nothing but pure confidence, all fearless and brave, but right now, she's human. Her head tips to the side, and she looks at me with labored breathing.

"Everything."

I take her hands in my own. "What can I do? What do you need?"

"Make it stop." More tears leak out as her grip tightens. "Please, Asher. Make me forget. I need you to distract me. I need you to take the pain away."

Taking a step closer, I pin her hands to the wall and cage her in. My subconscious is full of flashing red lights, screaming for me to run. She's weak. She's vulnerable. She's not in her right mind. But all I can focus on is the fact that she's hurting, and she needs me.

I press my lips to hers and she arches into me, skin against skin. Pulling away for a second, I stare deep into her eyes for any indication that this isn't what she wants but find none. All I can see is the painstaking need for relief, and fuck if I'm not going to give it to her.

"Are you sure?"

She exhales. "Please."

Between the anguish in her plea and the way she pulls her bottom lip between her teeth, my resolve snaps, and I'm heading full force into everything I swore I wouldn't do.

Our mouths collide in a kiss that's both needy and passionate as sin. I release her hand and move to hold her face while her nails dig into my shoulder blades. The water hits against my back in a warm stream but everything else is on fire. Now that I know I'm allowing myself to give in, every ounce of my focus is zeroed in on her.

"I've got you," I tell her softly.

She lets out a whimper that nearly rips me apart. I slide my hands down until I'm cupping her breasts. Her nipples harden to points the instant they register my touch, and I roll them between my fingertips. Tessa moans as I lightly suck one into my mouth while still teasing the other.

"Asher," she breathes, and my name sounds like a prayer slipping from her lips.

I reach over and turn off the water before scooping her into my arms. Her legs wrap around my waist, rubbing her pussy over my erection in ways that threaten to have me coming undone like some kind of virgin. We're both dripping wet as I carry her out of the bathroom and lower her onto my bed.

She looks like a goddess, all splayed out and waiting for me. She watches me with desire pooling in her eyes, and the only thing I want is to make her scream out in pleasure. With my hands on her knees, I spread her legs apart to show me that delicious center of hers. *How did I ever deny myself of this?*

"Fuck, Tess."

She grips the bedsheets, desperate for my touch, and I'm

more than willing to give it to her. I run two fingers over her sex. She's already so wet, and her body squirms at the contact. Bending down, I slip the two digits inside of her and run my tongue over her clit. The sounds she lets out are borderline animalistic and make me want to hear more of them. So much more.

Her fingers lace into my hair as I suck on the little bundle of nerves. My fingers rub against her G-spot, and I can tell by the way her grip tightens that she's going to come undone in record time.

"That's it, baby. Just like that."

I look up at her, and seeing the way her back is arched and she's biting her fist—it's everything. With a couple more flicks of my tongue, she screams out, and I feel as she clenches around my fingers. I keep going, not even slowing my movements until she stops convulsing. Then, I pull them out and raise to my feet.

"Please don't stop," she begs.

The corner of my mouth raises into a smirk. "I didn't plan on it."

Grabbing a condom from the nightstand, I slip it on and move until I'm hovering over her. My gaze meets hers, and I pause to give her every opportunity to back out. All she needs to do is say the word and I'll stop. It would fucking suck, but everything would end that instant. However, given the look in her eyes, she has no intentions of saying anything but go.

I line myself up and sink inside of her, loving the way her walls feel around me. Her nails scratch down my back as she arches her hips up to meet me. The way she craves every single inch of my cock—like it's somehow healing her—it's raw, and passionate, and real.

Thrusting into her, I keep my pace light. Slow. Careful not to hurt her in the fragile state she's already in. While every part of me wants to speed up, this isn't about me. It's about her.

The time it takes for the pressure to build inside me is embarrassingly quick. I reach down and press my thumb against Tessa's clit, rubbing it in a way that makes her voice raise a couple octaves. The two of us chase our high together, and the second she tightens around me, I can't hold back anymore. I let go, pulsing inside of her and emptying everything I've got into the condom.

WE'RE LAYING IN MY bed, with her head resting on my chest. I lightly graze my hand up and down her back in a comforting motion. I'm not even sure she's still awake, being as we've been like this for half an hour now and she's yet to say anything. The only indication I have is the small motion of her hand on my stomach.

"It was during the spring," she breathes. "My sister had stayed out all night, which was really unlike her, and my Uncle Dominic came to pick me up. He said he wanted to take us both out to breakfast."

"Tess, you don't have to…"

"I want to," she cuts me off. "If I don't tell someone, it's going to eat me alive."

I press a kiss into her hair. "Okay."

After a deep breath, she continues. "When I got into the car, I realized something was off with him. It's like he went from the loving uncle I always remembered to a monster in less than a minute. I tried to get away, but someone was in the back seat. They put something over my face and the next thing I knew, I was waking up in some type of wet basement."

My heart hurts listening to her, but I don't say anything.

Instead, I continue to rub her back and keep her as comfortable as possible.

"He spent the next however many hours abusing me and letting his friends do whatever they wanted to my body. If I didn't do what they said or what they wanted, they'd beat me. I lost count of how many times I blacked out, but it was enough to give me a concussion.

"My uncle forced me to call my sister. Apparently, her boyfriend had managed to piss him off, and when he couldn't find them, he planned on using me to lure them out. I tried to tell Delaney to stay away, but of course, she didn't listen. He tied me to a chair and looked at each one of my cuts and bruises with so much pride it made me sick."

She stops for a second to compose herself, wiping her tears with the blanket, and I take the time to kiss her forehead. Every word she's saying is like a knife straight to the heart.

"So, the house..."

"I'll get there," she tells me. "After Knox and Delaney got there, it was clear he had no intention of letting any of us get out of there alive. He was going to kill us all, and the sick part is, he probably would have gotten away with it. Knox somehow convinced him to let me and Delaney go. He was going to sacrifice himself for us.

"Just as he told his men to untie me, though, there was a commotion outside. Dominic was sure Knox and Delaney had brought the police with him, and he went off. He pointed a gun at my head to get Laney to stop hiding from behind her boyfriend and made her walk further away from Knox. I was completely convinced I was going to die that day. We all were." She pauses a moment, takes a deep breath, then continues.

"Thankfully, the FBI had already gotten a guy undercover in his fight ring, Jackson. He had been training Knox and

Grayson on how to fight for Dominic. It was a psychotic way to make money off the sick and deranged. He came out with his gun pointed at my uncle, and being as all his guys were dealing with the shit outside, he was defenseless.

Instead of surrendering, he did the unthinkable. He pointed the gun at Delaney and pulled the trigger."

Her whole body shudders, as if the memory of that part alone is enough to torment her for the rest of her life.

"It didn't even register that my uncle was shot ten times while standing right next to me. His blood splattered onto my face, but my attention was on my sister. Somehow, Knox managed to jump in front of her in time and took the bullet. It lodged itself in his chest, and he lost a lot of blood.

"He was in surgery for what felt like ages, and a coma for weeks after that, but he pulled through. I've never been more thankful for a person than I am for him, because losing my sister isn't something I'd be able to handle. Not now, not ever."

"Tessa," I whisper, feeling my heart break for her.

"I'm almost done," she replies. "I was dating Easton at the time, and he helped me through a lot. It's why no matter what, I'll never be able to have anything but respect for him. He did everything I needed him to do, whenever I needed it, but he was still something that connected me to that night. When he and I broke up, I was almost relieved. That relationship was one less thing to remind me of that day."

"And him coming back today brought that all back up?"

She nods. "He was supposed to be at UCLA, but he told me today he transferred to NHU and moved back. He told me he wants to get back together, but that's not what I want. When he got mad, he let it slip that my dad played a bigger part in everything than I knew. He wouldn't tell me more than that, so I went home to see what I could figure out."

My arms tighten around her involuntarily, and I have to

tamp down the anger at Easton's behavior. His careless shots could have killed her today.

She continues. "My father is a control freak, and went as far as putting surveillance cameras all over the inside of the house. I managed to get into his computer and found the footage from that day."

Her lip starts to quiver, and she moves until she's looking up at me. Her eyes are filled with tears and her cheeks are soaked. She takes in a shaky breath.

"My dad knew what my uncle was trying to do the whole time. He handed his own daughters over without a care in the world."

Just like that, she breaks again, and the sobs rip through her. I pull her in as close as possible, holding her tight as she comes apart in my arms.

AFTER CRYING AND SHAKING for hours, Tessa finally falls asleep in my arms—only after she explains the confrontation with her dad and that she started the fire in her uncle's house. A part of me is concerned for her mental state. It's one thing to break a few things; it's another to burn an entire house to the ground. However, knowing everything she's been through, I can't even begin to imagine the pain she's in.

I slip out of bed, careful not to wake her, and go to find my phone. As expected, a text from Colby waits for me when I open it.

> Tess's Lambo is in the parking garage. Fire trucks were already putting out by the time we got there. House is totally fucked though. She okay?

I look over at her sleeping form, seeing how she's curling in on herself and the pain you can still see etched across her face.

> No, I don't think she is, but she will be. I'll make sure of it.

Numb. Cold. Dark. That's the only way I can think to describe what I'm feeling. Don't get me wrong, I never liked my dad. He was never the kind of father that every child yearns for. The kind to show up at your T-ball games. The kind to threaten your first date but only because he doesn't want you to grow up. The kind that will walk you down the aisle and give you away because it's important to you. No, he was never like that. But still, no part of me ever considered how despicable he really is.

I sit on the couch, wrapped in a blanket and staring at the TV. I'm not actually paying any attention to it, but just staring into space was making Asher worry.

It felt good, telling him everything. It took a weight off my shoulders that was crushing me and making it hard to breathe. Not that it's gone completely now, but it's lighter, and I can handle lighter.

He gave me everything I needed yesterday. A distraction to stop the pain from swallowing me whole. A shoulder to cry on as I recited the worst day of my life. And he held me as I broke, keeping me grounded and giving me something to cling to. A reason to keep going when I needed it most.

I thought after watching that house go up in flames yesterday that I would feel some kind of relief. Every last materialistic thing he owned, every remaining physical part of him, burned inside that place. I should feel better. There isn't a single thing left of that monster. But, I don't. He's still there—haunting my every nightmare.

The elevator opens and Lennon steps out of it, sighing in relief when she sees me. I throw the blanket off me and run over to hug her. The feeling of her arms wrapped around me is soothing, like Asher's, only more. It's the closest thing I can get to the feeling Delaney would give me.

"What are you doing here?" I ask in disbelief.

"I invited her," Asher answers, coming out from the kitchen.

Lennon gives him a shy smile. "When you didn't come into school, I got worried. And then I noticed he wasn't either, so I figured you two were together. Why haven't you been answering your phone?"

I sigh, not sure how to answer that. There's been so much that's happened in the last twenty-four hours, I can't even wrap my head around it all.

Asher steps up and puts a gentle hand on my lower back. "I'm going to go get dinner from that Italian place you love. You two talk. I'll be back."

I nod and arch up on my toes to kiss him goodbye. It's nothing steamy or heated, but somehow, it still holds a level of intimacy I'm not used to. Once the elevator doors close behind him, Lennon and I make ourselves comfortable on the couch. I take a breath, exhaling quickly, and then I start explaining everything that went down yesterday.

It's difficult, reliving everything by repeating it all, but Lennon is patient and kind, and I know there isn't a single part of her judging me. My father, maybe. But not me.

"Wow," she says in shock when I'm finished. "I don't even know what to comment on first."

"Welcome to the club."

Her eyes narrow as it all plays through her head and then she snaps. "Okay, no. First of all, your dad is a fucking dick.

216

What the hell is wrong with him? And second, good for you for burning down that asshole's house! I mean, there were probably better ways to go about it, especially because arson is illegal, but you're right. Everything of his turning to ash is what he deserves."

I can't help but smile. "This is why I love you."

She chuckles and pulls me so I'm lying with my head in her lap. "Did you tell Delaney yet?"

I shake my head. "I haven't talked to her. I think I want to give Knox a heads-up beforehand. She's not going to take it well."

"That's probably a good idea."

The two of us are quiet for a minute, but it's a good kind of silence. The kind that lets you think and just bask in the fact that you're okay. You're alive. You're breathing. *You're safe.*

"Has your dad tried reaching out to you?"

I nod. "That's why I haven't been answering my phone. After the fifth time he called, I shoved it into Asher's dresser drawer. I don't want to hear what he has to say."

Her head tilts to the side and her lips purse. "Understandable, but just put his number on mute. I was so bored today without you."

"Well, we wouldn't want that." I chuckle and she rolls her eyes playfully.

ASHER ENDS UP BRINGING home enough food for the three of us, including my favorite chicken parmigiana. He introduced me to this place a couple weeks ago, and I fell in love with it. Now he knows that if he wants to get me to eat when I claim I'm not hungry, just get me this. The smell alone makes my mouth water.

We sit in the living room, eating and watching *The Vampire Diaries*—a show that Asher pretends he can't stand but still watches with me every time I turn it on. Having the two of them with me, I feel calmer. More relaxed. Like for the first time in a while, everything isn't going to shit. Sure, I may end up getting arrested for arson, but that's a problem for another day.

"Okay, but like, how does Elena even consider choosing Stefan over Damon?" Lennon voices what's probably on the mind of every girl to ever watch this show. "Just look at him!"

"You're preaching to the choir, honey."

Asher looks over at me and raises an eyebrow.

"Oh, come on. You can't possibly think I watch this show for the storyline."

He chuckles and pinches my ankle while my feet rest in his lap. It's so comfortable like this—so laid-back and carefree. I'd spend forever right here with no complaints.

IT'S AFTER ELEVEN WHEN Lennon says she needs to get going. She waves goodbye to Asher and I walk her over to the elevator. After a tight hug and making me promise I'll start texting her back, she leaves Asher and I alone together. I run my fingers through my hair and go back to the couch, standing in front of him.

"Feeling any better?" he asks.

I nod. "Thank you, for letting her come here, and for everything else. It helped more than you know."

A smile that threatens to take my breath away graces his face. "It was hardly a chore, Tess."

"Yeah, well, I know that was something you were trying to avoid, so I don't want you to think I expect it all the time now—especially since I'm going to be staying here with you. Are you sure that's okay, by the way? I can always go stay at Lennon's."

He grabs my wrist and pulls me toward him, making me fall into his lap. His hand cups my cheek, and he presses his lips to mine in a soft, sweet kiss. When he pulls away, the sincerity in his eyes is almost overwhelming.

"It's more than okay. I want you here, where I can know for sure that you're okay."

I kiss him again. "Thank you."

Tapping my hip twice, he gets me off his lap. "Thank me by helping shut everything down, and get your boyfriend off my TV."

"You're so possessive."

He winks at me, and I nearly die on the spot. Why does he have to be so goddamn good looking? I mean, really. Would it kill him to look a little more normal?

The two of us shut off all the lights and turn the key on the elevator so it locks—that way, even someone with the code can't come in. When we're finally ready for bed and I grab my phone from his dresser, I tell him goodnight and start heading for the hallway.

"Where are you going?" he asks.

I look back at him, confused. "The guest room."

"Oh." He sounds caught off guard for a second, but then nods. "Okay. Sweet dreams."

Giving him the best smile I can manage, I turn around and walk toward my bedroom for the time being. It's not exactly where I'd like to be, but I'm also not going to invite myself to share Asher's bed with him. Maybe a few weeks ago I would have, but I don't think now is the time to be pushy.

I get in bed and start messing around on my phone. I text Lennon back just so she knows I'm keeping my promise. I delete all the texts from my dad and put his contact on mute so at least my phone won't make a sound every time he sends another. And I text Knox, telling him to call me tomorrow after Delaney leaves for class. Letting him know what I found out—and what I did for that matter—is the smartest choice. He's her rock, and she's going to need him for this one.

I'm scrolling through social media when the door opens, revealing a bare-chested Asher in only a pair of low hanging sweatpants. He walks over to the bed and doesn't bother saying a word as he scoops me up and throws me over his shoulder.

"What are you doing?" I squeal, just barely holding onto my phone.

He carries me out of the room and back down the hallway. "I can't sleep, and I'm blaming you for that."

"Me? What did I do?"

Tossing me down on his bed, he pulls the covers over me and then gets in on his side. "You sleep there. Not on the other side of the penthouse. Right here, next to me."

"Oh? And don't I get a say in this?"

"Do you want one?"

I shrug. "I might. You're old, and old people tend to snore."

He lets out a deep belly laugh, one that makes me feel things I'm not sure I'm okay with. "There's the sass. I was afraid you lost it for a minute there."

"You wish," I quip. "Besides, I think you secretly love it when I fuck with you."

Wrapping an arm around me, he pulls me in close and kisses me before laying his head on the pillow and closing his eyes. "Goodnight, Cherry Bomb."

I roll my eyes and smile at the nickname. "Goodnight, Caveman."

THE NEXT MORNING, I wake up to find the bed empty beside me. The time on the alarm clock reads 9:13, telling me that Asher knew going to school today wasn't something I planned on doing. I know I'll need to go back soon, but the last thing I need right now is for Easton to try talking to me again, or worse, my dad showing up there. No. Laying low here is the best thing for me right now.

I get up and go into the living room in hopes to find Asher making breakfast, but instead, I find Colby. He's eating a bowl of cereal and watching a recording of some football game. Clearing my throat, it gets his attention and he smiles at me.

"Hey, Spyro."

A small chuckle bubbles out. "Spyro?"

His brows raise. "Uh, yeah. The little fire-breathing dragon!" He puts the bowl onto the coffee table. "Tell me you've heard of Spyro."

I shake my head, looking at him like he's lost his mind.

"Okay, well, now I know what we're doing today."

As he grabs the PlayStation controllers and switches something on the TV, I walk around to sit on the couch.

"Where's Asher?" I question.

He waves me off dismissively. "He had to work and told me you're staying home another day, so I figured I'd come over to keep you company."

I level him with a look. "You mean Asher asked you to come babysit me."

He stares at me with the guiltiest look on his face, and I groan. Of course, Asher told him to come here. It's like he doesn't trust me to be alone. Yesterday, when I told him I wasn't going to school, he called out without question. It was just immediately determined that he wasn't going in either. I understood it then, being as the day before I literally had a breakdown in front of him, but this?

I pull my phone out of my pocket and type out a text with a little more force than necessary.

> A babysitter? Really?

Just as I hit send, Colby sighs. "Don't be mad at him. I mean, you did burn a house down a couple days ago. He probably just wanted to make sure he has a home to come back to."

"Ha. Ha," I reply sarcastically.

He hands me a controller with a dimpled grin. "I promise to be fun, and I won't even make you eat your vegetables."

I take it from him just as my phone vibrates on my lap.

> Good morning to you, too.

Okay, he wants to play it that way.

> Well, at least Colby is nice to look at. You could have picked worse.

> Tessa. Don't you dare.

> I wonder if he'll let me model my lingerie for him. We both know your opinions weren't very helpful. 😬

Feeling accomplished as I hit send, I get comfortable and take the controller into my hands. Colby's phone dings only a couple minutes later, and as soon as he reads it, he throws his head back, laughing.

"You're Satan."

I smile sweetly. "I know."

DESPITE MY INITIAL FEELINGS about it, Colby actually ends up being good company. He doesn't push me for any information, and more importantly, he doesn't treat me like I'm damaged. He isn't afraid to make jokes about how young I am or even that I burned down my uncle's house. He's straightforward and real, which is something I need right now. The only way to stay whole is to genuinely believe I'm not already broken.

I'm texting Asher back during his lunch break when I notice the number of text messages my dad has sent me this morning. Even though I know I shouldn't look, curiosity gets the better of me and I open the thread.

> Where are you?

> Tessa Monroe.

> I called the school and you haven't been there the past two days.

> Answer me, young lady, or so help me God.

> If you want to throw your life away, fine, but you're not doing it in a car that I paid for.

The last one hits a nerve. My Lamborghini was a birthday present. Something my sister and I each got for our eighteenth. I always knew it was only a matter of time before he started holding it over my head, and I guess that time is up.

That's fine. I'll give him his car back. It's not like I want anything from him anyway.

"Hey, Colby?"

His head flops to the side against the couch pillow. "Yeah?"

"Can you follow me over to my dad's house? I need to drop off my car, and I'm going to need a ride back."

He exhales and pushes himself up to a sitting position. "All right. You want to go now?"

I nod. "Just let me grab my keys."

Going into the bedroom, I grab the couple things I need and head out. Colby is waiting for me by the elevator, and with an assuring grin, we step inside.

The whole ride to my dad's, I embrace how powerful this car is. I've loved it from the second I first sat behind the wheel. The black on black and the sound of the engine—it's heaven on wheels. It sucks that I have to use it to make a point, but it is what it is.

I pull into the driveway and feel slightly relieved when I see that my dad isn't home. *Good, I really don't want to see him.* Colby parks at the end and hops out of his car.

"All good?" he questions.

I smirk. "Not quite."

Walking around to the side of the house, I find the baseball bat Easton left here one day after baseball practice. I've never been so glad for his tendency to leave his things literally everywhere. I walk back toward my car, and the second Colby sees the bat in my hands, his eyes widen.

"Uh, whatcha doing with the bat, Tess?"

I don't answer him as I grip it in my hands and take the first swing, smashing the windshield and watching the glass spiderweb into a million tiny cracks.

"Oh! No!" Colby cries, clutching his hair. "Not the Lambo! What'd that precious baby ever do to you?"

"Has to be done, Hendrix."

I swing the bat repeatedly, beating the car I once loved to bits. With each one, I picture my dad and how pissed he'll be when he sees it. The look I know will be on his face only fuels my fire. I do it for me. I do it for Delaney. I do it to remind him that he's not the one in charge here—not anymore.

"Oh my God! I can't watch this." Colby covers his eyes like a big baby.

By the time I'm done, there isn't a single inch of the beauty undamaged. I toss the bat to the ground and pull the tube of red lipstick out of my pocket. Uncapping it, I apply the color to my lips and then write my message on the dented hood.

Here's your car. Go fuck yourself.

I bend down to kiss the hood, leaving my signature in a lipstick kiss.

Asher

"I'M SORRY, YOU LET HER DO WHAT?" I SHOUT INTO the phone.

Colby sighs. "Well, I didn't *let* her do it, per se. I didn't know what she was planning on doing until she did it."

I pinch the bridge of my nose, taking a deep breath. Leave it to my best friend to call me like it's no big deal and tell me that Tessa just took a baseball bat to her $400,000 car. I can hear her in the background, chuckling in the same way she did when watched her uncle's house go up in flames.

"Why didn't you try to stop her?"

He snorts. "Have you *met* her? If I had tried to get in her way, she probably would have beat me too."

I groan, knowing he's right. "Okay, well, get her back to my place and don't let her leave."

"He's so bossy," Tessa murmurs, and I find relief in the fact that at least she's still talking.

Colby assures me that there will be no more destruction for the day and we get off the phone. I toss the device onto my desk and rubs my hands over my face. To say I'm worried about her would be a massive understatement. It's like she's completely unraveling right in front of me and there's nothing I can do about it.

Well, that's a lie. There is something I can do, something I plan on doing. I just hope it helps.

———

TESSA SITS IN THE back of the Range Rover, trying to squeeze information out of Colby for the millionth time since we got in the car. She has no idea where we're going, or what we're going to be doing there, and I like it that way. It's a Saturday afternoon, and being as there's no school on Monday, I figured this weekend would be the perfect time.

"Oh, come on. Can't you just give me a clue?" she whines. "Wait, are you two turning me in? I can't go to jail, Asher. I'm strong, but I'm not prison strong. I'd become someone's bitch for a Snickers."

Colby laughs in the passenger seat, unable to contain himself. "A Snickers? Really? That's all it takes?"

She leans back and crosses her arms over her chest. "You'd be amazed what I'd be willing to do for the finer things in life."

He looks over at me. "Is that what you did? Gave her candy?"

I arch a brow at him with a scowl on my face that only amuses him even more.

"What? It's fitting, being as you keep saying she's too young for you."

"Fuck you," I grumble.

Tessa giggles in the back seat, and my eyes meet hers through the rearview mirror. She smirks in a way that tells me I'm not going to like what comes out of her mouth next. Just before I can tell her not to, she opens her mouth anyway.

"Asher *hates* when I have candy," she tells Colby. "Ask him what I can do with a lollipop."

A strangled sound leaves my mouth, and Colby straightens in his seat excitedly.

"Oh, I want to know!"

I reach up and pull my sunglasses over my eyes, then I raise the volume on the music. "We're not talking about it."

"You're such a buzzkill!" They both whine in unison,

making me groan.

I'm surrounded by children.

PULLING UP TO THE private jet, the car comes to a stop, and Tessa looks up from her phone. She looks around and her brows furrow.

"Are we here? Wait, where are we?"

Colby's face splits into a shit-eating grin, and he winks at her. "You're about to meet the boys."

The three of us get out of the car, and I hand my keys to the gentleman who is going to move it for me. Tessa walks around to the back of the SUV, and her jaw drops when she sees the plane in front of us.

"We're going on *that?*"

I smile, pulling the suitcase from the car. "You think you live the high life because you and your friends run around spending Daddy's money? Cherry Bomb, you haven't seen anything yet."

Our fingers lace together, and I pull her to the stairs of the jet, trying to ignore that I'm making a big move here— one that is as risky as it is serious. Introducing Tessa to the team was never a thought in my mind until it was. And once it was there, I couldn't seem to get it out.

We get onto the plane and the minute they see me, the energy level multiplies. Shouts of my name fill the small space, and I can't help but smile. I may not be on the team anymore, but for all intents and purposes, these guys are my family.

"Tess, you know Griffin and Colby, but these are the rest of the guys," I tell her, then turn to my team. "Guys, this is Tessa."

One by one, they each get up to give her a hug—greeting

her in a way that makes me super uncomfortable, but I know they're doing it to fuck with me. Once they're done, I pull her into my arms and hold her possessively. She rolls her eyes at the gesture, but I can see the smile she's trying to hide.

"All right, settle down," Coach says as he steps on board. His eyes meet mine, and he smiles. "Hawthorne. It's good to see you."

I shake his extended hand. "I've missed you, Coach."

"We've missed you, too. There hasn't been anyone to keep that one in line." His head nods toward Colby, and I laugh.

"Please. I couldn't keep him in line when we lived together. I sure as shit have no chance now."

Tessa laughs and throws herself in Colby's lap, much to my dismay.

"I think he's perfect," she coos playfully and pinches his cheeks.

He stands up with her in his arms, handing her over. "Sorry, babe. I like my balls attached."

She chuckles and bops me on the nose. "Yeah, he's a bit of a jealous one, isn't he?"

"I'm right here, and I can hear you."

"I know." She grins, and I put her down.

"Coach, this is Tessa."

His brow, which was knitted tightly during that whole scene, relaxes and he masks his previous expression with a smile. "It's nice to meet you, Tessa."

"You, too," she replies politely.

After making sure everyone's here, Coach heads up to the cockpit to tell the pilot we're ready for takeoff. I lead Tessa over to our seats and sit her between me and the window. She lets me buckle her in and rests her head back, turning to look at me.

"So, where are we going exactly?"

I smirk, knowing this is the best part of the whole thing. Well, second best. The best she'll get tomorrow night.

"Miami."

Her eyes widen excitedly. "For real?"

I nod, and she grabs my face in her hands to pull me in for a kiss. When she pulls away, I smile so wide I can feel my dimples popping. She bites her lip and pokes one of them with her finger.

"Put those away. They're dangerous," she quips.

"I know. That's why I like them."

HALFWAY THROUGH THE FLIGHT, Tessa is sound asleep in the seat. I kind of figured she would be. While she tries to play it off like she's getting better, her nightmares haven't gone unnoticed. I wake up almost every time she does, but after the first couple times of her having to lie to me about them, I started to pretend I'm still asleep. It seems to make her feel better about them, since she doesn't spend a half hour apologizing for waking me up, and that's all that matters.

I get up to grab a beer and on my way back, Coach nods to the seat beside him. I glance at Tessa to make sure she's still okay and sit down.

"What's up, Coach?"

He gives me a *no bullshit* look. "What are you doing, boy?"

My brows furrow. "What do you mean?"

"How old is that girl?"

I drop my head, realizing that if he figured it out in a millisecond, everyone else probably can, too. "She's eighteen."

"And?"

"And one of my students."

A heavy sigh leaves his mouth, and he shakes his head. "You're playing with fire, Asher. You've never been the type to take big risks. Why start now?"

I shake my head. "It isn't like that."

He laughs, but it lacks humor. "Sure it's not. Son, I've only ever seen you look at one other girl the way you look at her, and you almost married her."

My stomach churns at his words, and I think he notices because his tone changes.

"All I'm saying is be careful."

I nod. "Will do, Coach."

Just as I get up to go back to Tessa, he stops me with a hand on my wrist.

"And you may want to make sure the press doesn't get any pictures of her. You know how they can be."

Shit. I hadn't even thought about that. It's been months since I was forced into hiding to avoid them. With the exception of coming to the games I coach, they've left me alone, which has been nice. However, if they catch wind of me potentially dating someone, and especially if they find out who she is, it'll start a paparazzi free-for-all.

THE CAPTAIN ANNOUNCES THAT we're going to be landing in a minute, and I look over at Tessa, who is still fast asleep with her feet in my lap. I reach over and put a gentle hand on her shoulder.

"Tess, you have to wake up," I whisper, and thankfully, her eyes peek open. "We're almost there."

She sits up and rubs her eyes with the back of her hand. It's unnerving how adorable I find it and how beautiful she looks half asleep. I clear my throat and force myself to focus.

"Hey, listen," I start, "I'm going to need you to wear one of my hoodies, Colby's hat, and your sunglasses."

She cocks a brow at me and I can tell she's not happy. "In Miami? Asher, it's like 80 degrees."

"I know, but the press is going to be out there, and we can't have them seeing you. Your picture will end up everywhere."

That seems to get through to her, and she nods in understanding. "Okay."

I squeeze her hand and lean over to kiss her forehead, feeling grateful that she didn't fight me on it like I thought she would.

The pilot lands the plane with ease, and Colby comes over to help me with Tessa. I hand her my sweatshirt and she puts it on. It's no surprise that it swims on her—she's tiny. Colby puts his hat on her head and with her sunglasses, she's completely unrecognizable. Her hair is even tucked into the hoodie. The only way you can tell she's even female is from her petite size.

"Stay on the other side of her," I tell Colby. "I don't need one of those bloodhounds getting ahold of her. They're fucking ruthless."

He gives me a look that tells me he completely agrees, and the two of us lead Tessa to the door.

Lights flash the second Colby steps out of the plane. Tessa follows him with some confusion, and I bring up the rear. The second they notice me, they all go nuts. Shouts of my name and random questions are yelled from all angles as we make our way down the stairs.

Colby does what I asked, and the two of us cage her in for her safety. I don't even realize I have my hand on her lower back until someone mentions something about it. *Fuck.*

"Asher, is that your girlfriend? Is there a new special someone in your life?"

We ignore all questions and keep moving until we're safely inside the car. It isn't until we pull away that Tessa takes the hat off. She turns to look at me with a devilish grin on her face.

"Smooth move, Hawthorne. You couldn't keep your hands off me long enough to walk from the plane to the car?"

I drop my head and run my fingers through my hair. "I know. I fucked up."

The second Tessa puts a hand on my cheek, I stop my miniature freak-out.

"Hey," she says softly. "It's okay. It's not that big of a deal."

She tucks herself into my side, and I relax instantly, but I don't miss the look on Colby's face. He just watched that entire exchange, and he's never going to let me live it down. *Fuck.*

THE NEXT MORNING, COLBY wakes me up with a knock on the hotel suite door. As soon as I open it, he tosses a newspaper at me and steps inside. It only takes a second for me to notice the headline.

Asher Hawthorne: Taken by A Mystery Girl?

Right below it is a picture from yesterday, with my hand planted firmly against Tessa's lower back as I lead her to the car. Okay, so I knew this was going to happen. It probably would have happened even if I hadn't slipped up. For some reason, my love life has been a topic of fascination ever since Nikki and I called off our wedding six years ago.

"All right, it's not *that* bad."

He smirks. "Wait for it."

My brows furrow, until five seconds later when my phone starts to ring inside my pocket. Colby chuckles and takes a sip of his coffee.

"There it is."

Pulling it out of my pocket, I groan when I see Blaire's name lit up on the screen. Sure, I could always not answer, but she won't stop calling until she reaches me. And besides, she knows I'm with Colby. She'll use any excuse she can to get him on the phone, and he'd rat me out faster than I could blink.

"Hey, Blaire."

She scoffs. "Hey? Seriously? When were you going to tell me about this, Asher? Or do you find it amusing when I wake up to nearly 100 messages about something I know nothing about?"

I bite my lip to contain my laughter. "I mean..."

"Don't answer that," she groans. "It's too early in the morning to deal with your shit. Just tell me how you want me to spin this."

I think it over for a second but ultimately don't know the answer. "Give me options?"

"You're useless. She's just a friend. She's dating Colby. She's someone you're seeing casually but it's not serious. You're getting married next month. You eloped. Give me *something* to work with, Hawthorne."

Colby waggles his eyebrows at me when he hears the one about using him as an excuse. *Over my dead body.* I think over the rest of the choices and sigh.

"Go with just a friend."

"And in all actuality?" she inquires for the truth.

"It's complicated."

Okay, so that's not exactly a lie, but if I was blatantly honest with her, she would tell me to get rid of Tess. She'd have a flight back to California booked and a car here to pick her up within the hour. I can't let anything ruin this weekend. Tessa needs it.

She lets out an aggravated sound. "We're going to talk when you get back."

"Yes, ma'am."

As soon as I hang up the phone, I exhale, and Colby laughs. I almost smack him upside the head, and I would have if a familiar voice didn't distract me.

"What's so funny?"

I look over at the bedroom door, finding Tessa standing there in only my T-shirt. My hand flies to cover Colby's eyes as I let my gaze rake over her. My God, she's a fucking knockout.

"Nothing, babe. If you want a shower, go take one now. We're going to breakfast soon."

She nods and disappears back inside the room.

THE LOOK ON TESSA'S face when she realized we were going to a game was priceless, and it was even better to see how into it she got. From screaming Colby's name as he scored four touchdowns, and getting pissed off when the ref made a bad call, it was perfect. However, I know nothing will compare to what's about to come.

We pull up to the mansion the guys rented to celebrate in. After a 42 to 0 win, it was more than justified. I help Tessa out of the car, trying not to gawk at how she looks in that dress. I swear, the whole damn room could be on fire, and I would have no idea. My attention is entirely absorbed by her.

Stepping inside, the whole place is so upbeat, it's electric. Everyone is having the time of their lives, like they usually do after they take another team to the woodshed like they did. I grip Tessa's hand in mine and watch as she takes it all in.

"I don't know what's more amazing, this house or how happy everyone is. This is your life?"

A wide grin stretches across my face. "Unbelievable, right?"

She nods and looks around, mesmerized. "Incredible."

The two of us make our way around the party, stopping to congratulate the players I didn't manage to catch right after the game. Each one of them is completely taken by Tessa and her sassy charm. *They can get in line.* If I wasn't such a jealous prick when it comes to her, I'd probably find it amusing.

I'm in the middle of drinking a beer and listening to Tessa and Colby banter about how she could probably take him on the field, when I notice her surprise only steps behind her. The resemblance between them is too obvious for it to go unnoticed. The guy standing next to her looks nothing like I expected, but after hearing what he did, I have the utmost respect for him.

Delaney puts her finger to her mouth and quietly steps up behind Tessa. Once she's close enough, she chuckles.

"Typical Tessa. Always finding something to argue about."

Tess's eyes double in size and instantly water up as her sister's voice registers in her ear. In a split second, she turns around and throws herself into her arms. Delaney smiles brightly as they embrace, mouthing a silent *thank you* my way. I answer with a nod.

"Wait, there's two of them?" Colby practically salivates at the mouth. "Bruh."

Knox accepts the beer I hand him and takes a sip. "Yeah, there are, and I don't care how many people love you. Don't even fucking think about it."

He glances over at Knox and looks him up and down, then shrugs. "Fair enough."

When Tessa finally lets go of Delaney, she turns to me. "You did this?"

"I may have had *something* to do with it."

With the biggest smile, she lunges at me and leaps into my arms. Colby grabs my beer before I drop it, allowing me to hold her tightly. She murmurs a million thank you's with her head buried in my neck, but that's not what makes it worth it. The smile on her face is all the thanks I need.

I put her down and she takes a step back, slotting herself next to her sister. Delaney leans into her with her eyes stuck on me.

"Have I ever told you that you have *really* good taste?"

Tessa laughs. "Maybe once or twice."

I can't help but smile as Knox clears his throat and raises his eyebrows at Delaney. She smiles sweetly—in the same way I've seen Tessa do a million times when she knows she's in trouble—and blows him a kiss. Knox, even as strong as he is, seems to lose all his fight the second he pulls her into his arms and breathes in the smell of her hair. *Yeah, I know that feeling.*

I'M STANDING NEAR THE bar, watching from a distance as Tessa and Delaney sing *"Livin' on a Prayer"* at the top of their lungs. The whole place is full of people enjoying themselves, but nothing sticks out like she does. The glow in her eyes and the smile on her face—it's intoxicating. I could stand here and watch her for hours. Colby appears next to me and takes a swig of his beer.

"You know you're totally fucked, right?"

I sigh, finding no point in trying to deny it now. "Yeah, I know."

This girl is a storm—a tornado ready to wreak havoc on anything in her path—and I'm addicted to her chaos.

Tessa

IF I THOUGHT THE PARTIES ZAYN THREW WERE A good time, this is fucking Disneyland. Everyone is in such a good mood, it's impossible to be around them and not be happy. I don't know who gave Asher the idea for this weekend, or if he thought of it all on his own, but it's exactly what I needed. Plus, he gave me the one person who can manage to make anything better no matter what—my sister.

"Okay, but really," Knox says as he levels me with a look. "Why the fuck does it not surprise me one bit that you're dating your English teacher?"

I tilt my head to the side. "Eh, we're not *dating* per se."

Delaney laughs. "You're living at his place, kissing him because you can, and taking trips across the country together. Call it what you want, but you're dating."

There's no use in arguing with them, and besides, they have a point. However, I don't see the need to define things between us. Titles make things complicated, and what Asher and I have is so laid back; I'd hate to ruin that over something that really doesn't matter.

Colby comes up next to me and drapes his arm over my shoulder. "Spyro! Take a shot with me!"

He hands me a shot glass full of tequila, and the two of us throw them back. It only takes a couple minutes before Asher comes over. He puts out his hand and I take it, giggling as he pulls me out of Colby's hold and into his own. It's relieving to see he's not afraid to touch me here. A part of me was afraid that he would act like we were just friends in front of the guys. Instead, he acts just as possessive and hands-on as he does at home.

"Are you having a good time?" he questions.

I arch up on my tip-toes and kiss him quickly. "The best."

He shakes his head. "Good. You deserve to be happy."

My cheeks pink and I smile as I nod. "I am."

Knox slots himself next to Asher to talk football, and damn is it a pretty sight. I've never been one to deny that my sister's boyfriend is hot. If I wasn't ninety percent sure we would end up killing each other, I probably would've tried to get with him myself, but I'm glad I didn't. Him and Delaney make a perfect pair. They're totally different, with Knox being a badass and Delaney being the epitome of a good girl. Yet, somehow, they balance each other out. And I've never seen someone calm Knox down the way Laney can. It's fucking magical.

———

A COUPLE HOURS LATER, everyone is drunk—including my sister, which doesn't happen often. Her and Knox are all over each other in the corner of the room. I laugh and shake my head as Colby's jaw drops, looking at me while pointing to them.

"It's like he's never seen two people hook up before."

Asher chuckles. "That's drunk Colby. He has two different drunk personalities. We've figured out how to decipher between the two over the years."

My brows raise. "Okay, I've got to hear this."

"Well, when he's overly friendly and thinking everything is hilarious, that's Colby. When he's practically dry humping the leg of some chick and pulling her back to his room, that's Hendrix."

In a way, it makes sense. I've heard stories from both Asher and Colby himself about the thing he tends to do when he's intoxicated and horny. I'm slightly disappointed I haven't gotten the chance to see Hendrix in action. It sounds amusing.

"So, that's Colby?"

He nods.

I turn and stand directly in front of him, feeling braver now that I've got some liquid courage. "And what about you? Do *you* have two different drunk personalities?"

A smile graces his gorgeous face. "That would require getting drunk. I don't do that often anymore."

"Shame," I sigh. "Hawthorne could end up being my favorite."

"Oh yeah? And why's that?"

"Because I think he'd be fun. Less afraid to take what he wants."

He looks me up and down, a move he's done numerous times since we got here. "What makes you think I'm afraid?"

I step closer, arching up to place my mouth right next to his ear. "Because you've been undressing me with your eyes for last five hours, and you've yet to do anything about it."

"Maybe I'm just enjoying the view."

"You and every other guy in here," I sass.

I know my words hit their intended target when his jaw locks and he pulls me into his arms.

"What's the matter, Ash? Jealous?"

He masks his expression with a smirk. "Not at all."

"Oh, good," I feign relief. "Because I've been really hoping to hook up with one of your teammates."

"That's not funny."

Cocking one brow, I put on my best show. "Who's joking? Maybe I'll even grab a couple. Make it a ménage à trois."

The wink I send pisses him off, but my eyes scanning the

room for potential suitors turns him fucking livid. He steps in my way to block the view and glares down at me.

"Do you like making a sport out of seeing how far you can push me?"

I take a sip of my drink. "It passes the time, but I do have one serious question."

His eyes roll playfully. "And what's that?"

"What are you going to do when I find someone who doesn't hold back? Someone who isn't afraid to lay me down and fuck me into the mattress? Someone who will give me *exactly* what I'm craving?"

The grin falls from his face and I can see the dread that fills his mind. "Tess."

Shrugging, I keep my gaze locked on his. "I mean, you've said it yourself. I'm young and beautiful. It's bound to happen eventually."

"Not if I have anything to fucking say about it," he growls, then all bets are off.

He grabs the back of my neck and pulls me into him. Our lips crash together in a feverish kiss that threatens to suck the breath right from my lungs. It's as messy as it is needy, but nothing between us is ever anything but. The chemistry we have is explosive, and I'm surprised it took this long to get here. If I had it my way, we would have fucked in the car on the way to the airport yesterday, Colby be damned.

"Come with me."

He grabs my hand and pulls me through the party and into the first bedroom he finds. As soon as the door shuts, he pushes me up against it. We can still hear everyone on the other side of the thin wood, but he doesn't seem to care.

"What if someone walks in?"

His hand drags up my side, teasing and tantalizing. "Let them. You're mine, Tessa. I dare anyone to try to tell me otherwise."

Every word out of his mouth is like hearing my favorite song. It brings me to life and calms me down all at the same time. I grip the front of his shirt and tug him closer.

"In that case, do me one favor."

He licks his lips. "What's that?"

"Don't hold back."

His touch moves up until his fingers are toying with the strap on my shoulder. "Trust me, baby. There will be none of that."

He pulls the piece of fabric down my arm, repeating the same on the other side until the dress pools on the floor. His eyes rake over my body like I'm his favorite dessert and he's dying for a taste. He moves his mouth to my neck and presses soft kisses to the sensitive skin. It's almost like he's trying to torture me for pushing him, but no part of me is sorry. Not when this is the result.

He slowly moves down my body, kissing every inch on his way. He stops at my breasts just long enough to suck each one into his mouth. The way he looks up at me as he does it is the hottest fucking thing I've ever seen. When he's satisfied with the way they pucker, he continues his path.

Dropping down to his knees, his fingers loop into my thong, and he rips it off me like it's the easiest thing in the world. He raises my one leg and drapes it over his shoulder. Two fingers graze against my pussy, and he watches me as he sucks the moisture into his mouth.

"Always so fucking delicious," he murmurs.

The second that his tongue rubs against my clit, any coherent thoughts go straight out the window. If there's one thing this man knows how to do well, it's eating a girl out. He doesn't fuck around or think he's supposed to probe you with it. No. He knows that the little bundle of nerves between the lips is exactly where the pleasure is at.

In a move that catches me off guard, he slips his arms

behind me and scoops me up. Both my legs are over his shoulders as he holds me upright, still working magic with his mouth. He walks us over to the bed and lays us down, his hands still gripping my hips. As he pulls me down onto his face, I can tell I'm dripping, and he's loving every minute of it.

My fingers lace into his hair, and he moans against my sex. There's something desperate about the way his grip doesn't loosen at all, and it's hot as fuck. I throw my head back and let the pleasure take over my entire body as the orgasm hits.

I fall over onto the bed and Asher wipes his mouth with the back of my hand before standing up and undressing. I watch unashamedly as he pulls off each article of clothing until he's down to nothing. There's no way I could ever tire of looking at him. His body looks like it was sculpted from stone, and I want to trace his abs with my tongue.

"Shit!" His eyes widen as he spits the word. "I don't have a condom."

I've never been happier for birth control in my whole life. "I have the implant, and I'm clean. Are you?"

He nods slowly. "I've never gone without."

"Not even with your ex?"

"No," he chuckles. "She had some strange thing about messes."

He lines up, pinning my hands back as he sinks into me. His jaw drops, and his eyes practically roll into the back of his head. Feeling him like this, bare, nothing between us, it's pure bliss.

"Oh my God," he growls out. "You feel fucking amazing."

I can't even articulate a simple thought, let alone answer him with actual words. It's too much. Too real. Too good. I dig my heels into his back, and he quickens his pace. He pounds into me, unrelenting, his lip pulled between his teeth.

"Is this what you wanted? For someone to fuck you like this?"

The only reply to leave my mouth is a moan that he quickly muffles with his hand. The party may be loud, but he and I both know I can be louder.

A familiar pressure starts building again in my core, and I know Asher can tell. He smirks deviously and starts to go even harder. His thrusts are slow but each one is hard, slamming into me with a force that ripples all the way into my stomach.

Between the way he watches me start to come undone, and the way he's fucking me senseless, I don't stand a chance. My high rips through me, leaving utter destruction in its path. Asher thrusts harshly a couple more times before he lets go and fills me with his cum.

He pulls out and looks down at my pussy, watching the way he leaks out of me.

"Fuck, that's hot."

I giggle through bated breath and roll my eyes. "So possessive."

THE SUN PEAKS THROUGH the window and pulls me from my peaceful slumber. I glance beside me and notice the bed is empty. I don't remember how we got back to the hotel, or really much after Asher and I had wild sex with a party going on less than twenty feet away. All I know is that I've never felt better.

The sound of someone whistling grabs my attention. Asher is standing in the doorway, wearing only a pair of gray sweatpants with sweat glistening across his bare torso. He must have woken up to work out. His hands are gripping the top of the doorframe, putting each one of his muscles on full display. I let my eyes take in every inch of him without a bit of chagrin.

"I could get used to this," I tell him.

A dimpled smile stretches across his face, and he releases the doorway to walk toward me. "And I could get used to the sight of you in my clothes."

I glance down and, sure enough, I'm dressed in one of his T-shirts and a pair of panties. I must have kicked the blanket off while I was sleeping because there isn't a single part of me that's covered.

He bends down to kiss me, and somehow, this one is different. It's calmer. More natural. Like we've crossed some sort of invisible line that neither of us knew existed. When he pulls away, he runs his knuckle down the side of my face.

"I'm going to take a shower. Breakfast is in the other room."

"I could think of something more satisfying." I waggle my eyebrows and he shakes his head with a laugh.

"Get dressed and go eat, Cherry Bomb," he says with a bop to my nose. "We have a long flight ahead of us."

SAYING GOODBYE TO DELANEY isn't any easier the second time than it is the first. We hug for what feels like hours, until they call her flight and I have no choice but to let her go. Once she and Knox are out of sight, I retreat to the car where Asher is waiting. He would have gone inside, but the whole city knows he's here, and getting mobbed with me probably wouldn't be good for anyone.

"All good?" he asks.

I nod, trying to use my sunglasses to hide the fact that I've been crying. "Mm-hm."

As if he knows I don't want to talk about it, he says nothing but reaches over to grab my hand. I rest my head against his shoulder, and the chauffeur pulls out of the parking lot to bring us straight onto the tarmac. The benefits of flying private are very, very nice.

It's sad that this weekend came to an end as fast as it did. I could've spent forever in this place—a secret oasis where Asher and I seemed to connect on another level. It's something I've always been uncomfortable with—intimacy. Letting someone get that close to me usually causes more bad feelings than good. With him, though, it's different. I can't explain it.

Asher grabs our suitcase and hands it to the guy loading the baggage, then the two of us climb onto the plane. The energy is totally different going home than when we departed. I can understand why. Most of them are hungover, and the ones who aren't probably didn't go to sleep until after three in the morning.

We take our seats, and I immediately cuddle into Asher's side. He wraps his arm around me, pressing a kiss into the top of my hair as I stare out the window.

"Not happy to go back?"

I shake my head. "More like wondering what I'm going back *to*."

The two of us haven't even broached the topic of what happened last night, other than my failed, half-assed attempt at seducing him this morning. When we had sex a week ago, I knew exactly what it was. I needed a distraction to get through the pain of everything, and he was there to provide one. Cut and dried. Simple. Last night, however, was different. There was no reasoning for it other than the undeniable need for each other.

He lightly takes my chin between his knuckle and his thumb and turns my head toward him. "If you're worried it was a one-time thing, don't be."

"It wasn't?"

"No." He smirks. "I'm done denying myself of you, Tessa. I can't do it anymore. I want you too much."

Pulling me in, he kisses me slowly, like we have all the time in the world, and I meant what I said this morning—I could get used to this.

THE NEXT FEW WEEKS fly by quickly. My dad finally stops texting me, after a strongly worded voicemail about the condition of my Lamborghini. Kellan seems to finally be looking at Lennon the way he should, because let's be honest, the girl is a serious catch. He would be crazy not to notice her beauty. Asher and I spend our days in the penthouse, unable to keep our hands off each other. We've christened almost every inch of the place, including all four of his cars, and still, I crave him every second of the day.

My nightmares haven't stopped, but over time, they've become shorter and a little less traumatizing. Delaney and Lennon have been trying to convince me to see a therapist. They're the only ones who know about them. I know I should probably trust in Asher again, but I refuse to let one of the few good things I have left be tarnished by someone else's actions.

I'm sitting in class with my feet up on Oakley's desk. Asher is teaching some lesson I don't care about while Tanner and Kellan swipe through Micah's phone, insistent on finding him a girl. According to them, he's too uptight and needs to get laid. If you ask me, the only thing they're going to find him on that app is a one-way ticket to an STD.

"Look, Tess. It's your best friend." Kellan turns the phone to show me who it is, and Hailey's picture is on the screen.

Hailey is Knox's ex-girlfriend, and the girl I very publicly beat the shit out of last year. She had gotten ahold of a rather racy photo of my sister from Knox's phone and thought it was a good idea to send it to just about everyone. The day I got her within my grasp, I made an example of her, and everyone knew—you don't mess with Delaney or you'll have to answer to me.

"Ugh," I groan. "I hate that bitch."

"Tessa," Asher warns. "Language."

I chuckle and turn my head to look at him. "Oh, please. Like you haven't said worse. Don't be such a buzzkill, As—"

Alarm fills his eyes and I realize at the last second what's about to come out of my mouth. The only thing I can think to do is change direction to cover it up.

"—sshole."

Oakley chokes on air, and everyone snickers at the fact that I just called our teacher an asshole. However, it's much better than the alternative. If they had heard me call him by his first name, with the level of comfort it would've come out with, it wouldn't take long before everyone figured it out. Asher looks relieved yet unamused as he pinches the bridge of his nose.

"See me after class, Miss Callahan."

I sigh and glance back at Lennon. She laughs quietly while shaking her head at me. It's no surprise that I've gotten myself in trouble, again. I just hope he's not too mad. Since we got back from Miami, my mind has been wandering to places I never thought it would. The idea of what could end up happening after I graduate both excites me and scares the hell out of me all at the same time—and yet, the thought of not having him in my life is unbearably painful.

The bell rings, and I stay at my desk while everyone

leaves. When we're finally alone, I stand up and walk toward Asher's desk.

"Okay, I know calling you an asshole wasn't exactly smart, but it was the first thing that came to me."

He leans back in his chair, crossing his arms over his chest and smirking at me. "I think you secretly enjoyed it."

My brows furrow. "And why would I do that?"

"Because you've always loved pushing the limits."

Amusement sparks in his eyes, and I realize he's playing me. "You're not mad at all."

Laughter bubbles out of him, and he shakes his head. "Not even a little."

"You're insufferable."

"You like it."

Sticking my tongue in my cheek, I roll my eyes and turn toward the door. "I'll see you later, asshole."

"Wait," he calls out. "I got this in the mail this morning."

He opens his drawer and hands me an envelope. Scrolled across the front is handwritten fancy lettering.

Mr. Asher Hawthorne and Guest

I flip it over and open it, pulling out the invitation inside.

You are cordially invited to the Annual Lexington Benefit.
This year's theme is Hidden in Plain Sight.

"A masquerade party?" I ask as my eyes meet his once more.

He nods. "It's a benefit I go to every year. The Lexingtons are very wealthy and powerful people. They throw this massive event and every dollar earned goes to a charity they founded."

I look around to make sure no one has come in yet. "Are you out of your mind? I can't go with you there."

"Why not?"

"Uh, because we're supposed to be laying low? And you said it yourself, they're very powerful people, which means they're smart. What if they figure out I'm only eighteen?"

He reaches over and points to the word *masquerade* on the invitation that lies on his desk. "You'll be wearing a mask, and as for the age thing, just act older. You've done it before, *Miss Davenport*."

I try to hide my guilty smile as he uses that one against me. The corners of his mouth raise, bringing out his dimples and unfairly making it so I can't deny him.

"So, what do you say? Will you come with me?"

Asher

I STAND IN THE MIDDLE OF THE PLATFORM, looking at the suit in the multiple mirrors that all provide a different angle. It's simple. Charcoal gray with a white shirt and a light gray tie for contrast. The color will go well with the mask I've picked out.

"Oh, this one's good," Colby reads from his phone. "Rumor has it Asher Hawthorne secretly eloped with his mystery woman over the weekend."

For the past hour, while I tried on suits, Colby decided it would be a great idea to go over all the headlines that have been released since our trip to Miami. Some of them, like this one, are so absurd that they're actually amusing. Others, however, cut a little too close to the truth. Those ones make me uncomfortable.

Tessa and I have had to go through extra measures to ensure we don't get caught, especially with her currently living at my place. Don't get me wrong, it's been incredible. No matter how much time we spend together, I don't get the slightest bit tired of her. Somehow, she never loses her ability to keep me on my toes, and it always makes things interesting. However, I do sometimes wish we could go places.

The media has been tracking me since they saw me put my hand on Tessa's back. They call her my mystery woman, and it's become an internet wide thing where people try to figure out who she is. Even the kids on the team have picked up on it, trying to pry information out of me when I'm trying to run them through plays. They finally stopped asking when I threatened to make them do one hundred push-ups for every time they bring it up.

People have taken it a little far. One person even noticed me picking up food from the Italian place down the street and bribed the hostess to tell them how much I ordered. From there, they determined that I couldn't possibly be ordering all that for myself, and thus, must have someone at my place.

Thankfully, living in a penthouse has its perks. For example, it's full of excuses. No one can see in, and no one questions anything when they see her leave because she goes out through the lobby. There are hundreds of condos in that building. They probably assume she lives in one of those.

My biggest fear is that she's somehow going to get hurt in the process. She's strong, but I watched firsthand what Nikki went through—everything from people begging for my attention and trying to get it by any means necessary to people threatening her life. It was intense, and it took a while before she knew how to handle it. Hell, they could even think because she's young that they can get one over on her.

"So, should I say congratulations, or be pissed that I wasn't your best man?"

"Ha, ha," I deadpan. "You're hilarious."

His grin widens. "I know. But really, these are nuts. Why is there *this* much focus on your love life? They don't put this much attention on me."

I chuckle as I mess with the buttons on the jacket. "Because you hook up with so many women it would make their heads spin. Avoiding the whiplash is probably best for everyone."

"Yeah, yeah. We can't all be Mr. Exclusivity."

It's not that we meant to become exclusive, but I don't

think either one of us is complaining. It would just be a little hard to entertain other options when we're living in the same place. That and I'm pretty sure if either one of us brought someone else home, the other would lose their shit—me especially. I'm not usually the jealous type, but I'd knock someone out just for dreaming about her.

I take off the suit and pay for it. They assure me it will be delivered to my place by this evening. I thank them before leaving with Colby in tow. Tessa is spending the day being pampered, so he's the company I'm stuck with until she's done.

"So, you think you'll be discreet enough tonight?" he asks. "To be honest, I'm surprised you invited her."

"It comes with a little bit of risk—going anywhere with her does—but we should be okay. We'll be wearing masks for the theme, and you know how the Lexingtons are. Everything is top of the line and security is tight."

He nods slowly. "That's true. Well, as long as you two are careful."

It's surprising, really, to see how Tess has even managed to win over my best friend. And it's not in a way that makes me uncomfortable or worry about them together. He's super protective over her. He treats her like a little sister, and a part of me wonders if he'd fight even me if it came down to it. One thing I am sure of, is that in a situation where it's needed, I can count on him—always.

"You sure you don't want to come?"

Colby shakes his head rapidly. "No. After last year, I think it'll be a while before I show my face there again."

Laughter booms through me at the sudden memory.

Everything about the Lexington family drips wealth. It wouldn't be a bit surprising if they wiped their asses with hundred-dollar bills.

Well, Colby being Colby, he somehow got roped into

taking ecstasy by one of the cousins. It was all going well until he climbed up on the statue in the main foyer of the mansion and pretended he was riding the horse. There is normally a no-cellphone policy for the event, but everyone pulled them out to record that. The hashtag ColbyTheCowboy was trending for two straight weeks.

"Okay, fair enough," I give. "Well, let's go have a beer while I wait for Tess to finish up."

That makes him perk up. "Now you're speaking my language."

THE LIMO PULLS UP in front of Lennon's house. Her dad is away for the weekend, and we figured it was the safest place for me to get her from and not have outsiders put two and two together. I step out and walk up to the front door. The house is massive and even makes Tessa's childhood home look small. As I press the doorbell, a fancy musical tone echoes throughout the house.

A woman I've never met opens the door, and a little part of me starts to panic. However, Lennon quickly comes into view before I embarrass myself completely with trying to explain why I'm there to pick up Tessa.

"Thanks, Mel. I've got it."

The woman looks at me hesitantly, but after a reassuring smile from Lennon, she walks away and into the other room.

"Because that wasn't awkward at all."

She giggles, opening the door further to let me in. "That's just Melani. She's the housekeeper. I'll go get Tessa. Wait here."

As she runs up the stairs, I shove my hands in my pockets and rock on my heels. I glance around the room, seeing an actual full-size portrait of Lennon hanging over the fireplace in the living room. She must be an only child, and a part of me is honestly surprised she doesn't act as spoiled as she clearly is.

Movement at the top of the staircase catches my attention, and my jaw drops as soon as I see her. Tessa is wearing a white dress that goes down to just above her knees and sparkles in the lighting. The women I paid to do her hair and makeup deserve a hell of a lot more than I gave them, because she looks fucking breathtaking. Each one of her already beautiful features are accented with a little bit of makeup, making them pop, and her brown hair is loosely curled and flowing down her back. She looks like an actual angel.

As I stare at her, taking it all in, all I can think about is what a lucky son of a bitch I am.

"Wow," I breathe as she reaches the bottom. "You look stunning."

For the first time ever, she blushes and looks down at the floor. That reaction alone is different for her, and the fact that I'm able to cause something new sends a warmth all over my body.

"Are you ready to go?" I ask, offering her my arm.

She nods and looks back at Lennon. "Bye. Love you."

"Wait!" Lennon shouts. She pulls her phone out of her pocket. "I have to get a picture."

We stand against the one wall as instructed and I place my arm around her. Lennon snaps one picture after the next, until I can't hold back my amusement.

"Is it just me or does she look like one of those parents on prom night?"

Tessa bursts into laughter, pulling the same reaction out of me. Lennon rolls her eyes playfully but continues to smile as she takes the photos.

"Okay," she puts her phone down. "I think that'll do."

I watch as Tessa hugs her goodbye and makes her promise to send over the pictures, then she comes back to me. With a wave to Lennon, I lead Tessa outside and down the front steps. The driver is already standing outside and opens the door for the two of us. I thank him as we climb inside.

"Here," I say, handing her a glass of champagne then taking one for myself. "To a night of memories."

She smiles at me and takes a sip. "You're such a closet romantic; it's adorably sickening."

Okay, so usually I'm not. I always swore I wouldn't do this kind of stuff again, but with her I can't help it. Tonight is one of the rare times I get to treat her like she deserves, and I'm going to take full advantage of it.

THE HOUSE IS ALREADY full of people by the time we arrive. Just before we get out of the limo, I grab the box containing the masks and open it. The patterns match, showing they are the male and female counterparts of each other, but mine is a sleek gray while hers is white. She also has a small amount of lace around the edges. I pull hers out first and turn to her.

"This is for you."

A small gasp leaves her mouth. "Asher, it's gorgeous."

I smile, feeling accomplished. After she spent an entire evening searching through tons of different ideas, she still couldn't figure out what she wanted. I told her to leave it to me and only made her tell me what color dress she planned on wearing. And maybe I paid a small fortune to have these custom-made with actual diamonds in them. It made her happy, so in my book, that's a win.

Helping her put it on, I tie the back with a perfect bow and then lean back to look at her. *Gorgeous.* I make quick work of taking my own out and putting it on. Once I'm done and the two of us are ready, I kiss her once and slip out of the car. Tessa takes my hand, allowing me to help her out before lacing her fingers with my own.

"Whoa," she says as her eyes land on the mansion. "This is their *house?*"

I nod. "I told you, baby. You don't know the high life. Stick with me, I'll show you the ropes."

THE NIGHT IS EVERYTHING I could have hoped for. Tessa unsurprisingly charms every single person I introduce her to. For a moment, I wondered if she would get bored having to listen to Chase Lexington talk about his charity and all the good it's doing for a straight half hour, but she was actually enthralled.

Halfway through the night, I need to pull her away from Griffin after he managed to steal her from me and pull her out onto the dance floor. She leans into me as I guide her out of the room entirely and up a flight of stairs.

"Where are we going?"

I grin down at her. "To the best part of the house."

She exhales heavily. "Okay, we cannot have sex in these people's house. It's rude."

"Not what I was planning, but thanks for the etiquette tip."

It takes a few minutes to reach the other side of the overly sized abode, but once we do, I remember exactly why it's worth it. I open the door and allow Tessa to step out first, then I follow. She shivers from the chilly November air, making me wrap my arms around her.

"What are we looking at?" she wonders.

Walking her to the edge of the balcony, I spin her around

and point to the view in the distance. The Lexington Estate sits on top of a mountain, making it so you can see everything from below. The whole city is lit up, and with the stars above it, it's the most incredible view.

"It's beautiful." Her voice is soft, delicate.

I stand behind her with my arms casing her in, just admiring the beauty of it all and enjoying how I feel in this moment. Over all the years I played in the NFL, all the times I accomplished my dreams, I've never felt as content as I do right now, and it's because of her. She brings out the best in me.

Tessa turns in my hold and places her hands on my face. "Thank you for showing me this, and for everything today. You were right, this is a night I'll always remember."

I smile as I bend down and connect our lips in a sweet, passionate kiss. Every feeling in my body is electrified. My heart pounds against my rib cage, threatening to break free. It's like I've never kissed her before, but I guess that's partly true. Kissing may not be a new thing for us, but it's never been like this. There's something else to it. Something more.

THE NIGHT COMES TO an end, despite me mentally willing it to keep going, and Tessa and I say our goodbyes before climbing back inside the limo. She grabs her phone and sends a quick selfie to Delaney before texting Lennon back. The happiness that radiates off her is contagious, and I find myself just staring at how good it looks on her.

As the limo drives down the street, the loud sound of motorcycles vibrates the seats. They come up with one on each side before cameras start flashing. Tessa turns to me with a panicked look on her face—which is thankfully still covered by the mask. The windows are tinted, but it's better to be safe than sorry.

I wrap an arm around her and pull her closer while lowering the divide to the driver. Shouts of my name can just faintly be heard over the roar of their engines, and I've never been so glad to only hire the most experienced drivers.

"Try to lose them please, Elijah."

He nods and glances at me in the rear view. "Yes, sir."

The lights fill the backseat as Tessa burrows her face in my neck. I gently massage the back of her head to soothe her, but I know nothing can really be done until we get rid of these guys.

In one particularly ballsy move, one of the motorcycles goes ahead of the limo and tries slamming on its breaks to get us to stop. Elijah swerves out of the way and manages to avoid hitting him, but the whole car jerks as he has to correct the move. Tess screams and clings onto me tighter.

"It's okay," I whisper, kissing her head. "We're almost home."

Elijah pulls up to the gate and rolls down the window to enter the code. Even more chaos ensues as people scream my name and start running toward the car. Thankfully, the gates open and he pulls through before any damage can be done. He pulls around to the elevator that is thankfully out of view and brings the car to a stop.

"I am so sorry," I tell her, worried about how shaken up she is.

She pulls away and after glancing around, she sighs in relief. I reach behind her head to remove the mask and look her over to make sure she's all right. Then, once I'm satisfied with what I see, I pull her in for a desperately needed kiss.

"Are you okay?"

She nods. "Yeah. That was just unexpected. Does that happen a lot?"

"No." I get out of the car and wait for her. "They've just been eager for information on you. Apparently who I'm fucking is prime information, or at least that's how Colby put it."

Her laugh is everything I needed, and the tension leaves my body in an instant. I shake Elijah's hand and give him a rather large tip, keeping my attention on Tessa.

"Well, if Colby said it, it *must* be true," she quips.

"Is that right?"

The smile on her face gets brighter, yet more devious. "Yeah. I like him more than you."

My brows raise as I back her into the corner of the elevator. "Oh really? Well, I don't think that'll do. You know how possessive I can be."

"Maybe that's exactly why I said it."

Now *that* doesn't surprise me. She's always finding ways to mess with me, and secretly, I fucking love it.

"In that case…"

Her arms wrap around my neck as I pick her up and pin her to the wall. I press a button on the elevator and feel as it jerks to a stop. Our tongues tangle together and I get lost in everything her. After a night like tonight, ending it any other way would just be wrong.

SUNDAY FLIES BY, AND before I know it, it's Monday afternoon and I'm packing up my stuff to go home. The rain pouring down outside means practice is canceled. It's relieving, honestly. All I've wanted to do is go back to my place and spend time with my girl. *Fuck, Colby would call me a total sap right now.*

A knock at my classroom door makes me look up, and

Trent stands there, holding what looks like a newspaper. My brows furrow as I look at it and he steps inside.

"What's that?"

He holds it up. "This? This is the newest article about you and your mystery woman."

A mix of fear and frustration floods through me as I remember what happened Saturday night. He tosses it down on my desk, and I read the headline.

Hawthorne Takes Girlfriend to Annual Lexington Benefit

The picture underneath is fuzzy, obviously having been zoomed in a lot, but you can still make it out. I'm standing behind Tessa on the balcony, showing her the view of the city. Thanks to the mask, you can't tell who she is, but the photographer must have been hiding in the woods or on the cliffs. The picture next to it is of the kiss we shared after she turned around.

"I still can't believe you won't tell me who she is," he complains.

I shake my head as I toss the newspaper into the trash can. "It's not that big of a deal. I told you."

He rolls his eyes. "Please. You haven't dated anyone since Nicole, and all of a sudden there are all these pictures of you with some woman, and I'm not supposed to wonder about it?"

"Nope."

"Ugh," he groans. "I can't figure it out, but I feel like I know her. I don't know where from though."

Oh, you know her all right. "Trent, trust me. If it becomes something to tell, you'll know it."

It doesn't look like he believes a word I'm saying, but he sighs. "If you say so."

"I do."

Just then, in the worst possible fucking timing, Tessa comes walking in. Her attention is on her phone and she's already speaking as she walks into the door.

"Ash, I'm going to be a little late today. Lennon needs me to—"

Her words get cut off the second she looks up and notices both me and Trent staring back at her. He looks her up and down and then looks back at me, his eyes widening by the second. Reaching over, he pulls the newspaper out of the garbage can. I know then that he's officially put all the pieces together.

"Tessa, go," I tell her.

The fear and apology in her eyes is overwhelming, but I need her out of here before Trent flips out. And he's definitely going to flip out. I give her a reassuring, yet pleading, look and she leaves as quick as she came.

"Trent." His name comes out hesitantly, like I'm waiting for him to snap. "Buddy."

He steps back. "Don't fucking *buddy* me. Are you out of your damn mind? *Tessa* is your mystery woman? *Tessa?*"

"It's not what you think."

"The fuck it's not!"

I raise my hands in surrender and try to take a step toward him. "Just hear me out. I'm telling you, it's not as bad as what's going through your mind right now."

His glare is furious as he shakes his head. "No. No fucking way. I don't want to hear a damn word from you. You are her superior and she is a *child*!"

"She's eighteen, and legally allowed to make her own choices."

"Is that supposed to make it okay? Come on, Ash. You're better than this!" He pauses, then narrows his eyes on me. "Did she seduce you?"

"What?"

"Did she force herself on you?" he questions suspiciously, and my blood boils. "I know how psychotic she can be. If she pushed herself on you, you should have resisted, but I get it. She's fucking aggressive when she wants something. Is that what happened?"

My jaw locks and ever muscle in my body flexes. "Don't fucking talk about her like that. You don't know anything about that girl."

"Now you're defending her? To me? Unbelievable." Turning toward the door, he shakes his head. "You deserve whatever shit-storm is coming your way."

He storms out, ignoring my calls of his name. I flop down into my chair. Running my fingers through my hair, I pull angrily and groan. What the fuck am I going to do now?

AS I WALK INTO my place, I'm hoping Tessa is here so we can come up with some kind of game plan. A way to get out of this. However, that's not the girl I find sitting on my couch.

"What are you doing here?" I ask.

Blaire glares at me and stands up. "Trent called me. Are you fucking serious, Asher? A *high school student*? Seriously?"

Of course he did. Once a rat, always a rat. "Don't do that. Don't look at me like some kind of pedophile. She's eighteen."

"And your *student*! I don't think I need to tell you how badly this could ruin your reputation."

"Oh, please," I scoff. "Half the players in the NFL are dating younger women."

"None of them are in a position of authority with those women," she argues. "Not to mention their lives aren't as scrutinized as yours is right now."

I roll my eyes and go to the fridge to grab a beer. Lord knows I need one. Blaire follows behind me like a damn Chihuahua that doesn't know when to quit.

She places a hand on her hip and stares at me, clearly fed up. "You have to end it."

I snort. "Yeah, no. Not an option."

"It's the *only* option, Asher," she presses. "You're lucky Trent called *me* and not Jon Hyland. You can't have Tessa without throwing away everything you've spent your whole life working for."

The thought of not having her puts an actual pain in my chest. I've spent every single day with her for months, and now I'm expected to just end it? To go without her? No. Not happening.

A newfound determination flows through me as I realize what I need to do.

"Watch me," I tell her, putting my beer down and grabbing my keys. "I'm going to talk to Trent. You can show yourself out."

TWO HOURS LATER, I pull back into my parking garage and get out of the car. I literally spent the whole time at Trent's listening to him scream at me about how fucked up everything is. He said that I'm not only risking my reputation, but his as well, being as he was the one who recommended me in the first place. To be honest, I hadn't really thought of that, but it still doesn't change my mind. He's going to be pissed off for a while, but he promised he's not going to speak a word of it to anyone, and that's all I need.

I toss my keys down onto the counter. "Tess?"

No answer.

"Tessa?"

The sound of footsteps comes around the corner, but it's not Tessa who appears. I roll my eyes, wondering if calling security to have her escorted out of here would be worth it.

"She's not here."

"What are you still doing here, Blaire? I thought I told you to leave."

She grins, but it's nothing but fake. "I decided to stick around."

"Well, I'd rather you don't. Where's Tess?"

"I told you," she says slowly. "She's not here."

The look on her face makes my stomach drop. "What did you do?"

Her eyes glimmer with something wicked. "Exactly what you should have."

Dread fills my entire body as I race toward my bedroom. I yank open the closet to find half of it empty. The drawers on the dresser are still open from when she obviously hurriedly grabbed her stuff from them. The mask from Saturday night lies on my nightstand. I take it into my hand, feeling like it's the only thing I have of hers to hold onto.

"What the fuck did you say to her?" I shout as I come back into the living room.

Blaire brings a finger to her chin. "I can't remember exactly, but it did the trick."

Pulling my phone from my pocket, I dial her number and put it to my ear.

"Oh, I wouldn't bother. I can promise you, she won't pick up."

Sure enough, the phone rings twice before she hits ignore and I'm sent to her voicemail. I press end and my arm falls to my side.

"Get the fuck out of my house," I growl.

She rolls her eyes with a taunting smile on her face. "Asher, Asher. Always such a drama queen."

"I said get out! Now!"

My phone flies out of my hand and shatters against the wall. She flinches from the sudden outburst, then sighs.

"Look," she starts, her tone lighter, "I know you're mad now, but I did this for you. If the press found out you were dating one of your students, the public would eat you alive. You'd lose your job, both teaching and coaching. You'd be annihilated in the public eye, and everything you've worked for all your life would vanish in an instant. It might hurt now, but I always do what's best for you."

She grabs her bag off the couch and walks over to the elevator.

"Before I go, just answer me this. Have you introduced her to your dad yet?"

My brows furrow as I shake my head.

"Interesting. If she was important enough to throw away everything for, one would think you would've introduced her to the man who dedicated his life to helping you get where you are."

I don't say anything as she steps into the elevator and leaves me alone. The whole place feels empty. I feel empty. But as vile as she is, Blaire might actually have a point.

Tessa

I STARE OUT THE WINDOW AS WE DRIVE THROUGH town, watching as the rain flows down the glass. The storm outside matches the way I feel perfectly. Tears flow from my eyes and drip onto my sweatshirt. Everything she said was true, but that doesn't make it hurt any less. I want him. I *need* him. *He's better off without you.*

After rushing through helping Lennon, and freaking out while doing it, the only thing I want to do is get home and talk to Asher. I had no idea Mr. Englewood was with him this afternoon. I should have been paying more attention, but I was too caught up in Lennon freaking out because Kellan invited her over to watch a movie.

The elevator doors open, and as soon as I step out, I see a woman sitting on the couch. I rack my memory, trying to figure out where I know her from. Oh! She's the girl who came in and interrupted the argument with Asher the day after I was drugged.

"Uh, hi," I greet her.

She smiles sweetly. "You must be Tessa. I don't believe we've met. I'm Blaire."

I glance around the room. "Where's Asher?"

"Oh, he stepped out." She waves me over. "Come, sit."

Hesitantly, I walk over and take a seat. There's an uncomfortable feeling in the air— something that tells me as sweet as she's acting, she can't be trusted. Silence fills the room, and I pull my phone from my pocket to try texting Asher.

"If you're trying to reach him, I wouldn't. He's currently doing damage control."

"Damage control?"

She nods. "See, Trent found out about you two and he's livid. If Asher doesn't calm him down, he could lose everything."

My brows furrow. "I'm sorry. I don't think I understand."

"Well, you see, sweetie, when you're as widely known as Asher is, things that wouldn't be a huge deal for you is massive for him. If people find out he's been dating one of his students, that's like social suicide."

Okay, I tried to be nice, but I've had enough of this bitch. "Great. Thanks for your input. You can see yourself out now."

She chuckles darkly. "Yeah, I didn't think you'd get it. Trent said you can be a bit stubborn. So, I did some digging of my own."

"Digging?"

"Oh, yeah. You wouldn't believe the kind of stuff I can find." She reaches into her bag and pulls out a file, handing it to me. "Go ahead. Read it."

The file isn't thick, but the stuff inside it is damning. Everything I've been through is in my hands, from my report cards to a copy of the actual statement I gave to police after the incident with my uncle. She even has the documents from the rape kit exam from the hospital. All the noted vaginal tears stare back at me. I'm going to throw up.

"Yeah. That one was even hard for me to read."

I close the folder and toss it onto the coffee table. "So, I have a fucked-up past. Do you want a play by play of my shitty childhood, too?"

She scrunches her brows. "No, I've got all that, too. Your childhood therapist wrote very detailed notes. I just didn't want to take the time to print it. Waste of paper and all that."

"Why don't you just tell me what you want?"

"Isn't it obvious? You're no good for Asher."

My eyes roll. "Last time I checked, that's not for you to decide."

She tilts her head side to side. "Maybe not, but consider this. What are people going to think when they realize their favorite quarterback is dating his student, and one with as much emotional baggage as you come with? For all they know, he could be taking advantage of you."

"That's fucking bullshit."

Shrugging, she checks out her nails. "I've been in this business a long time, and protecting the image of my clients is my job. I'm just telling you what I know and what would be best for everyone involved."

"And if I don't listen?"

Her gaze meets mine and her lips pucker. "Then everyone will find out everything, and you and Asher will have to live through the whole world knowing all the horrid things you've been through. You think what's in that folder is a lot?"

She gestures to the coffee table.

"That's just what I found in a five-minute search. His fans are like the FBI. Every picture of you that's ever existed will be dug up, dusted off, and put on display for the whole world to see. Not to mention Asher will be publicly scrutinized. They'll call him a pervert and other names that will make him question if he was ever a good person. And he'll lose everything he's worked his whole life for, all for some broken eighteen-year-old girl whose own uncle disliked enough to want her dead. But don't worry, he probably won't resent you right away. It'll take some time."

My chest tightens so much it becomes hard to breath. She just threw the truth in my face, and now I'm trying not to choke on it. I do my best to hold it in, but I don't stand a chance. My eyes start to water and a stray tear leaks out.

"I know it's hard to hear, hun, but let's be honest—Asher is better off without you."

Getting up, I go into the laundry room and grab two duffel bags. Then, I go into the room we've shared together the past month. I toss everything I own into them until there's nothing left. I struggle to carry them both but I manage to get them over to the elevator.

Shit, my phone.

I walk over to the couch and grab it off the cushion. Just before I walk away, Blaire grabs my wrist.

"You're doing the right thing, Tessa."

Ripping myself from her grasp, I level her with a look. "Don't fucking touch me."

She doesn't say another word as I drag my bags into the elevator and hit the button to go down. I sag against the back wall, trying to stay calm. Everything she said was right. I'd only going to drag him down and make him lose everything. But still, that doesn't make it any easier to hear.

As soon as I reach the bottom, I'm reminded that I don't have a car anymore. And with the things running through my head, there's only one person I can think to call.

My phone vibrating on my lap brings my attention back to the present. Asher's name and the picture of the two of us from Saturday night appears on the screen. It takes everything I have not to answer. *He's better off without you.* I sigh as I hit ignore and flip the phone over so I'm not tempted to call him back.

"Tess," Easton says softly, and I turn to look at him. "We're here."

I hadn't even realized the car came to a stop, too lost in my own thoughts. It's a cute house, and a part of me is surprised he and Zayn can afford the rent for this place. It's not too big, but being so close to campus, it's practically prime real estate.

We get out of the car, and Easton grabs my bags from the trunk. I follow behind as he carries them inside. Zayn is sitting on the couch, and the second he sees me, his eyes widen.

"Tessa?" He gets up. "Holy shit, are you okay? What happened?"

I shake my head. "I don't really want to talk about it."

"I told her she can borrow the guest room," Easton tells him.

"Yeah, of course. It's all yours." Pausing for a second, he sighs. "Come here."

Zayn pulls me into his arms and holds me tightly. I have to admit, I missed this guy. We were always closer than we let on. Sometimes, when neither of us could sleep after one of his parties, we'd go downstairs and use the rest of the alcohol to make experimental cocktails. It was my favorite part of the night.

"Do I need to go kick someone's ass?"

A wet laugh leaves my mouth. "No."

He rubs my back before letting me go. "All right. Well, let me know if you need anything. Easton will show you where the guest room is."

"Thanks."

I follow my ex up the stairs and down the hallway. He points to a couple doors, telling me which room is his and which is Zayn's, and then he opens the one at the end. It's a small room, but it'll do. Especially since going home isn't an option.

Once he puts my bags down, he turns to me. "I'm glad you called. I don't know what happened, but I'm glad you still trust me enough to know I'm always going to be there for you."

Not knowing what to say, I give him a sheepish grin.

"I'll be downstairs if you need me."

He closes the door behind him, and the dam breaks. Every pain I tried not to feel, every tear I tried not to shed, it all rips through me with an intensity that has me gasping for air. I lie on the bed and curl into a ball, just wishing that I was enough.

Enough for my dad.

Enough for Asher.

Just enough.

THE FEELING OF SOMEONE lightly shaking me forces me awake. My eyes burn as I peel them open and find Zayn sitting on the side of my bed. I groan, throwing my arm over my face. Not only did it take forever for me to fall asleep last night, but my nightmares have come back with a vengeance. Therefore, I didn't get more than an hour of sleep last night.

"Time to wake up, Tess."

"No."

He chuckles. "You have to."

"Why?"

"Because you have to get to school. Easton had class this morning, so I said I'd drive you in."

I shake my head. "I'm not going."

He pulls the arm away from my face and looks down at me. "Yes, you are."

"No," I repeat. "I'm not."

"It's not an option. You're going."

I roll my eyes and sit up. "Why? What the hell does it matter to you?"

He shrugs. "It doesn't, but it *does* matter to you. Do you really want to have to repeat your senior year *again*? End up graduating with people who were sophomores when you were meant to get the hell out of there?"

As much as I'd rather spend the whole day in this bed, he has a point. I sigh and drop my head.

"Look, I don't know what happened, but I do know what a tough chick you are. Whatever it is, you'll get through it. Fuck knows you've been through worse. So, doll yourself all up, go sit in his class, and make him realize what a fuck-up he is for losing you."

My brows furrow. "How did you…"

He smirks. "Knox is my best friend, CBP. You really didn't think I'd call him after the shape you were in last night?"

"Ugh, not that fucking nickname again."

"You love it." He stands up from the bed. "Now get dressed. We leave in thirty minutes."

I SIT AT MY desk, looking anywhere but at Asher. It took a half-hour of getting ready and another fifteen-minute hype-up from Zayn before I felt strong enough to even walk in the front door of this place. I'm genuinely afraid that if I look at him, I'll lose it all over again.

Masking the way I feel with a smile, I distract myself with talking to Kellan and Oakley. However, that doesn't stop me from feeling someone's gaze burning into me throughout most of the class. Even Lennon keeps giving me odd looks, trying to understand what's going on.

Relief floods through me when the sound of the bell echoes throughout the room. I grab my things and go to leave, when a painfully familiar voice stops me.

"Tessa, can I talk to you for a minute?"

I stop. My back is to him, but every part of me is begging to turn around. I'm pulled to him, drawn in like fucking gravity, and it's hard to resist. *He's better off without you.*

At the last second, I grab Lennon's arm. "Hey, wait for me?"

She gives me an odd look but nods anyway. I take a deep

breath and turn around, knowing that Asher won't say much with Lennon standing right there. Still, I can't bring myself to look at him.

"What?"

"Tessa."

Reluctantly, I look up and my gaze locks with his. He looks as miserable as I feel. My breath hitches and a sob sits in my throat, threatening to wreck me once more. His eyes are begging me to talk to him. To tell Lennon to leave. To run right back into his arms.

He's better off without you.

I give him a pathetic, pleading look. "Don't. Please, just don't."

His shoulders sag and I turn to rush from the room. Lennon follows behind me, trying to keep up. When I finally reach my locker, I open it and grip onto the metal for dear life.

"What the hell was *that*?" she asks, confused as ever.

Shaking my head, I take a deep breath to try to get a handle on myself. "I love you, but I can't talk about it. If I talk about it, I'll break again, and I *really* can't break again."

Her bewildered expression turns to a concerned one. "Okay, babes. It's okay. Whenever you're ready."

I give her the best thankful smile as I can manage, but my eyes look past her, seeing Asher standing outside his classroom—watching me. And yeah, this fucking sucks.

I'M LYING IN BED, watching videos on my phone and mentally begging the world to swallow me whole. It's been four days since everything went to hell, and nothing has made me feel better. Not my favorite food. Not my favorite movie. Not even getting drunk. It's official, I'm stuck in a rut of my own making.

There's a light knock on the door and I whine quietly. *I just want to be alone.*

"What?"

Easton opens the door and pops his head in. "Can I come in?"

I shrug. "It's your house."

He chuckles and comes over to sit on the side of my bed. "We're about to order dinner. Do you want anything?"

"No, thanks. I'm not hungry."

His head drops before turning to look at me. "Tessa, you haven't been hungry all week. You need to eat something."

I roll my eyes. "I just don't feel well, okay? I have no fucking appetite, and if I eat, I'm only going to throw it up."

He thinks for a second before nodding. "Okay, I was trying to avoid this, but I guess I can't. It's necessary."

"What are you talking about?"

"I think I have something that will make you feel better."

My eyebrows furrow, and Easton pulls a small baggie from his pocket, holding it up and showing me the pills inside. He shakes it back and forth, and I sit up. I'll try anything to numb this pain.

Asher

THE MORE TIME THAT PASSES, THE MORE WORRIED I get about Tessa. Something is off with her and I can't seem to put my finger on it. The look on her face when I tried to talk to her has haunted me for the past few nights. She looked so hurt. So devastated. To know that I'm partially responsible for putting that look on her face makes me want to die a thousand deaths.

After Blaire left my house last Monday night, I drank a glass of whiskey and let my own mind torment me for hours. As much as I didn't want to admit it, she has a point. Tessa, as incredible as she is, is only eighteen. The chances of her knowing what she wants for the rest of her life right now are slim to none. So, what? I'm going to throw everything away for something that might not last more than a few months?

I was going to ask her—find out where her mind is on everything and decide what to do together—but whatever Blaire said must have done a number on her because she could barely stand to look at me. I decided then that I'd leave her alone, as difficult as that might be. However, that doesn't mean it hasn't killed me to see her get dropped off in the morning by her ex.

When she took her things and left the penthouse, I assumed she was going to stay at Lennon's. After all, that was her plan if I hadn't offered, or rather insisted, that she stay with me. It wasn't until I saw Easton dropping her off Wednesday and Thursday morning that I realized she must be shacking up with him. At first, I thought the worst—that she had run back to him the first chance she got—but it looks like they're just friends. Even so, I don't trust him.

After a weekend filled with sleepless nights and shutting out the world, I went back to work on Monday hoping to see her doing better. She's strong and I've never seen her let anything keep her down. Unfortunately, what I saw ended up being much worse, and it has only gone downhill from there.

The past few days, the bags under her eyes have grown. She comes to school but seems entirely strung out. On what, I don't know, but it has to be something. It's as if the world around her doesn't exist, and if she's even talking at all, she's lashing out. Skye made a comment yesterday, one that Tessa would normally roll her eyes out, and instead, she threw a pen at the back of her head. No fucks given.

I look down at the paper in front of me. The object of the assignment was to write a short essay about what your plans are for after graduation and why they appeal to you. Everyone did as they were instructed except for Tessa. Her answer is something that has me more worried than ever. I read it over for the tenth time since she handed it in.

Who actually gives a fuck? None of it matters anyway.

At the sound of the bell, everyone gets up. Tessa stands and nearly falls over, being caught by Oakley who luckily is built like a fucking brick house. I glance down at the paper and sigh.

"Bradwell, a word?"

Lennon nods and comes my way while Tess makes a face that shows her disapproval. She rolls her eyes and leaves the room with Kellan and the others.

"Is she okay?" I ask her best friend.

She sighs. "I'm not so sure. She's been really closed off, even to me."

Picking up the assignment, I hand it to her. "This was her answer to the short essay question today."

She reads it over quickly. "Wow."

"Yeah."

"I don't know." She runs her fingers through her hair. "I mean, I'm worried about her too, but there's a code. If I break it, she'll never trust me again."

I groan in frustration. "There has to be something we can do."

Lennon looks at the door and then back at my desk, grabbing the sharpie and a pad of post-its off of it. She writes something down quickly and places it down just in time for Tessa to reappear at the door.

"Len, are you coming?" she slurs.

A part of me wonders if she's drunk, but she absolutely refuses to make eye contact with me. Lennon nods, and with one last glance at me, she walks out and leaves with Tessa. My worry only builds knowing that her own best friend shares my concerns. I grab the post-its and read the words.

Call Delaney.

I'M STANDING ON THE side of the field, watching Tanner throw a perfect spiral down the length of the field. Oakley catches it in the end zone and celebrates like this isn't just a scrimmage against his own team members. I chuckle, unable to deny that I've actually grown to like these guys. They have a strong work ethic, and for some of them, if they push for it, I honestly believe they'll go pro one day.

"What the fuck is your deal?"

My eyes widen at the familiar voice, and I whip around to face her. Tessa stands there, for once meeting my gaze, but man does she look pissed. She raises one eyebrow at me, as if she's waiting for my answer. For a moment, I'm tongue-tied.

"Uh, did I do something?"

She scoffs. "Don't play fucking stupid, Asher. What did you say to Lennon?"

I raise my hands. "We were just discussing the assignment."

It's clear she doesn't buy a word I'm saying as she steps closer. I can practically feel the anger radiating off her. Gone is the girl I spent the last month tangled under the covers with.

"You don't see me talking to Colby about you behind *your* back, so don't talk to Lennon behind mine. I've already lost enough. I don't need you fucking shit up for me." She prods her index finger into the center of my chest. "I mean it, Asher. Leave her out of this."

"I'm not trying to mess anything up for you. I'd never— you know that."

She shakes her head. "I don't know anything. Not anymore."

Her eyes are glazed over, almost like they were when I pull her out of that fire, only worse. The only emotion in them is the hatred she seems to be directing straight at me. It could be a cover, a way to block out the pain, or her mind is tormenting her even more now.

"Tess," someone calls, and she glances back. Easton stands fifteen feet away from us, and based on the looks he's giving me, he knows exactly who I am. "You ready?"

Nodding, she goes to walk away.

"Wait," I grab her hand, and the feeling of it causes us both to freeze. She looks up at me, and I think I see a glimmer of the girl I've gotten to know so well. "Come over later. Talk to me."

For a second, I think she might actually agree, but that hope dies when she pulls her hand from mine and what I saw in her gaze vanishes. "There's nothing left to talk about."

She goes over to Easton, who gives me one last dirty look before draping his arm over her shoulders and walking her over to his car. Every inch of me wants to rid his touch from her body, but I can't. It's not my place. Not anymore.

———

THE WHISKEY SLIDES DOWN my throat, burning the whole way. No matter how much I drink, none of it seems to rid myself of the feeling like there's a gaping hole in my chest. I've never felt this unsettled. Not when I ended my engagement to Nikki. Not when my career ended a decade early. It's as if Tessa took every significant part of my life with her when she left.

"You could make her talk to you," Colby suggests. "Lord knows she did it enough to you."

I shake my head. "If I've learned anything about Tessa Callahan, it's that forcing her to do something only does more harm than good. And I respect her too much to break her even more."

"Fair enough."

He pours more of the amber liquid into my glass, and I sigh. "I don't get it. I mean, I can understand why I'm so worried about her, she's clearly going down the wrong path, but to feel *this* empty? It can't just be because she's not here."

"Of course, it can," he counters. "Because it's Tessa—the

psychotic little pyromaniac with a sassy attitude and comebacks that can keep up with the best of them—and you're in love with her. That's why you brought her to Miami and surprised her. Why she was able to break you down and get you to give in. And why you called her sister so she can make sure she's okay."

My mind instantly goes to the way her sister sounded when I filled her in on what's going on. Her first reaction was to get on a plane and fly here by tomorrow morning. However, Knox managed to talk her down from that when he reminded her that Tessa is staying with Zayn and Easton. From what it sounded like, those are two of Knox's best friends which gives Delaney a reason to trust them.

I remember the look on Tessa's face just before she walked away from me earlier: how detached she seemed from everything that has to do with me, like all she's trying to do is heal and I keep getting in the way of that. Maybe she's right—there's nothing left to talk about.

"You're probably right," I tell him, "but it doesn't matter anymore."

Bringing the glass to my lips, I take another swing and swallow it down, hoping to drown out the thoughts of her.

I GLANCE UP AND down the hallway, hoping to see the brunette I've been trying to avoid the past couple days. Even during class, I've kept my distance. All her assignments get perfect grades, regardless of if she turns them in. I make it a point not to talk to her friends, and I don't, under any circumstances, try to talk to her. Well, except now.

As the hallway clears, I sigh in relief when I see her standing at her locker, alone for once. I make my way over to her and stop only a couple feet away. My palms are clammy, telling me I'm nervous, but why wouldn't I be? This is the absolute last thing I wanted to do today, but I have no choice. If I don't talk to her before she leaves, I'll have to rely on her checking her voicemails, and that's no way for her to hear this.

"Do you have a second?" I ask her.

She freezes, and I can see as she takes a deep breath before turning around. "You can have ten."

Her voice is softer than it was the last time we spoke, and somehow, that soothes me. It's the first time she's looking at me without any pain or anger in her eyes. She even has a small amount of her sass back.

I swallow, realizing that maybe telling her this is a bad idea. If she's getting better, this could ruin that. Then again, after Blaire completely ambushed me this morning, I don't see another option. Well, unless I let her find out on her own, which could be catastrophic anyway.

"Are you going to talk, or just stand there staring at me?"

Snapping myself out of it, I rub the back of my neck. "I, uh…I have a date tonight."

She instantly looks like she was punched in the stomach, and I hurry up to explain.

"But it's not what you think. Blaire set it up as a PR thing. I've been pushing it off as much as I can, but she really wants to get ahead of this whole mystery woman thing, before they uncover the truth."

Her eyes look anywhere but at me. The floor, the walls, the ceiling. "Okay. Thanks for telling me."

There it is. The cold, shut-down tone that's meant to push me away.

"Please don't think it's anything more than it is," I press. "No part of me has any intentions of finding someone else right now. You meant more to me than that."

She shakes her head. "It's fine, Asher. You don't owe me any explanations."

"I do, though."

"No, you don't." Her shoulders sag, and she's never looked so defeated. "Have fun tonight. Who knows, maybe the two of you will hit it off."

She doesn't give me a chance to respond as she closes her locker and walks away, leaving me and what we had behind without looking back.

THE HOUSE IS FILLED WITH A BUNCH OF COLLEGE students just looking to have a good time. Music vibrates the floor and the alcohol flowing through my veins takes a little bit of the edge off, but it's not enough. The pictures from Asher's date last night are burned into my mind. I know, I know—I shouldn't have looked, but can you blame me? After he dropped that bomb, I felt like someone hit me with a battering ram. All the wind was knocked right out of me, and I had to resist the urge to vomit.

The internet is filled with photos from Asher's "first date in years," which is total bullshit, but of course, they're not allowed to know about me. To anyone who doesn't know him, he looks happy, sitting with the brunette who was selected because of her similarities to me. For those who have spent time with him, though, it's obvious he's not. His smile doesn't reach his eyes, and his dimples stay hidden from the world. He kept his hands to himself, which is a telling sign in itself. All these things remind me the date was fake—orchestrated by the devil in Gucci herself—but it doesn't stop the pain that came when I first saw them, because he should be on that date with me. He should be *happy* with me, not faking it with some lookalike.

I think I've managed to put on a decent front, with the help of Easton's *mood enhancers*. They keep a smile plastered on my face, and more importantly, make it so I'm not on the verge of a breakdown every second of the day. At least not visibly. Everyone thinks I'm perfect. That I've got it all put together. What they don't know is while I'm laughing with my friends, I'm dying inside.

I've never been one to put the reason for my happiness all on one person. Giving someone that kind of power over me was something I tried to avoid at all cost, but I couldn't help it with him. It's like one minute I was just enjoying our time together, and the next I was dependent on his attention. He's the antidote to my pain. When I'm with him, everything fades away, but when I'm not, I drown in the misery.

"You look like your best friend just died," Easton says, appearing at my side out of nowhere. He checks his own pulse. "Oh, nope. I'm still alive."

I feign disgust. "Who said you're my best friend?"

"Ouch," he hisses with a hand on his chest. "You're mean when you're moody."

"I promise I'll be nicer if you give me another."

He shakes his head. "Nope. No way. You just had one two hours ago."

"It's wearing off faster lately," I whine, but he doesn't budge.

Taking a step closer, he bites his lip. "I can think of another way to take the edge off."

Easton is hot, don't get me wrong. There's a reason I dated him for most of last year. However, all his words bring is an uncomfortable feeling in my stomach. Or maybe that's my liver begging me to stop drinking. My brows raise, and he waggles his own. Nope, definitely Easton.

"Tempting, but I think I'll pass." I smirk as I look him up and down. "Going back to old toys almost always ends in disappointment."

He throws his head back, laughing as I wink at him and walk away.

The last couple weeks, Easton has been everything I

always knew he would be. A friend, a shoulder to lean on, a confidant. The night he gave me the first pill, we laid there for hours. I told him everything that happened the last couple months, including how I ended up sleeping and living with my English teacher. It may have taken being high on oxy for me to talk about it, but he sat there and listened to every word.

I originally came here because I knew the first place Asher would look for me was at Lennon's, but I stayed because Easton ended up being everything I needed. He's one of my best friends, and I love him for that.

———————

THE MORE I DRINK, the hazier everything gets, but it does nothing to improve my mood. A part of me considers going to sleep, but I promised myself I would at least try to have fun tonight, and that's what I'm doing.

I'm walking through the living room when I trip and stumble directly into the back of some guy. I mumble an apology as I put my hand on his shoulder to find my balance. However, the second his face becomes clear, I yank it away as if it burned me.

"You don't look so good, babe," a guy I don't know says as he appears in front of me. *"Why don't you come with us? We'll make you feel better."*

"No, I'm waiting for my friend."

Him and his friend lift me up anyway. "I'll come back down to get her. Don't worry."

They bring me upstairs and lay me on the bed before locking the door. Asher. Where's Asher? Fuck. Everything is spinning.

"You," I gasp.

His brows furrow. "You okay?"

I walk backward, jumping when I bump into someone

else. I glance back with fear in my eyes that only calms slightly after noticing it's Easton. He grabs my waist.

"Tess?"

Shaking my head, I look back at the guy who has starred in almost as many nightmares as my uncle has over the last couple months.

"H-he…"

Everything is getting tight and suddenly, it feels like the air is too thick to breathe. Easton turns me around and places his hands on my face—focusing my attention on only him.

"Talk to me. What's wrong?"

My bottom lip starts to quiver. "He's the guy from the party. The one that drugged me."

He glances over my shoulder at the douchebag who still hasn't looked away from me. "Are you sure?"

I nod.

Releasing me, he moves me so I'm standing behind him. Once I'm out of his way, he storms over and grabs the guy by the front of his shirt. Asshole's eyes narrow.

"The fuck, man? Get the hell off me."

Easton pulls him through the house and out the front door, throwing him down on the grass. "You think you can drug my best friend and get away with it? What kind of sick fuck does that?"

He swings first, striking the guy in the side of the jaw. Everyone comes pouring out of the house to watch the fight go down, but no one makes an attempt to stop it. Fists fly as the two of them pummel each other. I try to scream Easton's name to stop him, but it's no use.

Thankfully, after what feels like forever, Zayn comes running out of the house and pulls Easton off the guy. He struggles in his hold, trying to get away as the douchebag stands up and spits blood onto the lawn.

"Let go of me! He fucking drugged Tessa!"

My breath hitches as Zayn looks at me with wide eyes. He must see the fear etched across my face because, in an instant, he releases Easton and goes after him himself. Having been trained by Knox, fighting Zayn is a losing battle for anyone, let alone someone who couldn't even hold his own with Easton. By the time they're done, the guy is curled up in a ball on the lawn, groaning in pain.

"Don't ever let me see you around here again, you got it?" Zayn growls, and the guy croaks out a faint *yeah*.

Easton shoves past Z and over to where I'm standing. He wraps an arm around me and brings me inside, going straight through the crowd that seems to jump out of his way. The two of us go upstairs and into his bedroom. He shuts the door behind him, leaning against it and sighing.

"Are you all right?"

I swallow harshly. "I think so. Are you? You're bleeding."

He wipes his chin with the back of his hand and hisses when he grazes the cut. I get up and go into the bathroom, grabbing a damp paper towel. Easton sits down on his bed, and I stand in front of him. I lightly dab at the cut to clean it and he whines.

"Don't be such a baby," I sass. "If you didn't want to get hurt, you shouldn't have fought."

"And let him get away with what he did to you? No fucking way."

I toss the bloodied cloth into the garbage and sit down next to him. "Well, thank you. You really didn't have to do that."

"Of course I did." He turns to me, using his finger to gently brush the hair out of my face. "Don't you get it? I'll do anything for you."

"Easton," I breathe with a shake of my head.

He sighs. "I know. I'm sorry. I just miss you, Tess, and I

hate everything about being without you. I want you back. Want *us* back."

I'm frozen in place as he leans in. Everything in me is screaming to move, but I can't. I'm too numb. Too damaged. Too broken. His lips brush mine, and I feel nothing. It lacks the excitement I got when Asher would do the same, the feeling of needing to breathe him in just to get a dose of him.

"E," I murmur, trying to push him away.

"Please," he begs. "I love you, Tess."

Those three words are everything I've been unknowingly dying to hear, but they're coming from the wrong person. I'm not enough for him. I'm never going to *be* enough for him. A tear flows down my cheek, and I don't put up a fight as Easton lays me down on the bed and kisses my neck.

"I love you," he repeats against my skin. "I love you so much."

RELEASING INTO THE CONDOM, Easton pulls out and crashes into the mattress next to me. I roll onto my side, away from him, and pull the covers up to my chin. The sound of his labored breathing fills the air, making my stomach churn. He pushes up onto his elbow and drapes his arm over me.

"I'm going to get a beer. You want one?"

I shake my head. "No, thanks."

He bends down and kisses the side of my head. "The pills are in the second drawer in the bathroom, pushed toward the back. It's been a few more hours. You can have another."

Climbing off the bed with a newfound energy, he throws a pair of sweatpants on and leaves the room. I wait until the coast is clear before I get up to put my clothes back on.

There's a half-full bottle of vodka on his dresser. I grab it and take a swig, hating the taste but needing the effects.

My bare feet pad across the floor into the bathroom. I lock the door behind me and place the bottle on the sink. Pulling open the drawer, I find the large prescription bottle filled nearly to the brim with oxy.

As I look up, my reflection stares back at me, but it's not someone I recognize. Mascara is running down her face, her hair a piled mess on top of her head. Her cheekbones pop out, as if she hasn't been eating, and there's no life left in her eyes. She looks cold. Dead to the world. Dead to herself.

Thoughts of everything I've been through flood my mind. Everything that happened in the underground, at the party, here. It's all too much. The trauma is an unbearable force that's constantly creeping up, threatening to break me at any given moment. This is no way to live.

I take a deep breath and open the bottle, grabbing the vodka to swallow them down.

One pill to numb the pain.

Five more to erase the memories.

And the rest to make it all just...stop.

Stumbling onto the floor, I sit down and lean against the bathtub, vodka bottle still clutched firmly in my hand. A small laugh bubbles out of me, and the tears turn to happy ones, knowing it's all about to stop. All the nightmares, all the pain. All the memories.

I'm going to be free.

Easton knocks on the door, calling my name, but I can't answer. The panic in his voice builds as the knocks turn to pounding. He kicks the door in, looking from the empty pill bottle lying in the sink to my place on the ground.

"No, no!"

He drops down beside me and grabs my face in his hands.

Unadulterated fear fills his eyes as he tries to get my attention.

"Tessa? Tessa! Answer me!"

He slaps my cheeks lightly but I can barely feel it. Everything is going numb—tingling. Flashes of everyone I love flicker in the distance. Lennon, Colby, Asher, *Delaney*. They won't have to worry about me anymore. They'll be able to live their lives, free of the burden of me. I'll watch over them and keep them safe. They'll be okay.

"Shit! Zayn!"

I start to slip into the darkness. *I'm going to be free.*

Asher

I SLAM THE CAR INTO DRIVE AND PEEL OUT OF THE parking garage. The street lights and lack of traffic remind me how early it is, but I don't care. I grab my phone and press the number I need to call, listening to the sound of ringing fill the car.

"Hello?" Blaire answers tiredly, though I'd expect nothing less at damn near four in the morning.

"I need you to cancel that interview for this morning. I'm not going to make it."

She sighs. "Uh, do I even want to ask why?"

"Tessa is in the hospital," I tell her. "Some kind of overdose. I don't know any more than that."

I pull up on the emergency brake and quickly spin the wheel, drifting around the turn. No part of me cares that the light is red, or that I cut off what was probably the only other car on the road. All I know is I need to get there, and now.

"Asher," Blaire says hesitantly. "Where are you?"

A dry laugh leaves my mouth. "That's a stupid fucking question. Where you do you *think* I am?"

She groans. "If you go to that hospital, you're risking everything."

"No!" I roar. "My everything is *in* that hospital! Don't you get it? I'm not risking it by going. I'm risking it by staying away."

My tone must tell her that no part of this is up for debate

because she goes completely silent for a moment. I'm almost pulling up to North Haven Medical Center when she speaks.

"Okay. Just try to stay out of sight. If the press finds out you're there, they'll have a field day."

"Yep. Thanks."

I press end without hearing anything else she has to say. If I stayed on the phone with her, I'd risk way too much time and energy that should be spent on Tessa. Doesn't she realize that my entire world is crashing down around me? I don't care if the media finds out everything at this point. All that matters is her.

I whip my car into a parking space and jump out, running in through the front doors. The security guard is sitting with the receptionist, and they both eye me suspiciously. I pull my license out and hand it to them so they can scan me in.

"I'm here to see Tessa Callahan. She was brought in by ambulance."

The receptionist hits a few buttons on the computer and the sympathy that flashes across her face scares the shit out of me. She fills out the pass and hands it to me.

"She's in the ICU, dear. Do you know where to go?"

I instantly feel like I'm going to throw up. My mouth seems to forget how to form words, so I simply shake my head. She tells me to get in the elevator, take it to the third floor, make a left and then a right at the end of the hall, and they will buzz me in. I'm not sure how, but I manage to absorb the words while taking back my license.

The walls of this place are as bleak as I feel. Pictures of happy and satisfied patients do nothing to stop my mind from thinking the absolute worst. If you ask me, they're a little insensitive, for all the people who have to leave this place without their loved ones. Having to walk through a hallway of smiling faces must feel like a punch in the gut.

As I reach the doors to the ICU, I hit the button and hold

up my visitors pass. The lock clicks and they open automatically. I walk through and up to the front desk.

"Tessa Callahan?" I ask.

The nurse looks down at her computer and sighs. "I'm afraid the doctors are still working on her. If you'd like to have a seat in the waiting room, I'll have someone update you as soon as possible."

I look at her pleadingly. "Can you at least tell me if she's all right?"

"Are you family?"

Fuck. "No."

She sighs, glancing from side to side before leaning in. "I shouldn't be telling you this, so if anyone asks, you know nothing."

I nod.

"EMTs responded to a call of an opiate overdose. When they arrived, she was unresponsive and not breathing. They managed to get her heart beating again and had to give her multiple doses of Narcan. Right now, she has the best doctors we have working on her. I can promise you, they'll do everything they can."

Everything goes quiet, except for the ringing in my ears that becomes deafeningly loud. Just then, a doctor moves a curtain for a second to step out and I get a glimpse inside. Tessa lies in the bed, looking completely lifeless except for the subtle beeping of the heart monitor. There are tubes coming from her mouth and nurses on both sides of her are working tirelessly.

I'm going to be sick.

"Just have a seat in the waiting room, Mr. Hawthorne," the nurse at the desk says kindly, and I realize I never told her who I am.

"Thank you for your help, and I'd appreciate it if my being here is kept under wraps."

"Absolutely. Let me know if you need anything at all."

I walk away and head toward the waiting room. How I'm expected to just sit and wait without completely losing my mind is beyond me. Just as I'm about to turn the corner, however, a familiar voice causes me to freeze.

"She has to be okay. She has to."

Another person exhales heavily. "Easton, sit down."

"I mean, they got her heart beating again. That's a good sign, right?"

I know I can't sit in there. He's the reason she had access to these pills in the first place. I'm sure of it. And judging by the way he looked at me the other day, I'm sure he's not my biggest fan either. All putting us in a room together will do is cause a fight, and I don't want to get kicked out of the hospital.

I turn around and walk away, knowing I'm going to have to find somewhere else to wait. Meanwhile, I pull my phone from my pocket. There's no way in hell I'm going to be somewhere further away from her, without a way to see what's going on. I press speed dial three and wait for an answer.

"The fuck you calling me this early for?" Colby barks, like I just woke him up.

"I'll explain everything later, but I need the name and number of the IT guy you use to delete pictures off girls' phones."

"Ooh," he coos. "Did Asher get himself in a bit of a pinch?"

I shake my head even though he can't see me. "Not even close. I'll explain everything later, I just need his info and I need it now."

306

AFTER PLACING THE PHONE call to a guy who solely goes by Sketch, it only takes a few minutes before I'm texted a link to a secure server by a blocked number. I click it and a window opens. Just like that, I've got access to the security camera placed right outside Tessa's room. *Thank you Sketch.*

I SPEND HOURS STARING at the camera feed and willing her to wake up. To have some kind of response. To give the doctors something to go off of so they stop walking out of her room with grim looks on their faces.

The coffee shop near the front lobby, where I've decided to take up temporary residence, fills with people trying to get something to eat before heading to work or visiting patients. I stay in the corner booth, keeping my attention focused on my phone. The sun peeks out from behind the building across the street and shines right in my face. I realize it's almost ten in the morning. It's been six hours, and we still don't know anything.

Just then, an alarm starts going off and doctors rush in, flooding her room. I can't stay away anymore. I need to know what's going on. Standing up from the table, I toss my empty cup into the trash and sprint out the door.

The ICU is chaos, with people running around and scrambling to grab the things they need. The nurse I spoke to before comes out of her room, seeing me standing there with a panicked look on my face. She glances back for a second and sighs.

"I tried coming to find you before but you weren't in the waiting room," she tells me. "I have to help your friend. Go wait there and I'll come talk to you as soon as I can."

My *friend*. Doesn't she realize she's so much more than that? The word friend is something I would use to describe

Griffin, or maybe even Colby on a bad day when he's pissed me off enough to drop him down from brother status. But Tessa? She deserves so much better than *friend*. Girlfriend, Fiancée, Wife...Lover even, but not friend. Definitely not friend.

Everything in my brain is foggy as I walk into the waiting room. I completely forget about the reason I didn't come wait here in the first place until I turn the corner. Easton's eyes land on me and his brows furrow.

"What the fuck are you doing here?"

I open my mouth to answer him, but someone else beats me to it.

"I asked him to come."

Delaney steps into the room with Knox in tow, and if looks could kill, Easton would be a rotting corpse by now.

The sound of my phone ringing pulls me from the only place I get to spend with Tessa—dreamland. Maybe that's pathetic, that I crave sleep so I can pretend we're still together, but it's all I've got. I glance at the clock. 3:43 a.m.

"Hello?" I ask, without even looking to see who's calling.

"Asher."

Pulling the phone away from my ear, I check to make sure it is who I think it is.

"Delaney?"

A sob rips through her. "Asher, something's wrong. Tessa's on her way to the hospital. It's bad. It's really bad."

I sit up, suddenly wide the fuck awake. "Wait, what? Calm down. Tell me what happened."

She's frantic, that much is clear. "I don't know. Zayn called Knox and woke us up. He said that something happened to Tessa and she's on her way to the emergency room. He thinks she overdosed."

I'm already out of bed and throwing on my clothes by the time she finishes talking. "Okay, Laney? I need you to put Knox on the phone. Don't worry, she's going to be all right. Just, put Knox on."

The sound of her crying fades as she hands the phone over. "Hello?"

"Where are you and what's the closest airport?"

"T.F. Green in Providence."

I scribble down the information on a notepad. "Okay. Pack a bag and start heading there. Tell them you have a private jet waiting for you. It'll get you here the fastest without having to worry about security and all that."

He thanks me and the two of us get off the phone. As I grab the things I need, I call the company Colby and I use whenever we fly private and put a jet on standby at T.F. Green.

"Delaney? How the hell are you even here? I thought you were in Rhode Island," he asks.

She scoffs. "And I thought you had some common fucking sense. I asked you to be there for her, not give her access to a whole damn pharmacy!"

"It's not...I didn't...It was an accident."

Taking a step closer, she genuinely looks like she's about to hit him. "I'll show you a fucking *accident*."

Sure enough, she rears back and kicks him directly in the balls. Every guy in the room winces as he hunches over and falls to the ground, only for her to stand above him.

"How could you be so stupid?"

He groans in pain as he looks up at Knox. "Dude, a little help here?"

Knox crosses his arms over his chest. "Yeah, I'm going to pass. And besides, I'm next."

Delaney smirks at Easton, as if she's mentally telling him

309

he's screwed. Meanwhile, Zayn walks over to Knox and gives him a hug. I don't know much about the black-haired guy, but he's not defending Easton, so it's that he's not happy with him either.

"I'm looking for the family of Tessa Callahan?"

Laney's whips around to face the doctor standing in the doorway. "I'm her sister."

The doctor tilts her head and glances at Easton, who is still on the ground and whimpering in pain. "Should I be concerned?"

"Nope," we all answer in unison.

Her brows raise and her lips pucker. "Okay, well, when your sister came in, she was in very bad shape. She wasn't responsive, and her pulse was very weak. She needed three rounds of NARCAN in the ambulance, and we pumped her stomach upon arrival."

A pained sound rumbles in the back of Delaney's throat.

"It's been very touch and go for the last few hours, but she finally started breathing over the ventilator, and her stats seem to be stabilizing. She's not out of the woods yet. We won't know if there any mental deficits until she wakes up, but it's looking up."

I sigh in relief as Delaney tears up and collapses into Knox's arms. When she gets ahold of herself, she wipes her face and turns back to the doctor.

"Are we able to go see her?"

She nods. "Just try to be quiet. Forcing her to wake up before she's ready could cause more damage than good."

We all follow her toward Tessa's room, including Easton, who limps behind us. Delaney stops at the door, covering her mouth as she cries at the vision of her sister. It's heartbreaking, honestly, to see someone so strong look so fragile.

"Go," I tell her. "She's going to want you when she wakes up."

She looks up at me and her brows furrow. "Aren't you coming?"

I shake my head. "I'll wait out here. I'm not entirely sure she'll want me in there, and I'd rather not make her uncomfortable."

It looks like she wants to argue, but instead, she nods and goes inside—taking up the seat at Tessa's bedside and grabbing her hand. I lean against the nurses' desk, staying where I can see her but making sure not to intrude. *Come on, Cherry Bomb. You're stronger than this.*

Tessa

I'M HONESTLY NOT SURE WHAT'S WORSE: THE stabbing pain that feels like it's piercing my brain, or that incessant beeping. I groan, trying to will it to stop. Someone gasps, and the hand holding mine tightens.

"Tessa?"

Delaney? It takes a minute, but I finally peel my eyes open to find my sister sitting beside me.

"Am I hallucinating?"

Tears spring to her eyes and she covers her mouth as she shakes her head. She practically jumps to hug me, only for her to pull away, give me a little shake, and then hug me again.

"You're such an idiot! What were you thinking?"

I don't get a chance to answer before she's back to hugging me.

"Ugh, I'm so glad you're okay."

As she sits back down, I see Knox beside her. He looks so relieved, yet so fed up with my shit. I smile as sweetly as I can manage, and it works like a charm. He chuckles and shakes his head, getting up to hug me.

"You're a pain in the ass, you know that?"

The room looks familiar, and it takes a minute before I realize, it's the same kind of room Knox was in after he was shot—or rather, after he jumped in front of a bullet to save my sister. *I'm in the ICU.*

My breath hitches as my eyes land on Asher. He's standing by the nurses' desk, with his gaze locked on mine.

"How long has he been standing there?" I ask Delaney.

She glances back at him and sighs. "Since they told us we could come see you. He won't move from that spot. He doesn't want to come in because he's not sure you want him here."

"If you don't want him here, just say the word, and I'll be more than happy to kick his ass out," Easton pipes up.

I hadn't even realized he was standing there. I don't have much recollection of what happened, but I remember something about him being there, frantically calling my name. *Pills.* Fuck, the pills.

"What did I tell you?" Delaney snaps at him. "Be seen but not heard. Or was that not clear enough for you?"

I try not to laugh at her, but it's nearly impossible. Delaney is one of the gentlest people I know, so to see her cracking orders with some invisible whip is amusing.

A woman in a white coat steps into the room. "Miss Callahan, it's nice to see you awake. I'm Dr. Josselyn, the lead doctor here. How are you feeling?"

"My head hurts."

She makes a face. "Well, with how much oxy was in your system, that's not surprising. I'm just going to do a few tests, okay?"

I nod and Delaney and Knox step out of the way. The routine checks she does are all things I've done before, and trigger the memories I was hoping to forget. When she's done, she types a few things into the computer.

"You got very lucky, Tessa. It seems there are no long term side effects of the overdose," she tells me. "However, I am going to order you stay overnight for observation. And I'll probably have them run a couple more tests just to be sure."

"And my head? Is there any way to get rid of this killer headache?"

She frowns. "Unfortunately, no. With the amount of oxycodone in your system when you came in, we have to make sure everything is cleared out before we can give you anything for pain."

Okay, I guess I deserve that.

Delaney thanks her for me and she leaves the room, stopping to talk to Asher, who is clearly worried. Looking to the other side of the room, Zayn and Easton are leaning against the windowsill, and Easton looks like he's on the verge of a mental breakdown. I need to put him out of his misery.

"Do you think you guys could give me a minute alone with Easton?"

Laney cocks an eyebrow. "No. Absolutely not."

"Lane," I plead.

Knox rubs a hand down her arm, and she glances at him before her shoulders sag. He and Zayn walk toward the door, but Delaney goes directly over to Easton.

"Stand up," she orders.

He instantly obeys her, and she starts patting him down, checking his pockets and all other parts of his body. Everyone watches her curiously, until Knox finally asks the question on everyone's minds.

"Bambi, what the hell are you doing?"

"Making sure he doesn't have any drugs on him," she tells him, as if it's obvious.

I swallow, hard. "Delaney—"

"No," she snaps at me. "The only reason I haven't screamed at you is because I can't do it while you're looking all sad and helpless in a hospital bed. Do *not* push me, Tessa."

Anything I was about to say is shoved right back inside as

Knox gives me a sympathetic smile and approaches his girlfriend with caution.

"Okay, Rambo. Let's go get you something to eat."

She takes a deep breath and nods, coming over to give me one more hug before leaving the room.

As soon as Easton and I are alone, it's as if he reads the unspoken question in my mind.

"Don't worry," he says quietly. "I made sure the doctors know it was an accident. Just partied too hard and it all went wrong."

I'm not sure if he's saying that because he thinks someone could be listening, or because he genuinely needs to believe that's the truth for his own peace of mind. Regardless, I'm not going to correct him.

"Thank you."

Silence fills the room as neither one of us knows what to say. Finally, when it becomes too much, he caves to the pressure.

"Did I...?"

I shake my head. "No. No, of course not."

"Everyone is blaming me. And I mean, why shouldn't they? I should have never started you on those pills in the first place. You just looked so sad, and I was desperate for something to bring back the Tessa I remember."

Honestly, it doesn't surprise me everyone is placing the blame on him. They all think that last night was an accident. Like I just happened to take one too many or mix it with too much alcohol. If that were the case, a part of me would probably blame him too, but it's not.

"Your heart was in the right place."

He rubs the back of his neck and looks up at me. "So, you don't hate me?"

"No."

Maybe he can see it on my face, or feel it in the air, but

the smile vanishes as soon as he realizes it.

"But you don't love me either."

There it is. The topic of conversation we were both trying to avoid.

I sigh. "Easton."

He takes a step back, keeping his hand against his chest as if my rejection physically causes pain. "Don't. Don't say my name like you're trying to let me down easy."

"I'm sorry."

"I love you, Tessa! I love you."

I'm trying not to get upset, but the tears come anyway. "I love you, too."

He pinches his lips together and looks down at the ground. After a few seconds, he nods.

"But you love him more."

I blink up at the ceiling, trying so hard not to break. Hurting Easton is the last thing I wanted to do, but I can't force myself to feel something I don't either. Last night was proof of that.

"I'm *so* sorry," I cry. "I can't help it. It's him. It's always going to be him."

With a huff, he shakes his head and walks out, storming past Asher without so much as looking at him. I close my eyes and take a few breaths to calm down. After I'm done drying my face, I exhale.

"Okay," I say without making eye contact. "You can stop pretending like you can't hear anything out there."

He drops his head and chuckles, pushing off the nurses' station and walking toward me. The closer he gets, the more I want him next to me. When he stops at the door, I know he's waiting for me to invite him in.

I roll my eyes. "Stop standing there like a creep and come sit next to me."

Doing as I say, he slips into the seat Delaney previously

occupied and slips his hand in mine. The contact alone is everything I've needed lately. Something to distract me. Something to ground me. Something to heal.

"How are you feeling?"

I crinkle my nose. "Like death."

His eyebrows raise and he tilts his head to the side. "Well, I mean, that's kinda fitting."

Involuntary laughter bubbles out of me. "You did *not* just make a joke about this."

"Well, someone had to." He smiles, and in the way I needed to see, his dimples come out of hiding. "Besides, I think your sister is angry enough for everyone."

Wincing at the thought of Delaney, I groan. "She's really pissed, isn't she?"

"Understatement of the year, but yes."

I side-eye him. "And I'm guessing I have you to thank for her being here?"

He sheepishly looks down. "I mean, we needed someone here who isn't afraid to lay into you. It was a tactical move. I made an executive decision."

"That teaching position has really gone to your head, hasn't it?"

"Aye," he mock-pouts. "I resent that."

"Sure you do, old man," I smirk.

He stands up, pretending like he's leaving. "I'm not going to take this abuse."

Just as he goes to walk away, I tighten my grip on his hand and pull. He doesn't fight it. Instead, he spins back around and falls into me, connecting our lips for the first time in weeks.

Everything in my body comes alive as his mouth moves against my own. He brings his hand up to rest it on my cheek, and I know he's needed this just as much as I have. As he breaks the kiss, he rests his forehead on mine.

"God, I've missed you."

"I've missed you, too," I breathe.

He goes to kiss me again, when Delaney, Knox, and Zayn come back.

"Good news," Delaney starts, acting oblivious to what she just walked in on. "The doctor said you're free to eat as soon as you're hungry. So, I grabbed all your favorites."

Knox pours out a bag onto the table and my brows furrow as I look at it all.

"Delaney, these are all *your* favorites."

She crosses her arms over her chest. "Yeah, well, I'm still mad at you."

"You and me both," Lennon's voice booms through the room, and all of a sudden, I have a strong urge to move to another continent.

I look at my sister. "I take it you called her?"

Her expression turns devious. "Yep."

"You," Lennon says to Asher pointedly. "Move."

He mouths a *sorry* at me and releases my hand to get out of her way. She marches up to my side, then glances out the door before smacking me over the head. It intensifies my pounding headache but it's nothing more than I deserve.

"Have you completely lost it? I mean, really. Do I need to knock some sense into you?"

I shy away from the loudness of her tone. "No more knocking anything please. It hurts."

"She has a bad headache, and they can't give her anything for it yet," Asher explains.

Lennon turns on her heels and zeros in on Asher. "Don't even get me started on you." She pushes him back with a hand to his chest. "Yeah, I saw those pictures from Friday night. PR date or not, don't be a douche. Just because you're my teacher doesn't mean I won't lay your ass out."

It's almost comical, seeing Lennon at five foot one and a

hundred pounds soaking wet threatening Asher, but it wouldn't surprise me if she actually did it. That girl is a damn firecracker.

"I have a better idea," I suggest. "You could hug me and tell me you're glad I'm okay."

She glares at me. "No."

Instead, she walks over to the windowsill and climbs up, curling into a ball and leaning against the wall. When she refuses to look at me, it becomes clear—she knows.

COLBY SHOWS UP AN hour or so later, with flowers and chocolates, because *"Asher doesn't know how to apologize."* It earns an elbow to the stomach from his best friend, but I find it amusing. I'd be lying if I said I didn't miss Colby. He's always been one of few people who didn't treat me like they need to tread carefully. Even now, he cracks jokes about how if I wanted a good time, I should've just called him. Lennon and Delaney may not see the humor in it, but it's comforting to know he's not looking at me any differently because of this.

We're all sitting around playing Never Have I Ever to pass the time when someone I never would have expected comes through the door.

"You know," Grayson says, looking around the room, "I'm getting really sick of coming to this place." His gaze lands on me and he tsks playfully. "Tessa, Tessa, Tessa. Always getting yourself into shit."

A disbelieving smile spreads across my face. "What the hell? When did you get here?"

"Our plane landed about a half hour ago," Savannah appears in the doorway. "The plane we got on as soon as I got Delaney's phone call."

"Sav?"

She shakes her head. "What? You think because I'm closer with Laney that makes you any less my sister? Hate me all you want, that's fine, but you're stuck with me."

My eyes water as all the animosity I had toward her goes right out the window. She comes closer and hugs me, and for the first time in years, I realize how much I've missed her. When she pulls away, Grayson sits on the other side of my bed.

"Psst," he whispers loudly, like everyone can't hear him. "Do you realize you have two professional football players in your hospital room?"

Everyone chuckles as I play along.

"Yes," I whisper-shout back.

His brows furrow. "Are they lost?"

"No. They're my little playthings. I kidnapped them and claimed them for myself."

His grin widens, and he high-fives me. "I'd expect nothing less from you, CBP."

I throw my head back, groaning. "Not you, too!"

Asher's confusion is evident as he looks at me. "What am I missing?"

"Knox started this nickname for me, CBP, and he absolutely refuses to tell me what it means."

He mouths each letter slowly as he tries to figure it out. Then, somehow unbeknownst to me, he gets it and starts cracking up. *Great, someone else in on the joke.*

"Babe, really? You haven't figured that out?"

I shake my head with a pout.

He leans in closer. "C–B–P. Cute But Psycho."

My jaw drops, and I look over at Knox, who is cackling. "You're an asshole, and if I wasn't in a hospital bed, I'd kick your ass."

Knox bends down and puts his hands on his knees, trying

to catch his breath. "Yeah, but he just figured it out with no help, so what's that say about you?"

I roll my eyes, trying my hardest not to laugh even though it really is funny. "It says I need new friends."

Looking around, I realize all the people who are here for me. Delaney, Lennon, and Savannah. Knox and Zayn. Asher and Colby. Last night I felt so alone that I allowed the past to convince me that I'm not good enough. That these people who love me would be better off if I wasn't around. But I don't think that's true. It can't be, not if they're here, coming from all over the country just to be there for me. I may not have been enough for my uncle, or even my dad, but I *am* enough for all of them, and *that* is enough for me.

One of the nurses comes in, her eyes focused on her tablet. When she looks up, she stops and her cheeks tint pink.

"Wow, that's a lot of attractive men," she tells me and I chuckle. Then, she turns to Asher. "We have a bit of a problem. It seems someone caught wind of you being here. Reporters are flooding the parking lot."

Asher's eyes meet mine before looking back at her. "Okay, thanks for telling me."

"That's it?" I ask. "That's all you're going to say?"

"What else did you expect? That I'm going to leave you here? No way in hell." His tone is full of assurance. "Besides, all they know is that I'm at a hospital, with thousands of patients."

"Uh," Colby chimes in, looking down at his phone. "That's not entirely true. Someone figured out that Tessa's one of those patients, and your student, and they're starting to put the pieces together on how much she looks like the woman you've been seen with lately."

Well, fuck.

Asher

THE SOUND OF HEELS CLICKING ON THE FLOOR gets annoying as Blaire paces across the room. She's been going on and on about how she told me so, and how coming here was a horrible idea. If I have to hear about her hatred for damage control one more time, I'm going to lose it.

Tessa still hasn't been able to have any pain meds, so with every tap of Blaire's shoe, it's clear her headache is getting worse. I grab her hand and run my thumb back and forth to comfort her. Delaney and Savannah watch my publicist like she's some kind of circus act. Though, that's probably because of their connection to Tessa. If she doesn't like someone, neither do they.

"Is she always like this?" Savannah questions.

Colby snorts. "She's worse."

"Okay." Blaire takes a deep breath. "Okay, I can spin this. There has to be a way to spin this."

I don't miss the way Tessa rolls her eyes. She's slowly starting to look better than she did this morning, with the color coming back into her. Blondie over there might be worried about my image, but my only concern is the girl in the hospital bed.

"And how do you intend to do that, all knowing one?" I quip.

She turns to glare at me, then her expression turns to disgust. "For starters, you can stop doing *that*."

Her hand gestures to where Tessa's hand and mine are

intertwined. Tess squirms uncomfortably and goes to pull away, but I tighten my grip, shaking my head when she looks at me. There's not a damn thing Blaire can say that will make me let go. Especially not when I just got her back and I almost lost her forever.

"I still don't understand how they found out." Delaney sighs. "You haven't left this room. Do you think it was one of the nurses?"

I shake my head. "They're under HIPPA and all that."

Colby sits up and runs his hands over his face. "The articles said it came from a reliable source."

Tessa gasps and turns to Zayn and Knox with wide eyes. "You don't think—"

"No," Knox stops her question before it's even asked. "He's not that fucked up."

Zayn, however, doesn't look so convinced. "I don't know, man. I was outside having a cigarette when he left, and he was pretty pissed off."

"Easton," Delaney says, annoyed. "Of course. I swear, when he doesn't get what he wants, he makes the stupidest fucking choices."

Blaire stops and crosses her arms over her chest. "Are you all done? Congratulations, you figured out the irrelevant."

"Irrelevant?" Savannah narrows her eyes at her.

"It doesn't matter *how* they know. The only thing that matters is *what* they know, and how we can twist it into a story we can deal with."

Everyone looks annoyed by the situation, except for Lennon, who is still curled up in the corner, though she's been annoyed since she got here. She hasn't left but she also hasn't said a single word to anyone. She just sits there, staring out the window and glancing at Tessa every now and then.

Blaire focuses all her attention solely on me. "It has to look like you were doing her a favor by being here."

"What?" Delaney balks. "No."

"Laney," Tessa tries, but her sister isn't hearing it.

"I said *no*. Absolutely not. You're not going to paint her as some desperate charity case."

As she rolls her eyes, Blaire looks bored. "Then please, enlighten me. What do you think we should do?"

Delaney stands and stalks toward her. "I think *you* should check your fucking attitude before I take your three-inch stiletto and jab it into your eye socket."

Colby watches her dreamily. "Have I mentioned how much I love that there are two of them?"

Tessa chuckles and lightly whacks him upside the head. Then, she looks over at Knox.

"Are you going to do something about this?"

He glances at where Blaire and Delaney are having an intense stare down and cocks a brow. "What? You think because she's in love with me that means I can get her to listen? I can't, and I don't want a heel in my eye either."

Everyone snickers while Savannah gets up. "I've got it."

She gently grabs Delaney and starts walking her toward the door.

"But I want to hit her," Delaney pouts as she's pulled out.

Savannah nods. "I know, love, but you're not very scrappy."

"I'm not?"

"No."

Tessa sighs, and as soon as they're gone, she looks at Blaire. "Just tell me what I have to do."

IT'S PAST SUNSET WHEN we're finally done. It took hours, but we managed to come up with a plan that satisfies Blaire and her obnoxious need to control everything. Tomorrow, when Tessa is discharged, she'll leave out a different door with Delaney and Knox. Meanwhile, I'll go out the main door and talk to the press—telling them that Tessa is a student of mine and that she had them call me because of the trust I've instilled in them. It essentially paints me as some kind of hero, and Delaney was right—it makes Tessa look like a damsel in distress.

A nurse pops her head in and smiles sympathetically. "I'm sorry, guys, but visiting hours are over."

"Can one person stay?" I ask.

She looks over at Tessa and sighs. "Just one."

I thank her and turn to Delaney, fully expecting her to be the one that's staying, but she shakes her head.

"She loves me, but I'm not who she wants with her tonight."

Tessa looks around the room, anywhere but at me, and I chuckle. "Tessa?"

"I wonder how many dots are on the ceiling."

"Tess."

She bites her lip and finally meets my gaze.

"Do you want me to stay or go?"

Her chest heaves with a deep breath and drops with the exhale. "Stay," she tells me, with vulnerability all over her face. "Always stay."

"Wait, what?" Blaire squawks. "You can't stay here. It'll give the wrong idea."

My head whips toward her, and I level her with a look. "No one asked you. I'm already going along with your ridiculous plan. Don't push it. If she wants me to stay, I'm staying."

Like a child throwing a temper tantrum, she rolls her eyes and storms out. *Good riddance.*

"Colby, can you take Knox and Delaney back to the penthouse?"

He nods a little too quickly, making Knox's brows raise. He steps closer and puts a hand on Colby's shoulder.

"Did I ever tell you I was trained to fight?"

Tessa laughs. "He's killed people."

"Tess!" Delaney hisses.

"What? He has."

Colby's eyes widen drastically as Knox winks. Meanwhile, Savannah side-eyes Grayson, and the amusement vanishes from his face. I don't know what the story is there, but I'm obviously out of the loop.

***

LYING IN BED NEXT to Tessa is something I never thought I'd be able to do again, but wished for every time I caught the clock at 11:11. Granted, I didn't think it would be in a hospital bed, but I'll take whatever path leads me to her. Tessa's head rests on my chest as I run my fingers through her hair.

"How's your head?"

She shrugs. "Not as bad as it was, but not as good as it could be either."

I press a kiss into her hair. "Do you want me to go see if you can have anything yet?"

"No, that's okay. I don't want you to move."

Holding her tighter, I think about everything we've been through. It's no secret that I wanted this girl from the start. She caught my attention at first glance and never let it go. The way she knew exactly what she was after and went for it without shame? It was the sexiest thing I've ever seen. And then, the universe threw in a curve ball.

I remember the look on her face when she walked into my classroom. I was already in a bad mood, having my arm twisted into taking a job I didn't want or need, and seeing her sent me into a whole different dimension. On one hand, I was furious. At no point during the eight or so hours we spent together did she mention anything about still being in high school. Then again, neither of us really said much of anything that night.

Despite wanting her, I tried to stay away. She's my student, and there are rules against this kind of thing. Rules I do think are important and valid. But, I couldn't. The more I pushed her away, the harder she came back. She broke down my walls, thinned my restraint, and gave me no choice but to fall in love with her.

I considered quitting. After the Lexington benefit, when I realized that the whole hiding thing didn't work for me anymore, I thought about it. I pictured all the places we could go together, all the things we could do, and I wanted it. Craved it like Colby with a girl in a short skirt. But before I even got a chance to really consider it, shit hit the fan.

"Can I ask you something?"

She peers up at me through her long lashes. "What's up?"

I cup her cheek. "What happened the night you left?"

Looking away, she sighs. "Blaire happened."

"I know that much. I mean, what'd she say to you?"

It takes a moment for her to speak, almost like she's questioning whether or not she should tell me at all. "Honestly? Nothing I didn't already know deep down."

My brows furrow. "Enlighten me."

She spends the next fifteen minutes telling me everything. How she came home hoping to find me there so we could talk about Trent. The folder that contained more information on Tessa's life than anyone should have access to. And even how much it killed her to hit ignore when I tried calling her.

"Why didn't you talk to me?"

Her lip quivers as she fiddles with the hospital gown. "Because everything she said had truth to it. It still does. And you're better off when I'm not in your life."

Fucking Blaire. "That's bullshit. That woman is a vile, disgusting human being who used information about your past to scare you away from me."

"Maybe so," she shrugs. "But she did it because it's in your best interest. Think about it, Ash. If the press finds out about us, they'll skin you alive. You'll be turned into the perverted teacher who couldn't keep it in his pants."

I shake my head and sit up. "What? No. I don't care about any of that. Can't you see that? I don't...I don't..."

"Shh, okay." She places a hand on my chest and lightly pushes me back down, cuddling into me. "We don't have to worry about that right now."

We shouldn't have to worry about it ever, but I'm not going to argue it right now. I pull her in closer and kiss her forehead.

THE CLOSER IT GETS to *"game time"*, the more Tessa seems to be on edge. We spent the night wrapped in each other's arms, even after the nurse came in to tell me those beds aren't meant for two people. Still, I can see how uncomfortable all this makes her, and I've got a fucking bone to pick with my publicist.

Tessa signs all the discharge papers, cringing at the pamphlets they give her for drug rehabs in the area. Once that's all done, she changes into a pair of sweatpants and a hoodie Delaney was nice enough to bring her. When she comes out of the bathroom, she looks a little bit more like the girl I fell for.

"Ready to go?"

She nods and laces her fingers with mine. Delaney walks on the other side of her while Knox waits in the car. Hopefully the press doesn't check the plates, being as that one is registered to me too.

When we get to where we're supposed to part ways, Tessa starts to tear up. A confused expression covers my face, and I notice Delaney is avoiding my gaze.

"Hey," I say to Tess, bending down with my hands on her cheeks. "I know it sucks, but I promise, I'll meet you back at the penthouse. You'll only be a couple minutes ahead of me."

She takes a deep breath, but my words only bring more tears. Something isn't adding up. I pull away and glance between her and her sister.

"What's going on?"

Delaney sighs, and the two of them share a look. It's like they've got some weird kind of twin telepathy or some shit, because they practically have a silent conversation with just their eyes.

I'm starting to get irritated. "One of you better tell me what the hell is going on."

Tessa pinches her lips together and grabs the front of my shirt. She arches up on her toes to kiss me but I hold her back by her shoulders. *Oh my God.*

"You're not *coming* back to the penthouse," I say as all the pieces fall together.

She wipes the tears with the sleeve of her sweatshirt and shakes her head. "Blaire had a point two weeks ago, and she still has one now. I'm no good for you."

"Fuck Blaire and her fucking opinion," I snap. "No. I don't care. We're doing this my way."

I grab her hand and pull her in the opposite direction,

332

toward the front door that she's meant to avoid at all costs. My car is waiting out front where the valet parked it, and I can see the plethora of people with microphones and cameras, waiting for a statement from me.

"Asher, what are you doing?" She tries to stop me, but I don't budge.

"I'm done letting that shrew control my life, and I'm sure as shit done being without you. I won't do it again."

As we walk through the front door, I release her and move my hand to her lower back. Cameras flash all around us, but my focus stays on Tessa. I lead her over to the car and open the passenger side to help her in. Once she's safely inside, I walk over to the crowd of reporters.

Asher, who is that?

Is she the mystery woman you've been spending time with?

What's her name?

I stand tall and clear my throat, pulling the notecards Blaire wrote for me from my pocket and tossing them straight in the trash can. The cameras are intimidating, and there are at least twenty of them.

"I know many of you have been worried, since I spent the past two days at this incredible medical facility," I start. "I'm sorry for the scare, but I can promise you, I'm in good health. There was a medical emergency with someone very close to me Saturday night."

"Is everything okay?" one of the reporters asks.

I nod. "Yes, thank you. The doctors here are outstanding, and I will be making a very generous donation to the hospital as soon as I get the chance."

Another holds out their microphone. "I'm sorry, Mr. Hawthorne, but I wouldn't be a reporter if I didn't ask. Who is that in your car? Some are saying that's Tessa Callahan, and she's a student of yours."

With a glance back at Tessa, I smile. "It is Tessa. She's my student…" I swallow down the lump in my throat. "…my girlfriend, and the woman I'm in love with."

The camera flashing intensifies, and the crowd of reporters go into an uproar. I hold up one hand.

"That's all the questions I will be answering today. I ask for privacy during this time. Thank you."

Turning around, I walk away and get into the driver's seat of my car, ignoring Tessa's jaw-dropped expression. I'm barely pulling out of the parking lot when my phone rings. I press the button to answer it on the steering wheel.

"Hi, Blaire."

"What the fuck do you think you're doing?" she screams into the phone. "Do you have any idea what you just did? You just flushed your career down the toilet! There's no possible way I'm going to be able to fix this."

I turn onto the road and merge into traffic. "Well it's a good thing you don't have to, then."

"Excuse me?"

My hand finds Tessa's and I intertwine our fingers once more. "In case it wasn't clear, you're fired, Blaire. I'll mail you your last check."

"What?" she shrieks. "You can't fire me! After all I've done for—"

The car goes quiet as I hit the button to end the call, until Tess starts to snicker, shaking her head.

"What?" I question.

She looks at me in disbelief. "Oh, I don't know. You just outed us to the entire damn world and fired your bitch of a publicist all in the last three minutes."

She's right, I did—and there isn't a single damn part of me that regrets it. My reputation may be in ruins by tomorrow, but as long as I have her by my side, nothing else matters.

I shrug. "What can I say? I took a page out of your playbook and went for what I want, no holds barred."

Her eyes roll as she huffs, but I can see a hint of the smile she's trying to hide. I drive through the city, finally feeling free. It isn't until I feel someone's gaze burning into me that I turn my head. I look over and find Tessa smirking.

"Care to share?"

She bites her lip. "So, you're in love with me, huh?"

I chuckle, bringing our conjoined hands up and kissing the back of hers. "Nah. You're way too young for me."

Laughter bubbles out of her, and it's like music to my ears. "You're such an old man. I'm obviously only dating you for the inheritance."

Tessa

THE PHONE RINGS CONSTANTLY FOR THE REST OF the day, and for a couple days after. Everyone wants to get a statement from Asher about his *forbidden relationship,* as they like to call it. With Blaire gone, we didn't have much experience on how to deal with it all. However, Colby was able to find someone who specializes in these kinds of situations.

She's nice, and a huge upgrade from the last one. When Asher mentioned another publicist was coming over to talk to him, I immediately shied away from the idea. I was so afraid she would come in and try to force me out the way Blaire did. Thankfully, that's not at all what happened.

She speaks to me like a human being and not a problem she needs to get rid of. She told Asher and I about how we can get all the records on my past sealed, and even how to get a restraining order against the paparazzi so they can't perch outside the building and follow us everywhere we go. She even managed to spin the narrative of our relationship so Asher doesn't look like a creepy pedophile. The fact of the matter is that I'm a legal adult and we're in a consenting relationship.

When we were leaving the hospital, I had no intentions to come back here. Despite how pissed she is at me, Lennon agreed to hide me at her house. I thought I was no good for Asher, and he was better off without me. Hell, I still do, but he's not taking no for an answer. He calls it *pulling a Tessa.* I call it being stubborn. Still, he kisses me in a way that throws my argument out the window.

"Babe, have you seen my black tie?" he asks me.

I shake my head. "But wear the gray one. It'll go better with that suit."

"This is why I love you."

"I love you, too," I answer honestly.

With a kiss to my nose, he retreats to the bedroom. Delaney sits across from me on the couch with a smirk on her face. I roll my eyes and flip her off.

"Not a word from you."

She chuckles. "I just think you're adorable. Love looks good on you."

I don't answer. Not because I think she's full of shit, but because there's no reason to deny it. I was always the first person to roll their eyes at happy couples. I had no interest in settling down and every interest in just having a good time. It wasn't until Asher came in and made me work for it, ruining me for everyone else, that I realized what the hype is all about.

Glancing at the clock, Delaney stands up. "I have to go. Dad is meeting me at the restaurant."

I stare down at my lap and nod. After I told her what I found out about him, Laney was devastated. It wasn't as surprising that he sacrificed me to the devil himself, but they didn't have the strained relationship that he and I did, so the knowledge of what he did was a hard hit for her. She's seen him a couple times over the last few days, but it's mainly because she's negotiating a deal. See, Delaney got early access to her trust fund when she graduated—a thank you present for not being such a fuck-up. I, however, still have to wait until I turn twenty-one, unless her plan works and she gets him to give it to me.

"You sure you don't want to come with me?"

I raise a single brow. "And spend over an hour with the father who knows I almost died and still hasn't asked if I'm okay? The father who set up me to be raped and tortured by my own uncle? No thanks, I'll pass."

My mom came to Asher's the day I was discharged. She apologized profusely for all the wrongdoing she indirectly played a part in, but it's going to be hard to come back from that. Her offer to divorce my dad if that's what I want is still something I'm considering—especially since he hasn't sent so much as a card.

Asher comes out, looking like the sexy millionaire he is. "We just have to wait for your babysitter to get here."

My eyes roll as I stand up to hug him. There are two things that Asher and Delaney have stood together on. One, Easton is out of my life for good, and two, I'm not allowed to be alone. I can't exactly say I blame them, but thanks to Easton's cover-up, everyone still thinks the overdose was accidental.

"Oh, good. That'll give me more time to seduce Colby," I tease.

Asher smirks. "Not Colby."

The elevator doors open behind me, and I turn around to see Lennon step out. My stomach churns, knowing we haven't been alone together since before everything happened. Hell, she's barely said a word to me since she stormed into the hospital and quite literally tried to smack sense into me.

"On second thought, lunch with dear old Dad doesn't sound so bad."

While Asher and Delaney chuckle, Lennon levels me with a look. "Sit your ass down."

I close my eyes and take a deep breath. "Well, my life was good while it lasted. Love life was a little short, but it is what it is."

My boyfriend presses a kiss to my lips and my sister hugs me before they both head out, leaving me alone with my best friend, and the one girl who isn't too blinded to see the truth. *Well, this should be fun.*

HOURS PASS AND I'M scrolling through my phone, looking at all the headlines Asher told me not to read. I can see why. Each one of them is cruel, making us both out to be monsters.

Asher Hawthorne: Closet Pervert, Borderline Pedophile.

Former Star Quarterback Throws Life Away For Drug Addict.

How a Night of Partying and Drugs Led to Asher Hawthorne Nearly Killing His Underage Girlfriend.

I throw my head back and groan. Lennon glances up at me from where she's been sitting silently since she got here.

"Stop Googling," she tells me.

I sigh. "I can't. It's obnoxious how they twist the truth. Some of these are even blatant lies. It's like they take one small piece of information and run with it."

She flips the page on the magazine. "That's the media for you."

Don't get me wrong, I love Lennon to death, but this dismissive attitude to everything I say is getting on my last damn nerve. This argument needs to be had, and until we force it out into the open, our friendship is going to continue to feel strained.

I get up from my spot on the couch and rip the magazine from her lap, throwing it across the room. She looks at me with no emotion whatsoever.

"I was reading that."

"Oops?"

She grabs another one from her purse and as soon as she

opens it, I do it again. I know her well enough to be able to see her restraint starting to slip, but she's not quite there yet. Finally, when I do the same thing with her phone, making sure it hits the couch and not the floor, she snaps.

"Fucking stop, Tess!"

"No," I push back. "Not until you talk to me."

She rolls her eyes and gets up to walk away. "I'm not doing this."

"Fine, then leave!" I point to the elevator. "There's the door! Just go!"

"I can't!" she yells. "You want me to talk to you? Fine! You hurt me! I was there for you! I would have supported you through anything, and instead, you pushed me away and just fucking quit!"

The tears in her eyes hit me straight in the chest. "Len."

"No! You don't get to do that. You wouldn't talk to me. I tried to help you, and you didn't want it." Her fight is weakening by the second, until she's down to just above a whisper. "You chose to self-destruct."

"I-I'm sorry," I cry. "I'm so sorry, but I'm better now."

She shakes her head. "You're not."

"I am, see?" I force myself to smile, despite the tears streaming down my face.

"And the nightmares? What about them?"

Even the mention of them makes me sick, reminding me that I'm broken. That I didn't escape the trauma. That I didn't rid myself of the pain.

"They'll go away."

Lennon looks as devastated and heartbroken as I feel. "You need help, Tess."

"No." I go to walk away. "No, I'm better now."

"You're not," she repeats. "You won't even admit what you did!"

Turning back around, I throw my hands in the air. "What

341

do you want me to say? That I took the pills on purpose? Fine! I did it!" I sob. "I did it because I'm weak. Because I'm a failure. I took a whole bottle of pills in an attempt to kill myself, and I couldn't even fucking succeed at that!"

At that moment, the elevator doors open behind me, and I freeze. Lennon's eyes stay locked on mine as the last piece of my heart breaks.

"You what?" Delaney breathes.

I turn around to find both my sister and Asher standing there, looking at me with unadulterated fear etched across their faces. I swallow hard and wipe the tears from my face only for them to instantly be replaced by more.

"I'm okay, I swear. I'm better now."

Asher

Two Hours Earlier

I sit in Jon's office, sweating as he rants and rages at me. When I admitted to dating one of my students, I knew shit was going to hit the fan, but that doesn't make it any easier to deal with. He's screaming loud enough for the whole school to hear him.

"What were you thinking?" he shouts. "How long has this been going on?"

I go to open my mouth, but he shakes his head.

"Don't answer that." Like a game of ping pong, he changes his mind. "No, do answer it."

"I met her in a club, the night after I was hired here," I explain. "It was an over-21 club. I had no idea she was even in high school until she walked into my classroom on the first day of school."

He rubs a hand over his face and sighs. "Well, that's at least better than my first thought, but it doesn't change the fact that you continued the relationship after you knew. The parents are in an uproar, and rightfully so. I have no choice but to fire you, from teaching *and* from coaching."

"I understand." I stand up and extend my hand. "I'm sorry to disappoint you."

He nods, accepting my handshake. "You're lucky she's over eighteen, son. Otherwise, I'd need to alert the authorities."

I chuckle. "Trust me, if she weren't, we wouldn't be having this conversation right now."

As I walk out of the office, I'm ready to leave and get home to my girl. When I get out the front doors, however, the whole football team is gathered on the sidewalk—Kellan and Tanner standing in front.

"So, it's true?" Kellan asks. "You're really leaving?"

I nod once. "I'm afraid so, buddy."

"This is bullshit!" Tanner exclaims. "Who's going to lead us to the championship?

"You are," I tell them, as if it's obvious. "You don't need me. You never did. Each one of you has potential. You just need to push yourselves. You'll get there, whether you have me as your coach or not."

One by one, each of them come up to say their goodbyes. I make a mental note to have every scout I know come check them out, because some of them have the ability to be incredible players. Once they're done, they all head to the field, while I go the other way.

"Asher," Trent calls. "Wait up."

I stop and lean against the back of my SUV. He jogs over to me.

"I heard what you said back there. That was really nice of you."

I shrug. "It's nothing I didn't mean. They're all good kids."

He nods. "Well, for what it's worth, I'm sorry. Not that you ever wanted this job in the first place."

"Eh, it kind of grew on me," I chuckle. "But my passion is always going to be football."

"Any hopes of getting back to it?"

"Who knows. We'll see what happens."

Rubbing the back of his neck, he hums. "Well, don't become a stranger. I'm here if you need anything."

"Thanks, man," I smile. "That means a lot. But I've got to get back to Tess."

"Yeah, of course." He steps back. "How's she doing by the way? Is she going to be all right?"

Honestly, I don't know the answer to that. She's seemed okay the past few days, but if I've learned anything, it's that she's a hurricane. For all I know, this could just be the eye of the storm.

"I'm not sure, but I really hope so."

I PULL INTO THE parking garage and park my car. Now that all that is out of the way, it's just a matter of waiting for Selena to handle the reputation fall out. Once all the media attention blows over, we should be free to do what we want for the most part.

Climbing out of my car, I find Delaney waiting by the elevators. When she sees me, she exhales and pulls the phone away from her ear.

"Thank God," she says. "I forgot the code for the elevator, and Tess isn't answering her phone."

My brows furrow. "You could have just called me."

Her expression drops, as if she hadn't thought about that. "Because that would have made sense."

I chuckle. "Come on."

The two of us step into the elevator, making small talk about how things went. However, the closer we get to the top of the building, the louder it gets.

"Is someone yelling?" Delaney tries harder to listen.

"Fine! I did it!" Tessa cries. "I did it because I'm weak. Because I'm a failure. I took a whole bottle of pills in an attempt to kill myself, and I couldn't even fucking succeed at that!"

Everything in me goes cold. Numb. Dead. I instantly have the urge to throw up as I realize the worst. The doors open and both Lennon and Tessa freeze. We step out, and I glance at a heartbroken Delaney.

"You what?" she breathes.

Tessa spins around to face us, and it's obvious she's been crying. She tries to dry her face but it's futile.

"I'm okay, I swear. I'm better now."

Delaney looks over at Lennon. "You knew about this?"

"I had my suspicions, but I wasn't sure."

"Ugh, stop! I'm fine!" Tessa comes over to me and grips the front of my shirt. "Asher, tell them. Tell them I'm okay."

I shake my head. "I'm sorry, Tess. I can't."

I can't, because everything is becoming increasingly clear by the second. The incident with her uncle caused catastrophic trauma. The guys at the frat party intensified it. Finding out about her dad pushed her to a breaking point. *The fire.* She was inside the house, sitting on the floor like the place wasn't burning down around her. It finally hits me— she had no intention of leaving.

"I think we need to get you help," I tell her.

She pushes me away in an instant. "You're supposed to love me!"

"I *do* love you!" I argue. "And it's because I love you that I'm saying this."

"Fuck this. I'm leaving."

Lennon runs over to the elevator and gets there just before Tessa does. She makes no attempt to move, blocking the exit.

"Get out of my way, Lennon."

"No." She stands her ground. "I didn't push harder. I let you cut me out because I thought you were healing in your own way and would talk about it when you were ready. I should have tried harder, and I am so sorry that I didn't, but I'm not making that mistake again."

Tears continue to stream down Tessa's cheeks as she turns around to face her sister. "Laney?"

She sniffles. "Sit down, Tess."

Reluctantly, and after realizing that Lennon has no plans on letting her out of here, she listens to her sister and flops down on the couch. I stay frozen in place until the sound of Tessa's sobs make me realize she needs me.

"I haven't asked you this question, and I think it's because a part of me was afraid of the answer, but I'm asking you now." Delaney sits on the coffee table in front of her. "What happened?"

Tess shakes her head, refusing to answer. I walk over and sit beside her.

"If you don't tell her, I'm going to get Easton over here, and we'll find out what happened from him."

She narrows her eyes at me. "You hate Easton."

I nod. "You're right, I do. But I hate the thought of losing you a million times more."

Tessa looks over at Lennon, and for the first time since she showed up at the hospital, I see her hard shell start to crack. She comes over and sits on the other side of Tess and holds her hand.

"You won't like hearing this," she tells me.

I push a stray hair away from her face. "If you're afraid of me leaving, you can forget about it. I'm not going anywhere, no matter what comes out of your mouth."

She sighs and looks down at her lap. "One of the guys who drugged me was at the party," she starts. "I panicked, and Easton could see it on my face. He and Zayn beat the shit out of the guy and then Easton brought me upstairs to his room."

349

As she pauses for a moment, I can already tell where this is going, and *fuck* it hurts.

"I helped clean a cut on his face and then we were just talking. He started saying stuff about wanting to get back together." She lets out a shaky breath. "When he kissed me, I tried to push him away, but then he started begging and saying he's in love with me and I broke. Not because I wanted him, but because hearing those words made me realize how much I wanted to be loved—just not by him. And then I realized it would probably never happen. Not after what Blaire said."

"I just laid there the whole time, and I don't even think he realized I was crying or that I wasn't into it. We were both pretty drunk, but when it was over, he told me where the oxy was so I could get another, and then went downstairs for a drink."

By this point, all three girls are crying heavily, and there is a tennis ball-sized lump in my throat. I lean over and press a kiss to Tessa's head, just so she knows I'm not angry. Does it hurt to hear she slept with Easton? Damn right, it does, but we were broken up and she was hurting. Tess looks up at me and I nod, willing her to continue. She drops her head again and exhales.

"I hadn't thought about it until I had the pill bottle in my hand and I saw how many were in it. All of a sudden I started thinking about how nice it would be to just not exist. The flashbacks and the nightmares, they all became too much. At first, the pills were enough to numb it until it was bearable, but I built up a tolerance pretty fast. I just wanted the pain to stop. I *needed* it to stop."

"Why didn't you tell me?" Delaney sobs.

She meets her sister's gaze and sighs. "Because I know you. You'd instantly drop everything to be by my side, just like you did when you found out I was in the hospital. I didn't want to burden you. You're finally away at college and living your life, moving on from everything that happened to us. I didn't want to take that from you."

"And what do you think it would have done to me if you died? Huh?" Her voice gets louder. "You think I would have been able to just move on with my life like you never existed? You're my *sister*, Tessa. My best friend. My other half. Losing you would be losing a part of me I can't live without. Did you think of that?"

"I just thought you'd all be better off if I was gone."

Delaney bends down, forcing Tessa to look at her. "Listen to me. No part of my life would be better if you weren't in it. Do you understand? *No. Part.*"

At the sound of her words, Tessa breaks completely and crumbles into my side. Emotions wrack her body, coming out in sobs and painful wails. I hold her as she cries while Delaney and Lennon let it out, too. By the time she calms down, Delaney looks at me.

"Do you know of any mental health facilities she can go to?"

Tess pulls away from my chest. "No, please. Don't put me in an institution. I promise, I'll get better."

"Shh, shh," I soothe her. "We're not going to lock you away. There are some really nice places that will give you the help you need. Therapists to talk with. Patients you can relate to. You said you took the pills because you wanted the pain to stop—this can help with that."

She seems wary but she's at least thinking about it. "Will you come visit me?"

I chuckle in relief. "Try and stop me." Pulling Tessa in close, I turn my attention to Delaney. "I'll make a few phone calls."

She looks completely wrecked, and I hope Knox gets back from Zayn's soon, because she's really going to need him.

However, we're going to get Tessa some help, and that's what matters most right now.

THAT NIGHT, I'M LYING in bed, cuddled up with Tessa. She seems restless, like she can't get comfortable, and if I know her, it's because something is on her mind. I rub my hand up and down her back.

"What's wrong?" I ask her.

She's quiet for a minute, and I'm starting to wonder if she finally fell asleep when she speaks. "I'm scared."

"Of?"

"Everything," she whispers. "Being away from you. Talking to people about what's wrong with me. Living at a facility for a month. It's all terrifying to me. What if I can't do it?"

It only took me two phone calls and a matter of an hour before I had the perfect place lined up and a bed on standby for tomorrow morning. The fact that this is our last night together for a while when I just got her back stings, but I know it's what's best for her. And best for us.

"You're going to be okay," I promise. "Maybe not by tomorrow or even by next week, but regardless of what you think, you are the strongest woman I know. You'll get better, like *actually* better, and I'll be cheering you on the whole way."

She pulls away to look at me. "I love you, Asher."

"I love you, too."

I slip my hand behind her neck and pull her in, sealing those words over her lips with a kiss, because I've never meant anything more.

THE WHOLE NEXT MORNING and the forty-five-minute drive to the facility go way too fast. I hold Tessa's hand in mine the whole way, while Delaney, Knox, and Lennon all try to make her laugh from the back seat. A few of their antics manage to work, but I think she's too nervous to find much amusement in anything.

I pull into the parking lot, and we all take in the gorgeous building. It doesn't look scary like the places you see in horror movies. This one is bright, with flowers and palm trees all around the outside. It looks like a place you can go to relax, and that's exactly what she needs.

We all get out of the car, and I grab her suitcases from the back. She hugs Knox first, being as he's the easiest to say goodbye to. He tells her that he will take care of Delaney and make sure she doesn't lose her mind at not being able to harass Tess every second of the day. Next, she moves onto Lennon. The two of them cry as they hold each other, and she promises to come visit when I do.

Then, she turns to Delaney, and even I start to break a little.

"I need you to do something for me," Tessa tells her.

"Anything."

She smiles. "I need you to go back to school."

Delaney shakes her head. "Okay, I should have specified. Anything *but that*."

Tessa giggles. "I'm serious, Lane. Go. I'll be in good hands, but I'll never forgive myself if I mess something up for you. I'm doing what I need to for me. You have to do what's needed for you."

It looks like she wants to tell her to go fuck herself, but she agrees anyway. They wrap their arms tightly around each other for a moment, and when they pull away, I know I'm next.

I turn my head up to the sky, blinking to try to keep in the tears. Tessa comes closer and reaches up to grab my face. She pulls my head down until I'm looking at her.

"Ash, don't cry."

"Psht, I'm not crying. I just have something in my eye."

She laughs at my horrible attempt to play it off. "It's just one month, right?"

"Right. It'll be over before we know it."

I bend down and press my lips to hers, kissing her in a way that hopefully relays everything I'm feeling. When we break it, her cheeks pink.

"I love you, Cherry Bomb. Now, go be incredible like I know you are."

She kisses me once more then takes her bags from me and walks toward the lady waiting at the door for her. Just before she goes in, she turns around and waves with a smile on her face that I'm going to hold onto the entire time she's gone. The smile that said she is going to face the trauma of her past, and she's going to beat it.

She's going to beat it.

Tessa

One Month Later

"I CAN'T BELIEVE YOU'RE GOING HOME TODAY," MY roommate, Paisley, whines. "I'm going to miss you."

Packing my stuff back into my suitcase, I smile. The last month hasn't been without struggles. It took a lot of work just to get me to open up, let alone make any real progress.

Paisley got here a couple weeks ago, and she's become like a little sister to me. She didn't want to be here at first, either. The seclusion. The pressure to talk about things that make you uncomfortable, that trigger feelings and memories that are excruciating. It's all a lot to handle, but she had me to help her through it.

When I think back to how I was when I got here, versus how I feel now, it's almost like I'm a different person. As much as I didn't want to admit it, everyone was right. I needed the help. I needed to learn how to cope with the sexual assaults, the betrayals, the violence I witnessed. I needed to learn how to deal, otherwise it was just going to continue controlling my life.

Once my bags are packed, I make my way downstairs to where all the counselors and other patients are waiting for me. As I walk in, everyone starts to clap—applauding not only my graduation from the treatment program, but the hard work I put in to get where I am. Tears spring to my eyes, and pride fills my chest. Paisley wraps her arms around me and holds me tightly.

"It's with great privilege and honor that I award Tessa Callahan with this certificate of completion," Danielle, my favorite therapist announces, coming closer and handing it to me. "I am so proud of you, Tess. You did the work, not only for the people you love who wanted you to get better, but for you. We're really going to miss you around here."

The hug she gives me hits different, and I don't want to let go. Danielle is the one who really got through to me in the beginning. I wanted to get better, but I honestly didn't believe I could. I thought I was too far gone. Too broken. Too hopeless. She showed me that it was possible to be better than my past, and I'll never be able to thank her, or any of the amazing people here, enough.

After I've said all my goodbyes, Paisley walks me to the front door. She's already crying by the time we get there.

"You have my number, right?" I ask, and she nods.

"And you're going to come back to visit?"

I smile. "Of course. I'll be here for *your* graduation, as long as you promise me you'll eat."

Paisley's problem was different from mine. She suffers from anorexia, and this is the first treatment program that is actually started to help her. I swear, the people here are like magic. They make you feel like you matter, while teaching you how to matter to yourself.

"I promise."

Pulling her close, I give her a hug that shows her even though I'm not going to be here, I'll always be available to her. When we pull away, I wave to everyone else and grab my bags. The second the door opens, I see Asher standing at the end of the walkway, leaning up against his car and making my heart stop just from the look of him.

I let out a shriek as my excitement skyrockets, and my

suitcases are left abandoned as I take off running. As soon as I'm close enough, I leap into Asher's arms. He catches me with ease and buries his face in my neck, breathing me in.

Over the last month, he's made good on his promise. Every week, he made the forty-five minute drive to come visit me, and we talked on the phone three times a week. But this — knowing there isn't a time limit and I'm able to leave with him—it's *such* a good feeling.

"You left your stuff at the door," he murmurs.

I chuckle. "I don't care."

It takes another couple minutes before I let go, but when I do, I go back to grab my things. Paisley stands in the doorway with a shocked look on her face.

"You seriously scored Asher Hawthorne."

A wide grin stretches across my face as I glance back at my boyfriend. "Nah, babes, Asher Hawthorne scored me."

THE WHOLE WAY HOME, all I can think about is getting back to his place and into his bed. We talk about everything I've missed and all the things I didn't want to waste time on during our short visits. Our hands stay firmly locked together as he tells me a million and one times how proud he is, and honestly, I'm proud of me, too.

When I took all those pills, I was in a place of despair. I honestly believed that the only way to escape was either to pretend like everything was fine, or to make it all go away— myself included. The last month has shown me just how wrong I really was.

We pull into the parking garage and I sigh happily, realizing how much I missed this place. Asher and I get out of the car. He grabs my suitcases from the back while I rush to the elevator. When he sees me itching to get upstairs, he laughs.

"You're like a sailor back from deployment."

I put a hand on my hip. "It's been a month, Asher. A whole damn month!"

He snickers. "Don't remind me. My hand needs a break."

We step into the elevator, and as soon as the doors close, he's got me pinned against the wall and he's kissing me like it's actually giving him life. I moan into his mouth, arching my hips to grind against him. He pulls away and rests his forehead on mine.

"Fuck, I've been wanting to do that so bad."

"Then why'd you stop?" I pant.

He steps back just as the doors open, and shouts of surprise scare the shit out of me. My jaw drops as I walk into the living room, seeing all my favorite people there waiting for me. Kellan, Tanner, Oakley, and Micah are standing in the back with their arms obnoxiously thrown in the air. Charleigh and Skye are to the side, watching them with amused grins. Lennon and Colby have the biggest smiles... almost. My heart explodes when I see her. Front and center, with the proudest fucking look on her face, is my sister.

"What are you doing here?"

A wet laugh echoes out of her as she comes over to hug me. "You really think I was going to miss this? Get real, Tess."

I accept her embrace and look back at Asher. He rolls his eyes as he hears my silent question.

"They're only here for the weekend," he tells me. "I already have a flight booked to bring them back to school on Sunday."

My brows furrow. "Them?"

Knox, Grayson, and Savannah stumble out of the kitchen, and Zayn isn't far behind. They all stop and look at where

Asher and I are standing with Delaney. Savannah huffs and crosses her arms over her chest.

"See what you idiots did? Now we missed the surprise!" She comes over and wraps her arms around me. "Look at you. You look so good!"

I smile at the compliment. "I feel good."

An actual damn waitress comes over with a tray of champagne flutes. Asher takes one before looking at the rest.

"Which one is…"

She points to a specific glass, and he hands it to me. My brows furrow as I look at him.

"It's sparkling apple cider," he explains.

And okay, maybe I fall for him just a little bit more. While I was in treatment, I learned that one of the things I try to do is drown out the pain—whether it be with alcohol or pills. After a lot of thought and putting my own feelings into perspective, I decided not to drink anymore. It may not be the right decision for some, and I respect that, but it's the right one for me.

"I'd like to make a toast," Asher announces, holding up his glass as everyone goes quiet. "Tessa, I am so incredibly proud of you for the huge strides and progress you've made. You continue to amaze me every single day, and I am so lucky to have you."

Everyone cheers their agreements as we all take a sip. Once they go back to their own conversations, I lean back into my boyfriend.

"I'm still sexually frustrated," I whisper.

He laughs and kisses my head. "Don't worry. I plan on kicking them out in two hours."

I turn my head to look up at him. "Make it one."

———

TRUE TO HIS WORD, Asher clears everyone out an hour later. He even threatens to set off the sprinklers in order to get Colby to leave. Of course, Colby makes some sarcastic comment about fire being my thing, which earns him a growl from Asher and a chuckle from me. As Asher lunges at him, Colby squeals and jumps away, running from the room.

"Make good choices!" he yells just before the elevator doors close.

Asher's eyes land on me, desire burning inside of them. "Oh, I intend to."

I take a step back, making his brows furrow, and fake a yawn. "I don't know. I'm kind of tired."

"Is that so?"

Concealing my amusement behind a clenched fist, I nod. "I think I need a nap. Your old age is rubbing off on me."

He smirks. "I'll show you old age."

Before I have a chance to react, he grabs me, lifting me up and pinning me against the wall. Our mouths clash together the same way they did in the elevator, only this time is more desperate. Needy. Like we're both going to self-destruct if we don't get enough of each other.

He pulls my shirt up over my head and instantly attaches his lips to my neck. After a full month of having to settle for PG-rated kisses, I'm craving him now more than ever. He grinds himself against me, and I can feel his cock, hard as steel and begging to be let free.

Carrying me into the bedroom, he sets me down and takes a step back. "Take your clothes off."

The authority in his tone goes straight to my core, and I clench around nothing. I drag my pants down my legs while feeling the intensity of his stare. Reaching behind me, I unclip my bra and watch as it falls from my body.

"Panties, too."

I bite my lip and watch as his pupils dilate just a little more. "Yes, sir."

Before I can do as he says, he's in my face with arms on either side of my head, caging me in. "Say it again."

Oh, so he has a kink after all.

"Say what, *sir*?" I tease.

A low growl emits from deep in his chest as he wraps a hand around my throat. "You like fucking with me, don't you?"

Completely rendered speechless by my own arousal, all I can do is nod. With his free hand, he reaches down and grabs my thong. The slightest sound of fabric being torn echoes into the room, and just like that, I'm stripped bare and his for the taking.

"This is hardly fair," I tell him. "I'm naked and *you* have way too many clothes on."

He smirks and releases me. "Go ahead, Cherry Bomb. Do something about it."

I don't need to be told twice. My fingers tease as I unbutton his shirt at a brutally slow pace, kissing the parts of his chest I expose. Once it's completely undone, I slide it down his arms and admire the body that only seems to get better each time I see it. He wasn't kidding when said he's been working out to get rid of some frustration. *God damn.*

Not able to wait any longer, I make quick work of his pants and boxers—immediately dropping to my knees. His cock springs free, only for me to take it into my mouth. Asher hisses as the contact and laces his fingers into my hair.

"Fuck," he groans.

I hum contently, and his whole body starts to quiver. He pulls me off him with a pop and glares down at me.

"It's been an entire month. If I cum anywhere but inside that pretty pussy of yours, I'm going to be an angry son of a bitch."

Standing up, I lick the precum from my lips. "By all means then, take what you want."

He spins me around and presses my back to his chest while his hand finds my neck once more. "Baby, I plan on it. I'm taking it all."

As he leads me over to the bed, all I can think about is how much I love this side of him. He's so demanding. In control. It reminds me of our first night together—when the only thing that mattered was how many times we could get each other off.

He pushes me face down over the bed and pins my hands behind my back. He uses his knees to spread my legs and I squirm as a cool brush of air meets my molten center. His free hand runs gently down my spine and over the curve of my ass, stopping just before where I want his touch the most.

"I've missed this the most." He drops down and licks a stripe from front to back. "The way you taste." His tongue flicks against my clit. "The sounds you make." He sucks the sensitive bud into his mouth. "The way you squirm. Fuck, Tessa. I've needed this more than the air I breathe."

"Then stop fucking talking and take it," I whine.

He chuckles. "Yes, ma'am."

He dives in without mercy, gripping my wrists tighter as his mouth creates what can only be defined as fucking magic. His tongue moves in all the right ways, and the second he adds his fingers, I'm a goner. He fucks into me in exactly the way I've needed it—hard, fast, and lacking any concern for my physical wellbeing. It only takes seconds before I'm screaming his name and being ripped apart by an overly intense orgasm.

Asher stands and releases my hands but it's only seconds before he's flipping me over. He climbs onto the bed and strokes himself a couple times.

"Ride me, baby. I want to watch you bounce on my cock."

I flip a leg over him and lower myself down on his length. The way he fills me is enough to shoot me back into sexual bliss. We both moan in unison, feeling connected in the best possible way once again. He grips my hips and lifts me up and down. His gaze locks on where we're connected, until the door opens behind us.

"Holy fuck," Colby breathes.

Asher's grasp tightens, and he tilts his head to the side. "What the hell? Get the fuck out!"

I glance back at Colby and smile, not feeling the least bit of shame. His eyes widen, and his jaw drops. He doesn't look away as he answers Asher.

"If you love me at all, you'll let me join."

Turning back to my boyfriend, my brows raise. "Well…"

He growls and flips us over, covering my body with his own and shielding me from view. "Hendrix, if you don't walk back out that door, I swear to God, the time your dick almost got bit off will be the least traumatizing thing you've ever been through."

Colby sighs. "It was worth a shot."

The door closes, and Asher focuses back on me. I can't help but chuckle at his glare.

"You think you're so cute, huh?" He thrusts harshly into me and shuts me up. "Thinking I'd actually let him anywhere fucking near you."

I pull my bottom lip between my teeth. "You're sexy when you get all possessive."

He sits up and grabs the backs of my legs. "Good, because you'll be dealing with it for the rest of your life."

Not giving me a chance to say anything else, he fucks me at an unmatched speed. The headboard slams against the wall and things start toppling off the nightstand. His thrusts become sloppy, and the look he gives me is enough to send me over the edge. The two of us reach our high together, him pulsing inside of me as I clench around him. His hot essence fills me as he marks me as his own.

Moments later, he collapses onto the bed beside me. The sound of our labored breathing is all that can be heard. The drywall is cracked. The alarm clock is broken on the floor. But the only thing either of us care about is that we're together. He leans over and presses a kiss to the side of my head.

"I love you."

I smile, finally believing I'm deserving of his affection. "I love you, too."

AFTER THE MOST COMFORTABLE sleep I've had in the last month, nightmare-free, by the way, I wake in the morning ready to take on the world. I grab a quick shower before throwing on an outfit that makes me look as powerful as I feel.

Delaney waits for me in the living room, and the two of us kiss our boyfriends goodbye before heading down to the car. The last thing Asher wanted to do was be away from me, but I have some things I have to do.

As the elevator descends, I pull out my phone and text Colby.

> Everything all set?

His response comes through just as I reach the bottom.

> All clear. He's expecting you.

> Thanks. I owe you.

Delaney and I get into Asher's Mercedes. She puts the key in the ignition, starting it up before turning to me.

"Where to first?"

I take a deep breath. "Levi's Stadium."

I STAND IN FRONT of the giant entrance. My heart is pounding inside my chest, and I feel like I may be sick, but that's okay. Like Michael Jordan once said, "Being nervous isn't a bad thing. It just means something important is happening."

Delaney waits for me in the car. I glance back at her and she gives me a nod of support before I step inside. A guard needs to clear me into the main office, but soon, I'm sitting in front of the head coach.

"Miss Callahan," he greets me. "I hope you're well."

I nod. "I am. Thank you."

"Glad to hear it. Colby said you have something you wanted to talk to me about."

"I do." I pause to take a deep breath. "I think you should get Asher back onto the field."

His brows raise. "And why's that?"

"Because he's one of the best damn players this league has ever seen, and you and I both know it." I keep my head held high, feeling the confidence I once lost for little while.

"I don't disagree with you," he says. "But Asher was taken out by an injury, and it doesn't seem like he has the same push to get better as he once did."

"Then make him an assistant coach, or a quarterback coach for that matter, but get him back where he belongs and with the guys who motivate him. It will push him to get better."

His gaze softens as he looks at me. "You're very adamant about this."

"I am," I confirm.

"Why?"

The question isn't one I didn't expect, but the answer chokes me up a little more than I thought it would.

"Because there was a time where I needed help becoming my best me, and he was there for me. I'd like to do the same for him."

The corners of his mouth raise. "Has anyone told you you're wiser than the average eighteen year old?"

I chuckle. "A few times."

He stands up and puts his hand out. "I'll see what I can do, and thank you for bringing the idea to my attention."

After I shake his hand and thank him for hearing me out, I leave feeling a little more accomplished than I did when I got here. *Task one, done.*

DELANEY PULLS INTO THE driveway of the house we grew up in. I haven't been back here since the day I took a baseball bat to my car—which, okay, may have been a little extreme, but I still think he deserved it. My knee bounces nervously in the passenger seat.

"Do you want me to go in with you?" Laney asks.

I shake my head. "No. This is something I need to do on my own."

She gives me a supportive hug and a half-joking promise that she'll keep the car running in case I want to make a quick getaway. I laugh and get out of the car, walking up to the door and stepping inside.

"Hello?"

"In here," my dad calls out.

I walk into the office I once destroyed. You can still see the scrapes in the wooden desk from where the golf club hit it. That day was one of the hardest. Maybe not *the* hardest, but it was definitely up there.

My dad looks up at me and smiles. "I'd get up to hug you, but I don't think you'd want that, so I'll stay right here."

"I appreciate that." Because he's right.

"You look good, Tess. Healthier. Brighter."

I smile, but it doesn't reach my eyes. "Thank you, but flattery isn't what I came here for."

He nods. "Understood, but if you don't mind, I have something to say first."

My brows furrow, but I sit down anyway to listen.

"My actions have been despicable," he begins, "not only this past year, but for as long as I can remember. I used to wonder where I went wrong with you and why you were so different from your sisters. It wasn't until Delaney told me everything that I finally understood. I *didn't* go wrong with you, because you're a survivor. You are strong, determined, and an incredible woman. I should have spent the last few years admiring you and cheering you on instead of tearing you down, and I am so very sorry that I haven't."

It's everything I've always wanted to hear from him, but it's tainted. Because it shouldn't have taken me nearly dying for him to see it.

"I forgive you," I tell him honestly. "But it's not for you. I forgive you for *me*, because I need it for my peace of mind. I forgive you because holding a grudge means carrying it with me, and I'm better than that."

He sighs and nods thoughtfully. "I understand, but I hope in time you'll give me a chance to build a relationship with you. The one we should have had to begin with."

"That is going to take a whole lot of time and work."

"I know," he assures me, "and I'm willing to do as much as it takes. Starting with this."

Opening a drawer, he pulls out a large envelope and hands it to me.

"This is everything you need to access your trust fund. I released the holds on it this morning," he explains. "And please don't think this is me trying to buy you. If you choose not to talk to me after you walk out that door, I'll respect that. But for what it's worth, I had no idea your uncle was planning to hurt you or your sister. I was blinded by the trust I had for my brother, and I should have paid more attention. Nothing I say or do can ever make up for that, which is why I had the arson you committed covered up. That house and everything in it should have been destroyed months ago, and you don't deserve jail-time for being the one to do it."

His confession is as shocking as it is relieving. At least I don't need to wonder when that will come back to bite me in the ass. I take the envelope and thank him before standing up.

"If you're willing to try, I'm willing to listen."

A smile forms on his face, like that actually makes him happy. "Thank you."

I go to leave when he calls my name.

"And Tessa?" I turn around. "Your mother told me what she offered you. Thank you for not taking her up on that."

With a nod, I leave the house and get back into the car with Delaney, feeling lighter. *Task two, check.*

I WALK THROUGH THE cemetery, finally coming to a headstone I've known was here but never saw in person. I never had the strength to come see it for myself.

Dominic Callahan
1974 – 2020

Taking a deep breath, I sit on the ground. There's no one around, which is good because they wouldn't understand what I'm about to say.

"I've played this moment over in my head a lot the past few weeks. How it went varied depending on my mood, but it usually always ended with me calling you some variation of a selfish asshole."

I look up at the sky to get a handle on my emotions.

"There was a point in my life when you were my favorite person, and I'm not sure you ever knew that. Maybe that's why it hurt so much when you turned against me. A small part of me tried to justify it. To tell myself that you were sick. That it wasn't you. But I know now that it was. You put yourself first in every aspect of your life, and when push came to shove, you were even willing to sacrifice your nieces to get what you wanted.

"You were my uncle, and I loved you. It took three counselors and hours of therapy for me to admit that. Over that time, I learned a few things. First, that it's okay to feel pain as long as you don't let it define you. Second, that you are bigger than the things that happen to you. And third, that you can overcome anything as long as you push through.

"I used to think that I wasn't allowed to acknowledge the heartache. That it would make me weak. That it would make it so you win—but it doesn't. Admitting that what you did caused damage doesn't make me weak. It makes me strong. Stronger than your men that rot in prison. Stronger than the memories that have haunted me at night. And a hell of a lot stronger than you.

"So, you don't get to break me, because I refuse to give you that power anymore. I'm taking it back, and I'm going to destroy you with it in the best way I know how—by forgetting you and living the best life you failed to steal from me."

A satisfied and liberated feeling rushes over me, and I get up from my place on the ground. I've said all I needed to say, and I'll leave here and never come back again. As I turn around to go back to the car, the corners of my mouth raise. Because standing there waiting isn't just Delaney, but Asher and Lennon, too.

I walk over to them and hug my sister. Asher drapes his arm over my shoulders and kisses my forehead while Lennon grabs my hand. The four of us walk away with smiles on our faces, knowing everything really is going to be okay. I may have fallen down, but I got back up again, and that's all that matters.

Always remember you're stronger than your demons.

Tessa

10 Months Later

TYPING THE ASSIGNMENT INTO MY COMPUTER, I make sure I have everything before I pack up my things. It's nice to finally be in college, especially being as I wasn't sure if this was going to be a thing for me. Until the end of last year, I never really knew what I wanted to do. Now, it's crystal clear.

Since I missed a month of school, I ended up needing to repeat all of my senior year instead of just half. I was a little annoyed by it, but I didn't mind it too much. I was able to graduate in June with Lennon and the rest of our friends, with Delaney, Asher, Colby, and even my parents cheering me on from the audience.

"Tessa?" The professor calls my name as I'm passing her desk. "Do you have a second?"

I nod and stop at her desk. "Is everything okay?"

"More than okay. I just wanted to tell you what a great job you did on your paper." She pulls out the assignment from last week. "Reading about your struggles and how you overcame them, I was so moved. Great job."

As she hands it back to me, I notice she graded it with an A+.

"Thank you so much."

She smiles. "No need to thank me. You are a pleasure to

have in class, and you're going to make a remarkable psychologist one day. We need people like you."

A warm feeling spreads through me as I make my way out of the classroom and to my car. Not wanting to leave Asher, I'm taking classes at NHU. My goal is to become a psychologist and specialize in PTSD. I want to help others never reach the point I was at, because they may not be as lucky as me to make it through it.

After a lot of consideration and talking it over with Asher, I ended up using my entire trust fund to open *Safe and Sound*— an outpatient facility where people can go for someone to talk to or just a place to breathe. Patients of all ages and social classes can come and choose to talk to someone, sit in on group sessions, or even just use some of the amazing resources it has to find the help they need. Danielle played a key part, staffing it with the best people she knows and running it for me. Eventually, when I'm done with my degree, the goal is for me to take over. It's something I take great pride in.

I GET OUT OF my car as soon as I see Lennon getting off the private plane. She takes her time, and I groan as I check my watch.

"Come on, come on. We're going to be late."

She rolls her eyes. "Don't rush me. I just had a long flight."

I chuckle. "Oh, yes. Flying in a private jet is such a tough life. You poor thing."

Climbing in and putting her seatbelt on, she smirks. "Perks of being best friends with Colby Hendrix."

Last summer, Lennon went through a lot and really managed to grow as a person. She was forced to make some pretty hard choices, and Colby was one of the people she had to lean on. For a while, Asher and I thought they would end up getting together, but instead, they became really close friends. We all are.

PARKING IN THE VIP section at Levi's Stadium is one of those things that will never get old. Lennon and I show the security guard our passes, even though he already knows who I am. After I came here to talk to Asher's coach, he ended up getting in touch a week later. They offered him an assistant coaching position with the stipulation that he continues to try to fix his shoulder.

Asher took the job and actually did really well with it. The guys responded to him and were glad to have him back—especially Colby, who looked like he was on cloud nine with his best friend by his side again. Meanwhile, we got in touch with the best doctors in the country, someone who specializes in nerve damage.

It was a few months later when I held Asher's hand and walked him down the hospital hallway as he went into surgery. I kissed him goodbye and spent the next five hours pacing. When he came out, they said everything went perfectly but only time would tell.

"Why are you running?" Lennon whines.

I look back at her and roll my eyes. "For such a great dancer, you're really slow."

We stand at the lowest level, just above the field where only VIPs are allowed to be. As they start to announce the players, I grip Lennon's arm tightly, barely able to contain my excitement.

"And now, playing for the first time in two years," the

announcer booms, building suspense, "let's give a big welcome back to quarterback Asher Hawthorne!"

The crowd cheers so loud it's deafening as he jogs out onto the field, jumping into the group of his teammates. I don't even need to be near him to feel the happiness and excitement radiating off him. Words can't even begin to describe how proud I am of him.

They all jog over to the bench and greet their coaches. Colby sees us first and points. Lennon and I laugh and wave in return. Asher turns around and smiles at me. He jogs over to the wall and jumps, pulling himself up and making it so I bend down to kiss him. Once he's gotten what he wants, he jumps back down and winks at me before walking away.

Our love story may not have been traditional, but it's ours —and like I said, I don't play by the rules.

THE ENEMY

Kensington Bradwell doesn't get told no often.

Not when he built an empire from the ground up.

Not when he became the most powerful man in North Haven.

And definitely not when he met my mother.

A picture-perfect relationship,

a happy family,

and twenty years of marriage—

all thrown away for a man with no morals.

Tearing him down won't be easy,

but I won't stop until his empire is in flames.

For my sister. For my father. For me.

I need to find a way to break him,

Lucky for me, the answer just fell into my lap.

Daddy's little princess may be innocent in all of this,

but Lennon's about to get caught in the crossfire of revenge.

The Enemy
Available Now

THANK YOU FOR READING!

I hope you enjoyed Asher & Tessa's story. If you did, I would greatly appreciate it if you could leave a review. :)

BONUS CONTENT

Want more Asher & Tessa?
Enjoy this bonus scene.

ACKNOWLEDGMENTS

I can't believe we're already at the third book in this series. I can honestly say I've never enjoyed writing books more than I have these. Each one pulls something out of me that I didn't know existed. The characters make my heart ache. Their pain is my pain, and Tessa's pain was very personal to me.

Thank you so much for reading The Rebel. I hope you enjoyed Tessa and Asher as much as I have. They truly are something else.

I'd like to thank my team. Christine Estevez, Mercedez Potts, and Christina Santos. You three literally keep me sane. Whether it's by doing the things that I don't have the time to do, reminding me of things I need to do, or just keeping me on track—you're all a very important part of my process and I love you for it.

To my street team, I know we've only just gotten started but you are all incredible. I love the way you push me and make it so I strive to make you proud. Thank you so much for all that you do. I know there are a million other books you could be promoting, and I'm incredibly grateful you chose mine.

To Kiezha, my editor, and my proofreaders Lauren, Elizabeth, and Heather. Thank you for helping me make this book as perfect as can be. Without you, this would probably be crap.

To my beta readers, Rita, Fay, Jill, Cathleen, and Kaylyn, you are all the best. Every time I finish a book, you all make me feel amazing with your love for my stories. Thank you so much!

To Lindsey, thank you for being there when I need someone to talk plots through with or someone to keep me from watching seventeen episodes of TVD. I'm so glad we've become so close in such little time. Also, get me my book. Melissa, thanks for letting me vent about everything under the sun and helping me when I need to just breathe. You may be thousands of miles away, but I love how close we are. Lastly, Thank YOU, my readers. Every single one of you plays a part in making my dreams come true. I can't believe where this has gone and the love it has received. Just know, you're all SO important to me, so thank you.

If you enjoyed this book and would like to leave a review, it would be greatly appreciated!

Until next time,
Kels

Who is she?
THAT GIRL, KELSEY CLAYTON

Kelsey Clayton is a USA Today bestselling author of Contemporary Romance novels. She lives in a small town in Delaware with her husband, two kids, and two dogs.

She is an avid reader of fall hard romance. She believes that books are the best escape you can find, and that if you feel a range of emotions while reading her stories - she succeeded. She loves writing and is only getting started on this life long journey.

Kelsey likes to keep things in her life simple. Her ideal night is one with sweatpants, a fluffy blanket, cheese fries, and wine. She holds her friends and family close to her heart and would do just about anything to make them happy.

For inquires: management@kelseyclayton.com

For social media links, scan below:

Books by
KELSEY CLAYTON

The Pretty Poison Trilogy

A Dose of Pretty Poison

A Drop of Pretty Poison

A Shot of Pretty Poison

Malvagio Mafia Duet

Suffer in Silence

Screams in Symphony

Haven Grace Prep

The Sinner *(Savannah & Grayson)*

The Saint *(Delaney & Knox)*

The Rebel *(Tessa & Asher)*

The Enemy *(Lennon & Cade)*

North Haven University

Corrupt My Mind *(Zayn & Amelia)*

Change My Game *(Jace & Paige)*

Wreck My Plans *(Carter & Tye)*

Waste My Time *(Easton & Kennedy)*

The Sleepless November Saga

Sleepless November

Endless December

Seamless Forever

Awakened in September

Standalones

Returning to Rockport

Hendrix *(Colby & Saige)*

Influenced

SIGNED PAPERBACKS

Want a signed Kelsey Clayton book?
You can purchase them on her website.
Check it out.

Printed in Great Britain
by Amazon